EBURY PRESS
THE CLOUD CHARIOT

Brijesh Singh is a senior IPS officer and principal secretary to the chief minister of Maharashtra. He was previously additional director-general of police in Maharashtra and has held the responsibility of Maharashtra Cyber, a unit looking after cybersecurity for the Government of Maharashtra for several years.

Brijesh contributes to newspapers and appears in the media on cybersecurity related issues. He has written the thriller *Quantum Siege* and co-authored *Dangerous Minds of India* with Hussain S. Zaidi.

THE
CLOUD
CHARIOT

BRIJESH SINGH

EBURY
PRESS

An imprint of Penguin Random House

EBURY PRESS

Ebury Press is an imprint of the Penguin Random House group of companies
whose addresses can be found at global.penguinrandomhouse.com

Published by Penguin Random House India Pvt. Ltd
4th Floor, Capital Tower 1, MG Road,
Gurugram 122 002, Haryana, India

First published in Ebury Press by Penguin Random House India 2024

10 9 8 7 6 5 4 3 2 1

ISBN 9780143470250

Typeset in Adobe Jenson Pro by MAP Systems, Bengaluru, India
Printed at Thomson Press India Ltd, New Delhi

www.penguin.co.in

Chapter 1

A Stranger in Tosali

'Halt! Who goes there?' shouted the *prahari* (watchman). The alarm rang clear and far in the night air. Archers immediately nocked their arrows and rushed to take positions atop the gates and turrets. Large torches burnt with a hissing sound and shadows danced like possessed spirits in the strong wind.

The traveller had arrived quite late at the gates of Tosali, capital of Kalinga Nagari. Was it a deliberate miscalculation? The traveller halted; he was searched for weapons and produced before the commander. He did not even resist and remained still.

He was not very tall, but his lean and lithe, yet muscular structure indicated that he could be a trained soldier. He looked sharp and walked with pride in his step, and the guards who had captured him guessed that he was no ordinary person.

It was unusual for people to travel at night-time, that too alone. Beyond the fortified cities and distant *janapadas* (countryside) were large tracts of forests, infested with wild animals and plagued with savage tribes, who not only looted the possessions of travellers, but also killed with impunity. It was virtually impossible for a person to cross these lawless tracts unescorted.

Inside the cities, there was always a curfew imposed at night; only a few were exempted. Any person reporting late at the main city gates was a definite suspect. Within the city, the king's administration kept a tab on every movement of strangers. Failure to report night movement was punishable for the watchmen too. The Arthashastra-based administration, existing from Mauryan times, had established a tightly knit system, and nothing escaped the attention of the authorities. Any transgression was severely punished.

The commander was a seasoned man, his ragged face betrayed no mercy. He observed the visitor closely with stern eyes for some time, then spoke in a firm voice. '*Arya*, or what do I address you as? Looking at your broad forehead and muscular arms, you appear to be from a high-born family. Or, are you an impostor pretending to be a Kshatriya? Tell the truth or your body will become a feast for the crocodiles of the river Daya.'

The visitor was wearing commoner's clothes that were in tatters, his white *antariya*, the lower body garment, was soiled with dirt and the crumpled *uttariya*, which clothed his upper body, smelled of dried sweat. His hair was matted and his skin looked rough. He had travelled a long distance and looked exhausted, but stood there unshaken and firm, his tired eyes sparkling earnestly.

'My lord, I am Rudravarman. I am no stranger to this country, I have come to my motherland,' he said respectfully.

The commander did not blink, his eyes slowly scanning the man.

'Was anything objectionable found in his possession?' he asked.

The guards said no. He then called one of them over and whispered something to him. Rudra didn't hear anything except for a reference to a 'dark prince' and his associates.

The commander continued, 'Your dress and appearance seem to be from the south-west, but your tongue seems to be native. We will deal with you tomorrow morning; till then you can rest at the guard quarters. And I wish you luck if you turn out to be from Magadha.'

'I too have not forgotten the massacre of our forefathers by Ashoka and the loot of the Kalinga Jina idol by the Nandas of Magadha a century before him. My blood boils at the very mention of that wretched land. I still see the blood of my ancestors flowing through the holy Daya,' said Rudra, pain and resolve apparent in his voice. He continued, 'Peace and prosperity have never returned to Kalinga after our protector, the Jina, was taken to Magadha. The idol used to appear in my grandfather's dreams; it always guided and blessed him in times of trouble. We should have foreseen our destruction at the hands of Ashoka.'

One of the guards spoke up, 'They destroyed us, but never could they conquer our spirit, even Ashoka called us *avijita* (unconquered).'

The commander stopped the guard from saying any more with stern a look. Then, he turned to the stranger and said after a pause, 'Guard, produce him before the chief tomorrow morning.'

The Kalinga capital, Tosali, was a large city with tall, fortified walls all around its square layout. It was surrounded by a moat filled with perennial waters from the holy Daya

River. Beautiful lotuses bloomed on its surface and hungry crocodiles lurked below in the deep green waters. It was said that the bottom of the moat had as many skeletons as the lotuses blooming in it.

Four large corner towers rose atop the city's walls, where keen-eyed archers kept vigil day and night. They could shoot at long distances with the dreaded Indian bow, of which even Alexander's army was afraid.

There were eight major gates, two on each wall, that led into the city, and eight smaller openings were distributed around the perimeter of the fort. Tosali was carefully designed according to the shastras and the tenets of the Arthashastra—streets with elaborate pavements were arranged in a grid pattern; every part of the city was connected by roads with widths depending on usage; commercial, residential and administrative areas could be clearly distinguished by their architecture.

As Rudra was led away, he reflected that Kalinga was indeed coming of age as a resurgent nation. It was carving a space for itself in the history of Bharatavarsha.

Rudra had faint memories of royal processions playing music as they passed through the main streets. They consisted of decorated elephants, followed by a train of elegant riders dressed in the Kalinga army colours. He would watch from the first floor of their house with his mother and sister as the spectacle passed . . . His memories had grown hazy with time, except for a few.

Rudra had already deposited the entry tax, payable by foreigners, and submitted his credentials. He was asked to rest in a large room in the guard quarters under the watchful eyes of the night guards.

Tosali had an elaborate system of royal seals, or mudras, in place. Every citizen desirous of going to the janapada outside the city gates had to establish his bona fides through a duly issued seal and there was a nominal tax on every entry or exit. Foreigners needed to carry similar documents from their place of origin, which were examined by expert officials at the gates. These officers were trained in the art of detecting forged mudras and documents, punishment for carrying which was very severe.

An elderly bearded man of affable appearance approached Rudra and asked him if he wanted to eat something. Rudra was hungry and tired; an offer for a meal was the last thing he'd expected here. He had heard about the strict authoritarian administration of the Kalingas, so he was surprised. Before he could answer, the man was gone. Rudra looked around, some soldiers who had later shifts were catching a quick nap in the dormitory near the guard room. He felt somewhat reassured to be in the company of humans again.

After a few minutes, the old man returned with karambha, a kind of porridge, and a preparation of barley meal stirred in curds. Rudra started eating without ceremony. The old man kept observing him in a warm, friendly way and struck up a conversation with him in a soft voice.

'You look very tired, how long have you been travelling my son?'

'I got delayed—I slept in the afternoon post my meal, and my fellow travellers left without waking me up.'

'Hmmm, thank God you came before midnight, there are too many wild animals roaming around in the forests. You don't seem to be carrying any arms for self-protection, aren't you afraid of them?' the man asked with concern.

Rudra smiled at the old man. He was aware that seasoned spies were employed at the city gates to verify the credentials of strangers and foreigners. In fact, spies were everywhere—in the guise of the deaf and dumb, hermits and ascetics, householders and merchants, painters and dancers. These spies were the backbone of the administration, for they ascertained the foul dealings of citizens as well as government officials and spared none. They gave the king an almost supernatural knowledge of happenings, which kept everyone in check. From apprehending thieves and robbers to baiting and entrapping other spies and suspicious persons, they carried out their clandestine work like the invisible hand of God. Nothing could be said without the fear of the spies hearing it, conveying it to the officials and causing retribution.

Rudra looked closely at the man. He wasn't a soldier, nor did he look like someone from the administration, the man's face had a kind of softness about it. His clothes were inexpensive but clean, this man surely didn't do any manual work.

Having worked in a royal administration earlier, Rudra was not new to the game. He nonchalantly played along.

'I am really fortunate to have been able to enter the city gates before midnight,' he said.

'Young man, you should actually thank your stars for being in Kalinga on this day. The great Mahameghavahana dynasty has risen and firmly taken command, with the illustrious king Aira Kharavela at the throne. He is righteous and just, as well as courageous and sagacious. He is the beloved of the people.' The old man's eyes shone with pride as he spoke.

'How did the mighty Mauryas fall?' Rudra asked the old man.

The man closed his eyes as if he was taking a deep dive into the past. In the dim, flickering light, he looked like a *rishi* (holy man) lost in meditation. After a brief pause, he said, 'The Kalinga War totally transformed Ashoka 125 years ago. He no longer remained the ferocious lion who was devouring smaller kingdoms. A changed man, he started preaching principles of non-violence to one and all. He increasingly laid more emphasis on religious duties than statecraft. Consequently, the army was neglected in his lifetime and the administration also suffered. The subjects were seemingly happy, but below the surface, there was simmering discontent. After him, there was a steady decline and the mighty empire quickly decomposed like a rotting corpse.

'By the time Ashoka's great grandson, Brihadratha, came to power, the empire had lost its former glory. It had virtually shrunk to the earlier borders of Magadha. The Satavahanas of Pratishthanpura had unequivocally declared their independence long back and the Chedis of Kalinga, who were originally the viceroys of Ashoka, reigned like an independent dynasty.'

'But this was in the recent past, wasn't it?' Rudra asked.

'Yes, my son, it was only last year that a Brahmin general of Magadha, Senapati Pushyamitra Shunga ended the line by killing the last Mauryan king, Brihadratha.'

'Yes, I remember. I was at Pratishthanpura, the capital of the Andhras, when this happened. There, they were wary of the change in guard at Magadha, and there were talks of a war between the Andhras and Magadha after Pushyamitra Shunga captured the throne,' Rudra said.

'Son, Magadha is a land of tragedies. It had a series of parricidal kings in ancient times. Its blood-soaked throne is cursed, and every dynastic bloodline has ended with the murder of the king, if his son hadn't already killed him. While he acts like a de facto ruler, Pushyamitra has still not declared himself the king, and he has not allowed anyone else to be coronated either. Once he stabilizes, he will start eyeing Kalinga and Pratishthanpura.'

'The Andhras of Pratishthanpura are quite capable of defending themselves. They have been holding sway over the large tract between the head of Dakshina Ganga River to Kachipuraka. None of Ashoka's successors has had the courage to question their independence. They have strong forts all along the bordering towns, with powerful independent allies, and the capital is well protected. I think Pushyamitra will find Kalinga to be an easier target,' Rudra baited the old man.

The old man smiled. Caressing his beard, he said, 'If Shunga attacks us now, it will be a lesson for them forever. We will avenge our past and there will be no future for Magadha.'

'What gives you such confidence, old man?'

'King Kharavela is a far-sighted man. He has already repaired all the ramparts and fortifications, increased the strength of the army and equipped it with the best elephants and horses. He is young, but wise beyond his years. He is as adept at playing the veena as he is with the sword. There is no king in Bharatavarsha today who can match him in strategy, foresight and wisdom. He is constantly watching other kings' moves very carefully; no one can catch him unawares.'

'Have you heard about King Satkarni of the Satavahana lineage of the Andhras, old man? He too is young, energetic and immensely popular amongst his subjects.'

'You have just come from Pratishthanpura, the capital of the Satavahanas, you are bound to sing his praises,' the old man retorted. 'But tell me one thing son, what brings you to Tosali?'

Rudra felt the old man's eyes piercing through him, and he suddenly realized that he had spoken much more than needed.

'I am looking for a job at the royal Kalinga court,' he said finally.

'And you are confident that you will get it?' There was a hint of sarcasm in the man's voice now.

Rudra drew a deep breath. 'I have faith in my abilities,' he said.

The night deepened, and before long the old man had slipped into slumber. Rudra too closed his eyes, but he did not fall asleep. His thoughts went to his journey, and his motive for being in Kalinga.

For Rudra, the return to his motherland was opportune in many ways: it was a chance for him to work for the kingdom in which he'd been born, to get to know his roots, and to explore the kingdom for which his father had worked so hard before he was consumed by fire. The flames had taken the life of his sister as well. Soon after their deaths, his mother had emigrated to Andhra territory where the Satavahanas ruled. Rudra was seven years old when his father and sister had died in that fire. Memories of that fateful night, when his mother had pulled him out of the smoke-filled room, coughing violently, flashed in his mind. Rudra suppressed the thoughts.

Growing up as an immigrant had its advantages and disadvantages. Though Rudra had maintained his cultural identity, there had always been a sense of profound rootlessness.

The deep void within him arose from the haze of his past. His mother had been secretive and guarded about their Tosali days till she died. Whatever little he knew about his late father and deceased sister was from her inadvertent references. He sensed in her a raw wound, hidden beneath layers of determination and grit. He too had inherited it. Any attempt to probe further was met with stoic silence from his mother and Rudra had learned not to inquire further. He never saw her grieving, but he knew that she silently experienced pain every moment. There was an uncomfortable dark silence at his home and within his heart.

As he grew up, a firm belief took root in him that one day, he alone would seek answers to his questions.

When Rudra arrived in Kalinga, the time was ripe for ideological subversion; Bharatavarsha had been simmering for the last 200 or more years.

The disintegration of the Mauryan Empire of Magadha had started soon after Ashoka's death. Though the Magadha Empire still controlled a large part of Bharatavarsha from Vanga to Avanti, each passing decade saw a decline in its power and reach. The adventurous Andhras were never subdued by Ashoka, though they acknowledged formal Magadhan suzerainty during his lifetime. The north-west of the Magadhan Empire had already gone independent.

Magadha saw the end of the great Maurya dynasty when Pushyamitra Shunga murdered King Brihadratha openly before the army. The murder was a coup in more ways than one. The Mauryas were predominantly followers of the Niganthas (Jains), except for Ashoka, who had leaned towards the teachings of Shakyamuni Buddha after the Kalinga War. The Maurya dynasty mainly supported the Niganthas, Ajivikas and other 'heretical' sects. Royal patronage meant a lot to these squabbling philosophical factions—kings would dedicate caves, provide food and shelter to one denomination or the other. The king's philosophical leaning also had an impact on state policies and relations with neighbouring kingdoms.

Ashoka had especially applied Buddhist teachings to state policy. However, Buddhism was not considered the state religion as all kinds of sects and denominations—such as the Sramanas, ascetics, Niganthas and Brahmins—were revered, given a special place and accorded privileges. However, the Buddhist sangha and its philosophy had the upper hand with ample state support, which resulted in spreading its teachings far and wide, the construction of places of worship such as *viharas* and *chaityas* and led to the general ascendancy of followers of the path of Shakyamuni.

After the death of Ashoka, his successors reverted to their original Nigantha faith, but state patronage to the Buddhists continued in some form. The rise of a Shunga dynasty under Pushyamitra was a Brahmanical resurgence and revenge. The deities of Shiva, Skanda and Vishaka were being returned to their past glory and many temples were built in their names. The enlightened one, Buddha, was proclaimed to be one of the avatars of Vishnu and placed in the pantheon of the Brahmanical gods. Pushyamitra would later be called 'Munihanta' due to his policy of persecution of the heretical ascetic Sramanas. On the other hand, Kharavela of the Mahameghavahana dynasty in Kalinga was himself a Nigantha, but he gave equal respect and credence to all denominations and sects; people were free to choose their religion, and the state did not interfere with it. Amongst all of them, the ascetics—of any denomination—were held in high esteem, even by the king.

The Vedic religion, with its strict emphasis on rituals and *varna* restrictions, had suffered a setback when the mighty Nandas established their empire in Magadha prior to the Mauryas. There were then sixteen *mahajanapadas* (independent states) in Bharatavarsha, Magadha being one of them. These were democracies of sorts before they were gobbled up into the expanding Magadha kingdom under an imperialist king, Bimbisara of the Shishunaga dynasty. The last king of the Shishunagas was assassinated by Mahapadma Nanda, who was of low birth, to establish the Nanda dynasty. The Nandas were known as the destroyers of Kshatriyas as they defeated the kings of Kashi, Panchala, Kalinga, Surasena, Mithila, Asmaka, Vitihora and the Kurus, amongst others.

The Vedic religion of these mahajanapadas became secondary as the Nandas clearly embraced the Nigantha path, which spread over the newly formed empire due to royal patronage.

There were tussles and battles, both ideological and literal, between the Ajivikas and Niganthas, Bhikkhus (Buddhists) and Brahmins, ascetics and Charvakas. The Kshatriyas were chafing about their dethroning as the first varna of Vedic times and the 'usurpation' (in their eyes) of their primary status by the ritualistic Brahmins. The Vaishyas had also benefited from the integration of smaller mahajanapadas under the Magadha Empire. This led to rising economic activity, resulting in their prosperity. They too resented the costly and time-consuming Brahmanical rituals of Vedic Hinduism.

The Vedic religion had initially taken a beating, but it was silently reforming, accommodating and evolving to the new realities. The end of the Mauryas signalled the resurgence of the old Vedic faith in Magadha and the vast areas under its influence.

With the steady decline of the Mauryan Empire, Kalinga had slowly but steadily regained its independence and become a powerful regional kingdom in its own right. The Mahameghavahanas emerged as the dominant power in Kalinga and established their rule in the region. Under the Mahameghavahanas and King Kharavela, Kalinga flourished as a centre of trade and culture, with the kingdom developing a sophisticated system of administration under the supreme authority of the king.

A shrill cry of horns broke Rudra's sleep. There was light in the room already. He got up and stretched near the window. Gusts of cold air soothed his aching body.

The guards at the city entrance were opening the gates in a military ceremony as a beautiful orange sun was slowly rising.

The imposing city gates and fort walls looked even more majestic from inside in the orange morning light. The grand *pratoli* (highway) gate had a permanent bridge over the deep moat. These walls, rising ten humans high at times, were examples of near-perfect fortification. The outer gate was connected to an inner gate by a broad paved street, so wide that five laden elephants could walk side by side on it. These were flanked by high walls with large terraces serving as platforms.

The old man had already been up for some time and had been observing Rudra silently. When Rudra turned, the man smiled at him and asked if he was ready to bathe and get ready.

'You have an audience with the chief of administration, the Nagaraka, today.'

Rudra nodded in agreement. This was exactly what he had hoped for. Having been dislodged from the Andhra court, it was his first priority to seek employment in the Kalinga court. Had he arrived like a regular visitor during the day, he would have never been put up before the Nagaraka. Being aware of the extra scrutiny late arrivals were subjected to, Rudra had used it as a ploy to gain an audience with the Nagaraka. The Nagaraka was his ladder to the court. If the Nagaraka approved of him, he would be put through higher levels of the court bureaucracy, which would examine him for suitability.

Rudra had heard that the king was a great admirer of talent, and people from many different nationalities served under him. He was confident of his own abilities, yet apprehensive of the future. Tosali was more than a place to earn his livelihood, it was his promised land. The land of his ancestors, of his mother, of his father . . .

The night shift guards came down from the ramparts in batches, looking weary-eyed and tired from continuous vigil, and deposited their arms—bows and arrows, spears of different lengths and swords—in the armoury.

A train of bullock carts laden with goods lined the exit gates for onward journey. The tinkling of bells tied around the necks of these animals, along with the beating of their hooves and the occasional snort created an air of expectation.

One could make out the difference between the traders, dressed in the head gears representative of their *srenis* or guilds, and the modestly dressed servants who drove the oxen in the caravan. Intermittently, one could spot riders who were armed and looked like soldiers. They were not in the military uniform of the royal Kalinga army, but their bearing and manner of riding conveyed that they were men meant for protection of convoys. These were hired mercenaries who travelled with bullock-cart caravans to protect the valuables and lives of the traders from robbers, thugs and marauders as well as hostile populations and errant tribes.

The roads leading to the city were being sprinkled with water by men carrying large leather water bags on their backs. They bowed in obeisance to the religious men who were returning after having taken a ritual dip in the holy river Daya, having performed their ablutions and said their morning prayers in praise of the sun god.

Rudra took a quick bath in the open, near the large community well. It was here that the old man accompanying him noticed his sacred thread, the *yagyopavita*.

'So arya you are, and that too a Kshatriya as I see from the knots of your *pavita* sacred thread.'

'It reminds me of the three debts that I have to pay, *pitra rina*, guru rina and the debt to the saints, as signified by each of the threads of my yagyopavita.'

Rudra lapsed into his thoughts as the old man kept speaking . . . Debts he had to pay, too many for him to count . . .

All had been going well for him, but he had never reconciled with his past. Life had been good at the Andhra court, and he had been rising in stature as days passed. Yet, a profound feeling of emptiness never left him. He always had a strong premonition that one day he would have to return to Kalinga and disentangle the threads. It was as if he had unknowingly been waiting for it to happen.

His mother had died a month ago, leaving him bereft. Calamity never strikes alone. To add to his grief, he had been dislodged from the Andhra court and left adrift. It was as if a poisoned dart was embedded deep in his heart, perpetually stinging like a burning ember, yet inaccessible to remedy.

Today, his identity had been obliterated, his future scorched and his loved ones taken away, again. Bereft of his mother, abandoned by friends, devoid of possessions, his motherland was his only hope, hope of survival, redemption and, maybe, revenge.

Chapter 2

Unanswered Questions

'May I ask you a question?'

'Yes, ask anything my son.'

'What is this talk about the dark prince?'

The old man abruptly stopped walking and took Rudra aside. 'Don't mention that name! Where did you hear it?'

'I just overheard people talking about him. Who is he?'

The old man seemed apprehensive. He came close to Rudra and whispered in his ear, 'He is a very dangerous man; he rules over the world of spirits, Yakshas and Gandharvas. He is an expert in casting spells and a master of black magic, but no one has ever seen him in flesh and blood.'

'But why is everybody afraid of speaking about him?'

'Arya, no one knows the extent of his magical powers. He has mastered the spells of the Shaunakiya Atharvaveda and the dark arts of the Black Yajurveda. He is invincible.'

'Where does he live?'

The old man gestured to Rudra to keep quiet and started to walk briskly. There was a palpable discomfort between them now. On the way, the man quietly handed him some sesame oil to anoint his body with after the bath. Rudra picked up his belongings from the depository where they had been left the previous night.

When Rudra was ready, the two walked towards the city centre. The main pathway was cobbled with large, flat stones, which were still wet from the water sprinkled to contain dust. The small roads that intersected the broad pathway were littered with people, pedestrians, riders and those pushing carts.

The buildings on both sides of the road were two- to three-storey high with thick, polished wooden poles supporting them. Women, seated in the upper reaches of the buildings, could observe the street while going about their domestic chores. There were a lot of *torana*s (decorative festoons) hung across the buildings and children played in the streets.

Rudra remembered running amok in the streets as a child, with his friend Mita. He had once collided with a potter carrying earthenware. The pots had shattered into small pieces and the angry potter had chased him for a full *krosha*! (two miles), but he had escaped. His sister and Mita had witnessed the chase and Mita had rolled on the floor in a fit of laughter. He had other faint recollections of his home in Tosali. His father carrying him on his shoulders along the streets as a child . . .

His heart suddenly grew heavy with the memories of his loved ones. Tosali had reopened his wounds. The loss of his sister had always felt like a gaping hole in his heart; time hadn't been able to heal it.

The old man accompanied him to a large building where a lot of people were waiting.

This was the office of the nagaraka. The building was a two-storeyed structure with a tiled roof, supported by fine polished-wood pillars that looked like stone from a distance. The windows had carved panels with elaborate designs, so constructed that the person inside could see outside, but nobody could glimpse the insides from the street. The upper storey had a balcony protected by a sturdy railing. The doors and windows were covered with curtains. Guards were posted at every entrance.

The old man asked him to remain outside and walked into the building. Rudra waited under the tree opposite the main entrance. Several people were waiting there already and the air was filled with the noise of their conversations. Rudra yawned as he closed his eyes and rested his back against the broad tree trunk.

Suddenly, there was a hushed silence as two riders appeared at the entrance, announcing the arrival of the nagaraka, who appeared moments later in a horse-drawn chariot, with his attendants in tow. The hum of conversation died down as the men got up from their seats and readied to present themselves for their appointments.

The nagaraka seemed like a serious person. He walked with graceful, deliberate movements. His clothes were crisp, and he wore a beautiful carved sword on the side. He alighted from the chariot and with measured steps, proceeded to his office.

In some time, the work at the office started. Minions of the bureaucracy could be seen moving in the corridors, entering and exiting from the nagaraka's chambers. Names were announced as people were summoned inside. After some time, it was Rudra's turn.

Back in the Andhra capital, Rudra was used to people being similarly ushered into *his* office. However, he was not finding it difficult to play a novice. He enjoyed the irony of the situation.

He keenly observed the overbearing demeanour of the guards posted outside the doors of the nagaraka's chambers.

The nagaraka was not at par with *amatyas* (ministers), but still a very important player in the scheme of things. He must have been chosen for the post very carefully and he seemed to do justice to his work.

When Rudra was ushered in, the nagaraka was writing something. Rudra stood motionless without disturbing him. He observed the man keenly. He was middle-aged and seemed to have had a strong physique at some point, though now Rudra could see his belly fat beneath the uttariya as it rose and fell synchronously with his breath. Peeking from the *mauli* (turban), his hair showed shades of grey at places.

After what seemed like a long time, the official asked, 'Tell us about yourself, arya.'

Rudra was impressed with his voice and demeanour. He replied, 'Shriman, I am a servant of Kalinga in the great lord Kharavela's dominion and have come back to my motherland as I heard that the great king is a patron of arts and an admirer of talent. I wish to seek employment with his royal highness.'

'How long have you lived in Andhra country, arya?'

'A long time, shriman—more than fifteen years.'

'Arya, how can you claim to be a citizen of Tosali, if you have been out for such a long time? Do you even know the local language?' He looked straight into Rudra's eyes.

'Shriman, I have not lost touch with my roots. In fact, my mother used to be very insistent upon maintaining links with our traditional identity.'

The nagaraka pondered for some time. Then, clearing his throat, he asked, 'We found a document with the Andhra king's seal in your belongings, what is that? It mentions Simhadhwaja. Are you the fabled Andhra minister Simhadhwaja?'

The air in the room thickened, and Rudra felt a slight flutter of panic in his stomach. He composed himself and replied, 'Shriman, I too have heard of the legendary Simhadhwaja, but I have never seen him. On my journey from the Andhra king's country to Tosali, I was with a group of travellers. This paper must belong to my companion, who went ahead when I was asleep in the afternoon.'

The man looked up at the ceiling as if trying to locate something, then he asked, 'What makes you suitable for employment in the great king's service? There must be hundreds like you dreaming to be a part of the royal court.'

Rudra couldn't help but notice a slight tinge of sarcasm in the nagaraka's voice. He decided not to react.

'I am well versed with both *shastra* (war) and *shaastra* (dharma). I have high integrity and a robust moral character. Having worked at a royal establishment, I carry years of practical experience in administrative affairs. Above all, I have a strong desire to serve my motherland, I shall be an asset to this kingdom.'

The nagaraka now seemed to exhibit some interest in him. 'You worked with the royal establishment in the Andhra country? What work did you do?'

'I was a record keeper in city administration of the Andhra capital at Pratishthanpura.'

'And what kind of records did you maintain?' he asked, locking his fingers.

Rudra had prepared his answer. 'I used to maintain records for the treasury storehouse. It involved inspection and counting of every article coming into and going out of the stores. The warehouse received various taxes in kind, so we had to maintain a very meticulous account of everything.'

'I see.' The nagaraka appeared to be bored yet satisfied with his replies; obviously he too had done his homework. Based on the documents that had been in his possession at the time of entering Tosali, Rudra's genealogy and ancestry had been traced, verified and nothing adverse was found. They had confirmed that Rudra had no relatives living in Tosali and that his family had moved out more than a decade before. The officer was also impressed with his manner of answering questions, his bearing and conduct.

Rudra was asked to wait outside. In some time, the old man emerged from the building, carrying a sealed letter. He handed over the letter to Rudra and wished him luck. Rudra thanked him earnestly.

As he walked through the town, Rudra saw that the town had changed from his childhood days. In fact, this was a time of great transformation. He remembered that before the rise of the Mahameghavahana dynasty under Kharavela, the king's father ruled Tosali, but it was not a flourishing state. The populace was still recovering from the rout of Kalinga by Ashoka. Although Ashoka had taken measures to ensure a very efficient, people-centred administration in the aftermath of the war, there were many new taxes and people had resented it. Ashoka had also prohibited any kind of celebrations and festivals. In his view, these made people lazy and took time away from productive endeavours.

The people of Kalinga Nagari were free-spirited and industrious. They had the thickest and best timber producing forests, in which fierce and independent forest tribes lived outside any government control. The forests also had the best elephants, unmatched in strength and quality in all of Bharatavarsha. On the eastern side, the port cities of Manikapatna, Palur, Chelitalo, Kalingapatnam, Pithunda and Khalkatapatna were sources of revenue through taxes like *samudrakara*, i.e. customs and other taxes. The Kalingodara Sea surrounded these ports and merchants from various countries visited them but were seldom allowed to enter the lofty city gates. Local ships sailed to Suvarnabhumi with goods produced in the country.

Rudra saw that festivities and celebrations had come back to the people of Kalinga, a sign that they had finally and firmly overthrown the Magadha yoke. He could see bards and artists of various kinds performing on the streets and in the markets, which were bustling with eateries and shops selling a variety of things, from earthenware to iron implements.

The king's officials were taking rounds on horseback, admonishing establishments that were creating litter. Rudra mentally compared this with the relaxed administration of Pratishthanpura, where people could roam freely and pursue their callings as they wished. King Satkarni was the ruler of the Andhra dominions at that time. He and his able companion Queen Nayanika ruled the kingdom with great benevolence and dignity. They were ambitious yet level-headed. They genuinely cared for the welfare of the subjects and patronized artist and soldier alike.

Was he feeling nostalgic about the life there? He brushed aside those thoughts. He was in Tosali for a very important reason. Rudra came from a family of valiant, proud and adventurous Kshatriyas who had served various dynasties and kingdoms. His father Indravarman had been an official at the Kalinga king's court—he did not remember exactly what he did, but he had very fond memories of him. He recollected how his father would tell him and his sister stories about his ancestors—valiant men, who had never even feared laying down their lives for the kingdom. He particularly remembered how his father would get serious when talking about the Kalinga War in which his forefathers had been martyred.

In a single stroke of misfortune, Rudra had lost his father, his beloved sister, his home and his motherland.

The sun was setting. By now he had walked to the southern part of Tosali city, where several *madiralayas* (drinking houses) and *ganikas* (courtseans) were located. This area's atmosphere was different. Attendants and charioteers waited outside noisy madiralayas, while traders, merchants and other classes of people, including Kshatriyas, were either immersed in heated discussions or making ribald jokes.

Rudra entered a considerably decent and quieter establishment; it seemed expensive too. He took his seat on a cushioned mattress beautifully decorated with long pillows. He rested his back and eased his legs, the street was in full view. He had been leading a precarious life for many days, and now, a sense of relief overcame him. Across the street lay a compound with large buildings housing the ganikas; he could hear music coming from there, and someone singing in a sweet but forlorn voice.

The attendant was very prompt and respectful. He asked, 'Arya, what will you partake of?' before giving a brief description of the liquors available. The house had medaka, prasanna, ásava, arista, maireya and madhu.

Rudra, being a Kshatriya, was allowed only certain kinds of drinks. He contemplated for some time and then called for a maireya sweetened with honey.

The sale of liquor was subject to very strict regulations. It was sold in small quantities only, such as half a *kudumba*, half a *prastha*, etc. Sale of intoxicants to persons of disreputable character was prohibited. Special licences, limited to four days, were granted for manufacturing liquor for festivals and fairs. Special occasions were also accounted for, and families could manufacture arista (white liquor) for medicinal purposes. Consumption of alcohol outside drinking houses was an exception, only allowed for those with stellar reputation. Rudra was thinking of the drunken brawls that used to take place in Andhra country, where regulation was not as strict. He missed the freedom of Pratishthanpura.

His contemplative mood was disrupted with the entry of two boisterous young men, who were engaged in a heated debate. They seemed to be high-born from the manner of their dressing and their demeanour and appeared to be close friends. For some strange reason, he felt a visceral distaste towards them.

'I can bet you on this, Kapidhwaj,' said the fellow with an elaborate headdress and a golden snake *bajuband* (armband) on his muscular arms.

'Girik, you still owe me money from the last bet, if you have forgotten?' said the handsome one with a boyish voice.

'Oh that! Hah! I haven't forgotten, but you had cheated. Don't you remember, I had protested so much? Still, I will pay for it. Let me bear the cost for today's evening as recompense.' Kapidhwaj agreed, laughing good naturedly.

'But what about today's bet? Are you still game for it?'

'Why not? I bet ten panas on this, she will indeed come this way today,' said Girik.

'Ten panas, that's a lot of money Girik. Why do you want to waste so much money on a simple bet?'

'My friend, if you lose the bet, I will get a glimpse of the heavenly beauty as well as ten panas,' said Girik. 'And even in losing the bet, you too get a chance to have a good look at her, isn't it worth it?'

Kapidhwaj nodded, laughing. They both then called for their liquor and settled comfortably on the mattress opposite Rudra's.

'Some people say she is more beautiful than the queen, and even more beautiful than Amrapali, whom Shakyamuni admitted to his fold,' said Girik.

'And you are aware how Bimbisara, the King of Magadha, had fallen for Amrapali and became her slave. He even retracted his army and stopped the war with Vaishali just to appease her, such is the power of women!' said Kapidhwaj. 'So beware, don't be bewitched by her beauty or you will lose your head, both figuratively and in reality.'

'Kapidhwaj, don't mention the inauspicious name of that country on this evening. It always makes me remember the tales that my late grandfather used to tell about the plight of our ancestors, due to that wretched Ashoka,' said Girik.

'But my friend, have you ever analysed why we lost the battle so miserably, despite having the best elephants and valiant soldiers? We, as a nation, are accursed, as we sided with the Kauravas in the Mahabharata. Out of the five great nations of the five sons of Raja Bali—Anga, Vanga, Kalinga, Pundra and Sumha—we openly sided with the evil Kauravas, and our king, Srutayudha, joined their camp in the battle. He was killed by Bhimasena along with his two heroic sons Bhanumana and Ketumana.'

'Till some time ago, it used to be said in other countries that we were Mlechchas and didn't have the blessings of learned Brahmins to guide us,' Girik replied.

Rudra agreed with the statement in his heart. He had heard many things about the Kalingas at Pratishthanpura, this was one of them.

'I don't know of the past, but today, we are a jewel amongst the nations. Our valiant and pious king respects the Sramanas, Bhikkhus and Niganthas alike. He venerates the learned Brahmins and adores the ascetics. Artisans, traders, Kshatriyas and even artists and performers are getting their due, everyone is happy in his rule,' Kapidhwaj said with pride in his eyes.

Suddenly, there was some tumult outside. Girik and Kapidhwaj rushed to the large window. Two armed riders were clearing the way for a decorated chariot, which was following them at some distance.

'Look! I won the bet, there she comes!' exclaimed Girik as they huddled together at the window to get a better view. Rudra too was curious. He casually got up and walked to the window. The sound of horse hooves was clearly heard as the chariot approached the madiralaya. A lady with female attendants was sitting majestically in the chariot. It was drawn by two stout black horses, barely visible in the night, except for the shine of their skin, which reflected the light from the large oil lamps outside the building.

The chariot stopped in its tracks just opposite the window. Girik and Kapidhwaj dived for cover and hid below the windowsill. Rudra continued to look on . . .

His eyes met a pair of eyes, and he felt a swooning sensation. The lady from the chariot was directly looking at him, her beautiful face appearing magical in the flickering light. She had an elaborate hairdo with a gold *makariya* (crocodile) covering the parting of her hair. Her eyes were like lotuses, her complexion as white as milk and her body as lithe as a tigress'. Time seemed to freeze; Rudra was bewitched by the sight. Before he could see more of her, she turned her face to the other side and said something to her assistant. The chariot moved, and she was gone . . .

Girik and Kapidhwaj came rushing to Rudra, 'Have you lost your mind, *agantuk* (stranger)? Why were you staring at her?' said Kapidhwaj.

'But what's the problem?' asked Rudra nonchalantly.

Girik was overcome with nervous excitement . . . 'Are you mad! She is Maitreyi, an amatya in the king's court.'

'So?' asked Rudra.

'She is known to be a ruthless and strict disciplinarian. She is in charge of the department of vice control—that is, all entertainment, madiralayas, *dyuta grihas* (gambling houses) and ganikas. Did you see any drunk person on the streets? You will never see that in Kalinga Nagari till she is in charge of these affairs. Her agents keep watch on the establishments, and no one is allowed to roam the streets in an inebriated state. Anyone found so is immediately apprehended and punished, and the madiralaya is also fined for being irresponsible with a client.'

'Seems like a very important person,' said Rudra.

'Important, ha! She is in the king's inner circle!' said Kapidhwaj, nudging Girik and sniggering.

Girik mockingly added, 'Don't say such scandalous things in public or the *nayaka* (police chief) will arrest you!' They both burst out into a hearty laugh.

Rudra didn't want to ask why they were laughing, but he felt that his heart was somehow already drawn to the lady. He didn't want to hear anything bad about her. He even felt annoyed that these characters had been trying to catch a glimpse at her. Undeserving lewd cowards, he thought, and wanted no further communication with them.

Given the circumstances, she seemed to be inaccessible; she was way above his current station in life. Yet, our paths will cross again, he thought, and laughed at his own audacity.

He returned to his place on the mattress, while the two friends, a bit astonished by Rudra's uncommunicative attitude, resumed their conversation in muffled tones. Rudra was lost in his own thoughts, but he overheard them talking about the arrest of a tribal chief by the nayaka. Then his thoughts caused him to drift him away.

On her way back to her residence, Amatya Maitreyi's thoughts continued to return to the handsome man who had boldly locked eyes with her at the madiralaya. It was an unusual experience for her; nobody in Tosali dared to do that. The incident incited a little anger, but deep within, she also felt intrigued by the man. 'Yamini' she called her attendant. 'I want some information . . .'

Chapter 3

The Bandit, the Soldier and the King

Rudra spent the night at a lodging house. He got up early in the morning and left for the royal palace for his appointment with the *mahamatya* (prime minister).

The palace complex had several lofty, ornate gates, with walls enclosing large lawns. Rudra passed by ponds and groves and saw peacocks pecking around. Occasionally, a peacock flew with great effort and sat atop one of the buildings. Visitors had limited access to the royal court, the rest was strictly off bounds. Compared to the Pratishthanpura palace, Rudra found the Tosali complex to be much more organized, militaristic and systematically planned.

The palace complex had a unique, elaborate security apparatus. Only the most trusted guards were posted inside, usually from families that had served the king's ancestors. They were loyal and willing to walk into fire at the king's orders.

Any visitors to the palace had to pass through several rounds of verification and scrutiny. The uniformed guards and spies in the guise of officials, servants and commoners kept a strict vigil on them. The whole environment had a solemn and official air.

A road inside the complex connected the courthouse to the king's residence, which was some distance away. The king arrived at the courthouse every morning in a small procession. An audience with him was a rarity, except when he heard petitions from the general public in an open session.

Rudra had presented his papers at the entrance that morning and was promptly taken to a large building inside the gates. The officials verified the seal of the nagaraka on the letter and Rudra was let into the second layer of security. Here, he was thoroughly frisked again. A series of senior officials questioned him repeatedly to verify his credentials and the authenticity of his purpose. He responded to them with sincerity and alacrity. Each one of them was to make an assessment and send a report to the next level, if a candidate was found suitable for recruitment. It was a long, repetitive and arduous process of interrogation, which Rudra endured with grace.

Finally, by late evening, he was led to the office of Mahamatya Nakiya. It was a large wooden building, which was barely decorated. There was an open courtyard inside the building where the mahamatya worked. As Rudra was about to enter the corridor leading to the courtyard, he heard a commotion. Before he could step inside, a man running at full speed collided with him and Rudra fell flat on his back. The man staggered, but quickly regained his balance. He stepped over Rudra and rushed forward. In the fleeting moment that

Rudra could see his face, he saw the burning eyes of a very angry man. The man mumbled an expletive at him before he vanished, a band of soldiers pursuing him with weapons drawn.

'What is happening?' Rudra asked a man at the door.

'That's the leader of the tribal bandits. He was captured by Nayaka Vikarna, the chief of police, and was to be brought before *Rajan*. But he has managed to escape!'

Rudra ran outside and saw some soldiers following the man at a distance. He was running at remarkable speed, jumping over obstacles like they were nothing. The soldiers, along with Nayaka Vikarna, were no match for his speed and agility.

Soon, the bandit reached a wall and started scaling it like a lizard. None of the soldiers could do it. He ran over the roofs of the buildings in the palace complex. Archers had joined the pursuit, but the brigand was moving so fast that they couldn't aim at him. Rudra decided to join the pursuit on the spur of the moment. He leapt down the stairs and ran after him.

'Shoot him down, now! Why can't you take aim, you idiots!' cried Vikarna. 'Isn't there a single fool who can shoot a straight arrow?' He snatched a bow from a soldier and aimed at the man. As he fired the arrow, the bandit anticipated it and ducked. He then jumped from the rooftop of one building to another.

Riders on horses had also joined the chase now. It was late evening, and daylight was fading fast. If he was not immediately apprehended, the man would vanish in the darkness. Unaware of the layout of the palace, he kept running helter-skelter to find a way out. He slipped twice over the terracotta tiles on the rooftops, but quickly recovered. Now, he was approaching the outer walls of the palace complex. One last jump and it would be impossible to trace him in the city. Volleys of arrows went waste as the man took cover behind a parapet wall. Rudra had now caught up with the rest. The bandit was weighing the risk of jumping from a three-storey building on to the narrow ledge of the outer wall. Rudra calculated that the distance was not impossible to cover, but the wall was very narrow at the top, leaving little space to land.

Rudra noticed a wooden ladder lying alongside a wall. He lifted it and started climbing the building. The bandit was taken aback. Before Rudra could scale the first floor, he leapt towards the wall, but lost his footing. He hung precariously on the outer side, his hands clutching the top of the wall.

Rudra quickly carried the ladder to the rooftop. Then, laying it horizontally between the wall and the roof, he walked over the ladder and bridged the gap. The soldiers below had stopped shooting arrows. They started encouraged him, shouting praises for his courage and swiftness. Rudra soon reached the bandit. He saw fear in the man's eyes; he was mumbling in a strange language. Rudra didn't say anything to him, he just offered his hand. The man hurriedly clutched his outstretched hand and climbed back on the wall.

The chief of police witnessed all that had happened. 'Arya, hand him over to us now, he will meet his fate today!' he said in a stern voice.

'Wait!' shouted Rudra. 'As I have apprehended him, I have given him an *abhay daan*, a guarantee of life, so nobody touches him.'

'Have you lost your mind, arya? Get down here, and hand him over to us; I command you as the nayaka of this city. If you refuse to obey, you too will face the consequences.'

Rudra's Kshatriya pride was hurt. 'Don't threaten me, nayaka. I've seen what you are capable of. You couldn't apprehend a mere fugitive by yourselves. If you don't agree to my conditions, I will set him free, and I know that you and your men will never be able to catch him again.'

'In that case, I will have to kill you too!' The nayaka now pulled the string of his bow and pointed the arrow towards Rudra.

'Nayaka Vikarna! Stop!' a voice shouted. 'I command you to put your bow down.'

Vikarna was startled. 'Mahamatya Nakiya! When did you arrive, arya?'

'You first comply with my orders and ask the stranger to come down safely with the prisoner. Nobody is to touch them.'

'As you wish, mahamatya,' said Vikarna in a sullen voice.

Rudra was brought down safely with the brigand, who was arrested immediately and fettered with irons.

'Send this arya to me tomorrow,' commanded the mahamatya as he left.

Humiliated, Vikarna spat on the ground and looked menacingly at Rudra, who merely smiled back.

The mahamatya was strolling in the corridor when Rudra was produced before him the next morning. He gestured for the guards to go away and gestured for Rudra to walk along. Rudra quietly joined him, walking a step behind the venerable figure. Nakiya was in his sixties, but he walked with a straight back and the confidence of a man half his age. He carried a bejewelled sword with an ornately crafted hilt which ended in an ivory head resembling a white peacock.

Nakiya had already seen a detailed assessment of Rudra's capabilities. The people who had been asked to place Rudra under surveillance had come back with very good opinions about him. He seemed to be a man with great potential, fit for responsibilities at a fairly senior level in the bureaucracy. Nakiya, however, wanted to make his assessments first-hand.

Nakiya cleared his throat and said, 'Please accept my gratitude for the help in apprehending the forest brigand.'

Rudra humbly shook his head but said nothing.

'I have been told that you want to work at the king's court.'

Rudra nodded in assent.

'Let me ask you a few questions then,' Nakiya said.

He stopped and looked at Rudra. 'What do you think is the single most important problem facing the country today?' he asked.

Rudra paused for a moment, mulled over the question and said, 'On the external front, it's the ambitious Satkarni of Andhra and the adventurous Yavanas in the north-west. The Shungas too are a weak yet potential threat. On the internal front, water is scarce in the city.'

'Go on,' Nakiya said.

'The repairs of the gateways, ramparts and palace damaged by storms in his father's reign have won the king great goodwill and fame. Now, if something is done to improve water tanks, especially along pathways, it will invite the blessings of gods as well as the goodwill of the people.'

'You have not been here since your childhood, how do you know all this?'

'Mahamatya, the glory of King Kharavela has spread far and wide. In the neighbouring kingdom, I heard tales of his sagacity, prudence and magnanimity almost every day.'

'How is it in Pratishthanpura?'

'Mahamatya, people are happy, the king is benevolent; taxes are not oppressive.'

'Then why did you leave their service?'

'Personal reasons, mahamatya. I am from Tosali and have always wanted to return to this place.'

'Hmm . . . why did our kingdom lose against Ashoka?' Nakiya changed the subject.

'Complacence, shriman, was the real reason, even Chandragupta Maurya couldn't conquer Kalinga, and his son Bindusara was also unsuccessful. We never thought that Ashoka would rout us like this. On the other hand, Ashoka wanted to outdo his grandfather, and he did what Chandragupta couldn't.'

Rudra waited with bated breath for the next question. This was his last chance to accomplish his goal. If the mahamatya didn't approve of him, he would be doomed. His future depended on the judgement of this one man.

The mahamatya then broke his silence. 'What kind of work would you like to do, arya?'

'You are a better judge of my competence, mahamatya,' said Rudra humbly.

Nakiya nodded. 'We will keep you informed about your candidature for employment in the royal court. Till then you may stay in a guest house in the royal palace premises. Don't venture out without an escort or permission. You may come to the royal court tomorrow to witness the proceedings. I will send someone to escort you.'

Rudra paid respects to him with folded hands and took his leave. He felt satisfied with the interaction. Things were going as per his plan, though he had unwittingly angered the city nayaka the previous day.

He knew that he would be under constant watch in these surroundings. Anyone striking up a conversation with him was bound to be a spy. He avoided speaking to anyone, headed directly to the guest house, ate his food and went to sleep early.

The next morning, he was escorted to the palace premises by an unarmed attendant. The palace was a study in splendour. It boasted of dark polished wooden pillars, carved with inlay work, which displayed exquisite embossing of flowers, plants and animals. The bell-shaped arches had lotuses in bloom engraved on them. The ceiling had geometrical patterns with small motifs in the centre. Brightly coloured silk curtains, tied neatly with tassels, moved gently with the wind.

A giant sculpture of Vyali the lion, who protected the kingdom and all its inhabitants, stood at the entrance of the royal court. Rudra took a deep breath as he passed under the majestic gaze of the lion protector.

In the court hall, the amatyas and other court officials sat according to their rank.

The royal attendant announced the arrival of the king. 'Rajadhiraja, Chedi Vansha Shiromani, Kalingadhipati, Aira Kharavela,' he called out, and everyone stood in obeisance, eyes down at the floor.

From the corner of his eyes, Rudra saw a tall figure gracefully walking in, followed by attendants holding an umbrella decorated with gold and gemstones over his head, two attendants holding *chauris* (fly whisks) and palm leaf fans, and the *shastradharini* (sword bearer), Saktimati, carrying the royal sword.

Saktimati was from a long line of loyal servants. It was said that, as the bearer of the royal sword, she did not take orders from anyone else, not even the queen. She was never seen talking to anyone. Ever vigilant, she accompanied the king on all excursions and visits, following him like a shadow. It was fabled that once, when a drunk cousin of the king was arguing with him, she pounced upon the poor wretch and held the blade at his throat. He was released only after the king ordered her to let go of him.

Her large eyes and dark complexion made her look like a *Yakshini* (spirit) except the fact that she had the height of a demon. Her uttariya was tied neatly at the waist where the *kayabandh* (waist sash) met it, barely concealing her supple body. She kept a keen eye on everyone around, ready to cut any threat to pieces.

The king sat on his *simhasan* (throne) and asked everyone to be seated. There was a hushed silence. The king then spoke in a measured but harsh voice. 'Mahamatya Nakiya, what are the issues to be discussed today?'

Mahamatya Nakiya rose and made his salutations with folded hands. 'Rajan, firstly we have to decide the fate of the forest brigand apprehended by the able nayaka.'

Hearing this, the tall and handsome police chief Vikarna beamed with pride. But, on noticing Rudra in the courtroom, his smile vanished. He whispered something to the amatya sitting next to him, who examined Rudra with a curious gaze.

'Nayaka Vikarna, I congratulate you for the success. How did you apprehend this outlaw? Rise and approach.' Saying this, the king indicated something to the female attendant standing behind him. She rushed out and returned with a *muktahara*, a pearl necklace, on a decorated plate. The king garlanded Vikarna with the string of pearls.

Rajguru Uddalaka, who was sitting next to the king, whispered something to him. The king's expression changed for a second before returning to being impassive. He indicated to the rajguru to wait for some time.

'Worthy Nayaka Vikarna, now tell me how you caught him?'

'Rajan, the forest tribes are a menace; apart from the protected forests and the elephant forests, these miscreants have infested all other ones. Not a single caravan of traders can pass through those areas without being looted. They also kill the poor travellers and maul the beasts of burden.

'You are aware that the Magadha Empire couldn't bring them under control, even Ashoka did not dare to disturb them and only levelled veiled threats at them. The rock edict at Samapa is a testimony to that.

'This man was trapped by us when we sent a decoy, a soldier in the guise of a merchant to the forest. The other bandits escaped, but we caught him. He is fast and dangerous, and we are fortunate to have caught him. It's all due to the clever planning and courage of my soldiers Rajan.'

There was a call of praise from the court. Rajan gestured for silence and asked Vikarna, 'How did he escape again?'

There was an uncomfortable silence. Amatya Maitreyi, who was in the court, looked disturbed. Vikarna went red with shame. He composed himself and said, 'Rajan, pardon the stupidity of my people, but this man was to be produced before you for his trial. However, he feigned unconsciousness, and my people thought he was dying. They said he had even stopped breathing. In panic, they sprinkled water on his face, and when he didn't respond, one of them poked him with a sword. Even then he lay motionless. The soldiers then removed his fetters and freed his hands too. But Rajan, as soon as he was freed, this criminal sprang to his feet and escaped before they could get him. I have already removed the soldiers who lapsed in their duties from service.'

'What happened then, nayaka?'

'With great difficulty he was apprehended again Rajan. I seek your forgiveness for the blunder.'

Nakiya spoke up. 'Rajan, there is one complication.'

'What is that, mahamatya?'

'The stranger who apprehended the brigand when he escaped claims that he offered an abhay daan to him. It is now up to you to decide if we should honour the promise given by a stranger to a criminal.'

'Mahamatya, this is a complex issue dealing with dharma and law. Let us consult the rajguru on this.'

Rajguru Uddalaka rose to speak, 'O learned Rajan, the prime lawgiver Manu says that, "A pure, truth-seeking, intelligent king, possessed of good allies and acting conformably to the teaching of the shastra, is alone capable of exercising the rod of punishment."

'Also, considering the wilful repetition of a crime by an offender, as well as the time, place and circumstances of its commission, the light or serious nature of the offence committed, and the bodily strength and pecuniary circumstances of the offender to bear the penalty, punishment should be inflicted on an offender,' said the venerable teacher.

The king quickly understood that this matter needed more consideration. He said, 'We will decide his fate in two days; put him in the *bandigriha* (prison) till then and take care that he does not escape this time.'

Nayaka Vikarna bowed to the king and returned to his seat. He cast a quick glance towards Maitreyi, who was keenly observing the proceedings.

After dealing with some other matters, the king finally turned to the rajguru, and sought his advice on the astrological predictions for the near future. He was informed of the *grahadasha* (astrological positions) of the planets according to *jyotishya* shastra. The king looked slightly worried. The rajguru said, 'It is futile to start digging the well after the house has caught fire! One has to be proactive. We should have appropriate response ready in hand before a problem arises.'

The king nodded in agreement and looked towards Senapati Bahushalin, who cast an assuring glance at him. The court was dismissed.

✦ ✦ ✦

Outside the courthouse, Nayaka Vikarna went up to Amatya Maitreyi and said, 'Did you see how Rajan undermined all my efforts?' He was livid.

'Vikarna, calm down and don't speak so loudly! You have done your duty and performed it well, why fret over small things?' she said, almost with affection. It was at these rare occasions that her beautiful face showed any signs of humanity.

'*Small things*, Maitreyi! How can you say that? My soldiers could have been killed apprehending the miscreant. In fact, three of them were injured by the tribals. And now, when I catch him, Rajan wants to defer putting him to death. How do I work like this!'

'Nayaka, let him take a decision. He is wise and will not let you down. Don't you see how he praised you in public?'

'Yes, he praised me indeed, and then asked me how the brigand escaped. It was such a slap on my face.'

'My dear one, you're overreacting. I understand your commitment to your work and your love for your soldiers, but please stop this. Do not get provoked for nothing. You're doing well; the king is happy with your performance, keep it like that. You know, Vikarna, sometimes I get worried about your excessive zeal . . .' Her grim exterior seemed to crack.

'Maitreyi, I understand all that, but why are they honouring the abhay daan given by that stranger who happened to help us? Would you believe it, I actually saw that man in the courthouse today! Do you have any idea who he is?'

'I too noticed him today. Doesn't seem to be a novice.' A sense of familiarity flickered in her mind.

'You know, Maitreyi, although he helped us capture the brigand, I somehow don't have a good feeling about him,' he said, holding his clenched fist in the palm of the other hand.

'Vikarna, would you stop being so irrational. You have a lot to handle anyway.' She took his hands into hers and caressed them.

'No Maitreyi, it's instinctual, you know. There are some people you don't like at first glance, and he is one of them.'

'You need some rest, Vikarna. Go home and take some time off work. Visit the Jina temple on your way and seek blessings.'

Vikarna nodded, still looking annoyed. He took his leave of Maitreyi and got into his chariot, exceptionally stiff and quiet.

Meanwhile, Nakiya had been asked to meet with the king for a briefing.

'Who is the stranger who apprehended the brigand?' the king asked.

'Rajan, I was going to talk about him in detail with you. He is originally from Tosali. He was in the service of the Andhras, but he has come back now and wants employment in the royal court. He seems to be highly talented and worth a look.'

'Mahamatya, get him thoroughly vetted. He should not turn out to be a spy. Check what made him come here so suddenly.'

'Indeed I will, Rajan. I have already asked our best spies to gather comprehensive information on him. Once that is done, I will send him to meet you.'

Chapter 4

Audience with the King

A few days later, as Nakiya had received no negative information about Rudra, King Kharavela asked to meet the stranger.

At noon, Rudra was escorted to the king's chamber by the ever-vigilant female guards of the palace. The room was not very large and it was austerely decorated with little furniture. While the pillars were ornate and embellished, they didn't seem to be polished.

Rudra's heart pounded in anticipation; he was meeting Aira Kharavela! The king had ascended the throne at the age of twenty-four and was renowned as an expert in civil and religious laws, finance, administration, military strategy and royal correspondence. He was known to be an accomplished player of the veena, who could outclass famed exponents of that art.

King Kharavela was sitting by the window, lost in thought, when Rudra was ushered in.

Rudra stole a glance at the king. He was a dark, handsome man with a stern face. He looked much more mature than his age. His broad chest and rounded shoulders looked imposing in his indigo uttariya.

'I heard about your brush with the forest brigand,' Kharavela said, without looking at Rudra. 'I also hear that you gave some good advice to Nakiya on constructing and repairing water tanks along the roads.'

'I did, Rajan.'

There was a long pause. 'Why did you give an abhay daan to the forest brigand, and on whose authority?' Kharavela turned and looked at him with his sharp penetrating eyes.

Rudra felt a chill run down his spine. He composed himself, drew a deep breath and spoke in a slow, deliberate manner. 'Rajan, you're well versed in ancient laws and dharma. When a man seeks sanctuary with a Kshatriya, it becomes his dharma to protect him. The man could have died—he would have fallen off the wall or been shot by archers. Such a death would not have served the purpose of either law or dharma. When I climbed on the wall to apprehend him, he was begging for mercy. I had no option but to allow him to live. I am ready to face suitable punishment for this, Rajan,' Rudra said with bowed head, but his voice was firm.

'Is that the only reason you saved him?' the king asked.

'Rajan, I am too ordinary a man to suggest this, but putting a forest brigand to death will further enrage the tribes. It will seriously endanger the movement of merchants across the forests and affect trade.'

'So you are suggesting that we leave him unpunished and further embolden these rogues?' Kharavela's eyes narrowed.

'On the contrary, Rajan, I beg to submit that we can use this opportunity to build goodwill amongst these people.

If we spare his life and take a promise from him not to molest our traders, it will go a long way in assuring the safety of our travellers.'

The king seemed to be lost in deep contemplation. He closed his eyes and rubbed his forehead. 'What if he fails to honour his commitment?'

'Rajan, this is the best strategy we have; a nest of gnats is best left undisturbed.'

Kharavela suddenly opened his eyes and blinked distractedly for some moments. 'I see the point in what you say arya, I will decide about his fate later.' The king now got up from his seat and stood at the window, looking out. 'I have been informed that you used to work for the Andhras at Pratishthanpura, in the service of King Satkarni, and now you wish to seek employment in my court.'

'That is correct, Rajan. This is my own country, I was born here. My mother always longed to return to her native place, but she died on foreign soil. I decided to come back here and serve my country after her death.'

There was a long pause, the king changed the topic. 'Tosali has been facing acute water shortage for some years. The wells have been deepened but rainfall has been less and less,' he said.

'Rajan, if I am permitted to speak?' said Rudra. The king gestured for him to go on. 'Rajan, if you consult the record-keepers, there was a canal through Thanasuli to Tosali built by Nanda Raja when Kalinga was under Magadha rule. It may have been buried over the years. If we excavate it, it will provide enough drinking water for the city as well as become a waterway for ships and boats.'

'How do you know about this canal? I don't remember ever hearing about it,' Kharavela asked, frowning.

'Rajan, when I was at the Andhra court, I had access to lots of old records, and in one of the documents from Magadha, the canal was mentioned.'

'I will have someone look into it,' the king said, nodding. 'What other abilities do you possess for which I should employ you in my court?'

Rudra paused, his eyes on the floor. 'Rajan, you performed the *rajasuya yagya* (consecration ceremony) on ascension to the throne, then the Vajapeya. It's time that you perform the Ashwamedha yagya.' The king looked at him curiously, wondering where Rudra was taking the conversation. 'Rajan, the Yavanas in the north-west are dreaming of conquering the mainland again, as the Magadhans grow weaker by the day. Although Senapati Pushyamitra is the de facto king, the Andhra king Satkarni is eyeing Magadha territory. He is valiant and ambitious and has been preparing his army for a long time. He has also been importing a large amount of iron and employing skilled blacksmiths to forge better, newer weapons and instruments.'

'This all sums up to what?'

'Rajan, if Kalinga doesn't make the first move in this geopolitical theatre, someone else will. Joining a war at the other party's chosen time and place is very bad strategy indeed.'

'So you're advocating war with a peaceful neighbour?' the king said, eyebrows raised.

'We do not have an option, Rajan. If you don't perform the Ashwamedha yagya, Satkarni will perform it, and Kalinga will be his first target. He will start right after Kartika, after the rains end. His *rajpurohit* (royal priest) has given him the *muhurta* (auspicious moment) for it.'

'Why should I believe you?' the king asked.

With his hands folded and head bowed, Rudra said, 'I indeed used to work in the Andhra court, but I have come back to serve my motherland.'

'Then you must know well that Satkarni's strength lies in his friend and minister, Simhadhwaja, who is a master statesman and a grand strategist. Can we match his wits?' retorted the king.

'Rajan, he will not have Simhadhwaja with him—it is the right time to strike,' said Rudra.

The king laughed incredulously. 'What do you mean he will not have Simhadhwaja with him?'

'Simhadhwaja is dead, Rajan! You may confirm it from your sources. He died two weeks ago.'

'What! Simhadhwaja, dead! How is it possible?'

'Rajan, I was in the Andhra kingdom on his last day. The king suspected him of treachery and wanted to put him to death instantly, but he escaped and was later killed by Amatya Dhavala's agents. I was with him when he was escaping, but was unaware of his identity, until his death.'

'This is fantastic information!' The king looked happy. 'Why did you leave Satkarni and come here?'

'I didn't want to fight against my own people in the impending war against Kalinga, hence I quit. There were other reasons for me leaving the Andhra court . . . this is the primary one.'

The king examined him closely, then, after a long silence, he asked Rudra to meet Mahamatya Nakiya the next day.

✦✦✦

'Why didn't you tell me that Simhadhwaja was dead?' Nakiya said, furious. He felt belittled.

Rudra was composed. 'Mahamatya, forgive me if I have done something wrong. The subject never came up in our discussions, and I limited myself to the questions being asked. Had you asked about Simhadhwaja, I would have told you the truth.'

Nakiya's eyes remained red with anger. 'What about the document you had with you, the one with the Andhra court seal. It had the name of Simhadhwaja, and you told the Nagaraka it belonged to a fellow traveller.'

Rudra requested in a sincere but firm voice, 'If you permit, I will narrate the whole story as it happened.'

Nakiya nodded tersely.

'Amatya Dhavala was Simhadhwaja's competitor in the Andhra court. He played a fair game for a long time but lost his patience in the end. He, along with other officers of the court, hatched a plan to bring Simhadhwaja down,' said Rudra.

'Last month, King Satkarni went on a hunting expedition. The best elephants were selected for it, along with the best archers and the king's trusted bodyguards. Dhavala accompanied the king. They were to come back in ten days. On the evening that the king left for the forest, spies informed Simhadhwaja that he should leave the kingdom and run away as far as possible because a conspiracy had been hatched that would condemn him to death. On digging deeper, he found out there was to be a feigned attempt on the king's life during the hunting expedition. Simhadhwaja's favourite bodyguard Pavaka would be caught for it, and he would confess that it was Simhadhwaja who had sent him to attack the king. Dhavala was to valiantly save the king's life, getting injured in the process.

'He couldn't believe his ears! How could Dhavala fall to such depths of treachery, and how had he convinced the loyal Pavaka to be a part of his deadly design? Simhadhwaja had no option but to leave the country. He told everyone that his guru was ailing and desirous of seeing him, and he had to go urgently. He left the kingdom before Dhavala could stage his dirty drama.

'When Dhavala came to know of this, he changed his plan. He didn't execute the feigned attack on the king's life, instead he sent *kapatikas* (undercover spy) and assassins to locate Simhadhwaja and finish him off. Being aware of such a possibility, Simhadhwaja took several precautions including changing his appearance and travelling under a false name.

'Meanwhile, I had left Pratishthanpura for Tosali. On the way to Kalinga, I met a man claiming to be an artist who was travelling to Tosali to perform. He later told me that he was being pursued by some enemies and took my clothes for a disguise. I kept travelling ahead as his associate. Unfortunately, the poor man was killed by Dhavala's agents. Before dying, the poor man told me who he was and asked me to trace his relatives in Tosali and inform them of his death. I escaped from the enemies and somehow reached the gates of Tosali. You may verify the facts through your sources, and I will remain your prisoner till then,' Rudra said solemnly.

Nakiya called the guards and asked Rudra to be taken away.

The mysterious figure moved gracefully; nobody, not even the personal guards of the king stopped the person. In a few minutes, the person was face to face with the king.

'So, what news do you bring today?' asked the king.

The person smiled. 'It's turning out much better than expected. This new player Rudravarman was a close associate of Simhadhwaja's. He met one of Simhadhwaja's men today and was informed that Satkarni's mind had been poisoned against the deceased man. He was also informed that Satkarni was deeply affected by Simhadhwaja's absence—he was confused, angry and sad at the same time. It was a major blow to Satkarni and when he was told that Simhadhwaja was killed by wild tribesmen while he was escaping from the kingdom, he had tears in his eyes.' The figure continued, 'this Rudravarman is reportedly deeply hurt at Satkarni's attitude. He has decided to teach him a lesson. He was expecting the king to have had absolute faith in Simhadhwaja; with loss of faith and his master dead, he now has nowhere to go, except Tosali where he is originally from.'

'Dhavala is doing a good job it seems,' said the king, with a sly smile across his face.

'Yes, without being aware that he is playing into our hands,' said the figure.

'Ah, this is what greed for power and ambition does to humans!' said the king. Both of them laughed.

'And one significant thing—we could successfully prevent a letter written by Simhadhwaja from reaching Satkarni's hands, here it is.' The figure held out a letter to the king. 'Had it reached Satkarni, it would have been the end of Dhavala and his followers. This letter talks in detail about the machinations of Dhavala and also provides proof. We intercepted it with the help of our spies in that kingdom and replaced it with a letter purportedly from Simhadhwaja asking for the king's forgiveness for his crimes.'

'This Rudravarman now believes that the king did not believe in Simhadhwaja despite receiving the letter he sent, hence his anger.'

'I think the circumstances are perfect. I see no harm in employing him in my court. He is a goldmine of information and has a very strong motive for taking revenge on the Andhras,' said the king.

'Indeed. The Nandas were destroyed by a single man burning with a desire for revenge. We can put him to good use Rajan.'

'I will tell the mahamatya to employ him from tomorrow but keep a close eye on him at all times. One thing more, I am very happy with your work.'

The figure bowed deeply and took leave of the king.

Chapter 5

Merchants of Cloth

The mahamatya asked Rudra to work directly under him. Everything he had said had been verified, and Nakiya did feel that the young man was very promising: he was not only good with analysis, but also had an exceptional knowledge base. The chief of spies too had cleared his appointment after due verification.

Nakiya had told Rudra that the announcement of his joining as a court functionary would be made at a suitable occasion later. Till then, Rudra was to get acquainted with different officials and be exposed to the working of the army as well as other administrative branches. Once well versed with the set-up and conversant with the workings, he would be given other work.

This interregnum of apprenticeship was to test him as regards his suitability and integrity.

Rudra had been provided with a lavish accommodation and personal guards. He was also given a personal chariot.

At the time of joining, the mahamatya had told him, 'You will be given five assistants of suitable rank; two of them will be chosen by us, the others you can appoint on your own. Their salaries will be paid by the royal treasury. I would like to assess the people you appoint personally before they are taken on. Please choose them carefully, keeping in mind their experience, personal habits and family background,' Nakiya had told Rudra.

The two assistants appointed by the administration were Jeemuthabahan and Devabrata. Both reported to him the next morning.

Devabrata was an elderly, frail fellow, who was surprisingly agile. He was short and walked with a characteristic limp of the left leg, so much so that given his briskness, it seemed a bit comic.

Jeemuthabahan was a quiet, middle-aged man with deep set eyes and a hoarse voice. Rudra knew at first glance that they were seasoned spies who would keep a watch on him while helping him with work. So be it, he thought; such arrangements were not new to him. He had played this game earlier at the Andhra court too.

Rudra talked to them about his work and himself and asked about prospective candidates for their team. They promised to revert to him with suggestions in three days.

Rudra felt a deep sense of satisfaction in getting employment in the Kalinga court. He finally had a chance to live a new life now. He decided to seek the blessings of Rajguru Uddalaka before he began work.

The rajguru lived in the palace premises. His house, situated in the north-east corner of the complex, was large but simple. The royal kitchen, storehouses and stables of the household were situated in the south-east.

The rajguru was learned in the Vedas and philosophical systems. He was an expert in the rituals that were performed on various occasions. The old man was also a reader of omens and portents. He had mastered the art of reading the movement of the sun and different planets through various constellations, and their effects.

Apart from this, he had been a mentor to the king and had taught him since his childhood. After the death of King Chetaraja, Kharavela treated him almost on par with his own father. The rajguru was a voice of reason in the royal household, giving advice on important matters. More than personages, such royal sages were institutions. They personified the duties of different varnas given in the holy Vedas. The Brahmins were supposed to be the spiritual guides and mentors to the warrior Kshatriya class. Across kingdoms, rulers rarely overlooked the good counsel of their rajgurus.

When Rudra reached the rajguru's house, he was just returning after performing the daily prayer at the king's residence. Seeing a stranger waiting for him, he inquired with the guards, who informed him of the visitor's request to see him. As he came close, the rajguru recognized Rudra. He asked, 'Are you the one I saw in the court the other day?'

Rudra nodded and then lay prostrate on the ground, touching his feet with both hands. The royal sage blessed him and asked him to get up. Rudra did so and accompanied him inside the house.

Two men had caught Rudra's eyes: one was Bhadrabahu, who had earlier worked as a mercenary soldier for the protection of travelling merchants, and the other was Vijayaka, who was in the service of the nayaka. Both men were capable, well-travelled and intelligent. Bhadrabahu could speak many tongues, while Vijayaka was a master of disguise. Rudra spoke to them individually and ascertained their willingness and suitability to work with him. On being satisfied with his choice, he asked Nakiya to appoint them in his team. He also got one of his old hands from Pratishthanpura, Kinshuk, to join him. Kinshuk had been with him through thick and thin and he had a relationship of absolute trust with him. With his team complete, Rudra set about preparing for his new assignment.

Statecraft was not new to him; it was now only a question of adjusting to a different work atmosphere. The basic principles remained the same—absolute loyalty to the king and the state, impeccable integrity in work and personal life, efficiency in every task and a positive orientation for common good.

His career path in Pratishthanpura had not been very different; he was noted for his qualities very early and picked up for higher assignments. At a young age, he was handling taxation in the city limits and advising the young King Satkarni on state matters related to revenue. The king, being a young man himself, had great faith in the energy of youth to make the Satavahana Empire greatest in the whole Bharatavarsha.

Nakiya saw that Rudra seemed to be performing his work well. He had struck a chord with the various heads of departments, city officials and other important functionaries. Despite his reticent nature, he had a way with people. His team too was working efficiently. Time and again, Nakiya would give them some tasks and they would accomplish them satisfactorily.

Rudra had met Amatya Maitreyi a few times in formal settings. She was professional and businesslike in her interactions. Rudra found her to be highly competent, though taciturn and generally introverted. He felt some kind of edginess in their interactions, but he didn't want to analyse it further.

It had been months now since Rudra had joined the court, and Nakiya had been considering giving him independent assignments. One particular day, a delegation of merchants had come to Nakiya.

Hiranyadatta, the chief of the weaver's guild, spoke up first. 'Worthy mahamatya, we have come to ask for your mercy and intervention.'

'What can I do for you, noble Hiranyadatta?' inquired Nakiya. Rudra was there too—Nakiya usually allowed him to be present during official dealings of non-confidential nature.

'It has become impossible to sell our muslin cloth in the Tosali market, mahamatya. This trader from outside is selling the fine cloth at throwaway prices!'

'Honourable Hiranyadatta, it would be difficult to intervene if he is neither cheating the customers on quality or quantity nor evading any taxes.'

'Most venerable Nakiya, I know that he is paying all the taxes and giving the right quantity too, but it is impossible to sell at such rates. I promise you, he would not be making any profit. Why should he be selling at a loss? This man has either got his goods by loot or he has received goods that have been stolen.'

'Let me examine this matter in detail. I will put my officer Rudravarman on this job. He will report to me in a week's time with all the details.'

There seemed to be some consternation amongst the traders at this statement. Hiranyadatta subtly indicated to them to be quiet. 'Very well then, mahamatya, we have full faith in your judgement,' he said.

The delegation took leave of Nakiya, and Rudra escorted them out. 'Please don't worry, venerable Hiranyadatta,' Rudra said politely. 'As ordered by mahamatya, I will examine the situation. You may see me again in a week's time.'

The merchants left the office premises filled with hope.

Senapati Bahushalin was at the riding grounds, checking a demonstration of the riders from the cavalry. Horses were an expensive commodity; good horses were imported by sea routes or brought from Gandhara. The latter were considered to be obedient and sturdy. The training of horses included movement following signals, galloping, jumping, kicking with forelegs and tight circling. The senapati was getting upset with the horses not being able to manoeuvre a particular jump. He got so agitated that he entered the arena and dragged the rider down, abusing him for his incompetence. Then, he mounted the horse and effortlessly scaled the jump. He also made the horse jump over the fence of the training ground. He gracefully led the horse back to the ground in front of scores of wide-eyed soldiers, who were awed by his skills and control over the horse.

Nayaka Vikarna was passing by when he witnessed the spectacle. 'Congratulations, senapati! I've never seen a defter horse rider, you're quite a talent in this field,' he called out.

'When did you come, nayaka?' the senapati said, greeting him happily.

'Oh, I was just passing by when I witnessed the incident, you were simply wonderful.'

'Come on, nayaka, if a senapati is not an expert at riding, who else will be? The rajpurohit?'

Both men laughed heartily. Then the senapati said, 'Nayaka, I really commend the act of capturing the forest brigand, it was a job well done. It has increased our respect manifold in the eyes of the people.'

Vikarna's face turned grim. 'But senapati, all my efforts have gone down the drain as the king decided to honour the abhay daan given by that stranger. To add insult to injury, that stranger has been appointed in royal service, that too directly under the mahamatya!'

'I did learn about the appointment of this fellow called Rudravarman, but it seems his appointment has nothing to do with the recapture of the forest brigand.'

'Senapati, don't try to console me. I also understand these games. I hate having to see that idiot's face almost daily at work.'

'He seems to be a reasonable person, Vikarna, why are you calling him an idiot?' The senapati's eyes narrowed.

'Let it be, senapati, let's talk of pleasant things . . .' Vikarna changed the topic and the two chatted for a while before parting ways.

Chapter 6

Machinations of the Asmakas

Rudra had sent Jeemuthabahan to buy some muslin from the foreign merchant's shop. The merchants had been right—it was of the finest quality but was being sold at dirt cheap prices. Rudra called his associates into the office to chart out a strategy.

'What do you think?' Rudra conferred with Bhadrabahu. 'Arya, I too had gone to the shop. The people there don't seem to be genuine traders.'

'What are you trying to say, Bhadrabahu?'

'It seems to be some kind of an operation in the guise of trade, arya,' he said.

Jeemuthabahan and Kinshuk—who had also visited the shop—seemed to be in agreement with the assessment.

'They claim to be from Bharukachcha, but their language seems to indicate that they are from Paundanyapura, the capital of the Asmakas,' Kinshuk said.

'Keep investigating, Kinshuk and Bhadrabahu, and keep me posted every evening,' Rudra said.

A few days later, the delegation of merchants came to thank Nakiya. 'Mahamatya, we are very grateful to you for your help. You are a man of your word. The foreigner has shut shop and gone away, we can resume our normal trade again. As a measure of our gratitude towards your efforts, we have decided to lower our own prices too, at least for some time.'

Nakiya accepted their acknowledgement with grace, and once they had left, he immediately called for Rudra. 'What did you do to scare away the muslin merchants?' His forehead betrayed worry lines.

'Mahamatya, take my word, nothing wrong has been done, but I will confirm with my team as to why the foreigner has shut shop and left.'

Rudra met his team, and they informed him that, as suspected, the foreign merchant was from the land of the Asmakas and not Bharukachcha, as claimed. They had probably got wind of the fact that there was some suspicion as to their antecedents, and had decamped overnight, leaving their wares behind.

Rudra dispatched Bhadrabahu and Kinshuk to Paundanyapura to get to the root of the matter. He told them to return in a month.

It was late afternoon when Rudra arrived at the king's palace. 'What brings you here, Rudravarman?' Rajan asked as Rudra was ushered in.

'Rajan, I have some disturbing news from the land of Asmakas,' Rudra said.

'What can the sons of Ikshvaku do that is a cause of concern to us?' the king laughed dismissively.

'Rajan, the lord of Paudanyapura was heard boasting in his court that he can crush the rising power of Kalinga any time. He also said that his ancestor Aruna and his minister Nandisena had once defeated the king of Kalinga after forcibly taking his four daughters as queens. They are good friends and neighbours of the Andhras. If they combine forces, it could create serious problems for us, Rajan,' Rudra said.

The king crossed his arms and thought for some time. 'Can you get information about what their plans are and whether they are cooperating with the Andhras? Let me also know the strength of their army, state of their preparations, weapons and tactics.'

'Yes, Rajan. I will find out everything I can about them.'

As he left the king's chambers, Rudra felt a slight sense of elation. Challenges somehow always made him happy.

✦ ✦ ✦

Another month passed and Rudra was summoned to the king's chambers. Mahamatya Nakiya was also present in the room.

'Your information is indeed true, Rudravarman. The Asmakas are planning something. They intend to cross the Dakshin Ganga and wage war with us,' said the king.

Multiple sources had independently confirmed Rudra's information. Mahamatya Nakiya indicated for Rudra to come and sit near the king. Rudra quickly recounted all the information he had collected in the last one month.

'Rajan, their army is well trained, and they have very hardy foot soldiers. Their country is prosperous and their treasury is full. Although they're a small country, they can actually put up a tough fight,' Rudra said.

'How are their terms with the Rathikas and Bhojakas? Will they join him, stay neutral or collaborate with us?' asked the king.

Nakiya interjected, 'As with any neighbours, the Rathikas and Bhojakas are not kindly inclined toward the Asmakas. The Andhras are also not likely to pitch in soon, but if there is a prolonged battle and we are seen as weak, the Andhras may attack us from the rear to take advantage of the situation.'

'Given the distance involved, we should go for a short and effective war, and crush them decisively. An element of surprise is the basic requirement for such a move, Rajan,' Rudra said.

'What do you have in mind, Arya Rudravarman?' asked Nakiya, as he handed over to him a wooden board and a writing implement. Rudra laid the board in front of the king and quickly drew a sketch map of Kalinga and its neighbouring kingdoms.

'Mahamatya, I propose that we silently make our preparations; no information should go out to anyone about our groundwork. We can put word out that the king is going on a long hunting expedition towards the north-east and will not be returning for two months.

'We will also make them believe that the senapati, along with a substantial part of the army, are away from the capital and the western border. This will encourage them to make a surprise move. At the same time we should move some of our elephants to the north-east to convince them of the king's absence from the capital.'

'But how do we fight without moving our elephants across Dakshin Ganga?' questioned the king, his broad forehead furrowed, his mind quickly evaluating multiple strategies, their consequences and costs.

'Rajan, given the great distances involved and the absolute necessity of surprise, it would be advisable to use only cavalry and light infantry.'

The king and mahamatya looked at each other. Rudra paused for a moment. Nakiya then asked him to continue. 'I propose that we send out troops ahead into their territory under the guise of trading caravans. A lot of merchants and traders cross their area to reach the Andhra country anyway, and the Asmakas derive a lot of tax revenue from them. As this is very usual, they will not suspect anything. Meanwhile, emboldened by the news of our hunting expedition, the Asmakas will try to make a swift move into our territory, thinking that they can achieve immediate success. We, on the other hand, will be sitting fully prepared for their attack. As they surge forward, we will bring out our elephants. They don't have many elephants to counter us. Meanwhile, our troops can capture their capital. They will be caught unawares and will be defeated decisively.' Rudra spoke animatedly, his mind racing ahead of his words.

'I like this strategy, Nakiya. Discuss it with the senapati in detail and tell me what he thinks of it.'

'One more thing, Rajan. The wild tribes of the Dandakaranya forests are very hostile to the Asmakas as their army recently cleared a large forest tract inhabited by them. A large number of their people were killed or tortured and their women dishonoured by the army. When we close in on them from front and rear, they will have no place to escape but to the jungles. The tribes will think that they are being attacked, and—as it is their own territory—they will fight with an advantage. I'm sure the Asmakas' army will suffer major losses on all fronts and will possibly surrender soon to avoid further damage.'

Rudra was furiously drawing on the map and the king too was looking charged.

'Mahamatya, work out the finer details of this strategy along with the senapati and Rudravarman and meet me in three days,' commanded the king.

Rudra and Nakiya had several meetings with the senapati. Bahushalin initially resented the fact that a newcomer was suggesting strategies for war. Then, seeing that the mahamatya was in full agreement with Rudra, he decided to cooperate. As the discussions advanced, the senapati saw the logic and beauty of it all. He in turn conferred with his commanders, who were also agreeable to the plan.

They finally met the king, and it was decided that they would go ahead with Rudra's strategy.

The sage had just taken a dip in the holy Dakshin Ganga, where the Murala River joined it. He had set up a hut at a point not far from the confluence of the rivers. He had meagre belongings and hardly any utensils, but he kept some herbs and medicines handy owing to his knowledge of Ayurveda. His beard was black, showing that he had taken the path of renunciation quite early in life, as he was still quite young.

The hermitage was in a clearing near the sandy banks of the rivers, visible from the nearby hills. It was also not far from the Dakshinapatha, a major lifeline of trade between various kingdoms, and large caravans would often pass here. Of late, traders would drop in to seek the blessings of the holy man. At times, he also gave them healing concoctions and herbs for their ailments. His fame was spreading fast, and people had started to come from distant quarters to visit him.

Over the last few days, the sage had noticed an unusually large caravan of traders proceeding to the south. They seemed to be originating from either Magadha or Kalinga Nagari. These caravans were well protected, with armed mercenary riders accompanying them.

The forest area surrounding the sage's hut was filled with hostile tribes who were lawless and did not accept the dominance of any king or state. They were independent minded and ferocious. The traders were at great risk of being robbed or murdered by these people, hence they travelled only during the day and carried enough protection with them.

Although the tribes were hostile to the traders and the soldiers, they were quite comfortable with the sage. In fact, some of their members used to visit the sage and they also provided him with rare herbs and roots from the jungles, of which they had intimate knowledge.

One evening, when the sage returned to his hut after collecting fruits from the forest, he found two tribesmen waiting for him. One seemed agitated and the other was lying down on the ground. The sage rushed to them. The tribesman lying down had a deep cut on his arm, and he had evidently bled a lot. His brother had brought him to the sage's hut in search of quick help. The sage cleaned the wound and applied a turmeric paste mixed with the pulp of the leaves of malati, katuki, neem, karanja and patala and put the wounded man to sleep.

'How did this happen?' asked the sage. 'Some soldiers were moving very speedily to the east through the forest. We were returning from the hunt when they saw us, and they attacked us unprovoked! I escaped but my brother got hurt.'

'Whose soldiers are they and where are they going?'

'They are Asmakas, going to attack Kalinga Nagari, as the king of Kalinga is out on a hunting expedition along with the senapati. He will not be able to return to his capital in the time the Asmakas overrun the city.'

'Strange are the ways of men . . . may god give them wisdom,' the sage said.

The tribesman said, 'We are worried that, on their return, those soldiers will attack us. But we are also prepared.'

Meanwhile at Tosali, Nakiya and Senapati Bahushalin had sought an urgent meeting with the king. The Asmakas were acting as per their expectations: there was confirmed intelligence on the sudden advance of the enemy soldiers through the forests towards Kalinga borders.

'The time has come!' he said. 'Senapati Bahushalin, rally your forces and give them a grand reception!'

'We will be victorious, Rajan, with your blessings!' said the elated senapati.

The tribesman had recovered and returned home two days back. The sage was getting ready for his evening prayers when he heard a large commotion outside his hut. Asmaka soldiers were running homewards, most of them wounded, some bleeding with sword and lance wounds, while others were injured by arrows fired by the tribesmen hiding in the trees, bushes and behind rocks. Some fell down bleeding, but the others did not stop to help them. The abandoned horses too bolted in various directions. Those shot by the tribesmen died soon as the poisons from the arrow tips spread into their blood. There were bodies everywhere; those who had not died were in the throes of death. The tribals had hunted down the wounded survivors. Night was falling now and there was an eerie silence around the place.

A soldier on horseback, who looked like a royal Kalinga bodyguard came to the sage's hut; he had an extra horse with him. 'Master, it's time we leave from here,' he said.

The sage smiled. He bundled his meagre belongings and threw them away. Then, he set fire to his hut and proceeded to leave. He was now wearing a soldier's uniform, which fitted his muscular body very well.

He effortlessly hopped atop the horse, face beaming with pride. *Things went exactly to plan*, thought Rudra happily.

Chapter 7

Unexpected Acquaintance

The court was resplendent. All the amatyas were present, and the king was presiding.

Nakiya arose with the king's permission and delivered a long speech on the recent war victory. He praised the king and his sagacity, and also praised the senapati for a valiant and brilliant war effort. There was no mention of Rudra's contribution.

The senapati stood up next. 'Rajan, the best moment was when the Asmakas reached our boundaries—they were caught absolutely unaware when we emerged from the hills. They didn't even fight, but simply turned back and began running at the sight of our magnificent elephants and armoured riders. They ran to the forests for cover, and the forest tribes gave them a memorable reception. Meanwhile, our contingent in Paudanyapura came out of their merchant disguise and conquered the capital. There was no resistance whatsoever. We have seized the Asmakas' treasury; carts of jewels and precious stones have been brought to Kalinga!'

Rudra secretly complimented himself on the achievement. He was intrigued by the fact that his contribution had not been mentioned, but then he saw that the mahamatya and the king were glancing at him with eyes full of appreciation. He kept his expression blank.

Everyone in the court cheered the news. Suddenly, a loud voice was heard. 'Shame on us as a nation! We are the same people who lost a hundred thousand men in the war against Ashoka, and we never adopted any tactics like these. Since when have wars been fought like this. This is worse than child's play, hiding like wild animals to pounce upon the prey. This is no war, no fight took place at all. What victory are we celebrating?' It was a handsome youth who was roaring like a lion, his face red with anger.

'Vajramitra!' shouted the senapati, getting up from his seat and rushing towards the young man. 'How dare you speak like this in the king's presence?'

Nayaka Vikarna also indicated to his soldiers to be ready for action as he too moved closer to Vajramitra.

The courtiers were aghast. There was a palpable tension in the air as the haughty man moved towards the throne. The senapati physically blocked him from reaching the king and Saktimati moved menacingly towards Vajramitra. Kharavela sat there unperturbed.

'Please don't intervene. I am talking to the king!' said Vajramitra with indignation as he jostled with the senapati.

Nayaka Vikarna thundered, 'Had you not been a friend of the king, Vajramitra, I would have severed your head from the body!' Vajramitra had been the king's classmate in the *gurukul* (traditional school) when they were young boys. They had been taught by the same guru, Uddalaka, who was now the rajguru.

Vajramitra stopped grappling with the senapati and laughed in a condescending way.

The king got up and asked Vajramitra to calm down. Then he spoke in a composed voice. 'Let us listen to Vajramitra. His family, which includes so many illustrious names, has served the nation for generations.'

Silence fell on the gathering, and the bodyguards cautiously took a few steps back.

'Tell me, Vajramitra, what do you have to say?'

'I do not approve of a "war" like this. It will make our soldiers cowards and cheats, rather than valiant fighters. It is against all principles of warfare to fight like foxes,' said Vajramitra.

The king said, 'It should be made clear to everyone that we were defending ourselves. The Asmakas were the aggressors, and we did all that was possible to secure the safety and well-being of our citizens, with a minimal loss of life from our side.'

Vajramitra was unconvinced. 'You approve of this cowardice? I would have never expected this from you!'

'You have spoken your mind, and I have heard you. Please go back to your seat,' the king said calmly.

Vajramitra hadn't expected this. He stood there for a few moments, looking at the king with burning eyes. Then, he turned and stormed out of the hall.

After the court was dismissed, Rudra was about to leave the palace premises when Amatya Maitreyi came up to him. As usual, Rudra was pleased to talk to her. All the negativity of the last half hour seemed to vanish. He felt that her grim exterior seemed to melt when she met him; he also felt that he was imagining these things.

'Arya Rudravarman, please don't lose heart, we are all aware of your efforts and contribution towards this victory. Do not pay heed to the detractors.'

'Devi Maitreyi, a million thanks to you. I thought that nobody noticed what my people have helped achieve. You're very perceptive.'

Maitreyi smiled gently and left. Rudra watched her for a few moments before turning to his chariot.

Everywhere in the capital, the victory was being celebrated. Houses had been decorated and different kinds of flags and colourful toranas could be seen all over. Shopkeepers had reduced the prices of commodities, and bards, singers and performers had come out on the streets in a mood of festivity. Rudra had decided to wander alone on foot this evening, despite the exhortations of his bodyguards to accompany him. He wanted to see life from the eyes of a commoner, so he had also dressed as one. He also wanted to explore the town and possibly locate where his old home had once stood before it had burnt down in his childhood.

He stopped by a betel leaf shop where some people were engaged in a discussion. A young merchant with long curly hair said, 'I hear that in ancient times the Asmakas had defeated Kalinga and had forcibly taken the daughters of the king as queens.'

'They will never dream of fighting with us in the future, so complete has been their rout!' another said.

'The king has arranged for victory celebrations for fifteen days! Come, I don't want to miss out on the singing and dancing.'

Rudra bought a paan and listened to the conversations of the people, soaking in the festive spirit. Suddenly, someone tapped him on his shoulder. He turned and saw an armed soldier.

'Arya, please come aside, the amatya wants to speak to you,' the soldier said.

Surprised, Rudra followed the soldier, and cautiously walked to a decorated chariot. It was as if lightning had struck him—it was Amatya Maitreyi again! She gestured for him to come up and sit in the chariot. Her bodyguards were aghast that a commoner was being asked to sit by her side.

Rudra climbed up, and a strange mix of intoxication, fear and yearning swirled in his stomach. She smelled like fresh flowers, he thought.

'Why are you moving around in disguise, Arya Rudravarman?'

He snapped back to reality. 'I . . . I . . .' Rudra stammered, 'I was wanting to see life as a commoner.'

She laughed a good-natured laugh, and her face was radiant. 'Oh! So what did you see? Which ganika did you like the most?'

'Ha, you arrested me before I could see anything,' Rudra said with a laugh, having regained his composure. He could not believe that he was sitting by her side. He felt terribly drawn to her and had a strange impulse to touch her hand.

She chuckled as if she could read his mind.

'I hear that you're very strict and unforgiving,' Rudra said.

'Do I look like a tyrant, Arya Rudravarman?'

Rudra looked at her large mesmerizing eyes, she looked like a goddess! He didn't reply, only blushed.

'I believe we are near your residence. You may proceed like a commoner from here,' she said mockingly.

Still, he couldn't respond to her as he alighted from the chariot.

'Arya Rudravarman,' she said suddenly in a hushed tone. 'Somehow, I feel that we have met somewhere before.'

The chariot sped away, and Rudra stood there stunned, remembering those eyes which shone like bright stars on that night at the madiralaya. He didn't move for a long time; the lingering fragrance of her presence was still fresh in the air.

Maitreyi was rather amazed at herself. Her favourite attendant and confidante, Yamini, broke the silence as she whispered in her ear, 'So this is the Arya Rudravarman you had been curious about? Your behaviour changes in his presence, amatya.'

Maitreyi shook her head dismissively, but she realized that this was true indeed. This was very different from her usual nature. Right since childhood, she had been reclusive and aloof, never opening up to people. Her mother had passed away at an early age, and as a single child, she was used to loneliness, which she had perfected into an art now. But she had a sense of comfort with this man, as if she had known him from before.

She had, despite her introverted nature, done very well for herself. Observant, unflappable and precise, she was an asset to the administration, and yes, she could be unforgiving too. Her father had been very particular with her education—she owed much to him. His own fastidiousness had influenced her, and she had grown up into a methodical yet versatile individual who could be unemotional. She sensed a change in herself of late though, and she liked it.

✦✦✦

As soon as Rudra reached home, he curled up on his bed and was about to sleep, when Kinshuk came in. 'Arya, there is an ascetic at the door, and he refuses to go away. He insists on seeing the master of this house. I told him that you are about to sleep and cannot be disturbed at this late hour, but he is adamant.'

'Bring him in,' Rudra said.

Some moments later, an ascetic with long matted hair and a beard was ushered in. Rudra touched his feet to seek his blessings. 'You will shine bright like the sun one day, no one will be able to look at you directly, such would be the fame of your deeds,' the ascetic said.

As soon as the attendant left, his tone and expression changed. He held on tightly to Rudra's arm and said, 'Arya, you must meet Vajramitra tomorrow, he has an important task for you. Do not miss the meeting for any reason. This is for your own good. Go in the guise of a messenger and meet him at this place.' The ascetic handed him a sealed letter.

Before Rudra could react, the ascetic had gotten up and left. Rudra stared at the letter he had been handed.

Chapter 8

The Scent of a Conspiracy

It was a nondescript house, but Rudra had no trouble locating it. He had taken precautions while making his way to this place, ensuring that no one was following him.

Vajramitra was already there, and he got up to welcome Rudra, who politely wished him as an equal. Rudra was apprehensive and cautious. Without much ado, Vajramitra said, 'Did you see that day, how the king behaved with me! I was speaking the truth. Which Kshatriya will tolerate such an insult?'

Rudra was taken aback but did not react.

'I am fully aware that it was all your strategy that led to an easy victory over the valiant Asmakas. I do not support such cowardice, but no one even mentioned your name Rudravarman! So, it was not me alone who was insulted, you too were deceived,' said Vajramitra, agitated. 'I want to avenge the insult, and I want you to support me. It is time that this dynasty of outsiders is uprooted from Kalinga. You're a master strategist, why don't we join hands?'

Rudra was stunned; he felt the blood freeze in his veins.

'If you don't support me, and if I am unsuccessful in overthrowing the king, I will say you were behind the conspiracy. If I succeed without you, you will be the first to be put under the elephant's feet for not helping me,' Vajramitra growled.

Rudra thought quickly. 'But Vajramitra, why me? I am an innocent person unconnected with all this,' he said.

'I am aware of your abilities, Rudravarman, and don't worry, you will be surprised to know who all are on my side. If we succeed with your help, you will be made the next senapati, with me as the king,' Vajramitra said. 'And one more thing, I know your secret—you're an associate of Simhadhwaja. So you don't really have many options. You could be arrested for being a traitor any day, I just need to feed the king's spies the information.'

Vajramitra's face had contorted into an evil smile. Rudra was shaken. He had just recently emerged from a crisis at Pratishthanpura and now he was caught in a quagmire once again.

What if I killed him right here? Would there be anyone to tell the world? Or has Vajramitra taken precautions and had people concealed in the house? Rudra was calculating possible courses of action in his mind. Finally, prudence prevailed and he composed himself.

'Arya Vajramitra, you have put me in a very difficult situation. I will need some time to think over it.'

Vajramitra studied him with a piercing gaze and then indicated for him to leave.

Rudra emerged out on the street, knowing that Vajramitra's spies would be all over. He had to be very vigilant now. Any word or action out of place would lead him to the executioner's axe, or worse, harm his motherland or the king. Trust no one, and don't take chances, he told himself. The faces of Nakiya, Maitreyi, Bahushalin, Uddalaka, Vikarna and the other amatyas flashed before his eyes. His mind did all the calculations—who could be trusted, who was a likely traitor and which players would be active in an endgame, if there was any.

He decided to keep his eyes and ears open and take the advice of Devabrata.

When he reached home, he called his assistant. 'Devabrata, I have a feeling that Arya Vajramitra is not on the right path. What is your information?'

'Arya, wise men get away from the ground where elephants play. Why do you want to get trampled by these heavyweights. I would advise you to not attract unnecessary attention by trying to gain any information about anyone in the court, you will not be spared.'

'But I have duties towards the king and my country.'

'The time will come, arya, when you would be able to do what you think is your duty. Right now, lie low and be vigilant.'

Rudra didn't like Devabrata's impassivity. 'What if it is too late, Devabrata?'

'Don't always act in haste like your father, son!' Devabrata said and then realized what had slipped out from his mouth. He got up and wanted to leave.

'What did you just say?' Rudra got up and held him by his arm.

'Nothing, son, nothing. I was just cautioning you.' Devabrata looked down as he talked, hiding his face.

'What was that about my father? Did you know him? Tell me, Devabrata, don't hide things from me!'

'It is not the right time to answer all this, arya; I do not know anything more,' he said and left. Rudra stared at his retreating back, shocked and confused.

The next morning, Rudra was about to enter the court when his attention was distracted by a guard who appeared to be in deep distress. Rudra couldn't ignore it and asked what was troubling him.

'I want to leave, master, but the guard in-charge is not allowing me. I have an emergency to attend to,' said the soldier.

'What emergency?' asked Rudra.

'My cousin has been bitten by a poisonous snake and is unconscious. There is no male member at home to attend to it,' the guard said with tears in his eyes.

'Please give me more information, maybe I can help,' said Rudra.

'My cousin works at the elephant kraal. This morning, he was found unconscious, bitten by a snake. His wife has sent a message for me. I don't know what his condition is now.' Tears rolled down the sturdy man's face.

Rudra was moved by his story and asked him to wait. Moments later, he returned with the guard commander and a replacement for the distressed soldier. 'Young man, you can go and attend to your cousin now,' said Rudra with compassion.

The soldier had tears of gratitude in his eyes as he thanked Rudra, and then he left.

As he walked away, Rudra felt that something was amiss. He beckoned Vijayaka and asked him to tail the soldier. Rudra then hurriedly took his seat in the court.

It was late afternoon when Vijayaka came back. He confirmed the soldier's story and said the cousin had died from the snake bite.

'What work did the deceased do at the kraal?' asked Rudra.

'Master, he used to train the royal elephants,' Vijayaka said.

Something seemed suspicious to Rudra, and he asked for the address of the soldier's cousin. On reaching the dead man's home, the guard approached Rudra and greeted him with tearful eyes. 'My cousin was a very good man. He was the one who tamed the largest and the wildest elephant in the kingdom,' he said.

Rudra asked if the body could be shown to him, and the soldier agreed. He approached the dead body and carefully lifted the cloth covering it. His eyes flashed with disbelief, but he immediately composed himself, paid his respects and departed.

Two days later, Rudra visited the elephant kraal after seeking the permission of the senapati. Rudra had some expertise in matters of training of elephants and horses. He talked to the mahouts and the camp commander, and visited the great Mahagiri, the largest elephant in the whole kingdom—it was the king's own favourite. Rudra also met the person taking care of the great elephant—this man was newly appointed in place of the guard's cousin.

After he was done, Rudra decided to discuss the matter with the nayaka and went to Vikarna's office.

'Oh, it's Arya Rudravarman! It looks like an auspicious day for me that such an important person has decided to pay me a visit. Whom are you catching today, arya? You seem to have all the qualities of a good policeman!' He laughed sarcastically and did not ask him to sit.

Rudra understood that it would be of no use to seek this man's intervention. He was too antagonistic towards him.

'I had come for a courtesy visit, arya, I thought it would be worthwhile to know you better.'

'Haha, that's quite unnecessary, arya. Anyway, I keep hearing praise for you from Amatya Maitreyi.'

Rudra bowed his head, acknowledging the compliment. 'I am thankful for your valuable time, arya. I understand that being the nayaka, you must be very busy. My apologies for barging in like this; may God bless you.' Rudra turned away.

'It is you who needs blessings Arya Rudravarman, don't worry about me,' Vikarna said, his voice harsh.

Rudra politely took his leave.

A week later, Rudra was talking to a trusted spy. It was late in the night. 'I feel that something very bad is going to happen. I see ill omens around us. As I had told you, last week when I checked the kraal, I found Mahagiri to be in an aggressive mood. Have you been keeping an eye on the kraal and its functionaries as I'd asked? What is your update?'

The spy replied, 'Nothing unusual till now, but I have put my own man as the cleaner of the place where Mahagiri and other large elephants are housed. He does not have access to them but is allowed to clean the place once the beasts are taken out for training.'

Rudra said, 'Can you ask him to bring me a small sample of the dirt from the floor after he sweeps it clean?'

'Yes master, it will be done from tomorrow.'

'Anything else unusual that you wish to tell me?'

The figure thought for a moment and then said, 'People say . . . that the dark prince's agents have entered the city and live amongst us in various disguises.'

'What does the dark prince want to achieve?' he asked.

'Arya, he wants the kingdom, nothing less, nothing more. He says that the Chedi Mahameghavahanas are outsiders, and they don't have any right to rule this land.'

'Tell me more about him.'

'Arya, nothing more is known about him, except that he has a lot of secret followers who follow the dark path of *Vama marga*.'

'I want to know everything you can find out about him.'

'Arya, I will work on it,' the spy said.

✦ ✦ ✦

Rudra went to the kraal the next morning. Tridib, the camp commander, approached him. 'The mahouts are preparing the elephants for a long journey—the king is going on a hunting expedition, Arya. I may not be able to assist you today, please forgive me.'

'I have just come to inspect and see if everything is in order, Tridib. I have been impressed by your work with the elephants and have brought a copy of the greatest work on elephant medicine, the *Hastayurveda* by Palakapya Muni, as a gift for you.'

Tridib was overjoyed and he gratefully accepted the neatly bound bark paper volume.

Tridib took leave of Rudra and went back to his work. Rudra headed to Mahagiri's enclosure. The beast was being decorated with gold embroidered cloth and being anointed with scented sandal paste. Rudra went up to the gentle beast, who raised its trunk in a blessing posture. At this moment, Rudra held its trunk as if accepting blessings and slipped a small ball of a paste into its snout. The animal promptly put it inside its mouth and consumed it.

Chapter 9

An Assassination Attempt

The royal procession was preparing to leave for the hunting expedition. Senapati Bahushalin had been instructed to remain in the capital and take care of the security of the city as well as the royal household. Mahamatya Nakiya was accompanying the king.

It was a huge procession, with hundreds of riders, foot soldiers and dozens of elephants. Rudra chose to ride ahead of the king, leading the right flank of the horsemen. His heart was pounding. He felt a looming threat in the air. Something terrible was going to happen any time now, but he was prepared. He rode forward with a hand on the hilt of his sword and the reins in the other. He crossed the narrow bridge over the deep ditch full of hungry crocodiles, turned back and waited for the king to emerge from the fort walls. Rudra quickly scanned all the people assembled for signs of disguise or unusual activity; he was focused and charged for action.

The king finally emerged, seated atop a howdah on the giant elephant Mahagiri, decorated with gold, silver and flaming colours, the royal flag fluttering high above him. It seemed as if Lord Indra himself was on the march. Mounted soldiers from the most trusted palace guards accompanied him in the procession. The riders wore brightly coloured uttariyas below light armour. They looked magnificent with their swords and spears.

As soon as the king reached the narrow portion of the bridge, a loud beating of drums and large metallic instruments began creating a terrible din. Mahagiri suddenly stopped in his tracks and took two steps back. The howdah got unbalanced, and the king was flung to the rear. He tightly grasped the vertical rods, struggling not to fall. By then, the mahout had sprung into action. He jumped and lay flat on the elephant's head, holding its large ears with bare hands. The beast shook its head vigorously from side to side, but the mahout was able to calm it. The music stopped due to this terrible scene, and the elephant steadied itself and crossed the bridge safely.

The king asked the mahout not to stop. He continued onwards as if nothing had happened.

The jungle camp had been established at a chosen place, elaborately laid out with provisions to repel any surprise attack. Divisions of sentinels kept a strict vigil with a defined timetable.

Late in the evening, Rudra was approaching his tent when he saw Maitreyi and the other amatyas coming into the camp. Vijayaka told him, 'Master, something serious is up, I will try and get more information on this. The king's head cook is my friend.'

Rudra asked him to be careful and retired to his tent.

It must have been very late at night when he suddenly woke up with a suffocating feeling. He realized that he was being forcefully carried out of his tent by four strong men. He tried to scream but one of them covered his mouth with his hand, almost gagging him. The men whispered to him to be silent, or he would be killed. Rudra saw that there was no point in struggling right now; he would conserve his energy for later. They tied his hands and dragged him into the deeper part of the forest.

Who were these men? Rudra wondered. Were they Vajramitra's men? Satkarni's spies? Asmakas' sympathizers? He could not place them.

They took him to a small hillock inside the forest, where a huge rock outcrop could be seen in the faint moonlight. They tied him to a large rock with ropes and stood there in silence before him. Then, their leader beckoned them to return.

Rudra knew that wild animals would devour him alive within hours. He decided to speak. 'Can I know who you are, and why you have tied me here?' he said.

The leader turned back and said in a grim voice. 'You should have thought of this before you fed opium to the royal elephant, you traitor!'

Rudra was stunned. Yes, he had done it, but for a different purpose.

He spoke in a composed voice. 'Give me an opportunity to explain. If Nakiya or the king is not convinced of my story, I will, as a Kshatriya, take my own life for my honour.'

The leader laughed and started walking towards the camp. Rudra shouted, 'The king's life is in danger. He may not go back alive and only I can help. If you are loyal to the king, give me one chance to speak to him. I swear heavens will fall if you don't heed my advice. Are you listening?'

The man turned around and stood squarely in front of Rudra, gazing into his eyes in the dim light. His assistant whispered something in the man's ear. He pondered for a moment, then untied Rudra and started taking him back.

It was hours before Rudra could see a ray of hope. He had been fettered and confined to a small tent, no one had spoken to him. At about noon, Nakiya came inside; his eyes were burning. Without saying a word, he indicated for him to be freed. Rudra was taken to the king's camp. He walked into the tent unshaken and saw that the king was alone there. However, he had the feeling that there were people hidden around, closely watching him.

'Rajan, at the cost of my life, I want to speak to you alone. No one else should hear what I am about to tell you,' Rudra said.

The king remained silent for a moment and then nodded curtly. Rudra heard rustling sounds in the background, as if several armed men were sheathing their swords back in their scabbards and withdrawing slowly.

'Rajan . . .' He cleared his throat and sat down on the floor. 'Ten days ago, the mahout who looked after Mahagiri died, ostensibly of a snakebite. I accidentally came to know of this from his cousin who is employed as a guard outside the royal court chamber. I felt something suspicious was going on, hence, I decided to personally visit the deceased's place.

'When I saw the dead body, I realized that it was not a case of snakebite—he had been tortured and then killed by administering snake poison. I gathered that something was amiss at the elephant kraal. There, I saw a new mahout who was in charge of Mahagiri. This man did not seem right to me, so I put my trusted aides to keep a watch on the activities in the elephant kraal, especially Mahagiri's enclosure, as I had seen that the elephant was having particularly bad moods.

'I got sweepings from his enclosure collected and sent to me. To my horror, I found that there were shells of kuchila seeds in it. I have studied elephant veterinary science and medicine and have mastered the sutras from Palakapya Muni's *Hastayurveda*. I knew that kuchila causes the victim to be very sensitive to the slightest of sounds and induces violent seizures. In fact, that was exactly what was happening to Mahagiri when you were crossing the bridge. The beast would have fallen into the waters filled with crocodiles, taking you along in what would have seemed to be a mere accident. The loud beating of drums was also planned to trigger the reaction in the elephant.'

The king's eyes widened. 'Why didn't you inform the mahamatya when you saw the kuchila seeds?' he asked now.

'I didn't know whom to trust. What if the senapati, mahamatya or anyone else I spoke to was involved? I didn't know which powerful forces were behind this. So, I decided to do something on my own when I learned that Rajan was to ride the same elephant on the hunting expedition. Had it not been for the lump of opium, the antidote to kuchila, which I had fed to it before the journey began, Rajan, it would have been a very unfortunate day for the nation.'

'Why should I believe you?' asked the king. 'You have fled from the Andhras after what they feel is bitter betrayal. No one here knows your real identity for sure, and then you're found feeding something to the king's elephant!'

'Rajan,' said Rudra, 'I have documented all that has happened and asked my trusted aides to deliver the letter to you in case of my death, so that you are warned in time. Yes, I fed opium to Mahagiri, but only as an antidote. All that I have done, Rajan, is to save you and my motherland from evil designs. If you disbelieve me, I have no option but to take my own life, right here and now!'

The king looked terribly distressed. 'Rudravarman,' he said in a sad voice, 'somehow, I am inclined to spare you today. Nobody except a few trusted people know what happened yesterday, so don't disclose your story to anyone at all. Now, go back as if nothing happened and keep a very close watch on everything. I want to know the forces behind this and deal with them suitably.'

Rudra returned to his camp, his head spinning from the events of the last few days.

✦ ✦ ✦

Rudra got up from the bed; a female attendant who was standing nearby saw his eyes open and rushed out.

'Where am I?' he said to himself. The place was unfamiliar but seemed to be a palace. It had high ceilings and carved woodwork on the beams and pillars. The objects in the room conveyed that the owner was an individual of fine taste. As he tried to get up, a stern-looking woman came into the room and asked him to lie down. He felt weak and dizzy, and his mouth felt dry and parched. He tried to get up again but collapsed on the bed due to weakness. His breath felt heavy. Rudra heard some noise in the adjoining corridor, as if people were hurriedly running around. He heard footsteps, and then smelt a familiar fragrance. He opened his eyes, and through the misty haze he saw Maitreyi! She was standing beside his bedside, looking at him with compassion.

Rudra thought he was hallucinating, he wanted to speak but couldn't utter a word. She indicated for him to keep silent and rest.

He closed his eyes, and he felt her hand on his forehead, checking for signs of fever. He kept still and slowly submerged into a dreamy delirium. He held her hand, his eyes still closed, and she didn't resist. It was deeply comforting. He lapsed into sleep.

Days passed, and Rudra's strength was returning. He could walk around the room and dress, bathe himself and eat properly. He was still in the dark about what had happened to him. Maitreyi did not return after that day's visit, but he knew that he was in her care, and probably, custody.

The attendants took good care of him but didn't speak a word or answer any questions; he began to feel a bit restless. Totally cut off from the external world, he was recovering in some form of captivity. He was grateful from the depths of his heart to Maitreyi for saving his life, but wanted to know what had happened at the hunting expedition for him to land in this condition? Was it the king's men who did this to him? Was it Andhra spies? Was it Vajramitra?

Had the culprits been identified and dealt with? Or were they still at large, waiting for a better opportunity to strike? Were they aware that it was he who had foiled their plans?

He examined himself in the polished bronze mirror to check for marks of injury but couldn't locate one. He ran trembling fingers again over his back, neck and thighs to feel any healing wound or scar but couldn't find anything. His mind was buzzing with confusion, what had befallen upon him? What was his future now?

He wrote down his feelings, apprehensions and surmises on the tree bark papers kept in his room. His writings had begun to pile up. One particular evening, when he was busy writing about his predicament, the room was suddenly was filled with a fragrance of fresh flowers; he had a strange feeling that someone was present in the room. He quickly turned around and saw her, standing behind him. God knows how long she had been standing there, studying him.

Startled and confused, he stuttered but couldn't speak. She came and gently sat beside him, looking directly into his eyes. He couldn't keep staring at her like that, nor could he take his eyes off her. He sat there spellbound and motionless.

'Rudra,' Maitreyi broke the silence.

He woke up from his trance, composed himself and said, 'Yes, Amatya Maitreyi?'

She continued in a soft voice. 'I know you must be having many questions. You're here on the king's orders. When you returned from the royal tent in the forest, there was an attempt to assassinate you. We have not been able to locate who the assassins were, but they fled after targeting you with a poisonous dart. You immediately lost consciousness and collapsed near your tent. Fortunately, the sentry located you in time and informed us about the incident. It was very hard to revive you. You are very lucky to have survived.'

Rudra checked himself again, and this time he noticed a small scar caused by a pointed object just below his left ear. He knew now that she was right, but could he trust her, and how much?

'Don't you have questions, Rudra?'

'Yes, amatya,' he said slowly. 'But please first continue, tell me whatever you know. I want to hear it all.'

She paused for a moment, as if gauging him, then continued, 'We have also verified that what you were saying was true, that there indeed was a conspiracy to kill Rajan by poisoning the elephant Mahagiri, and had it happened, it would have looked like a natural accident—nobody would have suspected foul play. The kingdom would have fallen into utter chaos as Rajan has no heir apparent; he himself is so young. He is grateful that you have saved his life, but we have not been able to unmask the real conspirators. Please tell me one thing, however. Why didn't you tell Rajan or Nakiya, me or Bahushalin about this conspiracy when you became aware of it?'

'How could I, worthy amatya? I did not know myself who was involved in the plot, and so I could trust no one. I thought of approaching Rajan but didn't have enough proof, so I decided to do what was possible within my power.'

'Rudra, not disclosing a conspiracy to assassinate the king is a capital offence—did you know that?' she said.

'Yes, amatya,' he said with lowered eyes. 'But I had no choice, I did the best I could in the given circumstances.'

He wanted to talk about Vajramitra but kept quiet. He was assessing her; *how much had she revealed, how much did she trust him.* He decided not to say anything about it.

'What happened to the new mahout of Mahagiri?' he asked.

'He committed suicide,' she said. 'As soon as he heard that Rajan had reached the jungle camp safely, he consumed the same kuchila seeds which he had fed the elephant. Rajan allowed you to live because the news of the mahout's suicide had just reached him when you were produced before him. He could gather that you were speaking the truth.

'All the cooks, guards and attendants have been changed, but nobody outside the limited circle knows anything about the assassination attempt—not even your trusted aides. I expect you to maintain secrecy as well.'

Rudra nodded. As she left, a deep sense of anguish, distress and anger filled Rudra's being. Someone had tried to kill him, probably the same person who wanted to assassinate Rajan, and he had absolutely no idea as to who it was! He had to track them down before they could inflict more damage to the king or him, and to the country. He had to be back in play as quickly as possible.

Over the next few days, his recovery was quicker. The medicines had also been reduced in dosage and frequency. One morning, as he sat meditating, he heard the voice of the royal physician. The old man entered the room and asked, 'How are you feeling now, arya?'

'As you can see, I am much better acharya, and I am perpetually indebted for what you have done for me.'

The old man had a happy smile on his face. 'You don't know how difficult it was Rudravarman.'

'May I ask acharya, what exactly was the poison used?'

'Arya, the arrow was laced with the poison of the water snake. We could not let your blood drain the poison as the wound was in your neck. Fortunately I was accompanying the king in the jungle camp and could locate fresh sarpagandha leaves and flowers to administer to you. We also fastened you on a plank of shalmali tree wood and bathed you continuously with cold water mixed with the juice of shalmali root and camphor. We were all losing hope, but Amatya Maitreyi insisted that we continue our attempts. You showed first signs of life only after three days! I must say you owe your life to her, she has been taking care of you till now.'

'Acharya, let me touch your feet and seek your blessings, for without you, I wouldn't have seen the light of day. My heart is also so full of gratitude for Amatya Maitreyi. I will thank her profusely and I promise that I will never forget your goodness till the last breath of my life.' Rudra had tears in his eyes.

'You need not thank me, arya, I was doing my duty as a physician.'

As the physician was leaving; something flashed in Rudra's mind. He could see the image of the deceased mahout, the cousin of the guard before his eyes. 'Just a moment, acharya. Can you tell me how does one differentiate between poisoning by a laced dart from an actual bite of a water snake?'

'Arya, water snake bites happen only to fishermen. Also, it is usually on their hands, because it happens while they're removing the snakes from the fishnets they're accidentally caught in.'

The dead mahout's face flashed before Rudra. He had been sure even then that the poor man had not died of a snake bite—he had an injury on his chest, no place for a snake to bite. It suddenly struck him that the same weapon was used against him! Could it be the same person?

Rudra longed to get back to work, and to the place that had become his home now. He met Maitreyi once or twice more. The meetings were formal and short—she checked on his condition and left in a short while. One morning, the female attendant taking care of him brought a new set of clothes for him. When he was bathed and ready, he was told that he was free to go without ceremony. Rudra had been waiting for this moment, but he wanted Maitreyi to be there. The attendants were tight lipped about her whereabouts though, and he left with a heavy heart.

Chapter 10

Trouble in the Provinces

Rudra reached his quarters. His trusted aide Kinshuk, who was not expecting to see him, was overjoyed. 'Arya, how was your journey to Avantikapuri? We heard that you directly proceeded to Avanti from the hunting expedition.' This was the story Rudra had sent as a message to his team, preferring that to revealing that he was poisoned.

'It was good, but I am happy to be back home after a long time.'

Rudra spent the next few days resting and getting updates from his aides about happenings in his absence. One afternoon, he got a message from the royal court—the king required his presence. Rudra immediately readied himself and accompanied the messenger. While happy to be working again, in a dark corner of his heart he had a seething desire to find out and punish those who had attempted to kill him.

When Rudra was admitted to the king's presence, a meeting was in progress, and clearly something of serious significance was being discussed. Nakiya beckoned Rudra to be seated, and Rudra obeyed. Maitreyi was there, so was Bahushalin, the treasurer and the head accountant.

Nakiya said, 'Rajan, you have been very lenient with the *rajvachanika* (governor) of Samapa province. I do understand that he has kept the hill tribes of Mahendragiri under control, which were a prime concern for Ashoka too.'

The king said, 'But there have been no issues with the administration of the Baruva Port.'

'Indeed,' said Nakiya. 'However, we have reports that there is something nefarious going on there; either you should visit it personally or send someone to check on the state of affairs.'

'What is your view?' the king asked the treasurer.

'Rajan, the Shadbhaga, Bali and Samudrakara tax accounts show no change in the last three years, yet something seems amiss.'

Bahushalin intervened. 'I have news that the rajvachanika's *yukta* (superintendent) has gifted a very expensive gemstone necklace to a courtesan. He was also inquiring about procuring expensive china silk from foreign traders; his habits are bad.'

The king said, 'He belongs to a very reputed family of the Samapa province. Even his ancestors were rajvachanikas under Ashoka. They could have easily declared independence when we or the Andhras did, but they chose to be a part of this great country. Whatever we do, we have to be aware of the consequences, and we must be doubly sure of the facts.'

Maitreyi spoke, 'He has become highly unpopular and is indulging in very oppressive practices. If there is no control over him, it will affect the reputation and glory of Kalinga itself.'

Rudra was pleased to see Maitreyi again, but noticed that she was not showing any signs of familiarity with him.

Having told them that he would consider their arguments, the king dismissed the meeting. As Rudra was leaving, he was told to wait. Nakiya, the king and Rudra were the only ones in the room now.

The king said, 'Worthy Rudravarman, I see that you have regained your health and have recovered fully from the effects of the poison. If you're willing to undertake some travel, Mahamatya Nakiya will brief you about an important task. You will have full authority to take decisions on my behalf. A small contingent of my best soldiers and spies will be with you all along, and you may also choose to take anyone you desire with you.'

'As Rajan desires,' said Rudra.

The journey began early the next morning. Rudra was moving with an entourage, which was armed and efficient. The riders ahead rode fast, and soon they had disappeared out of sight. Rudra's mind was on Maitreyi—*when would he see her again?*—but the call of duty had to be answered first.

A cart full of provisions, weapons, personal belongings as well as records and documents followed behind. They passed the main city gate, the Brahma gate, but Rudra didn't disclose his identity, allowing Bhadrabahu to complete the formalities required instead. They rode past the cremation grounds, the waterworks and then the *Bahidvaragma*, comprising settlements of heretics, pariahs and foreigners, till they reached the sanctuary forest.

Rudra and his team were travelling at good speed; Bhadrabahu was riding alongside him. 'Arya, I have sent a message to the chief of the Savara tribe. They will ensure that we have a safe passage during our transit through the Malati Hills forest. The journey will take two full days if we don't stop anywhere. If we are delayed and reach late at night, the Samapa Fort gates will be closed; what do you suggest?'

'We will travel only by day, Bhadrabahu. We can stay in safe villages at night. Two of our riders will move ahead of us to make arrangements on the way. In case of any danger or difficulty, they will alert us.'

Bhadrabahu nodded and updated Rudra on the plan for the day. 'Arya, today we will travel till Atthakutiko gama, the village of eight huts. It will be late afternoon when we reach. I have sent an advance rider to talk to the *bhojaka* (headman) of the village. He will arrange for food, water and some place to rest. Although it is a small village, it is one contributing tribute to the royal treasury.'

The forest was dense, yet the track was wide enough to accommodate a cart and a rider travelling side by side. At places it was dark due to the thick foliage preventing sunlight from penetrating. The sanctuary forest was a safe place though, it was free of wild tribes or large carnivores, but the vast jungle beyond—the deepest densest forest—was a dangerous place, inhabited by fierce tribes and wild animals.

When the band of travellers finally emerged out of the sanctuary, it was late afternoon, and a small village with a few huts was visible. The sky was clear and the air cold. As they approached the village, Rudra saw that a rider from their entourage was already there, along with the bhojaka of the village.

'We welcome you and your companions to this humble village, arya,' the bare-bodied bhojaka, who wore just a small loincloth, said with humility. He escorted them to a structure that was probably made to receive and entertain guests.

They all dismounted and took their places in the *pandal*. All around them were bamboo clusters and grass filled lands interspersed with farms. The bhojaka offered some cool water with sweet jaggery, which Rudra found very satiating. Bhadrabahu asked Rudra to remove his footwear and take a wash in the open, following which everyone freshened up and returned to the pandal. When the bhojaka returned, he was carrying freshly cooked food, including rice and pulses, with ghee and condiments. The smell of the food made everyone more hungry.

Waiting outside was a Savara tribal, dressed in deerskin, his black skin shining with sweat. He was short but muscular. He carried his bow over his shoulder and arrows of different lengths tied to his back. Bhadrabahu went out and talked to the Savara; Rudra could understand only a few words of the language spoken. He then came in and announced that the Savara had been sent to escort them as the chief of the tribe was happy to let them pass through his lands.

After a sumptuous meal and some rest for the riders and the horses, the band started again. Rudra thanked the Bhojaka, who while parting, disclosed that he was in the service of the king, and was responsible for the safety of these tracts. The Savara was asked to ride in the carriage but he declined to do so, instead he sprinted barefoot along with them at amazing speed.

The terrain was now becoming difficult and they slowed down a lot. Bhadrabahu kept chatting with the tribal and would brief Rudra from time to time.

The Savara had told Bhadrabahu that a very large lake, almost as big as the sea, would be on their left in the second half of their journey. He also described large ships that traversed the enormous water body. In the market near the great Baruva Port, the tribals would exchange animal skin, furs and meat for swords, metalware, ornaments and earthenware. The holy Rushikulya River flowed through Samapa and supplied water to the moat surrounding the fort.

While they moved, Rudra had an eerie feeling of being constantly under watch by invisible eyes.

Evening had fallen, the day was nearing an end, and the band traversed faster now. Suddenly, the Savara stopped. Bhadrabahu dismounted to consult him. He informed Rudra that the tribal escort had to go back as it was the boundary of his area, and from here the Pulinda territory started. Everyone thanked the man as he departed. Rudra gave him a small bag of silver coins as a token of appreciation, which the man reluctantly accepted before taking his leave.

'What now, Bhadrabahu? How are we going forward from here?'

Bhadrabahu was worried. The riders who had gone ahead were to meet them at a predesignated point on the way, but were nowhere to be seen.

The horses were also tired and breathing heavily. The travellers now came across a large wooden hut that appeared abandoned. A tall soldier travelling in the right flank informed them that it was a camping place for small contingents of the army on the move. It was also some sort of an outpost to provide security against the ferocious Pulindas.

They decided to camp there. They found a small spring with flowing water nearby and the horses drank heartily from it.

The place was spacious enough for all of them. They emptied the cart and kept their belongings inside the hut. Rudra still had the uncomfortable feeling of being under watch, of being pursued continuously, but he didn't want to share it with anyone else. A fire was lit, and food was cooked. It was quite dark now and sounds of wild animals could be heard at a distance. There was a chill in the foggy air that made the place look more mysterious. Everyone ate to their fill except Rudra, who partook of a small meal and retired early, beckoning Bhadrabahu to speak to him before he went to sleep.

It must have been the third quarter of the night when Vijayaka woke up with a shrill cry. Torches were quickly lit and when the soldiers went out, to their horror, they saw the place was surrounded by a raiding party of the wild and ferocious Pulinda tribals. They were encircling the hut with torches in their hands, some carried stretched bows with arrows mounted to shoot, others carried short swords, maces and sticks. They were making sharp, ear-piercing, high-pitched noises and moving menacingly to make a kill.

Vijayaka looked around in the hut, there was no sight of either Rudra or Bhadrabahu. Worried about them, he armed himself and readied for a fight to the death. Three Pulindas suddenly dropped from the rooftop and disarmed him and the others. Then, they called the rest of their band inside and began to rummage through their captives' belongings; however, they could not find anything valuable.

As the tribals couldn't speak the language of their captives, they kept asking them through gestures about the location of valuables and weapons. When they got no answer, they bound the soldiers together and began discussing something amongst themselves.

Vijayaka felt that they were about to kill them all, but his mind was on Rudra and Bhadrabahu who seemed to have disappeared. He thought that they had either been already held captive or killed by the assailants.

The Pulindas then settled down. Some of them started to eat whatever was available in the hut, while a few of them, probably their leaders, went out in the dark . . .

An hour must have passed like this. Vijayaka's arms and legs went sore with the pressure of the rope fastened around them. Suddenly, he heard a loud clamour, as if a fight had broken out between the Pulindas. He heard them argue in an agitated tone and guessed that there was some disagreement. Finally, he heard one of them shouting at the others in an authoritative tone, which was followed by silence. *This is the end!* Vijayaka thought. He looked at the others who were tied with him and cursed the moment he had decided to join this dangerous expedition. He remembered how his wife had tried to prevent him from going as she had seen a bad omen.

A man approached him with a sharp knife; he tried to struggle but couldn't move even a bit due to the tight ropes wound around his hands and feet. The Pulinda came up to him, bent down and cut open the rope binding his feet, then he cut the rope tied to his hands and indicated for him to keep quiet. He went on to release the others as well. The other Pulindas in the room stood by, doing nothing but continuing to stare at him threateningly.

Vijayaka could see dawn outside the hut now. The day had broken and birds were chirping loudly in the trees. He heard heavy footsteps and there entered Rudra and Bhadrabahu! They looked unperturbed by the presence of the Pulindas. A few steps behind them was a short but very stout and sturdy man, the chief of the Pulindas.

Bhadrabahu seemed to know the language of the tribals, he was talking to the chief, who then indicated to the others that they should leave the room. The Pulindas obediently exited.

Later, Bhadrabahu explained that, expecting the attack, he and Rudra had left the hut to seek out the chief of the Pulindas.

The chief had an old debt to pay to Rudra and had agreed to return with them and stop his men from attacking the soldiers.

The tribal chief had breakfast with Rudra and the others. When he left, Rudra gifted him with a pearl string, which pleased him immensely. Bhadrabahu informed everyone that there would be a Pulinda escort with them till they reached Samapa.

Vijayaka and the others were immensely curious—how had Rudra and Bhadrabahu survived the Pulinda attack? They had not just survived, but had befriended them so that they were now being escorted out of the forest by the Pulindas themselves? Vijayaka decided he would ask Bhadrabahu about last night's mystery at the first opportune moment.

Two riders, who had gone ahead of the group, now returned—the Pulindas had held them captive. Bhadrabahu then asked the others to go and fetch the horses, which had been hidden behind a very dense thicket of bushes, as planned by Rudra the previous night. The horses were rested, fresh and unscathed. The group, except for the two riders, now readied for onward journey, the sun was already shining bright in the clear sky.

As they went ahead, Rudra got down from the horse and went to a clearing in the forest. Anticipating trouble, he had hidden all their valuables and weapons there; he hadn't slept even for a moment the last night. He collected the things and distributed them as they were when they began the journey. Some half a *yojana* ahead, they met the Pulinda escort. Armed and nimble-footed, he was one of the men who had attacked the hut last night.

It was afternoon when they reached a lake in the forest. It was a serene water body with large outcropping rocks around it. The Pulinda told Bhadrabahu that this spot was considered sacred to the tribe. Rudra asked everybody to dismount and offer prayers to the spirits there.

They all sat down to have lunch, while the Pulinda excused himself to go and perform his rituals. Seeing that the moment was right, Vijayaka finally asked Bhadrabahu about last night's happenings. Bhadrabahu looked at Rudra, who signalled his approval and left to take a walk around the lake. 'Last night, when we were all having a dinner, Arya Rudravarman had called me to speak to him. He felt that we were being followed all along and feared that there would be an attack in the night. He was also apprehensive about the two riders not returning in time.

'He then planned a series of defensive countermeasures: Firstly, he removed the valuables, spare weapons, royal seals and documents and hid them at a distance. Then, he untied the horses and kept them behind a thicket where they couldn't be easily spotted. Lastly, he asked me to accompany him and act as a night guard. We both climbed a tree with our weapons and kept a watch on all sides.

'It was a very dark night and almost nothing was visible, we felt that wild animals were moving freely beneath us. It was very scary and cold outside, and it was difficult to stay awake—I must have dozed off. It must have been well past midnight when I was awakened by noises all around and saw the band of Pulindas moving towards the hut.

'Arya Rudravarman, who had been vigilant and focused, indicated to me to keep silent and not move. We saw the Pulindas attacking and then searching for valuables, which they obviously couldn't locate. I was shocked that the Pulindas had attacked a government caravan after their chief was spared by the king some months back. They must have surely mistaken us for wealthy traders or lay travellers. I couldn't do anything sitting there, and to my chagrin, Arya didn't allow me to get down and help. I was angry and helpless, but I could see that the raiding party was large and I would surely have been overpowered and killed had I tried to intervene. We watched you all being disarmed and held captive, and the Pulindas searching the hut, and then settling down. It was then that their chief came along with two of his bodyguards. As he was passing under the tree, Arya Rudravarman jumped on him and held a sword at his throat. I followed suit and disarmed his two bodyguards before they could react. They were caught totally unawares.

'The chief was indeed the same man who had been spared death penalty due to Arya Rudravarman granting him abhay daan! When he recognized Arya Rudravarman, he was overjoyed to meet him again. He realized the blunder he had committed, promised to release all our men and return any property seized. He also profusely apologized for his misadventure. Now, he has sent his own men to escort us for the rest of the journey.'

Vijayaka was moved. 'We are all alive only due to Arya Rudravarman,' he said.

It was late evening in the forest, they had been travelling for several hours now, and the sun had just set. The journey had been slow as it was uphill. The jungle had changed now—the trees were much taller and different. This also allowed more visibility unlike the earlier areas that were filled with dense thickets and shrubbery. Large rocky cliffs could be seen ahead in the twilight.

When they approached the rock face, now barely visible in the faint light, they realized that there was a small opening in the rock, enough for two people to pass through at a time. It was a cave, and they decided to halt there for the night.

They lit torches and found that it was a very large cave, with the ceiling as high as five men stacked one upon another. The Pulinda made some strange noises and beat the ground with a stick repeatedly. He explained to Bhadrabahu that he was ensuring that there were no wild animals or snakes hidden inside before they took up residence for the night. He was also seeking permission and protection of the benevolent jungle spirits.

Rudra asked two people to be on guard all night turn by turn and permitted them to prepare food. Not long after, tired and contented with the food, they were all in deep sleep.

It was late in the morning when Rudra woke up. The night had passed incident free and the two riders who had been left behind had also joined them.

The cave was at the higher part of the mountain, and beyond it lay a rocky path to the peak. Bhadrabahu told Rudra that if one could climb up to the summit, one could catch a glimpse of a very large water body, akin to the sea, in the south-east. If one was lucky, even large ships could be seen from there. The Pulinda had told Bhadrabahu that the water body was so large that it had four to five village-sized islands inside it. Rudra decided to check it out. He asked the others to eat breakfast and get ready while he, along with Bhadrabahu and the Pulinda, started trekking up the steep rocky path.

It took them much longer than expected to reach the summit. The sun was shining very bright now, and a very strong gust of wind was blowing. As they reached the top, they could see far and wide, and then suddenly, Rudra spotted water, shining at a great distance. It was one of the most beautiful sights of his life, and he was filled with a sudden joy. He breathed in the fresh cold air and didn't know why he suddenly remembered Maitreyi.

Chapter 11

A Game of Dice

The Pulinda had taken leave, and he had been handsomely rewarded too. The group had now reached a small village at the end of the forest, which had a small *sangrahana* fort, manned by soldiers called *antapalas* or boundary guards. These forts were built every ten villages or so for protection from invading armies and wild tribes. A *kharvatika* fort, much larger than a sangrahana, was built for every two hundred villages, a *dronamukha* for every four hundred and a large *sthaniya* at the centre of eight hundred villages.

This fort was built on a mid-sized mound, which gave a good vantage point to the guards. A single wall, around three humans high, ran along the boundary of the village. Before entering this village, Rudra had changed into the clothes of a commoner and briefed everyone not to disclose his identity in any case. Bhadrabahu led the group, produced their credentials and sought permission to stay for the night. They still had half a day's journey before they would reach Samapa.

Rudra woke up the next morning to see that the villagers had woken up quite early and set about doing their daily chores.

Most of them were farmers who had their farms outside the fortress. The shopkeepers had opened their shops and the artisans had started work in their small workshops. He called Bhadrabahu and others and told them about the next course of action. There were some queries, which he replied to, and then they broke away.

As Rudra wanted to tour the village, he headed towards the small marketplace in the centre. He observed the types of things sold, their prices and made small talk with the shopkeepers and their assistants. He then wandered towards the rear gate of the village. There was a noisy group of men sitting under a large banyan tree there and playing the game of *dyuta*.

Rudra sat near them and watched them. One of the men seemed to be adept at the game—he was winning repeatedly. This seemed to be giving impetus to the game, as the losers kept on betting more and more. The man smiled and chuckled loudly as his winning streak continued. When he noticed Rudra, he mockingly said, 'Welcome to the *deva sabha* (gambling meet) agantuk, do you also want to lose some money?'

Rudra smiled at him and decided to join in. The game was being played on an *atthapadi* (black and white board) with dice. The players were betting cowries on each throw. The dice were made from the nuts of the vibhidaka tree. Rudra realized that the man's ploy was to play his game calmly and distract the others when it was their turn, so they would commit mistakes.

It was Rudra's turn to throw the dice when the man broke into a song about the vibhidaka tree. It was about a magical tree under which weak men feared to sit, as demons resided on it. The magic flowed in the dice through its fruits, and as the fruits cured men of various ailments, the dice game would take care of all his worries. His wife hated it, but he was intoxicated by the vile smell of the tree's flowers. Rudra chuckled at the song.

'I am done, Nahush,' said one of the men getting up.

Nahush stopped singing and taunted him, 'Gunagya, you still have to make good your payment, are you running away?'

Gunagya turned back and peevishly took out two silver *kahapanas* from his money bag and handed them over to Nahush, who graciously accepted them.

They were playing with *sippikani* (cowry shells), which was the local petty coinage. For larger sums, they had to be converted into coins such as *pana, kahapana, kakanika, mashaka* or the very rare gold *shatamana*. Rudra exchanged two panas for 160 cowries with Nahush, and continued the play. Nahush didn't check the genuineness of the coins as they weren't of silver or of high value.

Rudra allowed Nahush to win the first game. Then, he lost a second and a third one in succession. Nahush was almost intoxicated with his victories, and kept on increasing the stakes. Rudra had lost the huge sum of five kahapanas, and the others present there urged him to stop as they cursed Nahush for taking advantage of a stranger. Rudra now exhibited signs of panic, he asked the people if he should make a last large bet and recover all his lost money. They unanimously asked him not to do so, but Nahush gently encouraged Rudra.

Rudra picked up the vibhidaka seeds and laid a bet for a very large sum of ten kahapanas, which Nahush immediately accepted. Rudra now closed his eyes, as if summoning some secret powers to help, muttered a mantra to himself, blew air over his closed fist and threw the dice.

There was an uproar. Rudra had thrown the perfect dice, and Nahush had lost ten kahapanas in a single throw.

Nahush couldn't believe his eyes, the stranger had beaten him at his own game. He looked at Rudra and said, 'I hope you're not the dark prince,' and laughed a sly laugh. Dejectedly, he parted with the ten kahapanas and left. As the others dispersed for lunch, Rudra asked one of the men for Nahush's address.

At Nahush's home, a frail child aged about ten years opened the door when Rudra knocked. Rudra smiled at the child and asked for his father Nahush. He told the boy to inform his father that his friend from the deva sabha had come.

Nahush came out in a hurry, looking worried. 'Arya, is there anything I can do for you? Why and how have you come to my home?' He closed the door behind him and anxiously stood on the street with Rudra.

'I have come to return your five kahapanas. I don't keep money from gambling in my home, it brings bad luck.'

'Arya, you must be joking. Please go away. My wife and mother are at home, and if they come to know about my gambling session, I will face their wrath.'

Rudra took out five kahapanas and placed them in Nahush's hands, who didn't know what to do with them. Rudra was insistent, and Nahush, who didn't want any scene at his residence, accepted them and requested Rudra to leave with folded hands.

The other members of the group left, as decided, the next morning. Rudra had asked Bhadrabahu to make arrangements for his independent travel to Samapa.

Rudra was about to leave, when he saw Nahush waiting out in the street with his son. He called them in. The boy politely wished Rudra who blessed him by touching his head. Nahush was asked to be seated comfortably.

After some silence, Nahush asked Rudra in a jittery voice, 'Arya, why did you return the very same five coins that I had given to you?'

'Do I need to answer that?'

Nahush seemed terrified. He asked his son to go out in the street and play. He fell down at Rudra's feet and started sobbing, 'Please forgive me arya, I will never do it again.'

'I am not concerned about the cheating that you do at the game, Nahush. You take advantage of the stupidity and greed of men, which is not as grave a crime as counterfeiting money.'

'Arya, I swear on the head of my only child that I have not counterfeited the money, but yes, I knew that the coins were fake when I gave them you. Forgive me, forgive me please. I promise that I will never ever play dyuta from today.'

Rudra was silent for a few moments. Then, he said, 'I will, but only on one condition . . .'

Rudra reached Samapa in the evening, as the majestic entry gate, the *gopura*, was being lit up. The gate walls were as high as those at Tosali, and the city appeared to be equally large. It was bustling with activity, but the strict governmental control seen everywhere at the capital was not visible here. A tired customs official perfunctorily verified Rudra's credentials and let him go after depositing taxes due.

As soon as he entered the gates of the city, he encountered a large rock outcrop, on which stairs and a pathway had been laid. As he walked towards the path, intending to go to the top, a soldier dressed in the royal Kalinga army uniform approached him.

'Where are you going?' he asked.

When Rudra expressed his desire to go atop the small mountain to see the view of the city from there, the soldier started laughing. 'You seem to be an outsider. Don't you know that there are rock-engraved orders of Devanampiya Ashoka at the top?'

'Oh the same ones as we have in Tosali?' asked Rudra.

The soldier laughed with contempt. 'It's only due to Tosali that these are here. You may go and see them but do not touch or destroy anything.'

The climb was quite steep, and once Rudra reached the top, he requested the soldier there to allow him to read the engravings. The soldier said, 'I was posted here three days back, will you please read them aloud for me as I haven't learned reading or writing.'

Rudra read aloud:

> By order of the Beloved of the Gods. At Tosali the prince and the officers at Samapa charged with announcing the royal decrees, are to be ordered thus: Whatever I approve of, that I desire either to achieve by taking action or to obtain . . .
>
> For this purpose I instruct you, that having done so I may discharge my debt to them, by making known to you my will, my resolve and my firm promise. By these actions, my work will advance, and they will be reassured and will realize that the king is like a father, and that he feels for them as for himself, for they are like his own children to him . . .

'Isn't that amazing. First he kills our brothers and sisters and then declares that he is our father!' the soldier fumed. 'I don't understand why we want to protect this . . . this piece of rock full of lies.'

Rudra didn't respond, and this angered the soldier further. 'Tosali didn't just lose its men, Ashoka also took away your Princess Charuwaki after killing her father, the great king Kaivarta.'

'I understand your anger my friend, I too feel very deeply about it,' Rudra said and moved away. Coming down the steep pathway, he felt that he and everyone else in his country had always been carrying the dead over their shoulders. They had never been able to forget what Ashoka had done to them. He had not only subjugated and destroyed a proud and independent people, but also decimated their culture and way of life.

Earlier, Kalinga had been under foreign yoke for a very small period under the Nandas, and had been fiercely independent before and after. Ashoka had crushed their pride. But things were changing now, Rudra thought. The decadent Maurya dynasty had just been finished by Pushyamitra Shunga, whose son now ruled over Avanti as a viceroy. And Kalinga was ascendant under Aira Kharavela.

Chapter 12

The Goldsmiths' Lane

In some ways, Rudra found Samapa to be better than Tosali. There was much less government presence, and the people appeared to be freer and easy going. Houses were adorned with beautiful patterns of creepers, flowers and animals. Their carved features were richly painted in blues, greens, red and golden. The wooden frontages, in the homes of those more well-off, carried statues of large demon Yakshas and beautiful Yakshinis.

There were two main intersecting streets called the *mahapathas*, on which carts, elephants and caravans could travel. They were paved with stone slabs and had wide footpaths along the sides with a drain to carry off the rainwater. A network of smaller roads branched periodically from these main highways. There were trees on the sides of all main roads. The smaller streets had beautiful wooden arches, exquisitely carved and decorated with symbols and mythical figures.

The broad paved street had uniformly placed houses on either side with sloping tiled roofs. These houses were single-storeyed in some areas and went up to three storeys in places where important functionaries or personages stayed. Houses were generally built on the pattern of a quadrangle surrounded by chambers, with the ground floor rooms facing the streets being used as shops in some cases. It seemed that the city had been planned well and the citizens had taken care to maintain it.

Every ten houses or so, there was a small well, and large earthen pots filled with water were kept at regular intervals, mostly as a precaution against fire.

Now, as night was approaching, people were returning indoors, wearied with the day's toils but eager to meet loved ones.

The next morning was a cloudy one and Rudra decided to visit the temple of Jina Sreyansanatha, the eleventh of the Nigantha *tirthankaras* (spiritual teachers), who was a native of Kalinga according to folklore. The temple sat in the centre of a beautiful lake; a path connected the banks of the lake to the temple entrance. It was a magnificent sight indeed; beautifully carved pillars of stone supported multiple small domes, and the main part of the temple that housed the deity was crowned with a high conical structure.

Two elderly men, who were sitting and idling after having completed their prayers, caught Rudra's attention. He greeted them and sat near them on the ground. The white curly-haired man lamented, 'Our faith has survived the invasion of Ashoka, but these new traditions will take us away from the holy path, nobody seems to be understanding this.'

The other one interjected. 'I don't see any problem. In fact, Setthi Ratnank's gifts will add to the glory of the temple and the fame of the deity.'

'This is what I am objecting to, the holy asceticism is getting replaced by pomp and show of the rich. Where was this Ratnank when this shrine was built? He wasn't even born, but now people know this temple by his name.'

The second one retorted, 'You're getting old and cynical, you should leave the thinking part to the new generation.'

'Yeah, and you're a young *kumara*?' They both laughed heartily.

'Forgive my ignorance venerable men, as I am a stranger. I don't know anything about this pious Ratnank,' Rudra said.

'Pious, ha! He is a social climber. He heads the guild of *kammaras* (smiths) and, just five years ago, he used to live on the outskirts of the town, near the workshops. You should see his residence now, it's a palace!'

'You're just jealous of him,' his companion rebuked.

The former became agitated. 'Why don't you go and beg alms at his door! I heard that he never disappoints anyone.'

'This is too much, how can you say that . . . ?'

Gently reminding the men that they were in a holy place, Rudra took leave of them.

As decided, Bhadrabahu had called everyone to a sacred grove in the city. They had done some preliminary work and were awaiting further instructions from Rudra.

Rudra needed leads before he could ask to inspect the records at the office of the yukta and the *nidhayaka* (treasurer). Vijayaka informed them that other than a very stringent tax regime, where the tax collectors were insistent and unforgiving, there was no visible distress in the populace. Bhadrabahu had undertaken visits to various guilds of smiths, weavers, ivory carvers; he had also visited various markets to find out if anything was amiss with the economy.

Rudra felt that something was indeed amiss, but he couldn't put his finger on what that was.

Kinshuk casually mentioned that the traders at Samapa highly respected Tosali coins, and they were ready to pay a higher value for them. At this moment, something occurred to Rudra in a flash. He instructed the team in detail and decided where and when to meet next with feedback.

They all dispersed then. Rudra had also been quite surprised by another piece of information: some officials from Tosali were seen in Samapa. They had probably arrived ahead of them by a different route. This meant that they had to take more precautions about their mission—the secrecy of their endeavour was at risk.

It was evening now, and Rudra headed towards the lanes of ganikas and *rupjivas* (prostitute) in the southern part of the city. There was much hustle-bustle there—vendors were selling garlands and flowers, paan and scents and jugglers, bards and street performers of all kinds were entertaining people. Pimps, musicians and clients were going about their work under the watchful eyes of the government officials. He walked for a while, soaking in the beautiful music and the happy atmosphere.

Suddenly, he heard a loud furore and, before he could realize it, he was flat on the ground. A man who was being chased by soldiers had collided with him head on and they had both fallen squarely on the road. He wasn't hurt too badly, and neither was the other man.

The soldiers running behind the man had now reached them. When Rudra got up, the man who had collided with him clung to his feet, asking for sanctuary. Rudra noted that the man was young and handsome.

'What is the matter? What has he done?' Rudra asked the soldiers.

'Arya, please believe me,' the young man said. 'I have done nothing wrong. They are accusing me of not making good, the payments due to the ganika, Sulasa. But she is lying and actually owes me money.'

The soldiers angrily asked Rudra to hand him over to them. They said that he was a habitual defaulter and a disreputable man, who had been escaping punishment. Rudra asked them how much he owed the ganika, and if he could make good the payment, would they release the man? The soldiers replied that they would have to ask the madam of the house. Rudra told them that he was ready to wait for the opinion of the madam; till then, the young man would be in his custody. Satisfied, the soldiers went to check what the madam had to say about it.

The young man was shivering with fear. With tears of gratitude in his eyes, he said, 'Arya, my name is Balmani, I am an apprentice at the guild of the ivory carvers, in the service of Acharya Dhritiman. Actually, I am in love with this ganika Sulasa. She had promised me that she would leave this profession and marry me. I have been collecting money to secure her release and have been working hard day and night for it.'

'Go on, what happened then?' Rudra asked, interested.

'The last few days, her behaviour has changed. She has been fighting a lot. Today, when I went to her place, she not only refused to see me, but called the soldiers and falsely accused me of not having made past payments. Such a liar she is! But she is beautiful, very beautiful, as delicate as a flower and as radiant as the moon . . . I think she is in love with someone else.' Balmani started muttering to himself. 'Who can that be . . . is it Chandrahas, the setthi's son, or Kaustav, the policeman . . . No, no it must surely be Fanindra—he has been calling her to his residence, it must be him.'

When the soldiers returned, they conveyed that Sulasa had claimed a large sum of fifteen *kasya* (bronze) panas. Balmani was belligerent, he contested the claim, but the soldiers were unmoved.

Balmani told Rudra, 'Arya, why should you suffer for the whims and fancies of a bad-charactered woman. I will suffer the punishment for my misdeeds and stupidity.' Rudra was moved. He paid the requisite sum to the soldiers, and secured Balmani's release. Balmani thanked him profusely for his kindness.

Over the next two days, Rudra moved about extensively in the city and obtained information about the conduct of the government servants, the state of trade, commerce and taxes, condition of agriculturists and *gahapatis* (householders–traders). He noticed that while there was some discomfort amongst the higher echelons of society, the poor appeared to be unaffected.

As he was getting ready to go out for the day, a smiling Balmani appeared at his door. 'Arya, I have come to return your fifteen kasya panas. While I can return the money, I cannot return your kindness.'

Rudra was reluctant to take the money back. 'It was not a loan, so there is no reason you should repay this.'

'Arya, don't put me in difficulty. I am a man of honour, I will have to live all my life with this feeling of being under debt.'

'Don't worry, my friend, I will give you a chance to repay me soon. Please keep the money.'

Balmani reluctantly kept the coins back in his purse.

'My hunch was right,' he said. 'It is that wretched Fanindra who is responsible for my predicament. Earlier, she was so kind that she used to shower gifts on me!'

'Good riddance then, Balmani. If the woman is not worthy, it's better that she stays away from you. Haven't you heard what Maharishi Yajnavalkya has said about receiving gifts?'

'No, arya, please tell me.'

'Maharishi says, one should avoid taking any gifts from a butcher, an oilman, a wine seller, a prostitute and the king. He says that each is ten times more wicked than the preceding one. And, my friend, you should know it's actually not about gifts, it's actually the association with these kind of people that has been prohibited. It's your own loss if you mingle with them.'

'I have indeed learnt my lesson, arya. I will never visit that part of the town again,' Balmani said. 'Are any of your friends staying nearby?' he asked.

'No, why?' Rudra asked.

'Actually, when I was searching for your place I met two men from Tosali, but their behaviour was very strange. When I asked them if they were with you, they ran away from here.'

Rudra was alarmed. 'What did they look like, Balmani?'

'They appeared to be normal householders; there was nothing striking about them.'

'How did you know that they're from Tosali?'

'Ah, I've never seen them here arya, so I guessed they must be from Tosali.'

'I see.' Rudra didn't want to show his concern to him. 'So, what else is going on in the city?'

'Yes, I forgot to tell. There is a very accomplished saint in the city, and he is carrying an *ichchadhari naag* (form-shifting cobra), who stays with him as a disciple and turns to a snake at will. People have gone crazy about it. Everyday hundreds of them throng to get a glimpse of the saint and his disciple, and suddenly in everyone's view, the disciple turns into a cobra.'

'Where is this? I would like to see it myself,' said Rudra.

Balmani promised to take him there in the evening, provided he could find out their location.

'Can you take me to your workshop today? I am very interested in seeing and purchasing valuable artefacts from different parts of the country.'

'I will have to take the permission of my Acharya Dhritiman. He should say yes if I vouch for you.'

'Let's try our luck then, Balmani.' Rudra bid farewell to him, with a promise to see him at the workshop during the day, subject to the acharya's assent.

The ivory carvers made various kinds of objects—bangles, vessels, statues, inlay works, pins, dolls, weapon handles and household objects like combs and small boxes. Their lane was called the *dantakara vithi*. It was one of the many lanes that were allotted to guilds manufacturing and selling their wares. Similarly, there was a perfumers' lane, a weavers' lane, a smiths' lane and a gem cutters' lane.

Not all occupations had a place in the city, however; some things came from the villages outside. Most villages specialized in a single commodity such as pottery or woodwork; these artisans could sell their products at the Samapa market.

Acharya Dhritiman had given permission to Balmani for Rudra's visit, and welcomed him courteously but he allowed Rudra to visit only the outer parts of the workshop. The guilds were very secretive about their craft, especially in case of valuable articles, and rightfully so. Rudra asked questions to various people Balmani introduced him to, who all seemed very friendly. But Rudra was coming to a strange conclusion.

The smiths' lane, the kammara vithi, was nearby. Rudra told Balmani that he wanted to purchase a gold necklace for his beloved at Tosali. This got Balmani excited, and he told Rudra that his childhood friend Vasuman worked in the goldsmiths' workshop.

The kammara vithi was devoid of people, and the path was covered with a thin layer of brackish ash and soot. Smoke was billowing from furnaces. All metals were worked with here—iron, copper, bronze, silver and gold too. Only the gold area had strict entry and exit restrictions, and each person was thoroughly frisked on entry and exit each time.

The furnaces and tools in the gold area were scaled down as compared to those in other parts. Rudra could watch the gold being worked on from a distance only, and was not allowed near the main furnaces and anvils. He noticed that the work here was of superior quality than Tosali, and the designs were more intricate. He purchased a gold ornament to maintain the credibility of his story. Somewhere deep in his heart he also felt a pang—he wished he could purchase something for Maitreyi.

As the work hours were now over, Balmani asked his friend Vasuman to accompany them on their visit to the great saint with the ichchadhari naag.

The trio walked leisurely for some time before they reached a grove where, on an elevated platform, an ascetic of the *jatila* (matted hair) kind sat in deep contemplation. A large number of people sat quietly before him. The ascetic had two disciples; one was meditating with him, while the other was managing the crowd and other sundry tasks. Rudra and his colleagues tried to get to the front so see more clearly. The second disciple had now lit a torch. The whole scene had an eerie feel to it. The disciple called out to the crowd, 'Be careful, watch closely, any time now the *ichchadhari naag* will appear to bless you in its real form. Don't miss this opportunity, and don't be afraid. Please don't attempt to run or do anything which will disturb the guru or the snake. If you want to offer money, don't do so unless you have a gold or silver coin.'

Vasuman was visibly excited, and when the disciple asked him to help hold a sheet between the devotees and the meditating ascetics, he readily agreed to do so. The disciple also asked Rudra's help in blowing the conch shell, which he refused, and Balmani offered his services with great enthusiasm instead.

Balmani blew the conch three times, and as he was finishing the third time, the disciple suddenly pulled the cloth away, and magic! The first disciple had turned into a snake! The people got very excited, but the second disciple kept them firmly under control. Some of them quietly made their offerings in gold and silver coins. Many were reciting mantras, others were dumbstruck; a small minority was sceptical, Rudra being one of them.

Chapter 13

A Secret Unfolds

The team was meeting again at a public garden, as decided. They had acquired lots of information now. Vijayaka felt that there was no visible oppressive practice or fraud in the collection of taxes under various heads. One thing was still inexplicable though—the extreme caution the traders exhibited when accepting currency of higher denominations.

Rudra asked Bhadrabahu, 'So what does your study of the coins say?'

'Arya, we have collected coins struck by various guilds from all the corners of the city, and we will be analysing them. One of our men is an expert in counterfeiting, he will check the coins and find out which ones are not genuine.' Bhadrabahu also informed him that they had properly classified the coins according to guilds, areas where they had been taken from, and their age.

'You will not be able to use fire or the touchstone here, so put half of the coins in acidic juice and the other half in salt water for the night. Also, check what they sound like when struck together and try and hammer out one or two,' suggested Rudra.

They decided to meet the next day at a safe place.

'And one more thing . . .' said Rudra mischievously. 'I don't want to see that false saint with that magical snake! Enough of that nonsense.'

Everyone started laughing and Rudra, in mock anger, scolded them, 'And imagine the guts of this Vijayaka. Last evening he chose me from the audience to blow the conch shell!' Now they were holding their stomachs with laughter. Rudra continued, 'Bhadrabahu, if you people keep doing this, you won't need any employment in the future; you have collected so many gold and silver coins!' He also began laughing. 'But I must say, Bhadrabahu as the ascetic was very convincing and the snake trick was very good. Congratulations, you scoundrels!'

There was a definite breakthrough on the next morning. Some of the coins kept in the acidic juice had become swollen, revealing a neat work of counterfeiting. A lead piece had been covered with gold or silver leaf using wax to make it look like a real coin.

Rudra asked them to arrange the fake coins by the marks of the guilds issuing them, and to his utter surprise, the one with the royal markings were the fake ones!

'Bhadrabahu, when I saw pieces of lead outside the goldsmiths' workshop, I suspected they were using the folding method of counterfeiting. That's why I'd asked you to put them in the acidic solution.'

'It was a quick and effective method, arya. We were wondering—where did you learn all this?'

'Stop flattering me and get back to serious work. In fact, the important part of the job begins now. We have to trace the culprit in the office of the superintendent, for without their connivance, this would not be possible. You must all be very careful now and keep collecting evidence. Those committing this crime might be very vigilant. I also hear that some officials from Tosali are here, so take care not to blow your covers.'

After everyone dispersed, Rudra went to the kammara vithi again and approached the goldsmiths' workshop. There, he asked for Vasuman. 'My dear friend, I regret to inform you that I have doubts about the purity of gold in the necklace I bought yesterday.'

Vasuman appeared hurt. He protested, 'Arya, we live by the trust of people, how can you allege something like this? You should know that there is a very severe punishment for practicing deception in my line of work.'

'The gold doesn't seem to be of the right colour. It seems to be a bit reddish, suggesting that copper might have been mixed in its making,' Rudra said.

'Arya, I beg you in the name of the Arhats, please don't make such allegations!' Tears started rolling down his face.

Hearing the commotion, the acharya of the workshop called them both inside his office. The old man listened patiently to Rudra and then responded, 'We can take back the article sold at the original price, cancelling the deal, but cannot accept an allegation of adulteration of precious metals. In fact, if you make this allegation and can't prove it, there is a provision for punishment.'

'And what happens, acharya, if my allegations are proved right? You will all suffer severe punishment and lose all your credibility.'

The acharya said patiently, 'Arya, I know that my gold is pure. I can go to any length to prove that.'

'All right. What about your *suvarna masha* (gold coins)?'

The acharya was taken aback, but quickly recovered from the shock. He asked Rudra politely what could be done that would satisfy him about the quality of the gold in the necklace. Rudra was belligerent, and more people from the workshop came in. They tried to convince him, but to no avail. Finally, he demanded a thorough inspection of the whole workshop— each crucible, anvil, furnace and implement. They couldn't agree on this.

The acharya told him, 'We will have to seek permission of the *jetthaka* (head of the guild) for that. Failing that, we cannot do anything as we do not have the authority to allow you on our own.'

Rudra agreed, and they asked him to come in the morning of the following day.

Rudra had just finished his breakfast at the guest house when he was informed that there were visitors for him. He dressed and went to the courtyard to receive them. He was warmly greeted by a handsome young man who appeared to be from a very rich family of traders.

'Oh, Arya Rudravarman, I've heard much about you! I cannot tell you how happy I am to meet you today,' the man dressed in finery said animatedly.

Rudra was taken aback—his cover had been blown. What else did these people know? The people along with the handsome man seemed to be some kind of soldiers, though not from the royal army. They stood expressionless, neither menacing nor interested in the conversation. Rudra knew from their body language that these men must be skilled fighters, employed for the personal security of this young man.

Rudra was calculating in his mind, three bodyguards and one young man; if things got bad, his best bet would be to quickly injure the young man and run as fast as possible.

The young man continued in a very affable voice. 'Arya, I am Ratnank, the sreshthin of various guilds dealing with valuables in this part of the country. By modest estimates, one tenth of the wealth of this city is owned by my guilds.'

The man moved so smoothly that it felt as if he was dancing, but despite the charming demeanour, there was something repulsive about him.

'I have come to apologize on their behalf and make good the damage done. You understand that, more than money, it's our name and credibility which is important to us. Please forgive us and keep that necklace with you for free. I have also brought a rare ruby, fit enough to be placed on a king's crown, as a personal gift for you. Please accept this and let the matter rest now.'

Rudra's mind was racing. Why was he trying to intervene in the transaction like this, especially when the necklace was of pure gold? He decided to keep talking and get more information. There seemed to be no immediate threat to his life. There was no ultimatum given, no harsh words used, yet he still felt uneasy.

'So how long do you intend to stay at Samapa, arya? Please shift to our exclusive guest houses, we will take very good care of you. And my bodyguards will escort you through the tribal territories on your journey back to Tosali.'

Rudra ignored his offer and said, 'Ratnank, it's not an issue of money, I have problems with the purity of the gold in the necklace, and I want to satisfy myself by personally seeing the process of manufacture.'

'Arya, that will not be possible. I have brought your money back. I have also profusely apologized for the mistake of my men. I will punish them personally, now please let go of your anger and accept our humble offering.'

Rudra noticed a tinge of exasperation in Ratnank's overly sweet voice and knew he would need to be cautious. Ratnank now produced a large, high-quality ruby, the likes of which were found in the Kirata countries of the Himalayas, and a purse containing coins worth the value of the necklace.

Things were getting difficult, Rudra thought. They were clearly not there for a negotiation—they were announcing a decree, a fiat to leave Samapa.

'Setthi Ratnank, I am thankful for your offer, and moved by your generosity, but I would appreciate it if you give me two days to think over it and then respond. I hope you're not in a hurry in this matter.'

Ratnank's face showed a flash of anger, but he immediately controlled himself and returned to his affable, compulsively smiling self. 'As you wish, arya, and please let me know if you need anything else here. Ah, and I will leave my assistant Lubdhaka here. He is very efficient and knows the city very well, he will be of great use to you.'

Rudra could see the noose tightening. These people were wanting no more trouble, and were putting him under constant surveillance. There was no point in protesting, he knew.

Ratnank left with his men, leaving the stone-faced Lubdhaka behind.

Chapter 14

The World of Ideas

Balmani was disturbed and angry. It was compounded by Lubdhaka trying to prevent him from meeting Rudra. When Rudra reached the front room, Balmani and Lubdhaka were about to get into a physical fight, and he had to restrain them.

'What happened Balmani? Why are you so agitated?' Rudra said, taking Balmani aside.

'Who is this man, arya? He is preventing me from entering this place. Have you employed him?'

'No, Balmani. I don't even know him. He is the personal bodyguard of Setthi Ratnank, who was here just some time ago. He has left him here to be of assistance to me, but it seems that he will cause more trouble than help.'

'Ratnank was here! He is a very rich man. He controls the gold, silver and gemstone business of Samapa.' Then, glancing at Lubdhaka, he lowered his voice and said softly, 'I had come to discuss the necklace incident with you. What happened?'

'Adulteration of gold by the kammaras is very unusual, and the laws about such crimes are very stringent,' Rudra said.

Balmani was clearly still annoyed with Lubdhaka. He said, 'If he is not your servant, why did he try and stop me from getting in?'

Lubdhaka moved menacingly towards him. Rudra seized the opportunity. 'Lubdhaka, you may please leave now. Rather than being of assistance to me, you have insulted my dear friend. You should immediately apologize to him!'

The muscleman was very upset. 'I will not apologize at any cost!' he said in a deep voice.

'You have no option but to do so, Lubdhaka.' Rudra raised his voice now, deliberately provoking the man.

'You're not my master. I will not take any orders from you, and about your friend, if he utters a word more, I will break his neck.'

'Get out of here immediately, Lubdhaka! First, you insult my guest, then you defy me and threaten him. Get out or I'll shout for help.'

Lubdhaka's eyes went red, he lunged towards Rudra in anger, but Rudra anticipated his attack, ducked in a swift move to the right, let him lose balance, caught him by his hair and slammed him flat on the floor. Rudra immediately pounced upon him and disarmed him, then shouted loudly for help. Balmani also rushed to pin him down, as people from the guest house rushed in. They saw that a stranger had been apprehended by Rudra and his guest.

They tied up his hands and feet. The monster of a man was difficult to handle, even when five people were restraining him. They then asked Rudra what had happened. He told them that an intruder had attacked him and Balmani. Balmani also added to the story as Rudra tried to suppress a smile.

✦✦✦

Rudra had arrived a bit early at the rendezvous point—a grove—to check if there was any surveillance on them.

The grove was one of the many gardens planted as public utilities. It was built around an excavated tank, with beautiful flowering trees. There were flowering madhavi climbers clinging on to mango, kachnar, parijata and mahua trees with scented blooms which created a scenic environment. There were raised pedestals where people could rest and chat and swings were also provided for children.

People were idling and chatting amongst themselves as it was late afternoon. Rudra approached a group of young men who were having a lively discussion. They turned out to be a group of travelling sophists. As he sat near them, he heard one of them say, 'Samarendra, what makes you say that there is no heaven and hell? You have started talking like a materialist.'

'Ardhendu, this question was actually answered by Ajit Keshkamblin when Ajatshatru, son of Bimbisar and King of Magadha, had asked it.'

'Tell us about it,' they all said, almost in a chorus.

Samarendra continued. 'It so happened that the king asked this question to the leading thinkers of his time. Each one of them replied to it differently. Ajit Keshkamblin, who used to wear a garment of hair—hence the name—said that there is no such thing as this world or the next; fools and wise suffer similarly and nothing remains of them after death.'

'Who else was there? And what did they say?' someone asked.

'Makkhali Gosala, Sanjaya Belathiputta, Nigantha Nataputta, Purana Kassapa and Pakudha Kachchayana were also part of this discussion,' Samarendra said. 'Sanjay Belathiputta was an agnostic, so he said that he could neither confirm, nor deny the existence of another world or otherwise. Makkhali Gosala was a confirmed fatalist, and he said that there is neither cause nor basis for human suffering, and everything from this birth to rebirth was controlled by destiny alone.'

'What did Nigantha Nataputta say?'

'He told the king about the endless cycle of life and death, and that the only way to attain freedom, *moksha*, was by living a life of fourfold self-restraints, which he elaborated upon.'

'So what is your opinion on this, Samarendra?' asked Ardhendu.

'I have already told you, there is no soul, no Yakshas, *Pisachas* (ghosts), *Rakshasas* (demons) or other such beings, and there is no other world than the one in which we live now.'

'How can you be so sure about it?' interjected Rudra.

'*Deshatithi*,' Samarendra said, referring to Rudra as 'stranger from another land', 'if it's about proof, who has seen heaven or hell? Has anyone come back from there to tell us about it? Has anyone seen a Yaksha or a Gandharva anywhere? If these beings are amongst us, why are they so shy as to not come before everybody in public? It's all a play of imagination, and a distraction for the dim-witted.'

Rudra wanted more of this intense conversation. He hadn't expected to get such a cerebral delight here in Samapa. He stoked the fires further. 'Samarendra, tell me then, are the Vedas incorrect, and the learned Brahmins and Shramanas in error when they teach us about the soul, karma and the cycle of death and rebirth.'

Samarendra got to his feet and cleared his throat, now addressing everyone. Some passersby had gathered and they too listened with keen interest.

'My dear friends, please don't feel offended about my views. I tell you the truth and only the absolute truth—there is no soul, god, afterlife, heaven or hell. All these are stories invented by Brahmins to fool you and let them live a parasite's life. Nature is not bothered with good or bad, kind or evil, virtue or vice. The sunshine falls equally on all.'

He continued, 'After death nothing remains, everything goes back to the four constituent elements, and there is no soul distinct from the body. Rishi Brihaspati has said, "If the beast slain in the *Jyotishtoma* rite will itself go to heaven, why doesn't the sacrificer forthwith offer his own father? All these expensive and wasteful rites of the Ashwamedha and other yagyas have been invented by the crafty to cheat unsuspecting idiots. The Vedas are a farce, there is no karma, and no knowledge other than that can be directly perceived through the senses."'

There was a lot of commotion. Rudra wanted to take this discussion to a logical conclusion. 'I have heard that Rishi Brihaspati has said: "*Yavajjivet sukham jivet | Rinam kritvaa ghritam pibet || Bhasmibhutasya dehasya | Punaraagamanam kutah ||* As long as you live happily, take a loan and drink ghee. After a body is reduced to ashes where will it come back from? So it's a theory of irresponsible living, focusing only on bodily pleasures, neglecting duties towards elders, society and state."'

'No!' said Samarendra. 'On the contrary, Brihaspatisutra is the only Arthashastra, long before the devious Chanakya expounded his theories on statecraft. You cannot run a state and society without applying rational, dispassionate thought. The stars and planets, ancestral souls, Yakshas and hundreds of gods will not save you when the enemy comes to your door with a naked sword. Only your intelligence and right thinking along with your skills will save you.' He added, 'And where were your gods when Ashoka killed millions and blood flowed in the Daya River instead of water? Why didn't they miraculously rescue everyone?'

Rudra felt a tug on his shoulder. Vijayaka was beckoning him to come with him. Rudra politely bowed to all the people present and turned to leave.

'Deshatitihi, stay please, it's getting interesting now,' Indushekhar urged.

But Rudra profusely apologized and left.

After a five-minute walk they reached the place where the team had assembled. Rudra apologized for being late.

'I got carried away, but it was a very invigorating discussion. I learnt much from it,' he said.

Bhadrabahu chuckled. 'Sometimes, I feel, you're too eager to change from a Kshatriya arya to a Brahmin acharya, especially when you launch into those theories of how things should be correctly done.'

Rudra smiled. 'So students, pay attention—today's session begins, thus.' Amidst light-hearted laughter, he began briefing them. 'It seems to me that the counterfeiting operation going on here is a large-scale one. As you may remember, I first suspected that there was such an operation when we were in the border village with a sangrahana fort and Nahush had given me five kahapanas in counterfeit coins after he lost in gambling. I had agreed to let him off if he revealed the source of the fake coins to me.'

He continued, 'Based on his information and the general preference for Tosali coins here, we've been able to collect coins, and analyse them to confirm that they are indeed being prepared by filling lead inside gold and silver sheets. Now, before we take any drastic step, we need some more proof, some concrete evidence.'

'Arya, we have been working hard, and we have much to share,' Bhadrabahu said. 'There has been lot of activity at the kammara guild during the night. It seems that they have wind of something and are shutting shop quickly. All this is not possible without the yukta knowing or being involved.'

'Bhadrabahu, I have also been observing the actions of Ratnank with great keenness. First, he comes to me with an offer of a ruby, then places me under surveillance! He is surely involved. You all must be extremely careful. I also understand that there is a team from Tosali, probably sent to keep a tab on us. It is also possible that they're working on the same issue; nevertheless, be extremely careful. This is not Tosali, and you may be at a severe disadvantage here. Meanwhile, I have sent three reports to Mahamatya Nakiya, and I'm sure he must have briefed Rajan.

'The endgame is near, don't leave anything to chance. When we have the proof we need, we will confront the culprits.'

They began to discuss their plan of action and when they dispersed, it was already dark.

Chapter 15

An Offer

Ratnank appeared at the guest house early the next morning, and Rudra was filled with extreme irritation when he saw him. As Rudra entered the visitors room, Ratnank stood up and rushed to him with folded hands.

'Arya, please beat me with your sandals for the folly of my man Lubdhaka. He is an idiot. I don't even know how to ask for your forgiveness, I am so ashamed!

Rudra remained quiet, and Ratnank continued.

'Let me recompense for the harm done, arya. Please do me the honour of joining me for a meal at my residence. I will also invite some prominent people from the king's administration.'

It would have been too much of an insult to reject the invitation. Seeing Rudra hesitate, Ratnank further pleaded, 'Don't refuse, please. I've already invited Fanindra, the yukta of this city. He will be so happy to meet you.'

The name sounded familiar . . . yes, Balmani had mentioned it. 'If you insist, I will be there Setthi Ratnank,' Rudra said finally.

'Thank you! I will send a chariot and my attendants to escort you, and don't worry, the fool Lubdhaka will not be anywhere near you.' They both laughed and the setthi took his leave.

When Rudra was ushered in, some people were already there, and Ratnank was prompt to introduce him as a guest from Tosali. Everyone welcomed him, and they sat down on mattresses and leaned back against fine silk pillows.

There were three guests apart from Rudra. Fanindra, he'd noted when he was introduced to him, had shifty eyes. The man was wearing a very fine yellow anatriya, secured by a *kassyaka* silk kayabandh with a many stringed golden *kalabuka* (girdle). The uttariya was a bleached white *patrona* silk, draped on his left shoulder, going diagonally across the chest and knotted at the waist, hanging loosely across the back. For an inexplicable reason, Rudra felt a visceral dislike for the man.

One of the other men seemed to be some kind of assistant to Fanindra. He was clothed in white, and his hairdo and turban were less elaborate. The third man had seemed vaguely familiar. Rudra's hunch was right; he was from Tosali, and was introduced to him as Manibhushan, a merchant of pearls.

Rudra looked around. It was a beautiful, large room. The wooden pillars had embossed figures of parrots and climbers, flowers and leaves. The walls were white with beautiful line drawings in a dark brown and the carved doors had curtains of dark green. The windows too had curtains, but they were of a fine semi-transparent type, covering a wooden grate.

The cloth was tied in the middle with a laced string ending in golden tassels.

Fanindra was talking to Manibhushan in a shrill voice, 'Then, I told them, if you don't pay in time, I will add a fine of one kahapana per day. The idiots immediately paid up!' He laughed loudly.

'But I think they must have been in some genuine difficulty. It is true that a ship on the way to Suvarnabhumi was lost and everyone on board is feared to be dead, all forty of them. Their merchandise was lost to the sea too. You could have given them some concession or extra time,' Manibhushan said.

'You don't know the local merchants, Manibhushan. They always have some story or the other to evade paying taxes. It's always Ratnank who comes up with a good compromise formula, otherwise half of them would be in the prison for defaulting on payments.'

Rudra decided to change the subject. 'Manibhushan, what are the types of pearls that you deal with?'

'Arya, there are eight sorts of pearls, *haya* (horse), *gaja* (elephant), *ratha* (chariot), *amalaka*, *valayanguli* (plum), *vethaka, kakudha phala* and *pakatika* (common/natural pearls). The other seven kinds are very rare, I have been dealing with pakatika pearls only.'

'Ah! So you're interested in gemstones, arya' quipped Ratnank. 'But I am sad that you refused my gift! The ruby was a one in a million kind.'

Rudra couldn't understand why Ratnank was talking of the ruby and his offer so openly.

'Can I have a look at it Setthi Ratnank?' asked Manibhushan.

'I think one shouldn't be excessively strict in matters of accepting gifts. In fact an excess anywhere is a cause of doom,'

Fanindra said with a trace of contempt in his voice. 'The rakshasa Bali was ruined due to his excessive charitable nature, Duryodhana was vanquished for his excessive pride and Ravana was destroyed due to his excessive interest in women.'

Rudra didn't reply or react to this. Manibhushan and Ratnank looked taken aback by Fanindra's haughtiness and pretended to be busy examining the ruby.

'Setthi Ratnank, I have some other work in the city to attend to. Would it be possible to serve the food early?' Rudra said, sensing a great deal of animosity emanating from Fanindra. He wanted to wriggle out of the unpleasant encounter.

'Oh, I see. What work do you have exactly, arya?' Fanindra asked aggressively.

Ratnank hurriedly intervened. 'Don't be angry with us, arya. Fanindra is a bit harsh in his manners, but he is a well-meaning person . . . Come, let me show you around the house, it's one of the most beautiful buildings in the city.' Ratnank held out his hand.

Rudra got up. Fanindra was staring at him with burning eyes and Rudra found his behaviour inexplicable.

Ratnank took him up a flight of wooden stairs which lead to a guest room. The room was spacious but less lavishly decorated. There were low tables placed around the room, with expensive soft cloth laid on them. As Rudra approached, he realized that each table had a collection of different gemstones, graded and sorted by type, colour, weight and quality into small clusters.

'This is a small store I maintain at home for discerning visitors, arya. Would you like to have a look at them?'

'What use does a Kshatriya have for jewels, Ratnank? I would be happier looking at weapons,' Rudra said.

There was a streak of exasperation on the setthis's face, but he immediately regained his composure. 'Arya, then let's come straight to the point. I and Fanindra are aware that you're snooping on us, we have been watching your movements closely,' he said in a cold voice. His bearing and manner had perceptibly changed.

Rudra sat down, forcing Ratnank also to sit. 'Go on,' he said. Rudra's mind was racing, he was evaluating the magnitude of the threat. Would there be an armed confrontation or was it just a pressure tactic designed to scare him into aborting his mission?

'We also believe you have gathered some information on the subject of currency and coinage . . .'

'Who is "we" setthi?' Rudra asked.

'I and Fanindra, the yukta of this province,' Ratnank answered impatiently.

'Hmmm, but I don't see the connection between you and him, setthi,' Rudra said.

'You know what you know, arya. Now stop pretending and talk business. We can work out a mutually beneficial solution for you and your entire team, believe me.'

'You're playing with fire, Ratnank. Aren't you aware of the punishment for bringing fake coins into the treasury?'

Ratnank shrugged. 'Look, arya let's stop this hide and seek now. We know all about you, and you know something about us.'

'That's interesting, setthi—what do you know about me?'

'Do you think we are little children playing marbles? Should I tell you some stories about magical snakes to fire up your imagination?'

Rudra took a blind shot. 'So you must also be aware that a second team from Tosali has been sent to investigate this matter?'

'Yes—the man introduced to you as Manibhushan, sitting down there, is actually a spy from Tosali, who is doing the same job as you are, and he knows everything about you. You seem to be rather in the dark about him though.'

'What is he doing here, setthi, at your residence?'

'He is helping us out.'

Rudra was dumbstruck. He suddenly became worried about the safety of his team. One thing he was sure of was their integrity—no one from his team would ever betray him or the king. His mind was working fast now, what were his alternatives? He wasn't even armed to defend himself and was unaware of the layout of the house to effect an escape.

'I can imagine what you must be thinking Rudravarman, and I am banking on your maturity and intellect. We don't want to hurt anyone; we're just looking for an amicable settlement, and that's not difficult my friend.' Ratnank was speaking very confidently now.

Rudra decided to show no overt signs of dissent. 'What have you offered to Manibhushan?'

'Oh, he is a mid-level spy. His appetite is not much, still we have taken good care of him. We are very generous people you know.' Ratnank smiled. 'I want to know your price, arya, please include the share of your team too.'

'How much can you pay?' Rudra said.

'Ah! so we're talking now . . . 10,000 kahapanas, five large gemstones of the highest quality, a pearl necklace and a safe passage through Samapa. And we're being very generous. The cash component is a bit more than your annual salary, you know.'

'Hmmm, and if I say that this offer is not good enough, what would you say, setthi?'

'We can better it. How about 12,000 kahapanas, ten glittering gemstones good enough to be fitted on a king's crown, three gutsa pearl necklaces of thirty-two strings each and the best ganika, Sulasa.'

Rudra thought of Balmani. Ratnank continued, '12,000 is the salary of a prince or governor, and we also promise that the counterfeiting will be stopped forthwith. You will never hear of a fake coin in Samapa again.'

There was a long pause.

'This is my final offer, arya. You don't have much choice, to be honest. What do you say?'

Rudra studied him for a moment, and then said, 'If this is the price for my integrity, I say no, setthi. I have been sending reports to the king every two days, and I am sure the man being called Manibhushan would be doing the same. I have a small army contingent at my beck and call here in Samapa and a larger reinforcement half a day away in the janapada. Any assault on me will have very deadly consequences, so make your next move wisely.'

Ratnank was aghast. He had not expected Rudra to have been so well prepared. He kept his calm. 'There must be some way, arya, please help us. I've already promised that we will stop this operation at once. We will also make good the loss we have caused to the treasury. Please forgive us, we have been very foolish.'

Out of the corner of his eye, Rudra saw a curtain on one end of the room move. He went up and pulled it to a side, and behold! The monster Lubdhaka was hiding there, armed. Before Rudra could react, Ratnank pounced on Lubdhaka, disarmed him, and started slapping him. 'You fool, who allowed you here, why did you come here? Get out!'

Rudra watched, astonished, as the brute walked away.

'Please, arya, forgive him too. You know he is so dim-witted. He is an utter fool who does not think of the consequences of his actions.' He was at Rudra's feet now, sobbing bitterly.

'Get up, setthi, it does not beget your position in society to act thus.'

'I will not leave your feet till you promise me that you will consider forgiving me with an open heart. I promise that we will make good all the lost gold and silver to the treasury and also pay fines, but it's all up to your magnanimity,' he sobbed helplessly.

'Yes, all right—get up now please. I promise that I will consider your case after consultation with my team.'

'I will take it as a true Kshatriya's words, arya, and I know you won't betray me,' Ratnank said, wiping away his tears.

The setthi descended the stairs and Rudra followed him down.

Fanindra looked up, trying to figure out the outcome. Manibhushan appeared unaffected, and Fanindra's assistant looked very anxious as he saw Ratnank's sunken face. The setthi went indoors and, some time later, a helper came from within the house and called Fanindra and his assistant inside. Manibhushan had realized that there was something seriously wrong and became guarded in his actions. Rudra broke the silence. 'When are you heading back to Tosali, Manibhushan? I can accompany you on your return journey.'

'Arya, I am not sure when, as the ship from Suvarnabhumi may arrive any time in the next four days or so. I don't want to inconvenience you till then.'

Rudra nodded. 'Have you known these people for a long time?'

'Yes, arya, my business keeps bringing me to these lands and they have been very helpful always.' Before he could say anything more, Ratnank appeared and called them in for their meal.

Fanindra and his assistant were already sitting on the small wooden seats provided. They washed their hands and feet and came back where the food had been laid out in bronze utensils. As Rudra was about to sit on one of the platforms, Ratnank requested him to sit next to him. He obliged.

The food looked delicious—Ratnank had made arrangements fit for a prince's reception. As they were about to start eating, Rudra said, 'In my society, we do not eat food which has not been offered to the gods. After making *naivedya* (supplication) to the gods, the food becomes *prasada* (blessing). When I was a child, my mother used to offer *ahuta*, a little naivedya to the fire that cooks and purifies our food, I have been following the practice ever since.' The others, being followers of heterodox systems, sneered at him.

'Would anyone mind if I offer some food to the fire god at the hearth?'

There was an awkward silence, as Ratnank looked at Fanindra in confusion. Rudra, taking advantage of this, picked up his plate and also that of his host and proceeded towards the kitchen. Ratnank hurriedly asked the women of the house to vacate the kitchen as Rudra walked in. He sat with closed eyes before the fire in the hearth, then recited a mantra—*Om pranay swaha, apanaya swaha, vyanaya swaha, udanaya swaha, samanaya swaha . . . brahmaneya swaha . . .* He threw grains of cooked rice in the fire, and they burnt with a hissing sound. He recited the mantra again and threw a few more grains. Then, he got up and brought both the plates back. Nobody had started eating. Rudra said, 'We also sprinkle water like this, and then commence eating,' and picked up his first morsel.

Fanindra started eating in silence, his contempt barely disguised. Ratnank kept staring at Rudra, who seemed to be thoroughly enjoying his meal.

Chapter 16

A Lot to Explain

The next day, soldiers searched everywhere for Rudra and his team. Given the differences in language and dressing, it was very difficult for an outsider to hide in Samapa, Fanindra knew this very well. But Rudra could not be found at the guest house, or at Balmani's, or at other probable spots. His associates were also missing.

Fanindra was fuming. 'I told this idiot Ratnank, we should have finished the matter last night. Kalahamsa, did you see how he bungled it up then?'

His attendant was deeply worried. 'If we don't find him by afternoon, it will be very difficult for us to answer the rajvachanika. We will be doomed!' he said.

The fact was, Ratnank had been found dead in the morning. It was his wife who had found him, when she went to wake him up. The news reached Fanindra, who called it a murder, and accused Rudra of poisoning Ratnank. A manhunt for Rudra and his friends had been launched immediately. The search had been futile though. There was no sign of the people from Tosali.

★★★

When Rudra reached the governor's palace, his team was waiting for him. He was quickly taken inside after verifying the royal seal he was carrying. Bhadrabahu ran towards Rudra and embraced him.

'Arya, we were so worried about you! We are so happy to see you unhurt. What happened at Setthi Ratnank's place? When I sent a messenger to your guest house, he was told that you had gone to fetch a white lotus flower for the Saraswati puja.

'We were confused at first but soon understood your message; the white lotus blooms only in the night and is not seen during the day. The coded message for us was to escape and not be seen during the day. Also, the mention of Goddess Saraswati indicated the need to be very wise. We acted accordingly, and as previously decided, we reached the governor's palace one by one. It was good that he had already had intimation that we would be arriving.

'It is here that we learned that Ratnank had been murdered and Fanindra was looking for you. He has also accused you of stealing valuable gemstones from the setthi's house last night. We know that this is all false, they're just trying to get even now. Let the governor meet us, we will tell him the real story.'

'Don't be so agitated, Bhadrabahu,' Rudra said. 'We will indeed meet the governor and tell him what has happened. But let me tell you about last night's events first.'

Everyone came close to him. They were confused and afraid, and he deliberately spoke in a calm voice to bring the tension down.

'Last noon, Yukta Fanindra was invited to Setthi Ratnank's place along with me and some others. It was a set-up, probably by Fanindra. They wanted to assess how much I knew about their crime and the extent of damage possible. Soon, they realized that the situation was very serious and needed extreme measures. I was offered a bribe, and I refused to take it. They made the offer very lucrative, but I still didn't budge. Then they showed repentance and asked for forgiveness. Seeing everything fail, they came up with a very drastic measure.'

'What was that, arya?' Vijayaka said, worried.

'Don't worry, no harm has been caused to me. But they did try and poison my food!'

'How did you find out, arya?'

'I suspected they would try and kill me because their plans to bribe and threaten me had failed. When they served our food, I told them that my religion doesn't allow me to eat anything that had has not been offered to the gods in naivedya and aahuti. They couldn't stop me from doing that. I took Ratnank's plate along with mine, and when I put rice from my plate into the fire, it burned with a hissing sound and a flash of green and blue; but the rice from his plate didn't do any such thing. I instantly realized that poison had been added to my food. So, I exchanged the plates. Setthi Ratnank died of his own poison, which acted late in the night.'

'Had it not been for your intuition, arya, we all would have been dead by now. We owe our lives to you,' said Bhadrabahu with tear-filled eyes.

'Tread with extreme caution now, we don't know who is a friend and who a foe, so don't go out till I order, and do not disclose anything to anyone. Bhadrabahu, send a message to summon the army contingent detailed for our protection and also alert the backup in the janapadas, we may need them.'

Rudra continued, 'I think the governor must have gotten the message from Tosali by now about the happenings here, but I still feel we should be circumspect with him when he comes back from Ratnank's last rites.'

As they waited, they were treated well by the staff, as per the governor's instructions.

It was late afternoon when the governor returned. He immediately called for Rudra.

Rudra was quick to notice the regional differences in the decor and furnishings in the governor's room. He particularly liked the blue Yaksha carved into the arch of the main door, as if it was simultaneously supporting the roof and hanging from it. For some reason, Rudra found it to be very comic.

The governor greeted him warmly, but Rudra could not help noticing the extreme caution with which the official was treating him. Fortunately, there was no hint of contempt. 'Arya, unprecedented things have happened, and I am still reeling from the shock of the loss of Setthi Ratnank. I don't understand why Yukta Fanindra is blaming it on you or why he is claiming you are behind the missing gemstones from the setthi's house.'

'Aryaputta, I was sad to hear about Ratnank's passing too. I think this is a case of poisoning. Have you interrogated the cook?'

'All the servants and family members are grieving deeply, how can I ask for the cook to be interrogated? It would be too cruel to the bereaved family,' he said. 'But wait . . . I could get some information covertly from my sources.'

'I would suggest you do so, aryaputta, before it is too late. You may have to depose and arrest Fanindra immediately.'

'Arya, I did get a wind of what you have unearthed, but I still have my doubts. He has been a loyal servant of the king for a very long time. I heard of his prodigal ways, but otherwise found him to be very efficient, prompt and versatile. I will need very concrete evidence before I take any action against him.'

'Your officers or you personally may talk to my men, who are now your guests, and they will give all the details required, but now, as per the orders of Rajan, I command you to immediately put Fanindra under arrest and throw him into the dungeon before he causes more damage.'

The governor was taken aback. He had not expected this kind of response from Rudra, he fumbled with the letter of authority bearing the royal seal on it, which Rudra had handed over to him. Rudra noticed that the governor was trembling; with fear or anger, he couldn't decide.

He had left few options open to the man. To begin with, he had arrived in the city unannounced, then successfully unearthed a counterfeiting operation happening right under his very nose, and now there had been the murder of an important figure, probably connected to this mess. Things couldn't have been worse for the governor.

Meanwhile, in Tosali, the king was in conference with the mysterious figure.

'Rajan, your information was indeed correct—there was a large-scale fraud being perpetrated at Samapa. It is yet not clear if the rajvachanika himself is involved, but the yukta is definitely a part of it. I know that you have already instructed the senapati to send backup to Samapa, in case there is a sudden revolt there,' the figure continued. 'Rudra has done a good job, I doubt if anyone else would have had the finesse to accomplish a task like this.'

The king smiled and said, 'You should know that he is actually a seasoned player from the court of Satkarni . . . What is the news from the frontiers? I hear that the Rathikas and Bhojakas are getting increasingly bold.'

'Rajan, I am getting even more serious news, but I will speak only after getting concrete information. Right now, we have to watch Samapa very closely, it is very important how the rajvachanika reacts to everything. The other team I had sent to keep watch on Rudra and his men has nothing adverse to note,' the figure said.

'Hmmm, anyways it was high time we tightened the rajvachanika's reins, he has been flying too high of late. Let's see, this will also test out his resilience and game plan.'

'Rajan, I'm confident that Rudra would have foreseen this possibility and taken precautions. It is good that you have vested him with power to take any decision on your behalf.'

'I think you're right. Tell the chiefs of the tribes to keep their soldiers in readiness, if the need arises. Keep me updated and apprise me of the Rathikas and Bhojakas in a week,' the king said. The figure bowed, and gracefully retreated.

✦ ✦ ✦

It was late evening, the dust kicked up by the hooves of horses announced that a small contingent of the army was reaching the governor's residence. Rudra received them and asked them to be at the ready, but not to make a move without his orders. He also ensured that this information was given to the governor, whose authority he didn't want to overtly undermine. After making arrangements for his team and plotting the next course of action, he changed into commoner's clothes and ventured out, despite the objections of the guards posted there. He had an important errand to run.

Balmani was simultaneously happy and angry to see Rudra. 'Where have you been, arya? Are you aware that there is so much disturbance in the city! Setthi Ratnank has died of poisoning, and his friend Fanindra has been looking for the assassin everywhere.' He paused and then, lowering his voice, asked, 'Should I tell you a secret?'

Rudra nodded.

'Some soldiers had come to meet me also, and they were asking about you! Do you have anything to do with the poisoning, arya? I am so afraid, but I believe that you're a very good and pious person and wouldn't be involved in anything like this. In fact, I told them that you had a small dispute with the kammaras, but it was such a petty issue that Ratnank wouldn't be bothered with it in any case.'

'My dear friend, please don't have any fear in your mind,' Rudra said. 'I am a commoner who has no connection with setthis. Please don't worry, nothing will happen to you.'

'There was a lot of activity at the kammaras. They have closed down the workshop for inspection; a large number of officials were seen there, most likely from the governor's office. They didn't allow anyone near the workshop—they closed the street . . .' he was breathless. 'Arya, you don't understand, they questioned Vasuman too, and this evening, another set of people came and asked me the same questions. I am so frightened! But I still believe that you are a good person, I cannot forget how you rescued me from the soldiers at the ganikas.'

'Calm down, Balmani. I have just come to say goodbye and to ask you a question.'

'And what is that, arya?' a bewildered Balmani asked.

'A very rich merchant has come to Samapa. He is a very old friend. Last night, I narrated your story to him and told him about your love for Sulasa. His heart melted and he has asked me to inquire if you would like to marry her. If so, he will pay the money to secure her release.'

Balmani was shocked. Then, with tears in his eyes, he said, 'Arya, I will never forget you and your friendship. I will go by the advice you gave me that day. I will live a purposeful life and marry a girl who is not fickle and genuinely cares for me.'

Rudra sat in silence for a couple of moments, then he blessed him and took his leave.

There was more trouble in store. It was night by the time he returned, and the governor was waiting impatiently for him.

'Venerable Rudravarman, where had you gone? I was so worried about you. There have been very serious developments.' Before Rudra could say anything, the governor continued. 'You were absolutely correct about the counterfeiting, arya! I am so ashamed that it happened under my watch. I have lost face before Rajan. What excuse do I have! We have found a hoard of counterfeit coins which had been shifted from the workshop by Ratnank last night. Had he been alive, I would have put him to death, that traitor! He and Fanindra were partners in this crime. I have sent soldiers to arrest Fanindra,' the governor spoke in one breath.

'And yes, we did investigate Ratnank's cook, as you suggested. He has confessed to preparing the poison.' There was a dark stillness in the room, Rudra felt sad for the young man who had died, but he also experienced a sense of relief at having survived the tumultuous turn of events. The governor was still speaking with a sense of urgency. 'I have to inform you with great regret, arya, that the plan was to poison *you*! But it seems your ancestor's blessings are with you, the plotter succumbed to his own machinations, and consumed the poison.'

'This is difficult to hear, aryaputta. He seemed to be a very amiable person. I forgive him for his wrongdoings—may his soul get *moksha*,' Rudra said quietly.

Just then, a servant informed them that a messenger had come with urgent news. The governor went out with the man, and when he returned, he looked shaken. He drank water and wiped the sweat off his forehead and kept staring at the wall. Rudra got up and put his hand on the governor's shoulder, 'Aryaputta, what is the matter? Please tell me.'

The governor took a breath. 'Arya, a small unit of my soldiers had gone to arrest Fanindra, but he escaped, and when they pursued him, he galloped to the ramparts and committed suicide by jumping into the ditch.'

'Aryaputta, this is very disturbing news, didn't your soldiers try to prevent him from doing this?'

'They tried and begged him to come down, but he threatened to cut his throat with the sword if they followed. And before they could react, he jumped off the high walls.'

'Compose yourself, aryaputta, you have a lot to handle. Does he have his own troops stationed here or any powerful relatives who could foment trouble in the coming days?'

'Arya, he was from a very reputed family, but his activities over the last several months have upset one and all, so there will neither be popular support for him nor any retaliation from his kinsmen.'

'That is a good thing. I suggest that you summon a meeting of the important people in the city—the head of the srenis, important Brahmins, Sramanas and priests of prominent temples—and explain this unfortunate turn of events to them. Then, you may separately brief the senior government officials. Meanwhile, your spies should immediately track and arrest anyone spreading rumours. This way you can pre-empt and contain anything that may go down an adverse path.'

'Arya Rudravarman, I've been too shaken by the incidents of the last few days. Please stay back here till things settle down, your counsel is of great value to me.'

'Please pardon me, but I do have to leave soon,' said Rudra with folded hands. 'I will take your leave now. I am very sure that you will handle the situation with great wisdom, astuteness and courage.'

Rudra, along with his team, left Samapa the next day. The governor had provided a detachment of soldiers for his protection despite his protests; he did not want to take any more risk with his security now.

Rudra's return through the forests was rather uneventful, except for some unconfirmed rumours of the destruction of a temple in the distant north-west. When he reached Tosali, his heart was heavy with memories of Samapa, but he also felt a sense of relief. He had finally come home. However, a storm was awaiting him.

Chapter 17

Rathikas and Bhojakas

He knew something really serious must have happened. Rudra had been waiting for the past few days to debrief the king and Nakiya about the Samapa assignment, but it appeared that something more pressing was occupying them. Everyone was summoned to the court early one morning and when Rudra entered the premises, he could hear the king shouting in anger. This was a rare occurrence. He had always seen him calm, composed and unfazed in the deepest of crises. Bahushalin was rushing in, Nakiya was already there, Vikarna had just reached, Rajguru Uddalaka was already seated and other amatyas started pouring in. There was no time for decorum; Mahamatya Nakiya asked everyone to be seated immediately. There was a hush as they waited for the king to address them.

'These Rathikas and Bhojakas have attempted to challenge our might, they are inciting us into a war. Our messengers have informed me that they have destroyed a sacred temple on the Vidyadhara borders. The Atavikas (forest dwellers) of Vidyadhara have been the biggest contributors of soldiers to our army, and there is a severe feeling of restlessness in that region. If we do not teach these Rathikas and Bhojakas a lesson immediately, there could be a rebellion!'

Nakiya said, 'Rajan, the Atavika soldiers have been loyal and valiant, they have even performed better than the fabled sreni soldiers; we cannot let them down, but I will advocate caution.'

'What caution, mahamatya! These people are not even kings. They are petty chieftains who have now started calling themselves Maharathis or something! We can straighten them out in no time,' the king said.

Senapati Bahushalin spoke up, 'Rajan, these people are indeed small chieftains under Satkarni, but they maintain their own armies and even mint their own coins. They also carry royal insignia like the *chauri* (fly whisk), *chattari* (umbrella) and a flag! It has gone into their heads that they are kings. I don't understand why the Andhras tolerate such nonsense.'

'Senapati, start assembling the troops, we march in two days' time,' said the king in a fierce tone.

Rudra felt distraught, they were rushing into a situation unprepared.

'What is your view, Rudravarman?' asked Nakiya, as if reading his mind.

'Mahamatya, Rajan, I request you all to think with a cool mind. Why should petty chiefs, who are the feudatories of Satkarni, dare challenge us? There must be something more to this.'

'Please elaborate,' commanded the king, a hint of impatience in his voice.

'Rajan, it may be a ploy of the Andhras to involve us in a proxy war. As Satkarni is related to Rajan from his mother's side, he may not want to have a direct confrontation with us, but he will have a valid excuse to join the war if we attack his feudatories. Also, as they have provoked us now, they must be expecting us to retaliate. We must not meet their expectation and wait for an opportune time to strike after weighing the possibility of the Andhras jumping in.'

Nakiya and the king's eyes met. Rajan closed his eyes for some time, and after some contemplation, he said, 'If we wait, we may have a rebellion to deal with in the Vidyadharas, if we act now, it may not be the most opportune moment. Rajguru, what do the planetary positions say?'

'Rajan, I will need some time to compute the planetary positions, but I do see a point in what Rudravarman has suggested. We can deal with our own people to prevent a rebellion, but rushing into a war may not be very wise.'

The king didn't seem to expect this reaction from the rajguru. Although he desisted from reacting sharply owing to the age and position of his teacher, his discomfiture was visible. He said, 'I will inspect the army today. Senapati Bahushalin, tell your people to be ready, Nakiya you may ask the storekeeper to open the storehouse in preparation for a march. You may disperse now.'

It was a wet morning. As Rudra left, he suddenly decided to visit Maitreyi and pay his respects to her. He asked his charioteer to turn towards her residence. As he neared her home, his heart started pounding, memories of his stay there after he was hit by the poison dart came afresh. When he reached, he saw that the help was sweeping and cleaning the courtyards, and a graceful old man with an affected gait was walking around. One of the female attendants immediately identified Rudra and asked him to wait in the guest room. He heard the old man outside inquire as to who the visitor was. In some time, an attendant came to Rudra and said in an apologetic tone, 'Arya, Amatya Maitreyi returned from a long journey late last night and she is in deep sleep. She must be very tired by the travel, should I wake her up?'

'Ah, no please, don't wake her up,' said Rudra. 'Just tell her that Rudravarman had come back from Samapa and wanted to thank her for saving his life.'

The attendant wanted to bring something for him to eat, but Rudra refused and quickly got up. As he was leaving, he passed the old man. Rudra greeted him respectfully and sought his blessings. The old man coldly put his hand on Rudra's head in a gesture of blessing. Rudra realized that he was a Brahman, and must surely have been Maitreyi's father, but he felt that there was something odd about him.

Leaving with a heavy heart, he asked his charioteer to drive him home. When he reached his residence, a messenger was waiting for him. Nakiya had called him immediately. In fact, the messenger had been waiting for some time and expressed anxiety about the late delivery of the message. Rudra immediately started for Mahamatya Nakiya's residence.

When he reached, Vikarna, Senapati Bahushalin, and the governor were already seated and seemed to be involved in an intense discussion. Rudra quietly took a seat. Vikarna gave him a dirty look.

Nakiya was saying, 'We primarily need to assess how bad the situation is. I do understand that the Vidyadharadiwas Temple has been constructed and maintained by the Kalinga royal families for centuries as a goodwill gesture towards the forest tribes, but someone needs to tell us what the extent of the damage is.'

The governor appeared to have gathered some information about it already. 'I have been told that the damage to the temple is quite extensive. Two pillars have collapsed, the sculpture on the eastern wall has been obliterated and the roof has been substantially weakened. Surprisingly, absolutely nothing happened to the idol, it's a miracle.'

'What is your update, senapati?' asked Nakiya.

'Mahamatya, Rajan is right in estimating the unrest in the Vidyadharas. I can see the discontentment in the soldiers from that area. They are watching us closely, if we don't act, we risk alienating a large and loyal chunk of our infantry. Apart from this, there will surely be severe disturbances in the forest tracts.'

'You should prepare the forces for Rajan's inspection today. Then, address them separately, inspire confidence in them and put spies on the job to find out if anyone is deliberately fomenting trouble or inciting the Vidyadharas in the army,' Nakiya instructed. 'And as for you Vikarna, arrest anyone who seems to be talking negatively or seems to be advocating subversion in the city; your men need to be everywhere.'

Nayaka Vikarna nodded. 'Mahamatya, all the dyuta grihas, madiralayas and centres of prostitution have been covered. Spies have been positioned in eateries, temples and all entry and exit points of the city. I am checking every report personally.'

'Arya Rudrvarman, what are your observations on this situation?' Nakiya asked. An expression of surprise and contempt passed on Vikrarna's face. Just as Rudra was about to begin, Maitreyi suddenly rushed in and Nakiya asked her to be seated. He then gestured to Rudra that he could speak.

'Mahamatya, we should first assess the situation and circumstances before deciding to march. I recommend sending a messenger with an ultimatum, this will give us a chance to ascertain their state of readiness, and also give sufficient time to read the reaction of their allies such as Satkarni. While the messenger moves, we can keep our forces in a state of readiness and place them strategically. Based on the reports of the messenger and spies, we then decide their fate.'

Senapati Bahushalin quipped, 'Mahamatya, Arya Rudravarman's suggestions are excellent, but who will explain this to Rajan? He seems to be too upset to hear anything except the sound of the war trumpet.'

'Let me handle that,' said Maitreyi, looking weary. 'I will talk to Rajan and request him to call a *mantriparishad* (assembly of ministers). He will then be bound by our decision.'

'Yes, yes,' they all echoed. 'Amatya Maitreyi, then it is your responsibility to talk to Rajan now and convince him to call a mantriparishad. Rajan will surely consult me after you make this request, and I will support your idea,' said Nakiya. 'So we disperse, everyone should get to their tasks without any delay.'

The amatyas started leaving one by one. Rudra was in the corridor when he heard Maitreyi calling him, 'Arya Rudravarman, please wait. I seek your forgiveness for not being able to meet you. My attendants didn't inform me, they thought I was too tired to be woken up. Please accept my apologies.'

'Amatya Maitreyi, it was my fault to have come unannounced, that too at such an early time of the day. I am the one who should apologize.'

He felt a mix of feelings, standing with her in the corridor. A soft breeze blew outside, and the curtains billowed rhythmically. She looked even more beautiful in this state, her hair unkempt and eyes reddened due to lack of sleep. Her elaborate hairdo and ornaments were absent today, making her look like a commoner, less intimidating, yet more enchanting.

Suddenly, Vikarna emerged from the doorway. He stopped in his tracks seeing Maitreyi and Rudra in a conversation. 'Hmmm, am I interrupting something important?' he said with a crooked smile.

'Not at all nayaka, you can join the conversation,' she said laughing.

'Maitreyi, if it is not so important, I want to discuss something significant with you.' Saying this, he took her aside. She looked apologetically at Rudra, who left the two and proceeded to the exit. He felt her eyes following him.

That afternoon, Rudra's team—Bhadrabahu, Vijayaka, Devabrata, Kinshuk, Jeemuthabahan—assembled for a meeting. When Rudra entered, Bhadrabahu immediately asked, 'Arya Rudravarman, do we hear the war drums or am I imagining things?'

'What you hear is correct, Bhadrabahu. The Rathikas and Bhojakas have caused great distress in the forested Vidyadhara region. They have attacked and destroyed the famous Vidyadharadiwas Temple. The Atavikas are upset, and if we don't teach the Rathika–Bhojakas a lesson quickly, there may be a revolt in the army too.'

'So we will march across the Vidyadhara forests in rain, and our chariots will get stuck for the enemy archers to feast upon?' Old Devabrata was sarcastic. He moved away and sat at a distance, as if dissociating himself from the discussion.

'I think venerable Devabrata is indeed correct, we should not jump into a war which has been foisted upon us,' Vijayaka said. Bhadrabahu nodded.

'Everyone, please understand, there are no simple solutions. The adversary has left us with few options, and he has played a very intelligent game. We have to chalk out a strategy which is beyond his calculations,' Rudra said.

'Given the distance, it would take us two to three weeks before our army can reach their territories. This will give them enough time to prepare and counter our moves.'

'But once we successfully reach there, our powerful and trained elephants will destroy their ragtag army in no time. Also, the rainy season will work to our advantage if we use elephants, as they fight very well in mud and slush when horses can't.'

'You expect the enemy to be standing with garlands in their hands when you reach, Arya Rudravarman?' said Devabrata with a smirk. He was slowly shaking his head in disapproval.

'No, Devabrata, we have to move our forces quickly without much pomp and show and maintain the element of surprise . . . Let's drop this for now. Tell me, what is the news from the city?'

Kinshuk spoke. 'Last night, a bard–jester was performing on the southern side of the city in the settlement of Vaishyas. He told a story about a band of dogs attacking and killing an elephant; the obvious reference being to these Rathika–Bhojakas.'

This worried Rudra; even the general populace was talking about the situation now. This could seriously affect the honour and dignity of the kingdom in the eyes of its own people.

Something needed to be done urgently, and more importantly, skilfully.

It was a bright morning when the army had been assembled for the king's inspection. What a great spectacle! The senapati had assembled the army in a *padmavyuha* (lotus formation), with the four types of troops—*pada* (infantry), *turanga* (cavalry), *ratha* (chariots) and gaja (elephants)—aligned in the forms of petals of the holy flower. The deputy commanders-in-chiefs were positioned at the tip of the petals, followed by the archers, behind whom were the javelin throwers and sword bearers, with the mounted riders of cavalry flanking them from the sides. The chariots stood in the inner layer enclosing the elephants.

The petals met at the base, where the king was positioned. In a war, if any enemy dared to move in the space between the petals, they would quickly close and swallow them up.

Five drummers mounted on chariots played the large war drums. The horses drawing them were specially trained not to react to the deafening sound. Three such chariots followed the royal chariot, with musicians, bards and trumpeters playing war songs.

The king moved through the petal formations. Whenever he halted to inspect something, the music would stop. He would ask the soldiers and officers a question or two and then move on. Saktimati the shastradharini moved deftly with the king. She would invariably place herself beside the king, a position which allowed her to strike immediately if something went wrong. Two of her female assistants accompanied her in a tight group, one of them held a bow with a quiver full of poisonous arrows. They also carried many small daggers and knives, hidden neatly between the pleats of their kayabandh. Senapati Bahushalin was on the same chariot as the king, explaining the formation to him.

The Kalinga royal army recruited from various sources, the Atavikas being one of them. There were well-trained *bhrata* (mercenaries), sreni soldiers from guilds who were part-time workers in the interregnum of wars, *maula* (hereditary soldiers), *mitra* (contributions from feudatories and friends), irregular soldiers and so on. Many ethnicities were represented too, the army had men from the Dramira (Tamil) Pandya County, Andhraites, Shakas, Khasas, Kiratas and even Yavanas.

Except the core unit, all others wore their traditional dresses. Thus the foresters wore next to nothing, with metal and bead ornaments in their ears and around their necks; the Shakas wore elaborate tunics, with buttons at the back; the remaining soldiers wore a protective uttariya of thick crude silk and a girdled kayabandh around the waist with a tight antariya.

The king's guards grew particularly alert when the king approached the Atavika soldiers. They, in turn, hailed him loudly, and he spoke to many of them.

The elephants were dressed in full armour, with a mount that carried a mahout, archers and javelin throwers. When the king stopped in front of an elephant, the mahout made it bend down and prostrate on its forelegs, while the soldiers atop balanced and held steadfast. The elephant was armed with a large iron sphere with spikes. A chain from the sphere was fastened to its trunk; one swing of the elephant's trunk could kill many enemy soldiers.

Some elephants also had poisoned swords and sharp metal points attached to their tusks, with which they would goad and maul enemy soldiers. The mahout always carried a sharp pike to control the animal by piercing its delicate ears or poking its head.

Following the inspection of the soldiers, the king proceeded to survey the army stores, armoury and the mess. He took a keen interest in the welfare of his men and gave specific instructions, such as sharpening the Khanda sword blades and tying bow strings properly. The train of bullock carts used to maintain supplies was also examined. King Kharavela spoke to the officers and motivated them, assuring them that the Rathikas and Bhojakas would not go unpunished. He also actively took their feedback from the conversations. After almost half a day of inspection, he asked the senapati to stand them down but keep them in battle-ready condition as they could move any time now.

✦ ✦ ✦

It was late night when the figure was in audience with the king again. 'So the plan is to force my hand at a mantriparishad?'

'It works in your favour, Rajan. This way you should be able to ward off a rebellion by blaming the mantriparishad for a delay, while getting more time for preparation.'

'Hmm, it looks like the old man is active again. He seems to be advising the daughter well.'

'He had been in the service of your father for a long time, Rajan. He is well versed in the dark arts as well as statecraft.'

'Keep a close watch on all the officials in the army, administration and the palace; these are delicate times. I also want a report on the probability of the Andhras jumping in or the Magadhans attacking from the north when we are at war with the Rathika–Bhojakas.'

'Indeed Rajan, I have tasked spies all around. They're swarming everywhere in the guise of ascetics, merchants, performers, ganikas and fortune tellers. I will update you before you address the mantriparishad. I would advise you oppose the council at first but grudgingly agree to their proposals later.'

'I will consider your point.'

'One more thing,' the figure went on. 'The Maharathis who head the Rathikas are related to the Andhras by blood, while the Bhojakas are not, so we can decide whom to hit harder. Andhra feudatories are fairly independent. They collect their own taxes, issue coins and carry royal insignia, as you are already aware. In this case, an attack on them is not exactly an attack on Satkarni, so we have some leeway. Our other significant neighbours and potential enemies, the Magadhans, are dealing with their own fears of an imminent Yavana attack from the north-west.'

The king gave a nod and ended the discussion. The figure moved away gracefully, and the king smiled as he watched the figure vanish from the doorway.

Three days later, the mantriparishad was held at Rajguru Uddalaka's residence. It was decided not to host it in the palace as secrecy was paramount. After everyone had assembled at the palace courthouse, they were asked to proceed to the residence of the royal sage immediately. Attendants received the amatyas, who quickly took seats according to their rank and importance. Nakiya had asked Rudra to assist him, so he sat with the mahamatya. The king was already seated.

As decided earlier, Maitreyi rose and proceeded to open the discussion. 'Rajan, all of us have unanimously decided to call this meeting. The dharmashastras say that the king is bound by the advice of the mantriparishad. We feel that everyone's views should be taken into consideration before we begin a war. We have consulted the rajguru too. Although he is not a member of the mantriparishad, he has a say in this matter.'

The king looked at the rajguru with a slight indication of hurt pride. 'What do you say, venerable rajguru?' he asked.

'*Kalaao vaa karnam ranjao rajaa vaa kalakarnam iti to samsyaao maa bhoota rajaa kalasya karnam* (Do not wonder whether time makes a king or whether the king creates time. Be assured that the king creates circumstances; good or bad.) Be aware of time and circumstance, Rajan, and pay heed to good advice.'

'Rajguru, that is precisely why I am here, to listen to you all. But tell me, is it binding by dharma for me to go by the advice of the mantriparishad?'

'Yes, Rajan. In case of a difference of opinion between the king and a mantriparishad that is unanimous, the king will have to go by the advice of the council. He has no choice, except if he dissolves the council.'

'You may start the discussions, Amatya Maitreyi,' the king said in a low voice.

'I would invite Mahamatya Nakiya to start the deliberations, Rajan. He is the eldest amongst all amatyas and is the best person to speak on the subject.'

Nakiya stood up, cleared his throat and said, 'Rajan, what we say may not make you happy, but we have thought much on this subject and feel that strategically we should not immediately jump into fire. War with the Asmakas was different; it brought us great riches. The Rathika–Bhojakas are petty chiefs under the Andhras, so a war now will not result in any major gain to the treasury.

'As far as the feelings of the Atavikas are concerned, we can buy some time as movement will be difficult due to the rains, and then decide with a cool head whether to attack if their resistance does not die a natural death.'

The other amatyas also spoke one by one.

Rudra listened to each one carefully, making a mental note of everyone's position. He felt that many of them, although earnest, were swayed by others' arguments, and not aware of all the facts.

He also felt that the king was participating but irritated. Interesting dynamic, he thought. The king was young, probably the same age as him, but possessed great maturity. Rudra compared him to Satkarni, who was a very different person, more quick-tempered, highly ambitious and a bit belligerent. It was strange that three great kings had taken charge almost simultaneously: Kharavela in Tosali, Satkarni in Pratishthanpura and Pushyamitra in Rajgriha. Their fates were somehow intertwined.

Satkarni was the third in the dynasty started by his father, Simuka. He had taken over the royal reigns from his uncle Krsna. Kharavela was also the third king in his line. His father Chetaraja had been the second of the Chedis. 'Senapati' Pushyamitra had usurped the throne and kingdom of Magadha from the decadent Maurya dynasty by killing his master, Brihadratha, in public view. In a way, all of them were new, struggling to establish their empires and their own rule in an unstable atmosphere.

'The enemy has enough time to monitor our movements, Rajan. It is a long distance and we cannot leave anything to chance. We have to be fully prepared before we move,' Senapati Bahushalin was saying. 'If you give me time, I can explain the tactics and logistics involved,' he said.

'We shall do so after the mantriparishad. Now, who else wants to speak on this subject?' the king inquired.

Rajguru Uddalaka indicated that he wanted to speak, and Rudra noticed that the king looked uncomfortable.

He began, 'Rajan, I have studied the *grahadasha* (planetary positions)'. There was a pregnant pause.

'Why on earth does the rajguru have to mention this in an open court, he could have informed me about it in a private session,' the king wondered.

Uddalaka continued in a foreboding tone, 'At the end of this Sravana month, there is a solar eclipse, and you know very well that no auspicious or new work can be undertaken on a solar eclipse. We should delay the expedition by fifteen days, at least till the first days of the month of Bhadra.'

It was a bolt out of blue, and given Uddalaka's status, the king couldn't even react. Rudra was reading his eyes—there were flashes of different emotions, but the face and body language were restrained and stoic. 'Rajguru, I respect your opinion, I would like you to go through the calculations again and then we will take a final decision on this.'

He turned to Bahushalin, 'Senapati, can you show me your plan now? Only those directly connected with war preparations will accompany me and mahamatya; the rest may disperse.'

The senapati, mahamatya and the king left the room. As the others made to leave, Uddalaka asked them to wait for some time. Once the king was out of sight, he lamented, 'This is why the Vedic religion of our ancestors is getting destroyed! These young kings don't understand the science behind astrological calculations, nor do they have appreciation for sound advice.'

Maitreyi was aghast. 'Rajguru, why do you say that! Rajan has always been respectful to you. He always listens to your good counsel and never does anything which is against dharma.'

'Amatya Maitreyi, a *dharmayudhdha* is a war conducted on principles of *Kshatradharma*, the law governing kings and warriors. It has to be a just and righteous war with the approval of society and for betterment of all. It cannot be started to satisfy someone's ego or desire for revenge. There are distinct stages of a war—the first is diplomacy, and only after diplomacy fails, can the option to use arms be exercised. This king is not ready to explore any possibilities, he wants to rush straight to the battlefield. This is improper and contravenes the teachings of the dharmashastras.'

Vikarna was visibly agitated by Uddalaka's words. 'Rajguru, we should leave the decision to the king. He is the best judge of the situation. Please allow me to leave now.' Saying this he paid his respects to the sage and left. Maitreyi too walked out and the others followed them.

Rudra was left behind, and the rajguru now directed his tirade at him. 'This king behaves like an *anarya* (inferior person). He has been a follower of those Niganthas, Annatithyas (heretics) and hardly follows any Vedic practices. What should I expect from him?'

Rudra didn't comment; he wanted the rajguru to continue so he could assess what was going on. The rajguru went on, 'There will be consequences! Any king who forgets dharma is bound to attract divine punishment. We should do something to save the country from such a misfortune.'

'What do you intend to do, acharya?' Rudra finally asked.

'If you're willing, arya, we can assemble like-minded people and prevail over the king. We can even force him not to embark upon such a misadventure.'

'I am listening, acharya, please go on. What if the king refuses to abide by our suggestions?'

'Then, he has no right to be on the throne. A king is actually a custodian of the people's well-being and welfare. If he violates the kshatradharma, he loses his right to rule.'

'Acharya, whatever you've spoken to me will never be revealed to anybody, but I pray to you to stop thinking like this and abandon any plans to oppose Rajan or gather people to oppose him. This, in my humble opinion, amounts to treachery, and you as rajguru should not indulge in it at any cost. Let's act as though this conversation never took place. Pardon my audacity if I have said anything wrong. Kindly allow me to leave now.'

Rudra got up, touched his feet and left. As he did so, he suddenly remembered Vajramitra.

The senapati had arranged for a detailed discussion on the march, provisioning, logistics, route, alternative routes, resources and dangers on the way, time required with and without contingencies, formations, manoeuvres, responsibilities of different officials, tasking, probable countermeasures by the enemy and responses of allies as well as other interested parties.

The king was looking over a miniature battleground modelled with mud. All possible natural and manmade features relevant to warfare had been represented—rivers, lakes, forests, open areas, routes of the enemy, campsites and other details had been shown with the help of static or movable miniatures. It looked like a *chaturanga* sprung into real life.

'How and when would we come to know if Satkarni makes a move to protect his feudatories?' the king asked.

'Rajan, presently, he is unprepared for a direct assault. By our estimates, neither he, not the Rathika–Bhojakas are expecting us to go on an offensive. Thus, he may send us a warning through a messenger before he advances, but if he doesn't, our spies will inform us if the Andhra army starts preparing to march. Fortunately, our route through the Vidyadhara region is fully covered with forests, which will help us to conceal our movements and preserve the element of surprise.'

'Mahamatya Nakiya, what is the preparedness of the physicians and medicine men to treat the wounded in war?'

'Rajan, all the physicians in the service of the army have been asked to be ready to move any time. They have been provided with funds to purchase medicines and equipment for the treatment of the soldiers. As the rules of warfare go, we will also have to treat their wounded soldiers and prisoners of war.'

'Make sure that all the requirements are arranged for— fodder for the bullocks pulling the supply carts, transportation of musicians, bards and singers, the auxiliary forces in tow and the camp treasury.'

'Rajan, not only that, we have made arrangements for the rupjivas to accompany the army,' said Nakiya in a low tone. 'The only question now, Rajan, is when do we start the assault.'

'I will inform you about that mahamatya,' said the king, and ended the meeting. Nakiya and Bahushalin were confused.

✦ ✦ ✦

Rudra had not been expecting this. He had received urgent summons from the king. It was already late evening when he reached the palace.

He was asked to wait in a small room in the palace complex, his weapon had earlier been deposited at the main gate. He was frisked again by the polite guards near the living quarters of the king. These were the scion's most trusted people, belonging to families that had served the palace for generations. However, even these guards were not allowed inside the quarters, only female guards held sway here. The female guards were fierce and ruthless. Cut off from any external contact, they exclusively focused on the protection of the king and the royal family with single-minded devotion. The queen had a separate guard of eunuchs, highly trained and cold blooded, they never allowed any male presence except the king and the princes in the ladies' quarters.

A female guard emerged from inside and commanded Rudra with her eyes to follow her. Nimble-footed, this girl was an Atavika forester, her brown skin looked like polished wood. She was tall for her race and looked strong enough to overpower a man with her bare hands.

Rudra began to walk and the guard fell in behind, weapon in hand, guiding him only with gestures. Rudra had a mischievous idea in his mind—he wanted to hear her voice and tried to think of some way of compelling her to speak, but a second look at her face made him drop his plan.

In the quarters—filled with the finest pieces of craft from various lands and perfumed with sandalwood and other oils—the king was relaxing. He was not wearing his royal clothes and jewellery, and initially Rudra couldn't identify him. He stood there perplexed. The king guessed his predicament. 'Arya Rudravarman, come and sit here,' he said, laughing in a light-hearted manner.

'I am extremely sorry, Rajan, please pardon me that I couldn't identify you, I have never seen you in these clothes.'

'Don't worry at all. Come take your seat, Rudravarman.'

Rudra politely wished him again and sat at a distance from the king.

'I hear that you did some good work in Samapa. I am pleased with you.'

'Rajan, I just did my duty. It was your trust which was paramount for me.'

'Hmmm. How is your health now? You seem to have fully recovered from the effects of the poison arrow. You should thank Amatya Maitreyi for bringing you out of the clutches of sure death.'

'Yes, Rajan, I am immensely grateful to her,' Rudra said.

'Coming to the point of today's discussion, I assume that you still have good contacts in the Andhras' territories, am I right?'

'I have worked there for a long time, Rajan. I definitely have some resources.'

'You have to only get me one piece of information, but you must be certain that it is absolutely factual.'

'What is that, Rajan?'

'. . . Whether Satkarni will join the war if we attack Rathika–Bhojakas.'

'Your wish is my command, Rajan. I will put all my efforts in gathering this information . . . One more thing Rajan, if you permit me, I would like to say something.'

The king indicated his approval, and Rudra continued. 'Forgive me for making this observation, but the rajguru seems to be upset about us going to war. He is a learned man who is entitled to his views and I am very sure he thinks for the common good.'

The king looked at him with searching eyes, but did not react.

When the conversation ended, the fierce female guard appeared. Rudra paid respects to the king who blessed him and accompanied her outside. They must have travelled some twenty steps in the corridor, when Rudra suddenly stopped. The female almost pounced on him, ready to attack. He turned back nonchalantly and asked her, 'Where can I get water to drink? I am very thirsty.'

She gave him a very stern look and said, 'Outside the palace.' Rudra couldn't stop smiling.

At home, Devabrata, Kinshuk and Bhadrabahu were waiting for Rudra.

'Arya! Is it true that the king himself had called you?' Kinshuk was very happy.

'Yes, Kinshuk, the king had summoned me today for discussion on war preparations.'

'Arya Rudravarman, please tell us what we can do to help you in this effort,' said Bhadrabahu.

'We need information from the Andhra country. Kinshuk, you will go to Pratishthanpura as soon as possible and arrange for information to come to me periodically. Our basic concern is to find out if the Andhras will join the war in the event of our attack on the Rathika–Bhojakas. You will need to set up an arrangement for passing information quickly without being detected. Observe the happenings closely—any movement of the army, any gossip in the madiralaya, any purchases by the government which may indicate a war programme. Also keep a watch on the discussions amongst common people as public opinion sometimes drives kings to action.'

Devabrata, an old intelligence hand, was working on a scheme already. 'Kinshuk, I will teach you the art of secret paintings. You will send these pictures across borders with traders and hide symbols in them that will be known only to you and me. So, even if someone intercepted them, they wouldn't understand anything that is being conveyed. You can send paintings of Shiva in Nataraja mudra, just keep on changing the objects in his hands depending upon the information you want to convey. Or, you can send different images of Shiva indicating the state of affairs there. So, if you see that they are about to attack, you can send me an image of Shiva in *roudra roopa* (angry), performing the *tandava nritya* (death dance).'

'Bhadrabahu, you and Devabrata will keep in touch with Kinshuk and inform me about the developments. I may have to go with the army to the battle, so be aware of my locations when we move. Maintain total confidentiality about your work. I am depending heavily on you.'

'Arya, have we ever let you down? Though you did leave me out on the Samapa trip,' Devabrata said with a tinge of sarcasm.

'You're old and surly, and you will never improve,' Rudra said fondly.

'Yes, arya, nobody cares for old people now. Even Amatya Maitreyi will leave her old father in some days.'

Rudra was amazed, 'Why do you say that, Devabrata?'

'Nayaka Vikarna is going to ask for her hand in marriage soon, then she will have to shift from her home. Anyway, the old man likes to live in the janapadas and comes here rarely.'

'How do you know that?' Rudra said, trying not to show how this statement had affected him.

'Arya, don't forget, I am an old man who has served for a very long time in this kingdom. I have also worked with her father when he used to be the chief of spies.'

'Devabrata! You never told me this.'

'Arya, you never asked me.'

'Oh you old fox; now quickly tell me when is Vikarna going to ask for Maitreyi's hand, and if she is also interested in marrying him.'

'Why are you getting so excited, arya? Such agitation is not good for a nobleman like you.' Devabrata was at his best now. 'By the way, arya, you never informed us that she saved your life. And that you were at her home for more than a month when everyone believed that you had gone to Avantikapuri. You never even told us that there was an assassination attempt on you, nor of the conspiracy to kill Rajan by poisoning Mahagiri, the royal elephant.'

Rudra fell silent.

'Arya, you should be thanking the Rathika–Bhojakas for postponing Vikarna's plans.'

Rudra looked up, his face brightening now.

'Arya, we all are loyal to you. You have seen that in Samapa and elsewhere. Now keep faith in us. We will not only help you with this upcoming war, but also unravel the mystery of the attack on your life.' Devabrata's voice was full of fatherly compassion. 'And arya, once we are through with all this, I will discuss your past with you, but on some other occasion.'

Rudra looked around—they all were staring at him, and somehow, he couldn't meet their gaze. He felt a heaviness inside and, at the same time, as if something wanted to come out, as if it was struggling to escape. He felt nauseated. With his head down, he rushed out of the room.

Dakshinadhipati Satkarni was seated in the court with his queen Nayanika beside him, watching a dance performance. The queen wore her hair in a coiffure with braids running back from her broad forehead pulled into a large bun on the left. She wore exquisite jewellery, a multi-stringed flat necklace of pearls, arm bands shaped like intertwined creepers, bracelets and bangles. Her antariya and kayabandh were of bright green silk, neatly pleated into folds. She rested her feet on a small wooden stool, her anklets chiming every time she moved them.

Satkarni wore his long black hair coiled in a knot above his forehead and wheel-shaped earrings. He too had a thick pearl necklace around his neck and a broad embossed arm band.

The shastradharini was not interested in the performance, she kept a sharp eye on the dancers and everyone around. In matters of royal security, no one was to be trusted. Everyone, including the queen, the princess, near relatives, amatyas—everyone—was a source of danger, and she knew it well. The three peacock feathers inserted in her headband made her look beautiful in a daunting way. The other ladies, including the chauri holder, the paan provider and the chattari holder had hair parted on the left side and they wore ivory bangles up to their elbows. They had veils over their heads, with large crescent-moon-shaped ornaments on their foreheads.

The royal couple sat on a large tiger skin placed on the throne, which was anointed daily with a thin paste of the most fragrant and sacred sandalwood. Fine drapery was wound around it, and the gemstones embedded in it shone through the semi-transparent cloth. A large enclosure surrounded the royal couple, no one except the royal priest and the king's personal entourage was allowed entry.

The dance performance was set to lively music from accompanying instrumentalists and singers, who varied the pitch and the tempo of the songs to the rhythm of the dance. The female dancers, eight in number, moved in unison in an improvized choreography of quick formations depicting the change in seasons. The king and queen were engrossed in the performance, and so were the courtiers who, at times, got so carried away that they shouted praises to the dancers.

The performance came to an end, and the leader of the troupe gathered the performers before the king. Some in the audience were discussing the amount of reward the king would bestow upon the artists in hushed tones. Satkarni was known as a patron of the arts, apart from being a successful statesman and an able leader. For many months, he had been making frequent trips to the Ajanta hills where, in a breathtaking horseshoe-shaped valley, he was creating something for future generations. These were the Ajanta caves, cut into a cliff overlooking a serene stream of water. Steps were cut from each cave to allow the pure water to flow, which frothed when it hit the rocks with fury. It was deep inside a forest where Sramanas could meditate upon the Buddha and his teachings in absolute isolation.

Satkarni had appointed skilled craftsmen and sculptors to chisel out pillars and decorate the entrances with emblems and motifs, and eminent painters had been summoned from all over the continent to paint scenes from the life of Buddha as murals on the walls. Unknown to him, the painters had also immortalized him on the walls by depicting him and the queen in some of the sequences they painted.

As the din died, Satkarni turned his gaze to the queen. 'Maharani, today you will reward the artists.'

'Yes indeed! I enjoyed it thoroughly and I will reward them suitably.'

The leader of the troupe moved forward to receive the reward. Queen Nayanika called for a large silver plate and placed two jewelled necklaces on it along with a silk bag full of gold coins. She asked the attendants to sprinkle some holy water of the Dakshin Ganga on these articles and adorn them with flowers before handing them over to the overjoyed artists.

The court was full of shouts of praise for the king and the queen, who gracefully asked them to calm down and be seated. As the day's work was getting over, a female attendant came and whispered something in the king's ear. He said, 'Send him at once.'

The royal attendant at the gate announced in a loud voice that a messenger from Kalinga, with a message from the great King Mahameghavahana Kharavela was being admitted to the king's audience; the whole court fell silent.

The messenger was dressed in Kalinga attire, with his hair tied up in a mauli with a side knot at the top.

'Victory to the great Satkarni, *dakshinadhipati* and *apratihatacakra* (wielder of the unchecked wheel of sovereignty). Please accept salutations from the great Mahameghavahana Aira Kharavela, the supreme lord of tri-kalinga (three Kalingas).'

'Welcome messenger, what news do you bring for us from the great king?'

'Rajan, Aira Kharavela wishes that you be informed that your feudatories, the Rathikas and Bhojakas, have not only attacked our border areas, but also destroyed an ancient and revered temple of the Atavikas in the Vidyadhara region.'

Satkarni was taken aback. Somehow, this news had escaped him. He looked at his mahamatya with burning eyes, then at the senapati. Both put their heads down in shame. The representatives of the Rathika–Bhojakas in the court tried to hide behind others in the audience.

'Go on, tell me the full story,' Satkarni thundered.

'Our king, being in the position of the father and protector of the people is now duty-bound to punish those who have committed this transgression. He wants to know if you would take the side of adharma or help punish the guilty.'

There was a dark silence. The die had been thrown, it was a veiled declaration of war against an ally . . .

Queen Nayanika intervened. 'Messenger, we would like to confirm this incident with our own sources. As you can see, we were in the dark about it. Please take rest today while we ascertain the facts, and then we will be in a better position to respond to your questions.'

There was confusion in the court. The Kalinga messenger had come with a declaration of a war, but it was not a threat directed at the Andhras. The future course of action was going to determine history. If the Andhras sided with the Rathika–Bhojakas, it would be a devastating war as both kingdoms were large, with well-equipped armies, horses, elephants and chariots. If they left their own feudatories high and dry in the event of an attack, it would seriously undermine not only the sovereignty, but also the legitimacy of the Satavahanas.

To complicate matters further, Queen Nayanika was from a Maharathi family, although not from ones who were at the centre of the controversy now, but they were still her distant relatives.

The king and queen retired to the palace, preoccupied with the probability of an unexpected war. Aira Kharavela's mother was from the Satavahana lineage, and they never had any issues with each other. The delicate balance of three large empires of India—the Shungas in Magadha, Satavahanas in Andhra and Mahameghavahanas in Kalinga—was about to be unsettled. The three giants existed in a perilous equilibrium, any one of them getting weakened was sure to be gobbled away by any or both of the other two. Perhaps, this kept the balance of power in Bharatavarsha. The three never had confrontation with each other in the reigns of the current kings. They were the product of the vacuum created by Ashoka's death and the petering out of the last Mauryas.

The king was angry at the Rathika–Bhojakas for creating this unusual impasse, and with the Kalingas for sending him this veiled ultimatum. Although the Rathika-Bhojakas were feudatories of the Andhra king, they existed as a kingdom within a kingdom. Not only did they have all the trappings of a king including the royal signs of chattari, chauri, swords and simhasanas, but they also minted their own coins and maintained their own armies. They had almost autonomous control in their own territories, except in the often-delicate matter of foreign relations. By contravening this understanding, the Rathika–Bhojakas had put Satkarni in a difficult situation.

The Andhras' administration was unique. While centralized rule applied to most areas, with officers having limited powers posted in the janapadas, the Mauryan system of dividing the janapadas into *aharas* continued under the Satavahanas. The five main aharas were Govardhana-ahara, Soparaka-ahara, Mamala-ahara, Satavahani-ahara and Kapurachara-ahara. Each functioned under an amatya who acted as a governor. The remaining areas were under feudatories of different ranks such as Mahabhojas and Maharathis, who held hereditary offices and even minted their own coins. Not only that, they maintained their own armies. Queen Nayanika was from the Maharathi family of the great warrior, Trinka Iyro, and thus had some soft corner for them.

'Had it been an amatya, I would have sacked him! Such foolishness! This is like throwing a stone at an elephant and running away, and now they want to hide in my home!' stormed the king.

Queen Nayanika was composed but troubled, 'There must be more to it than it meets the eye, Rajan. The Atavikas have always been a source of trouble to the bordering janapadas. We should know the full story before we decide to take any action.'

'Beloved queen, if the Atavikas were a problem, what was the need to destroy their temple, that too in the Kalinga territory? This has given the powerful Kharavela a legitimate excuse to enter our lands. Public sympathy will be with him for being a protector of dharma and waging a dharmayudhdha,' the king said with exasperation. 'Why did the Rathikas and Bhojakas not inform us about their trouble with the Atavikas? Now they have picked a fight with a much larger enemy and are drawing us into conflict.'

'Rajan, one thing is clear, there cannot be a decisive victory if we fight the mighty Kalingas. We will both be weakened and this will give an opportunity to the Yavanas, Shakas or the Shungas to subjugate us. A war with such a powerful enemy is not advisable at all. The Kalingas have made a very clever diplomatic move, if we don't take up the challenge of war, we lose the confidence of our feudatories and allies, if we take it up, we are seen as acting contrary to the principles of dharma—it is a double-bind situation. We need to come up with an innovative solution to this.'

Satkarni nodded. He felt the vacuum of Simhadhwaja's absence today, he missed him personally too.

The queen spoke again. 'Rajan, Agnimitra, son of Senapati Pushyamitra Shunga is ruling as a governor in neighbouring Vidisha, he has been eyeing Vidarbha and Andhra territories for a long time. The Yavana Milinda is making gains in Madhyamika and Saket, while Dimita, another Yavana king is getting a firm foothold in Gandhar. The Shakas are being driven out of their homes up north and looming large on the Bharatavarsha. In such a scenario, we have to be prepared for a larger escalation. We should ask the senapati to alert our allies and secretly get the army ready for a long-drawn war.'

'My dear queen, sometimes I think I don't need to go to anyone for good advice, you are quite capable of guiding me through any eventuality. Indeed, you play an important part in the affairs of the kingdom,' the king said with pride in his eyes.

He had always been very appreciative of his chief queen Nayanika, who took a keen interest in the affairs of the state. There was a hidden motive behind this, known only to a very few. Simhadhwaja, his close aide, knew this but he was dead now.

✦ ✦ ✦

Meanwhile in Tosali, Maitreyi's chariot was passing through a narrow street, as it took a turn, the charioteer saw another chariot blocking the way. Annoyed, her bodyguard jumped from his horse and approached the stationary chariot with his hand on the hilt of his sword.

Maitreyi looked at the man approaching the carriage and then suddenly wishing the person inside with reverence. He hurriedly came back to her and said, 'Amatya Maitreyi, the carriage standing in our way belongs to Arya Rudravarman, he says it's stranded and the horse is refusing to move. He has also sent his salutations to you.'

'Sumanta, ask Arya Rudravarman if he would like to come along with me in my chariot.'

'As you wish, amatya,' the man said and ran back to the first carriage.

Maitreyi saw Rudra jump out of the carriage with gusto. He looked handsome, and for some reason she felt happy to see him. Rudra came near the chariot and greeted her, 'Sometimes misfortune brings good luck, isn't it Amatya Maitreyi? If my cart had not been stranded, I would have missed the opportunity of meeting you.'

She laughed, and he felt her fragrance enveloping his senses. He looked into her light eyes and memories of his first encounter with her floated before his mind's eye. Strangely, that memory seemed to have come to her too. 'Ah! It was you staring at me from the madiralaya window that night, probably a year back,' she said. 'I have always wondered who the stranger was. Look, I solved that mystery today,' she said, smiling.

'Yes, indeed it was me, amatya. Somehow, I have also not forgotten that night. It was one of my first nights in the city of Tosali.' The chariot was moving now.

She said, 'And then I catch you on the streets pretending to be a commoner, just before the hunting expedition.'

'Or perhaps you were finding an excuse to give me a ride in your chariot,' he said jokingly. 'Or, who knows, perhaps you were following me at the king's behest.'

'Arya Rudra, let your imagination ride the clouds, no harm in daydreaming,' she chuckled. 'And then you land up at my place half dead, with almost no hope of survival.'

'Amatya Maitreyi, it seems gods are playing these tricks on purpose, there is some greater design hidden in this.'

'Like what, arya?' she asked, a look of curiosity on her face.

'Had I known it, I would have definitely shared it with you, amatya,' he said, looking deep into her eyes. Her face was covered with a deep blush but she said nothing and lowered her eyes. Rudra's hand brushed against hers, she slowly withdrew her hand.

'Where are you going, arya?' she said, changing the subject abruptly.

'Drop me wherever you feel like, Amatya Maitreyi.'

'No arya, where were you going when your chariot got stuck?'

'Oh yes . . . You can stop near the Jina temple, amatya.'

'Amatya? Why are you addressing me so formally, arya?'

'Devi, I hardly know you, apart from the fact that I am thoroughly indebted to you for bringing me back from the clutches of death. Despite having been your guest for more than a month, I know nothing of you. You didn't even bid me a proper farewell when I left your home. I can't fault you for that, you have done so much for me already, but I felt that you avoided talking to me when I left.'

She looked pained. For the first time, he saw her weak and vulnerable. 'There is a lot which I cannot share with you, Rudra, but you know that I always think good for you.'

Rudra remained silent.

'Someday I will tell you, things are not as they seem,' she said. She looked lost.

'Oh the Jina temple is there, let me get down Amatya Maitreyi . . . One thing more amatya, please invite me for your wedding. I don't want to attend it from the bridegroom's side.'

'*What?!*' she said, but Rudra had already alighted and disappeared into the crowd.

Aira Kharavela had played a masterly game. In one stroke he had not only put the Andhras in a fix but also reined in his council of ministers and silenced his critics. The declaration of war was a finality now, and no one could oppose it anymore. The Atavikas were convinced that the Rathika–Bhojakas were sure to be punished and they channelized their energies towards war preparations; the amatyas got their time to deliberate; the rajguru's apprehensions due to the solar eclipse were also accommodated and the king had his way too.

War preparations had begun, and Rudra was amazed to see Vajramitra being involved with them. Presumably, he would be given an important task. He didn't know what had transpired while he was in Samapa that had led to Vajramitra gaining ascendance now. He asked Kinshuk to dig deeper. 'Kinshuk, find out what Vajramitra's activities have been in the last few months. After the great and public displeasure he displayed over the Asmaka war, he went underground for some time. It is strange now that he is being given so much importance in the war preparations.'

After a few days, Kinshuk returned with some information. 'He has been maintaining close relations with the descendants of Tibar, who was a son of Ashoka by the Kalinga princess Karubaki. They live in the bordering regions of Mahakantar, as kings of the Atavikas of that area.'

'What does that mean clever Kinshuk?'

'Arya, it is unclear, but Karubaki, the daughter of King Padmanabha, was carried away by Ashoka, who had killed him in the Kalinga War. Later, he fell in love with her and married her as the second queen. Tibar was placed as a royal regent at Subarnagiri, his descendants have been there ever since. Not much is known about their activities.'

'Nothing that happens at Vajramitra's place should escape our attention, Kinshuk. I suspect that he is behind the attempt to kill me at the jungle camp. He may even have been a part of the plot to assassinate Rajan.'

'I have befriended his charioteer, arya. He is addicted to liquor, and I provide him with it illegally.'

Rudra nodded and after telling Kinshuk to be careful, dismissed him. 'Do what you have to do, we cannot afford another downfall. We have barely survived the disaster at the Andhra court.'

'Arya, I can lay down my life for you any time, please don't worry. I have learned from our past mistakes, those will never be repeated.'

✦✦✦

It was three days before the march. Everyone in Tosali seemed to be preoccupied by it. Traders and merchants had halved the prices of all commodities needed for the soldiers. Temples were full of devotees asking gods to bless the army with victory. Decorative festoons and flags were seen on houses and streets everywhere. Horse riders could be seen moving hurriedly through the streets. Dry fodder and grains from the janapadas were being brought inside in large quantities. There was a tense energy in the air and no one was left unaffected.

The king had called everyone for a final briefing at the palace. Uddalaka, Nakiya, Bahushalin, Maitreyi, Vikarna, other amatyas, governors and some nobles along with the relatives of the king were present. Nakiya had asked Rudra to accompany him, Vajramitra was also in attendance.

'The inauspicious solar eclipse has passed without any ill effects, the rains too have ceased. Rajguru Uddalaka and the astronomers inform me that all omens are good for a march,' the king said and then paused, gauging the reaction. Then he continued. 'We have sent messengers to the Andhras and the Magadhans about our intended march on the Rathika–Bhojakas, I am yet to hear anything adverse from them.'

Astrologically, the time was favourable; diplomatically, steps had been taken. Enough groundwork had been done to prepare the army for the march. Strategy and tactics were needed to be put in place now.

Nakiya had an excellent suggestion to make. 'Rajan, I propose that we move in two parts, one smaller component of the army can move along the Mahanadi River till it crosses Mahakantar and advance towards the Rathikas, while the larger portion can be positioned in the Vidyadharas and attack the Bhojakas from below. Such a move has another advantage, if the Andhras decide to join their feudatories, the second wing of the army can clash with them before they reach us, effectively slowing down their progress. We can then gather both sides and complete the assault.'

The senapati was not convinced. 'This will distribute our strength and delay our progress. It would also be difficult to coordinate the two marching columns.'

'Who will lead the section that will go along the Mahanadi?' asked the king.

'Rajan, I will do it,' said Vajramitra proudly.

'All right, Vajramitra, you will lead the first section. Create the illusion that I am leading that offensive, so tread like a king on the move.'

Rudra quickly glanced towards Nakiya, whose expression reassured him that the king's decision was apt. Maitreyi seemed to be at a loss for words; the others too didn't like the suggestion.

'However,' the king added, 'you will not actually attack the Rathikas till I send you a message.'

Vajramitra seemed overjoyed. 'Victory to Aira Kharavela!' he exclaimed. 'I will follow your instructions carefully, Rajan. Success will be ours.'

'The senapati has informed me about the army of the Rathika–Bhojakas,' said the king. 'They are hardy fighters, adept at the lance and sword, and they move fast on the horse. The quality of their horses is not as good as ours and they have a few elephants of middling quality. Their infantry is not a regular standing army, but a set of volunteers assembled according to need. Farmers otherwise, they are less trained and motivated than our valiant servicemen.

'I would like to add a word of caution: although it looks like an easy victory in sight, we cannot take anything for granted.

Fight them as if we were battling the fierce and devious Yavanas and be prepared for any surprises.'

The king then requested the rajguru to address the meeting. The rajguru said, '*Satyen lokam jayati, Danerjayati deenatam, Gurun sushrushya, Jiyadvanusha eva shatravan* (You can win over the whole world by truth, the poor by charity, elders by service and the enemies by archery). The enemy has destroyed ancient temples, and there is no worse adharma than this. Such impudence should not go unpunished. Our warriors will answer this audacity with their valour. All planetary positions are in our favour now, and the Devas, Gandharvas and spirits of ancestors are with us. We will come back victorious. *Vijayi bhava!*' he shouted. 'Vijayi bhava, Vijayi bhava!' the room resounded with a chorus.

There was a surge in the air, everyone was charged and raging to march. The king got up from his seat and touched the royal sage's feet, who blessed him. The gathering was dispersed.

Rudra quickly caught up with Nakiya. He smelled something sinister in Vajramitra's propositions. 'Mahamatya, may I speak to you in confidence for a moment?' he demanded. Nakiya indicated to his bodyguards and attendants to leave them alone.

The evening was a dark, cold one. As they started walking, Rudra hesitatingly opened the discussion, 'Mahamatya, Vajramitra has been spitting venom against the king everywhere. After the Asmaka war, he even publicly denounced Rajan. In this situation, giving him command over a large body of troops may be very dangerous.'

'Arya Rudravarman, Vajramitra is Rajan's childhood friend and a trusted person. He is just a bit unstable and haughty, don't take it so seriously.'

'Forgive me for my insolence, Mahamatya, but you have to stop this man from taking command of troops and leading an expedition.'

'Rudravarman! What has gotten into you, why are you saying such baseless things?' The mahamatya was angry now.

'Punish me for this mahamatya, but Vajramitra is not loyal. He is eyeing the throne.'

'Enough, Arya Rudravarman! You are crossing your limits now!'

Rudra fell at the mahamatya's feet, and pleaded in a desperate tone, 'Mahamatya, Vajramitra is truly planning an overthrow of the rule, he wants to assassinate the king! He offered to make me the senapati if he is successful!'

Nakiya was aghast. 'When did that happen Rudravarman, and why didn't you inform me or the king then?'

'Mahamatya, it happened just after the Asmaka War. I think the attempt to kill Rajan by poisoning the elephant Mahahgiri must also have been a part of this game. Even the effort to take my life at the jungle camp could be linked to this! After that I never got an opportunity to explain this to you or Rajan. I also never had any concrete proof.'

'Rudravarman, you don't have any proof still.'

'Mahamatya, I may not be having any proof, but the risk of handing over charge of a large section of the army will be disastrous! You may check with your trusted spies. I beg you for the sake of Kalinga and its people, please avert this disaster!'

'Go home Rudravarman, you seem to be tired. And beware, don't repeat this to anyone else. I will also forget that we had this conversation,' Nakiya said and left hurriedly.

Rudra kept staring at the diminishing figure merging into the darkness . . . He turned homewards with a heavy heart. In the distance, he could hear the bards singing victory songs.

Chapter 18

Drums of War

The day of the march had arrived. It was the third quarter of the night. Trikalingadhipati Mahameghavahana Aira Kharavela was woken up with the sound of auspicious mantras. Rajguru Uddalaka, along with a team of purohitas, Arhats, Sramanas, queens, amatyas and the king's relatives had gathered in the inner courtyard of the royal palace. The place was lit up with large torches burning brightly, all night the palace servants had been decorating the place with colourful garlands. A small, raised platform of wood had been created at the centre of the courtyard. It had been covered with a square awning entirely made of flowers. A flat stool smeared with sandal paste was kept in the centre of the platform. A flurry of activity started as the king moved from his chamber towards the place of ceremony. Attendants moved around carrying one object or another, much to the chagrin of the strict female bodyguards; the eunuchs guarding the female quarters were also annoyed by their constant movement.

Suddenly, conch shells started blowing, followed by trumpets and drums, filling the surroundings with an air of anticipation. The king was carried on an open palanquin, hoisted by eight men. He wore just a white antariya, with his bare upper body shining like a bronze idol. As the king came near, the Brahmins started chanting shlokas and mantras in a chorus, the drums had stopped now. It was still dark when the king descended on the platform and sat upon the stool. Rajguru Uddalaka came forward and applied sandalwood paste on the king's forehead, and the sound of conch shells rang in the air again. The two queens were called now, they came with scented scrubs in golden plates. Both of them applied the paste to his arms, shoulders and back, as the purohitas recited mantras. Water from five sacred rivers had been collected for the royal bath ceremony, and female attendants poured this water in small streams over the king's head from golden pots. His long curly hair stuck to his forehead and broad chest sat majestically.

Uddalaka chanted, '*Gange cha Yamune chaiva Godavari Saraswati, Narmade Sindhu Kaveri jalesmin sannidhim kuru* (I invoke the presence of holy waters from the rivers Ganga, Yamuna, Godavari, Saraswati, Narmada, Sindhu and Kaveri in these waters).'

The Niganthas chanted, '*Namo Arihantanam Namo Siddhanam Namo Ayriyanam Namo Uvajjhayanam Namo Loe Savva-sahunam Eso Panch Namokaro Savva-pavappanasano Manglananch Savvesim Padhamam Havei Mangalam* (I bow down to Arihanta, I bow down to Siddha, I bow down to Acharya, I bow down to Upadhyaya, I bow down to Sadhu and Sadhvi. These five bows with reverence, destroy all the sins, amongst all that is auspicious. This Navkar Mantra is the foremost.)

The Brahmins, Arhats, Bhikkhus and Sramanas all blessed the king as he got up from the seat. A temporary enclosure was promptly formed by holding cloth sheets, within which the king changed into silk clothes. He now wore a bright yellow antariya with a jewelled kayabandh, and an embroidered red uttariya on which motifs had been stitched with golden thread. He also wore his jewellery—a necklace of blood red rubies and earrings studded with small stones, which shone brightly in the lamp light.

As he emerged from the platform, everyone around threw rice grains mixed with vermillion on him, shouting chants for victory. He was now led to the prayer hall where *havanas* (fire oblations) were held. He sat there with both his queens and put offerings into the rising tongues of flames, in accordance with the mantras recited. His bow, covered in a red muslin cloth, was unveiled, and sandal paste was applied to it. His sword was also smeared with sandal paste and vermillion. Once the weapons were consecrated, the king sought blessings of all the holy men from different denominations, who received gifts from him in turn. He later held silver plates filled with pearls, golden articles and gems to be given away to temples and other religious institutions.

At the same time, on the banks of the holy Daya, in a large, open ground outside the city, the camp was being alerted for the march. Monstrous drums boomed as if the heavens were exploding, the sound reverberating in all directions. Then, there were ten distinct sharp strokes of smaller drums, which indicated the number of kroshas the army had to travel that day. Thousands of torches were lit, and assistants scampered around, waking up their masters in the tents. The stable and elephant attendants fetched saddles, leather straps, fastenings and charms to be put on the mounts. One could hear horses whinnying when being saddled by riders. Now, pegs were being uprooted and tents taken down to be neatly packed away. Elephants were being laden with bags full of fodder and other provisions. The large beasts trumpeted loudly in protest to the tightening of girth bands holding the materials, and their mahouts then tied bells around their necks.

The ringing of bells, beating of drums, tapping of mallets, blowing of trumpets, rhythmic tapping of hooves of the horses, shouting of officers, singing of bards, barking of the war dogs accompanying the warriors and marching of soldiers rose to a frenzy of deafening pitch and intensity. As the time for departure came close, the magnitude of the chaos increased. A huge blanket of dust slowly rose and enveloped the camp, looking like a dark ominous cloud in the light of a thousand torches.

Meanwhile, at the palace entrance, important nobles, relatives of the king and other generals had gathered—each riding a large female elephant covered in metallic armour, with attendants holding their large gold covered bows, javelins and swords. Tall riders flanked the palace guard which was to accompany the king. The royal standard was held high atop Mahagiri, who looked much larger than the other elephants. Mahagiri had been anointed with sandal paste and camphor, and the housing on top was fastened with thick leather straps and decorated in golden, violet and yellow colours. In the flickering lights of the lamps, the elephant looked like Yamaraj himself.

Rudra had been called to the palace by Nakiya. He waited, atop a horse. He spotted Bahushalin, the senapati, wearing a combination of a metal breastplate and leather armour. Rudra tried to locate Vajramitra, but he wasn't seen anywhere nearby. He assumed the man was inside the palace with the king.

A soldier came running with a message from Mahamatya Nakiya. Rudra was being summoned. He promptly dismounted and accompanied the huffing and puffing man, who took him to a huge armoured elephant, decorated brightly with blue and orange colours. Nakiya was sitting atop the elephant and asked Rudra to climb up. A small ladder was lowered for him and, within a moment, he was atop the elephant that was second only to Mahagiri.

The sound of magnificent conches filled the air, and Mahameghavahana Aira Kharavela emerged from the palace gates. He looked like a mythical figure in his majestic armour, his headdress studded with gemstones and his ancestral sword on his side in a golden scabbard. He walked confidently, looking all around with steady, proud eyes. The gems on his kayabandh looked like fireflies in the night.

A spirited soldier shouted at the top of his voice, 'Maharajadhiraj Trikalingadhipati Mahameghavahana, Aira Kharavela, Vijayi Bhava!' Cries rang all over in chorus, 'Vijayi bhava, vijayi bhava!' Citizens hearing this from their residences and gatherings on streets along the royal path followed it up with a loud hail, 'Maharaj vijayi bhava, Kalinga desh vijayi bhava.'

Cries echoed through the city as the king's procession started moving towards the city gates. People, half asleep but full of enthusiasm, had gathered all along the streets to catch a glimpse of their beloved king. They threw petals on the procession as it passed through the streets.

The Asmaka War had been a *kutayudha* (war by deceit), this was Kharavela's first major campaign. The fate of a resurgent

Kalinga under him was to be decided by this war. Ashoka had crushed their pride, but the Andhras had escaped such a treatment by surrendering to him. It was a great moment for the Kalinga nation that their king was marching westwards, disregarding the great powers of the day, the Andhras and the Magadhans.

The sky was lighting up now, the morning light colouring the clouds crimson on a background of orange and gold. Chirping birds rose in flocks from the trees as the procession progressed through the city.

When the king reached the camp outside the city, the first rays of the sun were beginning to illuminate the white umbrella atop Mahagiri's housing. Its radiance was dazzling. Gemstones shone like eyes of tigers and leopards as rays of light touched them. A huge procession of elephants, chariots and riders was meeting a sea of soldiers, like the mouth of a river merging into an ocean.

Bahushalin commanded the army to bow—the soldiers folded hands in namaskar, elephants lifted their trunks in a blessing posture, riders pulled the reins of the horses to bow their heads and the king raised his hand in approval. Hails of 'Vijayi bhava' rang through the great ocean assembled there.

The soldiers picked up their shields from the ground and awaited the orders to march, with their swords in their scabbards and their lances in their hands, some with bows slung over shoulders and quivers full of arrows tipped with mercury. Most soldiers were bare-chested, their broad torsos looked like the foreheads of elephants. The Atavikas wore feathers in their hair and carried their own smaller bows and arrows, under the able command of their tribal leaders.

The army had been assembled in two parts, a smaller part which was to be led by Vajramitra was to go north-west, while the main army led by the king was going to march west and then up north into the Bhojaka territory.

The king gestured to Nakiya to proceed. He broke off with a group of trusted riders, charioteers and elephant riders to meet the smaller part of the army stationed at some distance. Nobody spoke a word, only the sound of horses snorting, hooves tapping on the ground, creaking of the elephant housings, squeaking of the chariot wheels and the jangling of armour was heard. They moved fast till they reached the assembled contingent. Rudra's heart was pounding—how would he react at the sight of the wretched Vajramitra? And now it seemed, he had to travel with him!

The leader of the contingent was sitting atop a tusker, whose left tusk was broken and a sword had been affixed at the broken part, it looked intimidating. Rudra's muscles tightened with anger as the elephant came near them. The tusker stopped and raised its trunk in salutation while uttering a shrill loud sound.

'Durjaya, are your people ready?' Nakiya asked the leader of the force.

'Mahamatya, we are fully prepared and ready to march. We are just waiting for your command.'

'This is Arya Rudravarman, he will lead this expedition as the representative of the king. For this expedition, he will have all the rights and privileges of a senapati.'

Rudra couldn't believe his ears! He was to lead an expedition, that too through the dreaded Mahakantar region, full of hostile tribes, and passing through the dominion of the descendants of Tibar, living with them at the Subarnagiri.

He felt angry and elated at the same time, but where was Vajramitra?

Before he could ask any questions, he saw Nakiya blessing him and descending from the elephant. Rudra took a deep breath.

Vajramitra had not been sent to war at all. He was given a more important assignment—taking care of the city of Tosali and the royal household in the king's absence. Nakiya also remained behind, as a counterbalance. Vajramitra had nothing to complain about—he was to look after the kingdom in the king's absence. Unknown to him, Nakiya had made arrangements to take care of any eventuality; any mischief by anyone, and he would be quietly fed to the crocodiles in the moat.

Just before King Kharavela left on the expedition, a messenger hurriedly handed over a letter from Nakiya. It carried the personal seal of the mahamatya. The king opened it and read, 'Rudravarman informs that Satkarni will not attack'.

Unconsciously, the king touched his turban, he felt relieved inside.

Satkarni had taken a decision of waiting and watching. He didn't want to pay for the adventurism of his feudatories.

Satkarni had his own plans of expansion. He wanted to perform the Ashwamedha Yajna, declaring his suzerainty all across the Bharatavarsha. An untimely conflict with the Kalingas was the last thing he wanted to be drawn into. Not that Kalinga was not on his map of potential conquests, but he had not planned to do so in the immediate future.

Pushyamitra Shunga had been a constant irritant. He had assassinated his master but ruled under the title of senapati for some time now. His expansionist plans were hidden from no one. His son, the valiant Agnimitra, was virtually ruling like an independent sovereign from Vidisha. He maintained an army and a court. Not only that, him and his father bore all the signs and symbols of a king. They had a ̊chattari, chauri, sword, Conch shell, *lachhana* (a pictorial symbol) and a royal flag. It was only a matter of time before Andhra and Magadha clashed. The only question was, who would attack first.

Kalinga, on the other hand, seemed to be stabilizing and rising under Kharavela, who didn't appear to be an imminent threat. Unlike the Shungas, he was not on an expansionist policy. Satkarni didn't want to engage with him right now, so he decided to wait and watch.

It was to be a long journey, the army would have to travel ten kroshas on a good day. Going by this speed, it would take a month before they would reach the territory of the enemy. The main part of the army, commanded by the king, was to take a slightly longer route. Rudra was to threaten the Rathikas and draw them out while the actual assault was to take place in the Bhojakas' territory. This would divide their resources and reduce their strength. It would also strain their unity as each would attempt to protect his own interests first. There was one more reason for dealing more strongly with the Bhojakas—unlike the Rathikas, they were not related to Queen Nayanika. Their capital was far from Pratishthanpura, so the Andhras wouldn't rush to their help as eagerly as they would have done for the Rathikas. In case they did, there was sufficient time to not only counter them but sabotage their movement through a sudden manoeuvre by the contingent led by Rudra, as he was closer to Andhra territory.

The king had now shifted to a comfortable chariot which was surrounded by a cavalry guard from the most loyal palace sentinels. The outermost rings were composed of hereditary soldiers, tried and tested for their loyalty. The royal Kalinga flag with an elephant emblem flew high in the air above the king's chariot.

Riders had been sent ahead days in advance to locate campsites, scout for natural and safe sources of drinking water, food and fodder, make provision for fresh milk, honey and meat for the royal kitchen and other such tasks. Spies had been dispatched to enemy territory to get prior intelligence on their movement, state of preparedness and numerical strength. It was going to be a long and tiresome journey, for the army as well as the king, but he was young and raring to go.

Rudra's contingent, on the other hand, had to pass through very rough terrain. Fortunately, a path parallel to the great river Mahanadi had been chosen, which would constitute almost half of the distance. The only problem was that the tribes of Mahakantar and surrounding areas were more hostile and untamed than the Atavikas of Vidyadharas, and no one knew what lay in store for them.

Chapter 19

The March

It was the first night since the army had started its march from Tosali—tents had been pitched and a dry ditch was excavated in advance to encircle the king's tent for safety. The king's quarters were complete with a kitchen and a place for worship. The royal chefs were at work, and the air was filled with the sweet, spicy fragrance of the dishes that were to be served at dinner. It was a cold, clear night. The stars looked much bigger than they appeared in Tosali, and gusts of wind made the torches burn brighter. Bahushalin had asked for torches to be placed safely on poles away from the tents, and large water pots were kept everywhere to deal with any accidental fires.

When Bahushalin was ushered in, the king was being massaged by two stout musclemen, who were rolling wooden pins on his arms, soothing the pain of day-long travel. As the senapati walked in, the king indicated for the masseurs to go away. He then got up and received the senapati, who was still in his travel attire. 'Senapati, I hope everything is all right with the army after the first day of travel?'

'Rajan, with the blessings of Jinas and the good wishes of Brahmanas, Arhats and Sramanas, everything seems to be perfect. The soldiers have maintained good speed, the animals are tired but in good health and supplies are on their way. We have food and fodder for several days with us, and the contingent following us are carrying enough resources to last two months. We have identified additional sources of food, water and fodder on the path ahead. If we keep up this speed, we will reach the battleground in about a month.'

'Very good! Senapati Bahushalin, I wanted to discuss one more thing with you. The Magadhans have sent a messenger today.'

'What do the treacherous criminals say, Rajan?'

'They have declared their neutrality towards the Rathika–Bhojaka War. They have actually gone to the limits of expressing solidarity with the Atavikas, saying that as their temple has been destroyed, it needs to be avenged suitably.'

'Rajan, it reeks of lies.'

'Listen further, Pushyamitra has also offered to help us if Satkarni joins the war!'

'What! Rajan, he is playing Kalinga against the Andhras, so that they clash with each other and he can then defeat the victor who is weakened by war.'

'Yes, Bahushalin, I don't trust him. He who has killed his own master to usurp the throne is the last person whose words should be believed. How do you read the situation?'

'Rajan, Magadha will be keeping a close eye on the situation. We should avoid war with the Andhras at any cost. I feel the Magadhans would have sent a similar offer to the Andhras as well. If any one of us falls into this trap, it would be beneficial to the Magadhans alone. We should tell Satkarni that we do not intend to fight with him. I have no doubt that he will feel relieved; he is not ready for a sudden war. But, on the other hand, as the Rathikas are related to his chief queen, he might be under great pressure to help them. Being his feudatories, it is a natural expectation that he protect them from larger kingdoms.'

'It would be comforting for you to know that Satkarni will not join the war. Our spies have confirmed it.'

'That, Rajan, is great news! In that case, we need to concentrate on Pushyamitra and his son Agnimitra, who is sitting dangerously close at Avantikapuri.'

'Yes, Arya Rudravarman would be further north-west of us. He is in a good position to cut off any advances by Satkarni or Agnimitra. I think Agnimitra at Avantikapuri or Pushyamitra at Magadha will not dare to cross the Andhra territory unless they have a prior understanding, or they see an opportunity in exploiting the weakness of the losing side. So, they will not make a move until late in this war. We have to fully concentrate on the Rathika–Bhojakas. I am sure your scouts must have fanned their lands and we must be getting information on their strength, tactics and numbers.'

'Yes Rajan, we are getting information about them getting ready for the war. They're also hopeful that Satkarni will help them at the last moment.'

The king got up and reassuringly patted the senapati's shoulder. 'Let us see how it unfolds but be prepared for every eventuality. You may take rest now, you look tired.'

'Salutations to Rajan, good night.'

Once the senapati had left, the king read the reports of messengers and spies, and then fell asleep.

✦✦✦

It was now the fourth day of the march. Rudra didn't have much difficulty in navigation as he was moving along the banks of the Mahanadi River. A few horse riders swiftly went ahead, followed by the slow elephants, who also cleared the way ahead by uprooting trees, removing logs and fallen tree trunks and other impediments from the path of the infantry and chariots. Rudra had divided the contingent into three parts, and each was following a parallel but separate path. As they were within Kalinga's borders, there was no imminent threat of attack. Nonetheless, they moved carefully.

A group of scouts was travelling a day ahead to identify camping spots in advance. All three units kept in touch with each other through fast riders and assembled at the campsite every night. Rudra got detailed information from them about the day's happenings and took note of their difficulties and suggestions. He personally briefed the chiefs of the other two unit every morning.

That morning, Rudra had called the two chiefs for the daily briefing. Durjaya was fuming with anger, he had been informed about an officer misbehaving with a tribal woman.

'Arya, we need to punish him severely. If he is not chastized, indiscipline will spread through the army.'

As they talked, the soldiers brought the offending officer. His hands had been tied with a rope.

'Untie his hands,' commanded Rudra, to everyone's astonishment. 'Did you do it or not?' he asked the offender.

'Arya, these people are making false allegations because I scolded them for making noise last night,' said Devasena.

'Chief Durjaya, what do you have to say?'

'Arya, we have witnesses. His own bodyguard told us about the incident, and the tribals had also assembled to take revenge when they came to know of it. We had a tough time convincing them to let us march ahead.'

Rudra turned and went inside his tent. A few moments later, he came out with a whip in his hand.

'Don't move, Devasena, stand still,' he said in a cold voice. Before anyone understood what was happening, the sound of a whiplash rang in the air. Devasena cried out loud in pain and writhed on the ground.

'Get up, Devasena, it is not over yet.'

Devasena pleaded with tears in his eyes, 'Arya, forgive me this time, I will never repeat such behaviour. Please forgive me, please arya!'

Rudra moved forward and lashed again and again. The offender's cries could be heard all over the camp. Soldiers rushed towards Rudra's tents but were held back by the bodyguards. Something had gotten into Rudra; he kept whipping the man till he bled badly, his skin broke open into bloody gashes and he collapsed in pain. 'Take him away, he will remain a prisoner till the end of the war. Seat him on a donkey when we march tomorrow. It should be a lesson to everyone here, we will not tolerate any such thing!' Then, he returned to his tent.

His attendant came out later and asked everyone to disperse. As they were about to go away, a gust of wind blew and a beehive from a tree fell on the ground. Large bees burst out from it and attacked the men who had assembled. They all ran for cover, diving on the ground, covering their faces with their uttariyas and turban cloths. The only person who couldn't run to get away from them was Devasena. He became the target of those monstrously large bees. They stung him all over his face, eyes, neck, hands and feet, and he lost consciousness because of the pain. By evening, Devasena's body had swollen beyond recognition. He kept on falling into a comatose state. The vaidyas were worried for him. When they reached the campsite, they had given up hopes for his survival. Vaidya Chitrabhana was despondent and came to talk to Rudra about the patient's condition.

'Arya Rudravarman, we cannot let him die like this. There is a lot of concern in the army about his condition. They feel that whipping was too severe a punishment. They are also talking that not enough efforts were made to save him from the bee attack. If he dies, there may be a revolt. I feel he may not last more than a day in this condition.'

'Vaidyaraj Chitrabhana, is there anything that can be done to save his life?'

'Arya, we are trying hard, but nothing seems to be working. The giant bees have a very strong poison, we don't have an antidote with us. However . . .'

'What is it, vaidyaraj?'

'The local forest dwellers are used to these bee stings and they have an antidote for it. Hearing of a bee attack victim, the local tribal chief has come to the camp with a *mantrik*. He claims to have magical powers to cure the man.'

'Bring him to me immediately, vaidyaraj. We should try out all possible remedies. The man shouldn't die.'

Chitrabhana returned with the chief of the forest dwellers. The tribal headman was a diminutive figure and spoke a language that Rudra didn't understand. His mantrik looked like a boy, he had an innocent face, but he didn't look like a forest dweller. The mantrik spoke many tongues and could converse easily with Rudra in Prakrit.

'Where is the victim, arya?' the mantrik asked.

'He is inside this tent. Do you think you can do something to help him?'

'Arya, let me have a look at him, then I will question the spirits. If they say yes, I will help him, if they say no, he dies.'

Rudra didn't say anything further, he indicated to the attendants to allow the mantrik to see Devasena. The mantrik saw Devasena and started laughing, he laughed and laughed hysterically.

'What is the matter, mantrik? Why are you laughing?' asked Rudra.

'This man is undergoing divine punishment. He is a sinner.'

'Stop laughing and tell me if he will live!' shouted Rudra.

The mantrik continued to laugh uncontrollably. Then he stopped suddenly and went into a trance, only the whites of his eyes could be seen as he uttered incomprehensible guttural sounds. Then suddenly he emerged from it and said, 'Three days, in three days he will walk. The spirits have forgiven him, he will be all right.'

'The mantrik will have to accompany us for the next three days then,' Rudra said, looking at the headman.

The mantrik said something to the headman in their native language, who nodded in agreement and said a few words as well. 'The headman says that you may take me along and keep me as long as you want,' informed the mantrik. 'He suggests I take seven of our village men with me.'

Chitrabhana whispered in Rudra's ears, 'He will also be a great help in navigating through the jungle. Let him travel with us till the end. He will be of some use if anyone has a problem similar to Devasena.'

Rudra nodded and rewarded the headman with five gold kahapanas.

Ten days had passed since they had left Tosali, Rudra's army was now well acclimatized to the march. There had been no untoward incident and, surprisingly, Devasena had survived. Rudra saw him recovering well, his strength was returning too.

Rudra called for the mantrik. It was noon already, and Bhadrabahu had asked his permission to halt and have lunch. Rudra was about to commence eating when the mantrik came to meet him.

'Worthy mantrik, you seem to have performed a miracle! Devasena has not only survived, he has also improved a lot. I think he should be able to fight in the war by the end of the month.'

'Arya, I am just a conduit, the spirits have the power to heal, they have cured him. He will be perfectly fit to fight a war in less than ten days.'

'When would you like to return home, mantrik?'

'Arya, I think you will need my services in future. The jungle is denser ahead. I am very familiar with this area, and have detailed knowledge of the plants and animals in this forest. I will continue as long as I can be of some use to you.'

'I am overwhelmed by your kindness mantrik. Bhadrabahu, reward him with five silver kahapanas and a deerskin. He has rendered great service to us and the Kalinga nation by saving the life of our officer.'

'Arya, thank you, but I don't want any reward. I do what I do for the love of Kalinga,' the mantrik said.

The Rathikas and Bhojakas had heard of the march. Some traders who had returned from Kalinga to Pratishthanpura had mentioned about massive preparations, but there was no substantial corroboration from any quarters. Spies and scouts were of no use as the Atavikas were not allowing any outsiders in their territories. Five scouts had already been hit by those lethal small arrows of the foresters that everyone dreaded, and now, no one was ready to enter the forest to gather information.

Satkarni had informed them that a Kalinga messenger had come with the declaration of war, but the Rathika–Bhojakas had also received similar communication. This left them without any concrete information on the Kalinga army's strength, how far they had moved and when they would attack.

Aira Kharavela was moving steadily ahead, his scouts and spies were keeping him informed about the movements of the enemy and the disposition of the Andhras, Shungas and the Yavanas beyond. He had ensured that the other side didn't get an exact idea of their movements and had sent spies to spread disinformation about the exact location of assault and the progress of the army.

Back in Tosali, Vajramitra was happy to be in charge of the kingdom in the absence of the king. He had also sent messengers to the king conveying that everything was in order it the capital. Nakiya remained vigilant. After whatever Rudra had told him, he had instructed his spies to immediately assassinate Vajramitra if he played any tricks. His every movement and conversation were monitored.

The king received regular advice from Nakiya and Uddalaka from Tosali through messengers. The morale and motivation of his army was at its peak and the Atavikas from the Vidyadharas were crossing their own territory now, they were striding with great pride.

✦✦✦

Rudra's contingent had reached a point where it became impossible to carry on along the banks of the Mahanadi River. Rudra wondered if they should continue the earlier strategy of having three contingents moving in parallel, and meeting at a designated point by evening, or converge. As Rudra and Durjaya discussed this, they saw the cheerful mantrik coming their way. As he was a local, they decided to take his views too.

'Mantrik, do you know what the terrain ahead is like?' asked Durjaya.

'Salutations to Arya Rudravarman. If you permit, I will tell you the best way forward.'

'Please do, mantrik. You have been of great help to us.'

'Arya, as you can see, the terrain along the river is difficult and when we deviate from it, it becomes more dangerous. I suggest that you now travel as one group because you're getting closer to enemy territory. The tribes of this Mahakantar region are very different from those in the Vidyadharas, they may not be as welcoming as them.'

'Durjaya, I see a point in what the mantrik is suggesting. What do you say?'

'Arya, you're right, the scouts have been making this suggestion for the past two days. We also need a very good local guide as the terrain is difficult to cross.'

'I can serve as a guide as I have been in this area several times while going to other border kingdoms,' said the mantrik.

'Thank you, mantrik. Durjaya, inform everyone about the change in plans.'

As they continued their march, the forest got thicker and the trees taller. There was a lot of shrubbery and undergrowth too, which made travel difficult. At times, the path was so narrow that only two men could pass at a time. The elephants, horses, chariots and bullock cart trains of supplies had to be sent by a longer route. Still, they didn't slow down. Their spirits were high and their hearts were burning with a desire for revenge.

While Satkarni had decided to refrain from an unnecessary involvement, he had to protect his assets and interests. Queen Nayanika had suggested that the towns bordering the Rathika–Bhojaka territories be fortified, without attracting much attention. The other feudatories, who maintained independent armies of their own, were asked to make arrangements for their defence. If the Kalingas crossed the borders of the feudatories into any province of the Andhras, they would have to face tough resistance from fortified cities, slowing down their advance, in turn giving sufficient time to the rulers of Pratishthanpura to organize a massive counterattack.

Satkarni had sent his spies to the border areas and beyond to get accurate information about the Kalinga army movements. It was indeed a tricky situation, Aira Kharavela had declared a holy war against an offending ally. Satkarni could neither rush and help his feudatories to fight the mighty Kalingas, nor sit quietly and watch the war unfold. He needed time and a lot of patience.

Aira Kharavela was now more than halfway to the Bhojakas' fort. His spies brought news from the enemy territory that rather than consolidating, the adversary was scattering its resources all over, which was unusual.

Kharavela's spies had been spreading misinformation, thus, the Rathika–Bhojakas were getting various kinds of news. They were told of hundreds of chariots, elephants and thousands of riders and an infantry of an uncountable number of foot soldiers being on the way. They heard about the advances from the south, the east and the north. They decided to conceal their assets, fortify the towns and villages and scatter the infantry in small groups that could close in quickly at short notice. Advice from Satkarni also mandated them to do so.

Rudra's contingent had now reached the heart of the dark forests in the dreaded Mahakantar region. He knew that the tribes must be following their movements closely, but given the size of the army, they wouldn't dare harass or interfere with them. The mantrik was a marvellous guide and Rudra felt indebted to him for the assistance he had been rendering all these days.

It was late afternoon but the jungle was so dense that it felt as if it was night already. Sunlight could hardly penetrate the dense foliage, and the army marched slowly. The elephants and chariots that had taken a longer circuitous route were tired. Many soldiers had been stung by insects and pricked by thorns from bushes and creepers, it was also getting unbearably cold.

When the contingent finally reached the campsite, it was quite dark already. The site was on a small hillock which was flat on the top, adjoining it was a pond of water that had sufficient water for all the men and animals. The tents were pitched quickly, kitchens were set up in a hurry and attendants rushed to bring water from the pond. The whole camp was under a shadow of severe fatigue. Rudra too felt tired after a long day of gruelling travel, he ate a light meal and quickly fell asleep.

Was it a bad dream? Rudra heard the name of Simhadhwaja being called in a low guttural voice. He tried to open his eyes, but nothing was visible in the pitch dark. He dismissed it as an illusion and closed his eyes again.

'Simhadhwaja, get up. I want to talk to you,' the voice commanded.

Rudra sat up with a start. He hurriedly got up from his bed and rushed out of the tent, but there was nobody outside. He picked up a lit torch from outside and came back to his tent. As he entered, he saw the mantrik sitting at his bedside, his eyes shining devilishly in the flickering light. In his tribal attire, he looked like a ghost. His body was painted with ash, as if he had come straight from some ghastly ritual.

'Sit down,' commanded the mantrik.

'What has gotten into you, mantrik?' Rudra said as he tried to reach for his sword hidden by his bedside. It wasn't there.

'Why don't you sit down?' the mantrik said softly.

'Was it you whispering in the dark at my bedside? How dare you sneak into my tent. Didn't the guards stop you?'

'They all need some rest, they're so, so tired. Are you so heartless, arya? Let them sleep.'

'Who are you, mantrik? Disclose your identity now!'

'Arya, I know your real identity . . . and you would have heard a lot about me. Let me see if you can guess correctly.'

'Stop this silly game of yours. Are you not afraid of the consequences of your audacity?'

'We are two similar people, arya. You too are aware of the dangers in the game you're playing.'

'I could get you arrested right now and put you under the elephant's feet in the morning!'

'Calm down, arya. We have a lot to talk about. It is just the second *prahar* of the night.'

'What are you up to, mantrik?'

'If you calm down, arya, we can have a meaningful discussion.'

'What do you want, whoever you are?'

'First, let us vow to answer all questions truthfully— in fact, you don't have any other option, as you will come to know soon.'

'All right. Ask your questions,' Rudra said reluctantly.

'Actually, I don't need to ask you anything. I will tell you some things which will be beneficial to you.'

Rudra didn't answer, but kept looking at the mantrik, whose innocent face had now transformed into a demon's countenance. 'Firstly, you will stay here tomorrow and the army will not move ahead. Secondly, you will hand over your personal seal. Not the one in your right hand, but the one in your left hand from the Andhra days. Thirdly . . .'

'What makes you think I will do all this, mantrik?'

'Oh, it hurts so much when you address me by that name, Simhadhwaja. Haven't you learnt to respect royalty? From now on mind your manners and call me honourable prince, understood?'

'Which prince masquerades as a mantrik?' Rudra remained nonchalant outwardly, but his heart was beating hard and his mind racing.

'I am the royal prince of Suvarnagiri, a direct descendant of Ashoka and Karubaki, the princess of Kalinga.'

'You are the dark prince?'

'Do I look dark to you, Simhadhwaja? Now let's come to the instructions I have prepared for you. As I was saying, thirdly . . .'

Rudra interrupted. 'And if I refuse?'

'Simhadhwaja, let me outline the situation for you. The pond from where you, your men, and your beasts drank water was poisoned by my people before you reached. It is a slow acting poison. You have only three days to live, if I don't give you the antidote. There is only one way out of this campsite— the path which you came from. Further down, the hillock is surrounded by a deep swamp, so no one can escape from there. The only exit has been blocked by my archers, who are hiding in the trees. They are armed with fire arrows that can burn your tents down in no time.'

'Why should I believe you, dark prince?'

'Do you have an option, Simhadhwaja? I have been following you since you left Pratishthanpura and came to Kalinga as Rudravarman. Our fates seem to be intertwined. You foiled my attempt to get to the throne of Kalinga by saving the elephant Mahagiri from being poisoned. Then, I tried to kill you with a poisoned dart in the jungle camp, but you survived. I saw your skills in the Asmaka War too. As things stand now, you're one of my most serious concerns, the biggest impediment in my path to the seat of Kalinga. You should understand that the throne of Kalinga is rightfully mine. I am the descendant of Princess Karubaki, the original heiress to the kingdom. And I have the blood of Ashoka in my veins too. The Chedis who call themselves Meghavahanas are outsiders, their ancestors didn't die in the Kalinga War. They've contributed *nothing* to this land.'

The light from the torch was dying, they were now staring at each other in near darkness. Rudra surreptitiously tried to search for the knife concealed under his bed with his feet. The dark prince laughed.

'Arya, I have been living in the darkness for decades now, it's like a friend to me. Don't even think of trying something stupid, you will lose your life in an instant. Listen to me and do as I say, that is your only chance for survival. Any unwise action will cause the loss of hundreds of lives.'

'I am listening,' said Rudra.

'As I was saying, you have very limited options. But I will be generous with you. To begin with, let me make you a good offer. You join me in my plan to capture Kalinga, and I will make you the mahamatya when I succeed. Surrender to me without a fight and I will save those who agree to join me, the rest will die a quick death in the next three days.'

'And if I say no?'

'Arya Simhadhwaja, you should listen to me fully before making up your mind. I will give you one more reason for helping me out. Apart from the riches that I will shower upon you, it will be the revenge for the death of your father, who was killed at the behest of Chetaraja, Kharavela's father.'

'You're a wretched liar, dark prince. Just like your name, your heart is dark too.'

'Well said, arya, but I have no reason to lie. If you survive the coming three days, which you won't, you will find out on your own.'

'Liar, liar, liar!' Rudra was hysterical now. He got up in an instant and lunged towards the dark prince, who effortlessly dodged and pinned Rudra down. Rudra felt something cold against his neck, the dark prince had a knife at his throat. He gently moved the knife across his skin, Rudra felt burning pain and cried out in agony.

The dark prince released him and said, 'Arya, you're wasting your time. If I had to kill you, I could've done it when you were fast asleep. Now be rational—tell me do you accept my offer or not?'

'No, no, no. A thousand times NO!'

'Very well, you're forcing my hand, arya. We come to the other options now, you can hardly call them options actually. You must hand over your Andhra seal and declare unconditional surrender, then, I will choose who all get to live and join me in my plan to be the king of Kalinga. You will get to live and save the lives of all your men if you write a letter to Satkarni, saying that you're Simhadhwaja and that you're not dead as he assumes. Warn him of Aira Kharavela's plan to attack Pratishthanpura and take over the Andhra country.'

'What wretched designs do you have behind this?' asked Rudra with anger.

'You need not apply your fertile mind to the problems of kings, Simhadhwaja. It should suffice to say that Aira Kharavela and Satkarni will fight when your letter reaches the hands of the dakshinadhipati. Pushyamitra's son, Agnimitra, who is on the borders of Mahakantar, will then defeat and kill the survivor with my help. He has promised me the throne of Kalinga in return. He wants to keep Andhra for himself, which is a legitimate demand. What do you think, arya?'

'You will die a painful death, dark prince. You are playing a very foolish game. Satkarni will never fight with Kalinga, even if he gets my letter, I can assure you of that.'

'What makes you so confident, arya?'

'Satkarni has a rare and terminal illness, he will not live more than the next five years. He wants to accomplish a lot in that time, so he will not get into a war in which his victory is not certain. Only his queen, the mahamatya and I know this, no one else is privy to this information. I have not revealed this to anyone in Kalinga.'

'Nice loyalties you maintain, Simhadhwaja—I appreciate that. But here I am in charge and I know how things will roll out in future. So give me your seal and write the letter now!'

'Don't threaten me, dark prince. I am here to fight a war and I am ready to die. It's a pity that I may die at the hands of a coward like you. I will not betray my master even at the cost of my life. You will not gain anything by killing me like this or taking the lives of my soldiers. I have lived my life by principles, I am ready to die for them. When I was at the Andhra court, I was loyal to them, but circumstances drove me out of Pratishthanpura. I have returned to my motherland to rise again, but not at the cost of my integrity. I refuse to do as you say. You may go ahead and kill me right now.'

'Ah Simhadhwaja, I didn't think you'd be so weak. Here I am, giving you an opportunity of a lifetime to be a mahamatya, and you're not only throwing it away but being stupid enough to lay down your life for a king who doesn't even care for you. What happened after the Asmaka War? Did anyone acknowledge your contribution? And how about Samapa? They didn't even realize what you have done for them, and here you are singing praises in their honour . . . You are a confused person, arya. We will discuss this again tomorrow, but mind you—it will be a rest day for all, nobody moves from here. Good night.'

'Gods will punish you for your misdeeds, dark prince. Your karma will catch up with you soon.'

Rudra couldn't sleep till the morning. He thought hard but couldn't think of a way out. If he did as the dark prince said, it would be treachery. If he didn't, the whole army would die, including him. If he could somehow kill the dark prince, it still wouldn't help as the army had been poisoned already. The only person who could save them was the dark prince.

When he heard the drums sound for departure, Rudra quickly got up and went to Durjaya's tent. Durjaya was already up and getting ready. 'Salutations, Arya Rudravarman. What brings you here so early?'

'Durjaya, call off the march for today. The army is looking very tired. Let's give them a day's break. In any case, we are more than halfway through and have been walking continuously without a stop.'

'Why, arya, we are doing fine. Do you think it is really necessary?'

Rudra nodded curtly. 'We are ahead of schedule Durjaya, and I can see a little fatigue setting in now. If they take a break, they will be fresh for the remaining march and war.'

'As you command, arya.' Durjaya rushed out and informed the trumpeter about the change in plan, a predetermined signal was given through the beating of drums. Rudra could hear the cheers of the soldiers at getting a day off, and he thought, 'Poor fellows, they don't know they hardly have a couple of days left to live . . .'

Bhadrabahu came running in, panting. 'Arya, the fish in the pond are dead. Ask everyone to stop drinking water from there,' he said in a rushed voice.

'Come with me,' Rudra said, and ran towards the pond to confirm the news. He could see the silver bellies of the dead fish floating on calm waters as he approached the pond. He asked Bhadrabahu to place a sentry at the pond to prevent anyone from using the water. He rushed back to his tent and called for Kinshuk, Vijayaka, Devabrata and Jeemuthabahan to meet him immediately. He also sent word for the vaidyaraj to come to his tent.

'The pond has been poisoned,' Rudra told his team. He was starting to feel a bit queasy now. 'Once we take the suggestion of Vaidyaraj Chitrabhana, we need to quickly organize the medicine in large quantities. Vijayaka, you go and talk to each senior officer and assure him that help is at hand and there is no need to panic. Jeemuthabahan, call the leaders of the other two parties to my tent for an emergency meeting. Devabrata, rush to the stables and see how the animals are doing. Check with the caretakers about medicines for the animals. Everyone hurry up now, there is no time to waste.'

They all rushed out to carry the instructions, except Devabrata. When Rudra saw him still sitting, he shouted, 'You old log, why are you not moving?'

'Where is the mantrik, arya? He can help us with this. He is a local and has very good knowledge of the medicinal plants around. Why don't you take his help?'

'Devabrata, there is no time for that. You first go and carry out the instructions given to you.'

'Arya, you knew about this beforehand, didn't you? Why else did you cancel today's march?'

'Devabrata, I will tell you everything and seek your advice too. There is much that is unknown to you, but you must rush now.'

'I think I can help you by listening to the truth, arya' said Devabrata stubbornly.

'Well then, listen to this. The mantrik is actually the dreaded dark prince. He has made a fool of us by travelling with us in the disguise of the mantrik. He is the one who has poisoned the pond.'

'I was always suspicious of him, arya. He didn't look like a forester to me. Now, tell me, what does he want?'

'He wants the army to surrender to him, else everyone dies. He also wants the throne of Kalinga to which he thinks he has a natural right.'

'What else, arya?'

'He is in touch with the Magadhans and wants to involve Satkarni in the war. Once Andhra or Kalinga is defeated, he will get the victor killed and take the kingdom of Kalinga. He has promised Andhra to the Magadhans.'

'Sounds quite complicated, arya. What will he get by killing an entire army?'

'He has the antidote and he will give it to only those who surrender and join him. Meanwhile, if Satkarni does join the war, our contingent, which was supposed to cut any advances by the Andhras, will be totally ineffective, leaving the Kalinga army open to a sure defeat by the better prepared Satkarni.'

'What does he want you to do?'

'He wants me to write a letter to Satkarni, saying that I am an ex-employee of the Andhra court, and I am writing to him to inform him of the real purpose of the Kalinga attack—to capture Pratishthanpura!'

'How about all of us escaping from here?'

'The dark prince has locked us in, there are marshes on three sides of the hillock and his archers are blocking the only exit route with fire arrows.'

Devabrata was pensive. Then, he said, 'Arya, listen to me, I will do my best to locate the antidote cache; he must have kept it hidden somewhere in the camp. I have been doing my homework too. I never trusted the mantrik from day one.'

'So what do you suggest?'

'I will let you know by evening, but if he shows up before that, keep him engaged in conversation. Have faith in me, we will fight it out. We won't die like this.'

'Go Devabrata, do your best. Please forgive me as I have failed in my duties as a leader . . .'

'Arya, don't give up so easily, we have time till this evening.'

By the time Devabrata left, Rudra was feeling very nauseated. He retched and pangs of pain ran like hot needles through his stomach, he ran out and vomited. When he recovered, he saw that there were a lot of other people vomiting. Vaidyaraj Chitrabhana was administering salt water to induce vomiting so that the stomach of those affected would be cleaned out, but he still wasn't able to figure out what poison had been used, and hence couldn't administer any antidote.

All day long men and animals had been vomiting and purging, they had grown exhausted and weak. Two soldiers had already died from the poisoning. Rudra had been working all day long to provide medicine and help to all the men affected. He was about to collapse with fatigue when Kinshuk came with a message from Devabrata.

'Arya, Devabrata has told me to convey to you the following message—"Agree to whatever the mantrik says, but don't allow him to get out of your sight at any cost".'

'Kinshuk, this is a very confusing message. What does it mean. I don't have time for riddles!'

'He only asked me to convey this and return.'

'Return where?'

'To the forest. He is busy there, I have to go back quickly as he needs me.'

Before Rudra could question him more, Kinshuk left. He now saw that some soldiers were carrying vessels of water from the pond, he rushed and accosted them.

'Are you mad, didn't the guard at the pond stop you from taking water?'

'Arya, this is not for drinking. Arya Durjaya has commanded us to bring this water.'

Rudra felt confused and frustrated. One stupid misstep and he had ruined his destiny. Not only his own fate, but the fate of his motherland too. The lives of hundreds of men were in jeopardy due to him. His heart sank, there was no hope left, time was slipping out of his hands.

Night had fallen. Rudra felt lost and despondent. His health was rapidly deteriorating. When he approached his tent, he felt dizzy, and rushing inside, he collapsed on his bed.

When he opened his eyes, he saw that there were others in the tent. Startled, he got up to find the dark prince there, as expected. He had a benevolent smile on his face. 'You should thank me, Simhadhwaja,' he said.

'You expect to be thanked for killing me and my army, dark prince? I have never seen a more wretched character than you, shame on you!'

'Peace, peace, peace, Simhadhwaja. Your problem is that you jump to conclusions before hearing the whole story. When I tell you that I have administered the antidote to you, and your life is safe now, will you thank me then?'

Rudra scowled with anger. He wanted to clobber the rascal to death. 'Dark Prince, all day long I have been tending to my men, who are dying. Two were already dead by evening, and many more must have succumbed by now. All these bad deeds and the blood of innocents will not go waste, you will have to repay ten times of what you're doing. I spit on you.'

'Ah, I saw you working hard during the day, but you didn't remember me. You could have asked for the antidote any time. It's not too late, why do you want to kill so many men Simhadhwaja, you're so cruel.'

'Even the Asuras were not as cruel as you dark prince. You intend to be a king! A king is like a father, he can't see his sons dying like this!'

'Simhadhwaja, you're a strange person. You are taking these men to a war to kill people and get butchered themselves, and you're calling them innocents. It looks like you're wasting my time, arya. Why don't we meet later at night, when you're in a better state of mind?'

'Okay, dark prince, don't go, I surrender.'

'Ah, you make me happy! But you know, that is not what I want.'

'I will write that letter and give you my Andhra seal too.'

'Now you talk like a sensible man. See I always knew, this man would do anything to save the lives of his men,' said the dark prince to his assistant.

'But I would like to consult my old colleague first. Will you give me some time to discuss it with him before I do as you say?'

'You take all the time you want, arya. I thank you from the depths of my heart for your contribution in my noble cause. Your services will not go unrewarded.'

'I don't even want to live after this dark prince, what reward do you speak of?'

'What kind of Kshatriya says that, arya? Don't be disheartened. It's always the darkest before dawn. So don't lose hope, I am with you,' the dark prince said and left.

The antidote had worked, and Rudra was feeling much better. He was worried about his men though. Just then, Devabrata entered the tent with Bhadrabahu and Kinshuk. Rudra couldn't help noticing that they were all looking surprisingly agile.

'What is the situation, Devabrata? How many more men have succumbed?' Rudra asked.

'Arya, don't worry. I have revealed everything to Bhadrabahu, Vijayaka, Kinshuk and Jeemuthabahan. We have worked out a scheme together. I think the positions of the stars are not as bad as it looks today.'

'Tell me quickly, Devabrata. That demon is waiting for me to call him.'

'Arya, there is no time for details. Just keep him inside the tent and do as he says, we will manage the rest.'

'But what is this scheme? He is asking me to commit treachery. How do I do that? How do I save the lives of my men? How do I complete our mission? Let me know now, I am dying of despair.'

'Arya, please just do as we say. Keep faith in us, remember how these people have worked miracles for you during the Asmaka War and the Samapa mission,' said Bhadrabahu confidently.

'And one more thing,' said Devabrata, 'if you hear the sound of the kokila bird, it would be an indication that our work is done. We will be ready to rush inside your tent any time after that. You just have to call Kinshuk and we will capture the dark prince.'

Rudra was feeling a bit reassured now, he knew his team was very capable. They had certainly worked something out, but how effective would that be? His head was still reeling. He decided to stabilize himself and face the task squarely. If they were so confident, they must have taken care of the possible fallouts of whatever was going to happen now.

Rudra went out and, seeing the dark prince's assistant, asked him to tell his master that he was ready for him. When the dark prince came, he hugged Rudra, much to his annoyance.

'Tell me dark prince, where is the antidote to save my men?' Rudra asked. The exasperation in his voice couldn't be concealed.

'Let me first express my heartfelt gratitude. Arya, you are not aware of what you're doing for me. All my life I have had this dream, of ascending to the throne of Kalinga. I was born to be a king. My ancestors also waited throughout their lives, you don't know how happy their souls will be to see me achieve what they couldn't.'

He continued. 'Simhadhwaja, you are an instrument of fate, you are about to change history. Devas, Asuras, Yakshas, Pisachas and Gandharvas may be witnessing this moment, you are blessed.'

He lovingly caressed Rudra's forehead. Rudra felt like spitting on his face. Such brazenness! He was aghast. This man was mad. Rudra wanted the ordeal to end as soon as possible. A strange thought suddenly crossed his mind, these may actually be his last moments. He would not live to see tomorrow. He remembered his beloved mother; he saw her face and she was weeping. He felt sad and angry. He also remembered Maitreyi, he wanted to see her at least once before he died, but that would be impossible.

'So this may be our last meeting, Arya Simhadhwaja,' the dark prince said, as if reading his mind. 'You see, you are rejecting the offer to be mahamatya of my kingdom. In that case, I don't think we will meet again. If you intend to change your decision, I am still ready to consider.'

'Dark prince, you already know my answer. As we are meeting for the last time, I would like to hear from you about how you managed to sabotage us, and what are your further plans?' Rudra said trying to buy time.

'*Shubhasta sheeghram* Simhadhwaja, good deeds should not wait. So, first things first, and I will explain to you as we go on.' Saying this, the dark prince produced a bark paper and a reed pen.

'You will write a letter to Satkarni, your old master and friend. He can identify your handwriting, so the authenticity of the letter will not be questioned. Then, we will endorse and close it with your Andhra ring seal, which will further reassure Satkarni of its genuineness.

'Satkarni will then make arrangements to counter Kharavela, learning of which, Kalinga will be prompted to react, setting off the war I have been waiting for. Agnimitra will then wipe out the victorious of the two and give me Kalinga. Isn't it a wonderful scheme? I am so pleased with myself.' The dark prince was in a state of feverish excitement.

'What happens to my army, dark prince?'

'I am a man of my word, and you told me that a king is like a father, so those of my children who want to join me will get the antidote and live. I will take care of them like my own children.'

'Where is the antidote dark prince? I will not write the letter until I see the antidote,' Rudra said.

The dark prince lost his temper. 'Why don't you understand! I already gave the antidote to you, what more proof do you want?'

'I want to see the antidote in a quantity sufficient for all my men and animals.'

'You are unnecessarily delaying things Simhadhwaja and you will be responsible for their deaths, why don't you believe me? Why should I lie to you?'

'Believe you! Are you joking? You have poisoned me and my entire army deceitfully and you want me to believe you? I will not write anything until you show me the antidote.'

'Arya Simhadhwaja, the antidote is kept in the marshes, hidden in seventeen large earthen pots. Once you write the letter, I will assemble the army, show your letter of surrender and ask for the support of the people who want to live. It's so simple, arya, don't complicate things. Now don't go back on your word—begin writing the two letters immediately. One to Satkarni and the other to your own army announcing unconditional surrender.'

'You think I am an idiot dark prince? What if you don't actually possess the antidote?'

'Oh, you're acting like a child, Simhadhwaja. Let me prove it to you now.' Saying this, he called for his assistant and asked him to produce a portion of the antidote. The man complied and furnished the antidote in a small earthen pot.

'Arya Simhadhwaja, this is *ajeya ghrita*, it can cure this poison. It is like the Sanjeevani herb which can revive the dead.'

'How do I know that it's genuine and effective, dark prince?'

Arya, my men made this three days before you arrived here, it's a wet paste of vidanga, yashti madhu, priyangu, both kinds of haridra, vrihati and sariva, slowly cooked in clear ghee for a whole day. It cannot go wrong, you see it has already cured you fully.'

Rudra thought, *If I could kill this man right now, it would still be difficult to search for the antidote hidden in the marshes. If Vaidyaraj Chitrabhana was to prepare it, it would still take a day. By that time, most of my people would be dead.* He had no option other than to comply with the demands of the dark prince.

'Arya, I promise, that after you give me the letter to Satkarni, I will send my people to get the antidote, but not all at once. We will ask the army to surrender their weapons before the administration of the medicine. So without wasting any more time, write!'

He forcibly thrust the reed pen in Rudra's hands.

Rudra didn't resist, and now laid down the bark paper before him. The dark prince started dictating the letter. 'Write as follows:

> Salutations to Dakshinadhipati, Simuka putra Satkarni,
> I, Simhadhwaja, your loyal and trusted amatya, am still
> alive. I am writing this to warn you that Aira Kharavela's
> real mission is to conquer Prathishthanpura. He has
> sent me with an army through Mahakantar forests to
> encircle you before he arrives. I am also supposed to cut
> off any help from your allies and feudatories. Kharavela
> will reach the borders of Rathika–Bhojaka in another
> fourteen days. If you're caught unawares, you will lose
> your kingdom and your throne . . . Written under the
> hand of Simhadhwaja.

Rudra wrote rapidly. As he was completing the letter, the dark prince grabbed his left hand and tried to remove his seal.

As they grappled with each other, Rudra heard the distinct sound of the kokila bird, and he immediately let go of the ring.

The dark prince angrily took his ring and applied his seal at the end of the letter. He then carefully sealed it and applied the seal to the covering of the letter and called upon his assistant to take the letter for delivery. 'Ah, I am so relieved. Now, for my part of the promise as a benevolent king, I will send my men to bring the first batch of the antidote. You have to do the remaining work fast as your men are dying. And please ask your men not to do anything adventurous, my archers with fire arrows are up in the trees on the only exit route. A single command from me will reduce your camp to ashes, you understand?'

The dark prince asked another assistant to bring the first five pots of the antidote from the marshes. Rudra saw him disappear in the flickering lights of the torches. He realized, all of a sudden, that the night was very cold, and he found himself shivering. He wondered if it was only due to the cold.

'Now, we get ready for the second letter,' proclaimed the dark prince.

'I will write two more letters, dark prince,' said Rudra.

'To whom do you want to address the third letter, Simhadhwaja?'

'After this defeat, even if I survive, I won't be able to show my face to my near and dear ones. So I want to write a confession seeking the pardon of everybody.'

'Very well.'

Rudra started writing. *Devi Maitreyi, I don't know with what words I should seek your forgiveness . . .'*

The dark prince peered over his shoulder and said with mock sympathy, 'Oh, it seems that you love her very much.'

When Rudra ignored him, he continued. 'You tell me what is to be conveyed to her, and I will get your message communicated to her. You have done so much for me, I have to repay your debt in some way.'

'Will you really do that for me, dark prince?'

'Arya, you can take the word of the future king of Kalinga on this.'

Rudra hurriedly completed the letter and then put the seal of the ring from his right hand on it. Then he handed it over to the dark prince, tears streaming from his eyes.

'Oh, don't cry warrior, you have such a soft heart. What message do I give to her when this letter is delivered to her?'

'Tell her that Rudravarman was loyal to Kalinga and he fought valiantly . . . before he . . .'

'Before what, arya?'

Rudra suddenly turned and thrust the reed pen in the right eye of the dark prince. The dark prince screamed and retreated quickly, he was writhing in pain. He took out a large knife hidden under his clothes and lunged at Rudra. Rudra ducked and called out, 'Kinshuk, Kinshuk!'

The dark prince covered the bleeding eye with the reed stuck inside it with one hand and roared, 'AGNIVARSHA, AGNIVARSHA.'

Before anyone could react, fire arrows started raining from the trees. Rudra's tent caught fire. The dark prince looked more sinister with his right eye burst open and his uttariya red with blood. He charged towards Rudra in a violent rage but Rudra was ready for the assault and kicked him hard in the groin. The dark prince fell like a log, but he grabbed Rudra's leg, taking him down too. The dark prince quickly spun around and moved like an alligator towards

Rudra, who rolled on the floor to escape the knife thrusts. The burning tent produced a bright light in which Rudra could see the bloodied face of the dark prince, the reed still in his right eye. Smoke started billowing inside. Out of nowhere, Bhadrabahu caught Rudra from behind and pulled him out of the burning tent.

Outside, the clang and swish of bows and arrows was everywhere. His men hauled Rudra to another tent at some distance. Suddenly, the wind started to blow and the volley of fire arrows from the trees stopped. A terrible swarm of monstrous bees had descended on the camp, and everyone went into hiding.

No one said anything, as Rudra watched his tent burn to ashes . . . 'Goodbye dark prince,' he muttered.

They went into hiding till dawn broke, the bees could still be heard buzzing angrily, though their fury had subsided now. There was no time for explanations. An exhausted Rudra fell asleep almost immediately. In the morning, he got up and looked around. Arrows from the attackers' bows were stuck in tree trunks, tent cloths and the ground. They were all at a vertical angle, indicating that they had been fired from a height. 'The dark prince was right, he indeed had an army of archers up in the trees,' he thought. He walked around the camp and found, to his surprise, that the fire arrows, though fired at the tents, had had no effect on them. He asked a soldier standing near a tent about last night's happenings.

The soldier saluted him and said, 'Arya, Shriman Durjaya had told us to wet our tents in the evening with pond water. We did not understand why, but he had asked us to comply without questions. I now realize that he was aware of a possible attack from the trees with fire arrows. When the enemy fired the arrows, they didn't have any effect as the tents were dripping wet.'

'How did we counter the enemy attack, soldier?'

'Arya, it was with God's help, as soon as the enemy archers fired from the trees, a swarm of angry bees burst upon them. They dropped like ripe fruit from the trees, it was amusing to see them. Most of them died due to the fall, the remaining were killed by bee stings. We found no survivors when we went to check this morning. I pity the fate of our poor enemy.'

'Tell me one more thing soldier, how is everyone free from the effects of the poisoned water?'

'Vaidyaraj Chitrabhana gave an antidote to everyone by last evening. However, nine men have succumbed to the poison. I hear that a bullock and two horses have also died. But the antidote has really worked like magic, arya. We have been cured completely.'

'We will move out of this accursed place very soon soldier, ask your colleagues to get ready fast.'

'As you command, arya,' the soldier said.

Apart from mild bee stings and sporadic arrow injuries, the army was intact. Rudra breathed a sigh of relief at getting rid of the dreaded dark prince. The terrible villain had not only fooled him but put his army through such an ordeal. The soldiers looked happy to have survived, some were praying to their gods, some feverishly discussing last night's incidents, while others solemnly set about packing their things and dismantling the tents for marching on. Rudra went to Durjaya's tent and called Bhadrabahu and Devabrata there. Durjaya requested Rudra to rest for some time and left the tent to organize the departure.

Devabrata and Bhadrabahu came along with Kinshuk in some time. They wished Rudra, and he asked them to be seated. 'Tell me now, Devabrata, how did it all happen? What did you do yesterday that made you so confident when we met last evening?'

'Arya, I have been following the dark prince like a shadow. I realized quite early that there was something sinister going on. I told Kinshuk and Bhadrabahu to keep a close watch on his men through the night when we arrived here. Kinshuk saw one of them moving to and fro towards the marshes that night. The next morning, we found out that the dark prince had poisoned the pond, and it is then that we realized that there was something hidden in the marshes.

'Initially, we couldn't locate anything, but later in the morning, we found that the assistant had hidden something in an earthen pot. He had made a sign on the tree to locate it again. With the help of such signs, we located three pots filled with some medicine by the end of the day. We showed it to Vaidyaraj Chitrabhana, who immediately identified it as ajeya ghrita, the surefire antidote to the poison. He immediately set about making it himself for the whole army. By the time you met the villain again at night, almost everyone had been given the antidote. We had mixed the antidote found from the marshes with your breakfast on the advice of the vaidyaraj, hence you did not develop more serious symptoms like everyone else. We did not share our plans with you as you were under close watch of the dark prince. As he concentrated on you, we were left unmarked.'

'Oh, I see now, how we have all survived. Congratulations Devabrata, Bhadrabahu, I applaud your effort!'

'It is the will of God, arya, that we are all alive. Our ancestors must have done some really good deeds or our parents' blessings have acted as a shield against a treacherous death and destruction.'

'Indeed, Devabrata. Now tell me what about the letter I had to write to Satkarni? The dark prince must have had it sent to the Andhras by now,' said a tormented Rudra.

'Don't worry, arya. We kept two of our best men to lay ambush on the route of his riders. They waylaid and killed them, the letter has been recovered and is safe with us now,' said Bhadrabahu.

'I am so relieved, Bhadrabahu! Had it not been for you, the dark prince would have killed me in the burning tent.'

'How would we have allowed anyone to harm you, arya? It's our duty to protect you, even at the cost of our lives.'

'I will ever be indebted to you all. Tell me one thing—how did you counter the archers perched up in the trees?'

Devabrata's face lit up as he described what happened to the archers. 'When our watchers informed us about them being armed with fire arrows, Arya Durjaya instructed all of us to wet our tents. When they rained a volley of fire arrows, nothing at all happened, but we could locate them up in the trees, each one of them.'

'Then what did you do, Devabrata?' Rudra asked.

'We didn't shoot at them, arya. Instead, we shot at the large hives of those demonic bees that almost killed Devasena. The bees did the rest of work for us and the archers fell down like hailstones from the sky. Ah what a sight it was! It all happened so fast that it was over before we could make sense of it.'

Rudra breathed a sigh of relief. A heavy weight had lifted off his chest. He looked at his team with eyes full of gratitude.

'We should now leave this place fast, arya. We don't know what else lies in store for us here.'

'Yes, Bhadrabahu. Beat the drums, give the signal to march. We shall leave as soon as possible.'

When the soldiers heard the marching signals, they had already taken down the tents, packed their things and were ready to go. Rudra, sitting on a horse, led the advance.

His thoughts drifted to his Andhra days. Those were his days of glory as Simhadhwaja, when King Satkarani would not take any decision without consulting him. Not only that, Queen Nayanika also reposed a lot of confidence in his counsel—she would call upon him separately to discuss matters of importance.

This had upset many people, and Simhadhwaja's closeness with the royal family, his meteoric rise in the court, his astuteness and alacrity had won him enemies. At a young age, he had learnt the art of statecraft well, and knew that his enemies would not spare even the slightest mistake on his part. Not that he was unaware of the machinations of his detractors, but eternal vigilance was impossible. Proximity to kings is akin to walking on fire, if you slip once, you are engulfed by the flames. His enemies had waited for him to rise and rise, util the inevitable slip.

Chapter 20

War

The terrain was undulating, slowing down Aira Kharavela's advance. He was now reaching the edge of Bhojaka territory. His spies reported that enemy scouts had been seen keeping an eye on their movements. The soil had turned black and the forest appeared to be denser. Large outcrops of black rocks gave the landscape a foreboding feel. On the last day of the march, the Kalinga army was camping in these dense jungles. Senapati Bahushalin seemed upset, and the king inquired about the cause of his distress.

'Rajan, this area is infested with wild animals. Our people have seen tigers roaming around and they even come close to the camp at night. Our supply trains have been affected due to attacks by these wild animals, and to make things worse, there are so many wild bears roaming around in this area that it is highly unsafe for any soldier to go out alone in the forest. In fact, two of our soldiers have already been badly mauled.'

'Senapati, tell all soldiers not to venture out of the camp alone. Sentries will beat drums in the night to keep wild animals away, but nobody will hunt or kill any animal without reason or for pleasure.' He paused for some time and then asked, 'What is the news from Arya Rudravarman's camp?'

'Rajan, Arya Rudravarman's contingent faced the worst possible crisis, but they have survived it with minimal losses.'

'What happened, Bahushalin? Are Arya Rudravarman and his army safe?'

'They had a serious problem some days back when the army drank poisoned water. About ten of their soldiers died due to it. They also had to face an attack by the tribes of Subarnagiri.'

'How dare the tribes of Subarnagiri attack my army, aren't they afraid of my wrath?'

'Rajan, it has transpired that the dark prince was behind these incidents. First, he poisoned a water source at a campsite and then attacked our soldiers with fire arrows at night. He is reportedly in touch with the Magadhans and has hatched this plan at their behest. Fortunately, Arya Rudravarman and his commander Durjaya have successfully overcome these acts of sabotage. They identified the poison early and administered the right antidote with the help of Vaidyaraj Chitrabhana, saving the lives of the entire contingent. Not only that, they anticipated the attack by tribals at night and repelled it well. Arya Rudravarman sends a message that the dark prince has been killed in a fire at the campsite.'

'What? The dark prince has been killed? Impossible, that vile fellow is said to be immortal, senapati.'

'I too have heard similar things about the dark prince, Rajan. Whatever be the truth, the army is safe now, they're rapidly advancing towards the Rathika borders.'

'Once the war is over, I want a detailed analysis of this episode senapati. It is a very serious incident which could have jeopardized all our efforts. It could have even led to a defeat!' The king sat there perturbed, slowly pounding his head with his fist. Then he said, 'Now tell me, how do we attack the Bhojakas?'

'Rajan, a forest fort of the Bhojakas lies at a distance of about one day's march. It is a large fort with arrangements to keep the army inside for a long time. The Bhojakas, learning of our advance, have gathered their army in sufficient strength to receive us there. Their scouts and spies are all around.'

'Senapati, you need to get information about a suitable battleground where we can meet them. It should be free of obstructions from shrubbery and rocks so that our chariots and elephants can move. They don't seem to have a large infantry but they're reputed to be good riders. We will have to match their riders with our chariots and elephants.'

Suddenly, they heard a huge commotion outside. The senapati asked the king to wait as he rushed out of the tent to find out the cause of the disturbance.

To his shock, he found that the Bhojakas had suddenly struck—a swift group of enemy riders had conducted a quick raid on the camp, injuring the sentries and carrying away their weapons. They had withdrawn with the same lightning speed they attacked with, and the Kalinga army was found unprepared for such an assault. There was a terrible hue and cry as riders got ready to pursue them.

The king quickly took stock of the situation and prevented any hasty pursuit. It could have been a larger trap—he was a trained strategist, who couldn't be fooled with such tricks. He assembled the senior commanders and instructed, 'The enemy knows the terrain better than us. It knows that we are far more superior on the battleground in a frontal combat, but our size is our weakness. They will harass us before we reach their strongholds by making these surprise raids and retreating quickly. What countermeasures should we take?'

Jishnu, who was leading the weak auxiliary forces, had an apprehension, 'Rajan, I suspect that they will target the weaker sections of the army at the rear. Any successes will embolden them and affect our morale.'

'We should form smaller groups with a mix of different types of soldiers. Each unit can then operate independently,' said Lohitaksha, a veteran.

'Rajan, I think what Lohitaksha has suggested makes sense. From now onwards, we break the army into units of a chariot, an elephant, three riders and five foot soldiers. Three units will make an independent *sena mukha*. The *gulma* (army unit) will consist of three sena mukhas. The higher orders of arrangements in *gana*, *vahini*, *pratana*, *camu* and *ani kini* (each three times larger than the previous formation) will be suspended till we reach the battleground.'

'Senapati, I agree with your suggestions. Let each gulma be led by an officer from the hereditary forces. Keep the heavy weapons aside and let all carry lighter ones to keep mobility high. The supplies will follow through safer but longer routes. We have to reach the front fast as the war has begun. The longer we stay in the forest, the more advantage they have.

'Apart from this, keep a small contingent of dispersed riders ready for hot pursuits, tell them not to go too far in the chase but repel attacks effectively.'

The commanders appreciated the need for a quick change in tactics, they consulted amongst themselves and then swiftly dispersed to implement the instructions.

Before the army could fully regroup according to the new plan, the Bhojakas struck again, but this time the army had anticipated it. There was no substantial damage, but the attackers receded with great speed and agility.

Aira Kharavela was getting worried, he had not anticipated this kind of warfare. Although the forest tribes did adopt such ambush tactics now and then, this was like a war before a war, and he had been caught off-guard.

The dispersal of the army into self-contained groups seemed to be working well as there were no weak flanks or tails left to be attacked at will. The units moved quickly under able commanders, advancing in loose coordination with each other. They had reached the end of a large plateau, from where a deep valley could be seen. The Bhojaka forest fort was said to be located on the hill at the other end. The question was, how could the army safely cross the valley?

The Bhojaka riders appeared suddenly from nowhere, like apparitions and inflicted damage before disappearing into the thickets, giving no chance for retaliation. In these conditions, it was seemingly impossible to cross the valley and attack the Bhojaka fort. Something needed to be done urgently.

The army was now stuck at the top of this huge cliff overlooking the valley. The Bhojakas had struck three more times. The army, now being better prepared, retaliated and injured at least two of their riders, but they were successful in escaping capture.

Things had come to an impasse, any further movement was out of question, and staying put there was no option at all. Attacks of wild bears, snake bites and the fear of surprise attacks by highly agile Bhojaka riders had put the army in a quandary. Aira Kharavela called forth his experienced strategists to break this stalemate. They discussed for a long time into the night; the lights in the king's tents went out only at dawn.

Before sunrise, there were two separate attacks by the Bhojakas. There was better anticipation and response now, but the army was getting tired owing to the constant vigil. This state of affairs couldn't continue for long, the mighty Kalinga elephant was not to be grounded by a bunch of wasps stinging and disappearing at will.

It was late afternoon when war horns broke the silence of the jungle with a screeching sound. The calls were a predetermined signal and the commanders rallied their units by yelling their slogans. The army was now rapidly descending the slopes into the valley. The elephants were kept back. Riders and foot soldiers rushed forward, filling the valley with war cries, their shouts echoing through the hills.

Then began the ascent, the slope was steeper on this side, but they met hardly any resistance as the Bhojaka raiders had disappeared. Senapati Bahushalin was leading the assault while the king was commanding from the rear.

Soon the uphill climb ended, a flat plateau was visible. A powerful stream cut through, falling into a beautiful waterfall at the left of the cliff. Right beside the stream was the Bhojaka fort, ensconced in a thicket of trees and climbers. It looked like an abode of demons. The ground around the fort was fairly level, and once the Kalinga army climbed up to the flat terrain, it realized that there were no visible enemy formations protecting the fort. The commanders consulted the senapati, who decided to hold the ground gained. By evening, supplies and the other parts of the army reached; a message was sent to the king to join, as surroundings were rendered safe. There was enough visibility to prevent a surprise attack, no high ground from where the enemy could launch an assault with advantage, no thickets where assailants could come close unnoticed and no visual or other obstructions which could be used as a cover to shoot arrows from.

Aira Kharavela decided to camp there, and the tents were pitched. A system of defences was put in place, guard duties were assigned in shifts and even those off duty were to sleep with arms nearby, in readiness to fight when required.

Watchers were despatched in all directions, each given a predetermined signal to alert the guards at the enemy's approach. The king, having set the defences in place, called for the senapati to determine the assault strategy.

'Rajan, the Bhojakas are playing some strange game. They attacked us before we reached their territory, but now they've gone into hiding. Probably, they didn't expect us to come this far. If they decide to hole in, we will have to deploy siege-craft.'

'Senapati, did you see the fort? There is virtually no access to it. It is well protected by dense forests. I hear that it has several secret passages. How do we attack such a fort?'

'We have to let them make the first move, Rajan. That will pretty much decide the course of this war.'

'How many of our soldiers have been injured today, Senapati Bahushalin? What is the count on the other side?'

'We have very few injuries, Rajan. On the other hand we entirely destroyed a raiding party of theirs. As decided last night, we spread our scouts deep into the enemy territory. In the morning, when we repelled a sudden attack, two of their soldiers were badly injured, but they escaped. We later found one of them badly injured and dying alone in the forest. We brought him to the camp and gave him medication. He later told us that the Bhojaka riders came out of secret passages from the fort and split into groups to attack us. Our scouts then surveyed the narrow mountain trails and realized that they were emerging into the valley from a very narrow pass. We sent our foot soldiers disguised as commoners, to lay ambush on this path. When the Bhojakas returned after their afternoon raids, they were in for a rude shock—our men had cut down trees and blocked their path completely. They didn't know what to do, and before they could respond, out archers brought them down one by one. The few survivors ran off into the valley, while none of ours was injured. Once the raiding party was destroyed, they gave the signal for us to march. We quickly surged ahead behind the retreating enemy.'

'That's good. How do you evaluate their options now?'

'Rajan, they don't seem to have the strength or a design for a full-frontal combat. They know that we are better equipped and much larger in size. They will either hide in the fort to tire us out and then mount a surprise attack or buy time to consolidate their resources, team with allies and then attack.'

'Get an estimate of their numbers inside the fort. I also want an idea of their resources, weapons and allies. Do this quickly. Till then ask everyone to be vigilant, there can be an attack any time.'

News had come from Pratishthanpura, the Andhras were secretly augmenting their defences. Weapons were being readied, perhaps as a precautionary measure against the Kalinga elephant romping in the vicinity. The Rathikas on the other hand, had been rallying all their minor allies and local chiefs to counter Rudravarman's contingent, which was hovering ominously at some distance, threatening attack. Fortunately for Kharavela, the Rathikas, being deadlocked by

Rudra, would not rush to help their beleaguered neighbours. The other neighbours of the Bhojakas were the Asmakas, who were not kindly disposed to them, and were not likely to join the fray. A punishing defeat in the recent war with Kalinga was also a prime consideration in the Asmakas' eyes.

The Bhojaka fort was a medium-sized fort, less than a krosha in dimensions on both sides. It had abundant supply of water through the perennial mountain stream which fell into the gorge, making a spectacular waterfall on the side of the plateau. There was no regular moat, but bodies of water fed the stream around the outer walls. There were at least three sets of walls, one enclosing the other, each with a gate and separate defences. Almost entirely made of the local black rock, the fort looked formidable and forbidding at the same time.

Anticipating the attack, the Bhojakas had relocated their resources and people. Thus, the janapadas around the fort had been vacated and the population had been moved to the interiors, while hardened fighters waited inside the fort without their families. Food, water, weaponry and other resources for months of siege were in place. The Bhojakas seemed to have decided to wait and tire out the Kalingas. It was evident that sustaining a very prolonged siege was out of question for the Kalinga army as their supplies were limited and came from afar, the terrain too was unfamiliar to them, putting them in a situation of great disadvantage.

The morning began with a strong cold wind blowing from the direction of the fort to the Kalinga camp. As the sentry duties changed, a sudden volley of arrows came from the fort, taking advantage of the wind. These arrows were surprisingly large, almost as big as spears. They went straight through the tough tent cloths, earthen pots and wooden objects. A soldier was hit in the head and his skull burst open, spattering his brains out. Another one was pinned down at the hip with the spear-like arrow completely piercing through him; they both died instantaneously.

After an initial volley of twenty or twenty-five arrows, the attack stopped. As the Kalingas regained their senses, another barrage of massive arrows started. This time, the commanders alerted the army to take suitable cover and horns were sounded for alert. The arrows could be spotted from a distance, which gave the Kalingas enough time to get out of their path.

Kalinga soldiers hid behind trees and in trenches away from the range of the arrows. The volley stopped again and a band of Bhojaka riders was seen emerging from the woods and charging in a full-frontal assault. As they neared the Kalinga camp, the horses suddenly got out of control, trying to turn back. The Kalinga strategists had planted sharp bamboo stakes in the ground, which the Bhojaka riders hadn't anticipated. Their horses saw the spikes and revolted, tipping some riders off balance. Kalinga archers were ready and waiting and they shot a torrent of arrows which hit the animals and riders alike. The party quickly decided to retreat in the face of a strong counterattack, leaving behind their dead and wounded. Kalinga soldiers chased them back on foot, but they managed to vanish into the forests quickly. The wounded Bhojakas were writhing in pain and bleeding heavily. Many of their horses had been badly injured and some had succumbed to the wounds.

Aira Kharavela quickly sent for water and medical aid for the wounded. After stabilization, the wounded were brought to the camp for treatment, while the animals were killed on the spot. The first attempt by the enemy had failed miserably. The wounded prisoners included a man named Bhoopat, who had a severe arrow injury in his ribs. He was treated by the vaidyas and was now stable and able to speak. Senapati Bahushalin, while visiting his own wounded, also met this man. An interpreter who could speak the local language was with the senapati. Bhoopat was grateful for his life being saved.

As the senapati was leaving the tent, he turned back and addressed the wounded man, 'Tell him that I really appreciate the skill with which his men ride.' Bhoopat smiled when he was told what the senapati had said. Bahushalin then asked the vaidyas to pay special attention to Bhoopat. The senapati came back to the infirmary in the evening. He came to Bhoopat's bed and then addressed the man through the interpreter, 'I have never seen arrows as large as spears, your archers must be magicians or gods to shoot so far.'

Bhoopat became animated. He tried to get up, but the pain was too much for him. He said, 'We have these large *yantra*s (machines), five in number. They are mounted on a mobile platform. We can string very large arrows, like javelins on to them. They can propel arrows up to 100 dhanus, that is one-tenth of a krosha.' Suddenly he realized that he had been tricked into revealing important tactical information. He fell silent and hid his head under the blanket. The senapati casually moved on, inquiring of the health of other wounded.

Everything was not going well at Tosali. Vajramitra was getting increasingly exasperated with Nakiya and his style of functioning. Whatever he ordered in the capacity of a caretaker king was rejected by the palace bureaucracy under Mahamatya

Nakiya. He had been informed that the contingent of hereditary troops under Rudra, which he had contributed to from his own men, had been poisoned and barely managed to survive. He wanted to seek an explanation from the mahamatya and summoned him. When a fuming Vajramitra reached the conference hall, he found that Maitreyi and Vikarna were already there along with Mahamatya Nakiya. As he barged in, trembling with anger, his rage was further fuelled by the fact that none of them got up to wish or salute him.

'What nonsense is this, mahamatya? Don't you know I am the ruling monarch here, in the absence of the king?'

'Vajramitra, sit down. There is no use throwing tantrums,' Nakiya said calmly.

Vajramitra was dumbstruck, he had not expected such a cold response. He took his seat, but sat in a very casual and disrespectful manner and looked at Maitreyi and Vikarna with burning eyes, 'You parrot and mynah, do you do something other than courting each other?'

Vikarna turned red and got up from his seat. 'What has gotten into you, Arya Vajramitra? Why are you being so insufferable?'

'Insufferable? My soldiers are dying out there due to the stupidity of that fool Rudravarman. I was supposed to lead that contingent, but at the last moment that incompetent man was sent, and he not only gets my loyal soldiers killed without a war, but also gets into a conflict with the peaceful prince of Subarnagiri.'

Maitreyi intervened, 'Arya Vajramitra, as far as I understand, Rudravarman has exhibited great valour and maturity in dealing with the crisis. He has successfully saved his army from the sabotage of the tribes of Subarnagiri. Not only that now he is critically poised to counterbalance the Rathikas and Andhras at the outskirts of the dreaded Mahakantar region.'

'Oh Vikarna, look now, your mynah is singing praises of that idiot. Why don't you keep silent, Maitreyi, don't interfere in things you have no idea about.'

'Arya Vajramitra, control your tongue, or I shall forget our years of friendship,' said Vikarna.

Nakiya got up and asked everyone to control their tempers. It was timely as Rajguru Uddalaka was entering the room. He was dressed in white and his bearing conveyed grace and dignity. Everybody other than Vajramitra got up to seek blessings of the royal sage. 'Vajramitra! Don't forget that you are not the king! Get up and seek the blessings of the rajguru,' shouted Nakiya in anger.

'Keep quiet you old fool, you people have messed up this kingdom. You should be taught a lesson!' Saying this he removed his right shoe and was about to throw it at Nakiya.

Before he could blink an eyelid, a sharp knife had pinned the shoe in his hand to the wooden pillar behind him—it was thrown by Maitreyi. She had sprung like a tigress with a drawn sword in her hand, ready to kill.

'Stop Maitreyi,' said Uddalaka. 'I command you to retreat.'

With burning eyes, Maitreyi retreated, breathing heavily. She scornfully sheathed the sword. Her beautiful face had transformed into the face of Devi Nirrti, the goddess of death! She looked menacing in her black attire. Composing herself, she spat on the floor with disgust.

Vikarna was astounded, but Nakiya had kept his cool and said in a firm voice, 'Arya Vajramitra, it would be appropriate if you respectfully retire for the day today. We will call for you if we require your assistance. But let me caution you as a friend, do not try anything adventurous, your stars may not favour you all the time.'

Insulted and discredited, Vajramitra got up from his seat and left. He took out the knife embedded in the shoe to free it from the wooden pillar and wore it as it was. As he walked away, he removed his headdress. His hair were entangled in it, and he struggled with it in disgust. His walk was laboured but determined.

Uddalaka told the others that he did not have a good feeling about the incident. He asked them to be extremely careful henceforth.

Vikarna asked Maitreyi to join him in his carriage while returning. 'What got into you? Why did you throw a knife at him? Have you gone mad?'

'Vikarna, I expected you to react but you didn't! You lost all respect in my eyes today!'

'What do you mean, Maitreyi? He is ruling in place of the king!'

'So he is allowed to commit any crime? How could he have insulted the rajguru, and how did you and Mahamatya Nakiya tolerate it! I am so ashamed of you all. Tell me one thing, Vikarna, and don't lie. Had he dared to insult me, how would have you reacted?'

Vikarna kept silent. Maitreyi's eyes were red with anger. She asked the charioteer to stop. Vikarna feebly tried to hold her hand but she brushed him off and got down from the chariot in revulsion.

✦✦✦

The siege had continued for a week now, with intermittent attacks of those deadly spear-like arrows. The Kalingas had formed a good idea of the attack patterns by now, and consequently their casualties were at a minimum. It had rained a little in the morning, making the ground slushy as the black soil stuck to everything. A sentry had blown the alarm, informing the soldiers that there was some movement in the valley. There were different types of signals of the shrill sringa instrument— short bursts to alert troops of enemy movement and long, high-pitched wails indicating the need to take shelter from a torrent of arrows in the air.

Riders mounted and quickly moved towards the east where the movement had been spotted. Seeing sizeable enemy formations, they thought it better to call the archers for support. Then, the combined team of archers and riders surged forward to attack the enemy.

As they went near it, they realized that it was not a body of troops but a supply train, which had gotten stuck in the sticky black soil due to the sudden rains. The soldiers accompanying it for security had run away seeing the Kalinga riders charge at them in large numbers. It was a lucky catch—livestock along with other foodstuff were being transported to the Bhojaka fort. These had been collected from the janapadas. It was fifteen days' worth of ration and meat. The Kalingas spared the lives of the carriers and confiscated the supplies for their own use. They also drove the oxen and cattle back to their own camp.

The senapati was bouncing with joy despite his age, and went to the king to inform him about the sudden windfall. 'Rajan, the sudden rain has done us good. The Bhojaka supply trains got stuck in the soil—we just had to go and retrieve them! Nobody even offered resistance. It seems they also miscalculated the time as it was morning and the supplies could not reach the fort.'

'How many men have been captured, senapati?' the king asked.

'Fifteen, Rajan. At least half of them are seasoned soldiers, three are guides and the rest are attendants. We left the merchants and drivers of the carts unharmed.'

'Good. We are fighting a dharmayuddha, and we should not harm the innocent in any case. However, you should try and gain information from the combatants about the secret routes to the fort, the strength of the enemy and their plans.'

'Rajan, rather than the soldiers, the guides will give us more valuable information. First, we will talk to them and ask for their cooperation. If it does not work, we will offer them a sufficient price for the information, and if they still don't agree, force will have to be used.'

'Senapati, use *sama-dama-danda-bheda* (convincing, bribery, punishment and dissension) to gain the information as quickly as possible. I am not too sure of the Andhras and the Shungas. If we are stuck here for too long, one of them will exploit the situation to his own advantage.'

'Rajan, I will try to break them by all means. This may be a serious blow to the Bhojakas, the apprehension of their supplies.'

'The constellations are indicating positive signs for us, Senapati Bahushalin. Let's not lose the advantage. We need to act fast and embrace victory.'

'Victory will be ours, Rajan!' the senapati said reverently and left.

It had been three days since the supply train had been apprehended. The senior commanders had come up with a final assault plan. The guides had provided ample information to plan for a final onslaught. Two days of preparatory time was given to all the commanders. They had to complete all the stages of the plan before the final and decisive strike. Countermeasures for enemy tactics had also been put in place.

Step one began with reaching a point where the source rivulet of the mountain stream encircling the Bhojaka fort split into two, before one of the larger branches went to the fort and the other went off in a different direction.

Miners were called with digging equipment, and they began to cut and transport large rocks from the surrounding hills and fill them into the stream going towards the fort. As each new rock was added, the flow of water decreased in this stream and increased in the other one. In some time, there was a veritable dam of sorts, from which very little water trickled into the stream going towards the fort. The other branch now was flooding with water. Its flow tripled and water rushed through it with great fury.

Step two was to spread a layer of highly inflammable oil on the stream and the areas surrounding the fort. This was done too, in the night; on the stagnant flow, oil was discharged slowly so as to spread it evenly and afar.

In step three, large arrow-throwing yantras were built from local resources, with the help of artisans and captured soldiers.

Aira Kharavela, having made these arrangements, sent his messenger Bhargav to deliver the final ultimatum for surrender in the afternoon. Bhargav was a committed and level-headed spy. He could get vital information of tactical advantage on the pretext of delivering the message. The mood of the enemy, it's readiness to fight, and even kind of weapons and provisions could be known in some measure by the messenger in his interactions with the enemy officials. Kharavela waited eagerly for the return of his messenger.

A chill dark evening had settled on the camp when the disturbing sounds of angry shouts and shrill cries tore through the silence.

'Rajan! Look what they have done!' Senapati Bahushalin said, as he entered the tent. He was livid. Bhargav, who was severely injured, was brought into the king's tent as well.

'Bhargav! What happened to him, who has done this? Is he alive? Answer me immediately!'

'Rajan, the Bhojakas tortured him till the evening, and sent his body back assuming he was dead. The vaidyaraj is attending to him, but he does not have much hope of his survival.'

'He cannot die! Senapati, vaidyaraj, are you listening? He will not die! Light up the stream! No more waiting now, we will go for the assault!'

'Rajan, it may be a trap. They are inciting us to attack them. Should we fall prey to their tactics?'

'I command you, senapati, the attack should begin in half a prahar from now.'

A streak of fire ran from the fort stream, gaining momentum and magnitude as it rushed forward like a thousand snakes intertwining into each other. Soon, the fire assumed massive proportions and the jungle near the fort walls, with all its thorn bushes, woody climbers and densely branched trees, was up in flames. The sky was lit a bright orange, and an indiscriminate volley of arrows were fired from the fort. Those large, spear like arrows, fell like rain from the sky. The Kalinga army had anticipated it and hence decided to attack from the rear. The senapati was leading the section of riders who had taken a detour and were circling around the fort from a distance. The forest fire provided the right kind of distraction to make this movement. They moved swiftly, and unnoticed by the enemy, they positioned themselves to the rear side of the fort. As they were away from the line of fire of the arrows, no one was injured. They had been instructed to await further orders from the king.

The jungle burnt like oblations in a ritual fire and was soon reduced to ashes. One could see the smouldering stumps and scattered logs emitting smoke until morning. The fort was clearly visible now. Shorn of its cover and devoid of the water body around it, it looked abandoned. The shower of arrows was intermittent now—the Bhojakas were probably conserving their arsenal for later battles.

The first light of the sun shone brightly on Kharavela's face. He now asked for the yantras to be set up. These monstrous machines were prepared in large numbers. Arrows, larger than those of the Bhojakas', were mounted on them. At the sound of the war horn, all yantras simultaneously fired the arrows inside the fort.

Hundreds of arrows converged at the fort, hitting the people inside like lightning bolts. The Bhojakas were absolutely unaware of this tactical catastrophe; their own weapon had been successfully copied by the Kalingas, and they had even improvized it! With the forests burnt down and the stream almost dry, the fort was badly exposed. The secret pathways were of no use as there was no cover of vegetation. The Kalingas could come close and strike, not only that, they were moving their heavily armoured elephants to breach the fort defences. Sentries and watchers who attempted to take a look from the ramparts were instantly shot down by skilled Kalinga archers who had moved close to the fort walls now. The Kalinga army was closing in on the fort from all directions, it seemed like a flood of soldiers, chariots and riders. They moved with a menacing speed and the Bhojakas were stuck inside their own fort like rats in a hole. The Kalinga army would shoot the arrows and then move under cover; when the Bhojakas tried to retaliate, they would stop and hide behind the shields. The Kalingas were now closing in for the kill.

Slowly, Bhojaka resources were depleted. They had exhausted them in the last few days, and new supplies hadn't arrived. The Rathikas, despite their promise, had not been able to arrive for help.

Till mid-afternoon, the balance tilted heavily in favour of the Kalingas, who were poised for a victory. The volley of arrows from the fort was intermittent now, but skilled Bhojaka archers were trying to shoot riders and important officers from the ramparts. It was about late afternoon when the shooting from the fort finally stopped. The Kalinga army kept on moving ahead cautiously. Suddenly, warning alarms were heard from all sides—enemy riders unexpectedly emerged from the woods behind the Kalinga army and charged straight at them. They made deafening noises as they rode straight towards the Kalinga army.

The senapati instantly fell back to inform King Kharavela about the sudden manoeuvre. Aira Kharavela asked the senapati to quickly move to the rear and assume the *apratihata* formation.

Senapati Bahushalin moved like the wind. He sounded the signals. As the Bhojaka riders charged and attacked, the foot soldiers started retreating, while the elephants, followed by the chariots and riders, inched out towards the point of skirmish.

The foot soldiers had successfully resisted the advance of the Bhojakas, and now the armoured elephants had arrived. This was an excellent tactical move by Kharavela, who used the peculiar battle formation that was a subtype of a mandala configuration. In this formation, the elephants formed an outer wall, behind which were the chariots and riders, who could attack at will from within the mobile fortress formed by the elephants and quickly retreat to safety.

At the front, Kharavela shaped the army into an *ardhachandrika* (half-moon) formation and continued moving towards the fort. The rear was now safe as the elephants had stymied the advance of the Bhojaka riders. Kharavela commanded the foot soldiers from his favourite elephant, Mahagiri. He had kept an array of the best archers and a team of his loyal guard with him.

The fort gates were in sight now. Kharavela was contemplating as to how he would breach them when the large doors opened and a horde of Bhojaka riders, footmen and archers emerged. Kharavela commanded his foot soldiers to stop and take cover behind their shields. He then asked the archers to swing into action. The Kalinga archers were carrying the famous Indian bows that were as tall as men. They fixed the base of the bows on the soil with their toes and strung the deadly arrows. As the sringa blew, a coordinated swarm of arrows flew from the Kalingas' side. In a few moments, the Bhojaka horde got hit hard. Riders fell off the beasts and foot soldiers were knocked down like hare. A brief pause followed while the fort gates behind were being closed. Then the surviving enemy soldiers gathered together and started to charge again. The sringa signalled death once more. The archers were already in position, with arrows strung and bows firmly planted in the ground. A storm of arrows hit the charging enemy. This time barely anyone survived as they were straight in the line of fire.

Kharavela now signalled his men to advance, and they soon closed in on the Bhojaka contingent and finished off the remaining fighters. The wounded were left unharmed. They then crossed the bodies of the slain Bhojakas and reached the gates of the fort. Kharavela called for two of his best elephants trained in breaching doors. The two animals moved in tandem, they first approached the gates and then suddenly retreated. The mahouts sensed that there were special arrangements at the gates for final protection. As they moved back, Bhojaka soldiers hidden at the top of the gates poured burning hot oil, which narrowly missed the elephants and the mahouts.

The elephants stepped back, turned to their sides and approached the gates again at a slanted angle. They butted fiercely against the huge wooden doors but nothing happened. They retreated and started again in unison, butting hard against the massive wooden doors, which rattled. Meanwhile, foot soldiers started scaling the outer walls from the sides, there was hardly any resistance as most of the Bhojaka soldiers had been killed in their last effort to charge at the Kalingas.

The gates started creaking. The iron hinges were making sharp sounds with each blow. The elephants were made to change the mode of breach now, they both stood together and pushed at the obstacle. The gates fell with a loud sound.

Foot soldiers waited for a moment and then rushed inside shouting war cries of victory. King Kharavela waited outside cautiously. Soon, news came from inside that this was only the first gate. There were multiple walls inside, enclosing specific areas within the fort, in a concentric fashion. The king already had some inkling of this, hence he had waited as his soldiers had rushed in.

The Bhojaka riders at the rear had been surmounted. They couldn't breach the mobile bastion of the elephants and were in turn vulnerable to the Kalinga archers and riders . They were exhausted and wounded. When they heard of the breach of the fort gates, they lost the will to fight and indicated surrender.

The senapati handled the surrender like a seasoned warrior. The riders were allowed to dismount, then to remove their armour. Finally, they were asked to deposit their weapons. Everyone was instructed not to harm the soldiers who had surrendered. The horses were taken away to the camp first, followed by the Bhojaka soldiers, walking with their heads down in shame and grief. They smelled of blood, sweat and dust, and barely said anything. They were allowed to help their wounded, and those needing immediate attention were tended to by the accompanying Kalinga vaidyas.

Kharavela had decided not to go further inside. Astute warrior that he was, he knew that the Bhojakas were left with virtually no options. The water supply to the fort had been cut off, and a large part of the army, especially the cavalry, had been defeated and captured. He called the senapati to discuss.

'Rajan, it may take days before we breach all the walls and reach the innermost part of the Bhojaka fort. In the meantime, we would be vulnerable to any surprise attack by the enemy or their allies.'

'Senapati, what will they sustain on? We have seized their supplies and cut off access to any external help. Their best riders are our prisoners, what can they do now?'

'Rajan, these people are very tenacious fighters. When Lord Krishna had abducted Rukmini, her brother Rukmi refused to return home and went on to establish a new city. They are proud and warlike. We should give them a reasonable exit route. If we delay further, Tosali would be unsafe, and our army too is tired and longing to return. I submit that we may send a messenger and ask for a surrender on honourable terms.'

'Senapati, don't you remember what they did to my beloved messenger Bhargav! How can we send another messenger to these wretched people?'

Aira Kharavela had played all the elements of siege warfare well—he had begun with a blockade, followed it with a breach and used scaling ladders too for the escalade. Only two options were left with him to end the siege and conquer the enemy: mining and trickery. He was considering all possible means as he was in no mood for conciliation now.

Senapati Bhaushalin was troubled. The other commanders who had been called for the consultation had maintained silence and the senapati was upset about this. He came out looking disturbed and left for his tent without saying a word to the others.

The king returned to the camp. It was already night, the chill in the air was severe, and soldiers were seen lighting bonfires and celebrating the victory of the day's battle.

Meanwhile, scouts had returned with extremely disturbing news for Rudravarman. Andhra soldiers had been surreptitiously moving towards the Bhojaka territory under the guise of cattle herders and nomads. They were effectively poised to encircle the Kalinga army on return. It was obvious that they did not seek direct confrontation but were ready to take advantage of any weaknesses or misstep by the Kalingas. The place where Rudra had held back the Rathikas was a flat valley which separated the Andhra territory from the Rathika areas. They had not dared to attack or come out of their forts to counter the Kalinga forces under Rudra.

Kinshuk had come with bad news, Devabrata and Bhadrabahu were also worried. The siege at the Bhojaka fort was going to continue for a while. Rudra thought this was a bad idea, as holding the Rathikas and Andhras back for a very long time would be impossible. He decided to convey his predicament to the king through a letter. Meanwhile, he had to come up with a counter tactic to prevent the encirclement by the Andhras.

Aira Kharavela received Rudra's letter but decided not to disclose its contents to anyone. Instead, he called upon the senapati and his commanders for consultation. 'I have decided to go for the final assault tomorrow morning. We have in our possession complete details about their secret pathways from the captured soldiers.'

'Rajan, I have some news that the Andhras have started to mobilize their forces. Whatever we do, we have to do in a day or two.'

'Senapati, I fully endorse your views. So this is what we do tomorrow. We send in our soldiers through their secret pathways and finish this war.'

'Rajan, pardon my impudence, but such a move would be expected by the enemy. They would be prepared for it.'

'Yes, senapati, I too anticipate that. That is why we send in the captured soldiers first.'

'Brilliant move, Rajan, it is indeed a gem of a strategy.'

'Now you all get to work, keep the details a secret from anyone outside.'

'As you command,' they all said and dispersed.

The morning broke with no assault from either side, they waited and watched. The Bhojakas were up for a major surprise when they found their own soldiers coming in from the secret pathways. They were in a fix, neither could they attack them, nor could they defend, as behind the human wall of the Bhojaka captives were the Kalinga soldiers.

The trick had worked, and by afternoon, the Bhojakas surrendered. They had to surrender their chattaris and their crowns as a sign of defeat. The same would apply to the Rathikas, who had also laid down their arms. They were to surrender their treasury to the victor and repair the Vidyadharadiwas Temple with their own funds. Their territories, army, lands, women and forts were to be left unmolested. The senapati was commanded to prepare for the return journey. Rudra was also notified.

This was the first major victory in which the king had himself commanded the army. After this war, Kharavela's name and fame spread through all neighbouring kingdoms and beyond.

Chapter 21

Friends and Enemies

A wave of celebration swept through Kalinga, and the festivities continued for weeks after the return of the victorious army. The faith of the Kalinga people in their king and his prowess was at a new high. From being a vanquished nation, they were rising to determine the future of the land. Soldiers returning from the war talked endlessly about the valour, ingenuity and brilliance displayed by the king in the war. The crowns and umbrellas of the Rathika–Bhojakas, as well as the seized gems, pearls, gold and silver were was put up for public display, and the Atavikas in the army walked with a pride in their step.

Everyone who had participated in the war was handsomely rewarded. But there was something else going on in Rudra's life. A letter had arrived for him. The handwriting was familiar, and Rudra's heart fluttered at the sight of it.

It read:

Beloved Master Simhadhwaja, I know what you must be thinking now, that what a treacherous person I must have been to betray you! I have no face to show, I am a man without honour. I have been unfaithful to a person who is like pure gold. Sure enough, arya, God has punished me for my sins. Fetid sores have broken all over my skin, and I have been banished out of human society due to my ailment. Dhavala had promised me that after you were arrested, he would get me pardon from the King Satkarni and give me a hoard of gemstones and gold-silver ornaments. Not only did he renege on his promise but when the plan to assault King Satkarni was abandoned, he also sent men to arrest me! I escaped from Pratishthanpura and wandered from place to place like a nomad. Then I was informed that you had been killed on that very day. I was so struck with grief and repentance that my whole body swelled. It itched badly all over, and the more I scratched, the more it swelled. By the third day, a yellowish-green pus which was very putrid started to ooze out from my raw skin. The smell was so rancid that even dogs would run away from me. Nobody gave me shelter, and I have been wandering ever since.

Most of my skin has fallen off now. My face is disfigured and I am dying. My last wish is to meet you and ask for your forgiveness. It has given me immense relief to know that you are alive. You cannot imagine the extent of my happiness when one of the captured commanders from the Rathika–Bhojaka war, after he was released, told me that you're alive and serving under the Kalingas. I want to die peacefully. I don't know whether God will forgive me for my sins, but I want to meet you and seek your forgiveness personally. Please don't refuse my last wish, and please don't take pity on my state when you meet me. I deserve this living hell, and only asking for pardon at your feet will set me free.

I know you're compassionate and kind-hearted, please don't turn down my request. I am lying hidden at the ruins of the abandoned courthouse of the Magadhans near the smaller water tank in the centre of the city. I cannot come out on the street as people pelt stones at me thinking that I am some pisacha. So I lie covered in bandages and secretly come out in the night to scavenge for food. I do not wish to live more. Come tonight and liberate me from this wretched existence.

Your unworthy servant,
Pavaka

Rudra stared into the dark after reading this letter. A strange brew of emotions rushed through his mind—anger, bitterness, vengeance and disbelief. As his breath settled gradually, he started feeling bad for poor Pavaka, who had been afflicted with such a malady and was dying. He tried to imagine his face as it must look now but what came to his mind was the fresh face of an energetic and enthusiastic man, who never said no to any task. Rudra remembered how Pavaka would walk with him like a shadow in Pratishthanpura when he was Simhadhwaja. He had never in his dreams imagined that he would be betrayed by his trusted Pavaka!

'For old times' sake,' he muttered to himself, 'I have to go and see the dying man.'

It was a full moon night. The winter was particularly harsh and a thick fog had settled over the city, obscuring the moonlight. Lights from the oil lamps in the street flickered with a halo around them. The streets were still littered with dry flower petals and leaves from the day's celebrations. As Rudra walked, shrouded in a thick blanket, some street dogs reluctantly barked at him and went back to sleep. Unfazed by them, he kept walking.

The Magadhan courthouse was a huge building, gone into disuse after the Mahameghavahanas took charge. The new dynasty had a deep abhorrence of any Magadhan signs and symbols. It was understandable as they had risen by shaking off the yoke of the conquerors. They were harbingers of a resurgent Kalinga nation, how could they use the buildings of their conqueror–oppressors. Perhaps, the Mahameghavahanas wanted everyone to witness how the symbols of their defeat and subjugation were disintegrating, or perhaps they desired to remind everyone about the grim past. Whatever their motives, they had neither destroyed, nor continued using the buildings. Instead, they let them rot and crumble. The old courthouse, palace and other buildings now stood as ruins, much like the edifice of the Magadhan Empire, which was a pale shade of its former glory under the Mauryas. The multi-storey courthouse must have been a magnificent building, but now its bright colours had faded and the exterior walls were covered with green moss and creepers. The surrounding vacant land was covered with bushes and undergrowth, making the building inaccessible. The people of the city detested these structures, hence nobody entered them ever. There were many stories about evil spirits residing there. There were anecdotes about people who dared to enter, but never returned.

Rudra had now reached the entrance of the grand, dilapidated structure. It had the eerie appearance of a haunted place. It was situated next to an artificial lake which had now turned to a marsh. He struggled through the bushes as his blanket got caught in the thorns of the shrubbery. He struggled to free it, then decided to dispense with the blanket. As he left the blanket, a very cold draft hit him and a shiver ran down to his bones. He rushed inside, the large wooden door was half open and had been stuck in that condition for years now.

It was pitch-dark, damp and cold inside. For a brief moment, he felt as if there were many people there. He even thought of the evil spirits lurking around. He imagined sounds, echoing through the dark, whispers and murmurs. He brushed these thoughts aside and moved ahead. The floor was muddy but the wood below creaked as he walked.

His eyes were getting used to the dark now, as he searched for Pavaka. He felt a whiff of a very putrid smell in the clammy air. Pavaka must be somewhere near, but why wasn't he speaking? Rudra felt that something was amiss. As he moved ahead, he saw that a moonbeam from a hole in the wall was lighting the floor. The white beam of light across the room seemed ghostly. On taking the next step, he was startled to see a human being lying supine on the floor, covered in a white shroud, as if it were a corpse. Rudra's heart skipped a beat as he walked towards it.

The stench grew stronger as he approached the body. He guessed that Pavaka was sleeping. He went near him and said, 'Pavaka, get up—I am Simhadhwaja.'

'You have finally come, Simhadhwaja?' The voice was guttural and strange. The smell was unbearable, and Rudra tried to hold his breath to prevent himself from vomiting. His mind was reeling with fear and repugnance.

'Yes, Pavaka, I am here.'

As he said this, the figure lying down sat up. When Rudra saw the face in the moonlight, he shrieked in revulsion. It was the face of a man who had no features. The nose, lips and ears were all absent. He looked like a ghost.

'Do you recognize me, Simhadhwaja?'

'You are not Pavaka! Who are you? Tell me or I will cut off your head right now!'

'Patience, Simhadhwaja, patience. How many times have I told you not to be so rash. You don't seem to heed good advice.'

'Who are you? Tell me right now!' Rudra screamed.

'Ah I love your impatience, Simhadhwaja. How can you forget me, we met only some days back.'

'Dark prince!' Rudra shrieked. The ghost of the demon had returned to haunt him. 'You cannot be real, so I have nothing to fear. You are a dead man dark prince.'

'We have a lot of time to discuss this,' the demon said, in a patronizing tone. 'Why don't we talk about how you have been betraying everyone?'

'You talking of betrayal is like the Asur reciting the Vedas, *narpishach*! How do you speak of morality!'

'I love the way you lie, Simhadhwaja. First you betray Satkarni, then you escape to Kalinga, where you maintain a false identity to infiltrate into the royal court. You're a liar and traitor—just like your father Indravarman!'

'You wretch!' Rudra lost his temper, and lunged at the throat of the ghostly figure. The villain didn't move. He just whipped out a sharp knife that shone like a firefly in the moonbeam. Before Rudra could realize, he had slashed him, making a gash on his face from below his earlobe to his left eyebrow.

Rudra cried out in pain, he had not anticipated the wretch to attack him physically, as he looked so weak and frail. His eye had barely survived the attack, spurts of blood oozed from the open wound and he had fallen flat on the floor. He realized that the enemy was going for the kill, and he lay still. Before the man could stab his chest, Rudra kicked him in the groin. The dark prince fell backwards, and as he fell, Rudra took out his dagger and jumped to pin him down. He saw him writhing in pain and climbed over him, firmly pinning him down like a wrestler. The man's knife had been thrown away and he was unarmed now. A sudden rage was overcoming Rudra and he wanted to cut his head off. He was torn between an urge to kill him and the restraint against attacking an unarmed adversary.

Suddenly, he felt a cold, sharp object against his neck and realized it was a sword. He froze, realizing there was someone else there. He dropped his dagger and slowly got up. The man with the sword now held his left hand at the back and dragged him away from the dark prince. The injured man cowered on the floor. Rudra was steady now, waiting for the next move of his captor.

'Do you have any other weapon on you?' a tough voice asked.

'No,' Rudra lied. It was a known voice, and it suddenly occurred to Rudra—it was Vikarna, the police chief.

'Vikarna,' he said, 'what are you doing here with this traitor?'

'*You* are a traitor, Rudravarman, trying to eat out our kingdom from within like a white ant. Your dirty game ends now!'

'You are mistaken, nayaka. He is the traitor. I have never, not even in my dreams, done anything against my motherland.'

'The dark dungeons will extract the truth out of your intestines, traitor. I was apprehensive of you from day one, but you were successful in winning the trust of Rajan and the mahamatya, so I kept quiet.'

'Nayaka, release me now. I can prove my innocence, just give me a chance. Arrest this traitor immediately before he can do any more damage to the kingdom. I plead with you, please don't come under his evil influence.'

'Be quiet, imposter. We have heard the communication between you and him. Now surrender or get killed.'

'I will not surrender to falsehood like this nayaka!' Rudra suddenly bent down and flipped Vikarna over his shoulders. The nayaka was not prepared for the sudden assault and he landed straight on his face. His sword fell and Rudra grabbed it in a quick move. The nayaka lay unconscious, and Rudra now rushed towards the dark prince who was trying to get up, his knife in his hands.

Rudra's face was drenched in blood and his uttariya was soaking wet. He had been losing blood and his vision was getting blurred. The scrawny figure of the dark prince rushed at Rudra again, not knowing that he held Vikarna's sword. In one stroke, Rudra swung the sword and cut off his left hand from the elbow. It fell down on the floor, still grasping the knife. The dark prince bellowed in pain, and retreated towards the door but Rudra pounced upon him.

Now, for once, he had the dark prince within full striking distance. He raised his sword for the kill, but before he could strike at him, sparks flew as his sword struck against the sword of an assailant.

Grave miscalculation, he thought. There must be many more of them hidden around. It was now in his best interest to escape. He quickly parried with the assailant who struck at him with vigour. He kept on moving towards the door as he clashed with this new entity. This one moved quite swiftly and struck with great ease, evidently a skilled fighter. Rudra understood that there was no point in engaging with this man as he was already getting weak. He ducked again, fighting defensively now to secure the exit route. He suddenly turned amid the fierce sword fight and rushed to the door and, in four jumps, he was out of the door.

The thick fog outside engulfed him as he ran over the thorny bushes towards the road. When he reached the road he looked back to see his adversary emerge from the fog like an apparition. Before the man could attack him, Rudra played a classic move. He swiftly sat down and did a leg tackle. The man stumbled and tottered. Before he could regain his balance, Rudra struck at his sword and disarmed him. Now he held the point of the sword at the throat of the combatant, and asked, 'Who are you, who has sent you here?'

'I am Maitreyi, Rudra,' the voice said.

Aghast, Rudra came near her to look at her face. Yes, it was her indeed. He threw away the sword and asked in a grieving voice, 'Maitreyi, what are you doing here, with these people?'

'Answers you have to give, arya, not me.' Saying so, she suddenly picked up the sword Rudra had dropped and held it at his chest.

'You don't need to do that, Maitreyi. I will come with you.' His voice sank as blood mixed with tears on his face and caused an intense burning sensation. The cold felt like jabs of needles all over his body and he fell unconscious.

When he regained consciousness, the first thing Rudra felt was immense pain. His whole face was swollen and the gash hurt immensely. He tried to move his hands in an attempt to feel his face in the darkness but realized that he had been chained.

His hands were manacled into thick cuffs and his feet were bound in iron shackles. The metal clanked as he attempted to move. He was totally nude, bound in iron chains and held captive in the cold dark dungeon. The stone floor was as cold as ice and Rudra could feel that his skin was going numb where it touched the floor.

Hours passed like this. There was no sign of another human being, nor any guards or other officials. He understood that this was a very secure location, away from the prison where other offenders were kept. He was cold, hungry, alone and weak, his breath was heavy and his eyes strained due to staring in the dark.

After many hours, he finally heard some sound at a distance, as if someone was opening the locks of the cell. Then he heard footsteps. As there was some light in the room, he squinted to see who had arrived. His heart simultaneously jumped with delight and sank in despair to see Maitreyi walking towards him. He hadn't been given food and a strong headache prevented him from opening his eyes fully. He saw Maitreyi sitting beside him and then felt her running her fingers through his hair.

Excruciating pain brought him back to senses. His hair was being pulled violently. His eyes opened wide to see Vikarna dragging him by the hair. He shrieked in pain. 'Maitreyi, where are you?' he cried out.

There was no limit to Vikarna's anger now. He slammed Rudra's head on the floor. Then he called for cold water. Without a word, he started pouring ice cold water on his head. The wound on Rudra's face stung and smarted like a scorpion bite. He held his breath, as Vikarna kept pouring water on his face, making it difficult to breathe. Rudra tried to move his head from side to side, but to no avail. He took a breath and a large gulp of water went into his airpipe, causing a paroxysm of coughing. Vikarna stopped momentarily.

'Would you repeat what you said just now, traitor?'

'I . . . am . . . not a traitor, nayaka . . . you are . . . mistaken,' said Rudra, wheezing for air.

'Oh yes, I forgot, you're the patriot we were looking for, forever!' Vikarna laughed, and again poured cold water over Rudra's head. The water had flowed over the ground, making it wet and cold. Rudra felt the cold stinging like needles. He decided to calm down, conserve his breath and fight for his life.

'How did you even utter the name of Amatya Maitreyi, you traitor?' Vikarna was unstoppable now. At that very moment, something changed inside Rudra. He chose to live, to endure the torture and survive at any cost. Come what may, he had to prove his innocence, at least to Maitreyi and the king if no one else. He wouldn't allow Vikarna to come between him and his goal. He was much calmer now and allowed Vikarna to torture him without resistance. He was conserving his energy, he didn't want to die.

The old man felt helpless and remorseful. Devabrata had given him some information which had shaken his conscience. Something buried deep down in his heart had resurfaced to haunt him. Tears flowed down his cheeks, tears of repentance. This man had never cried in his life, but today, his grim exterior had cracked and he sobbed unconsolably. Devabrata let him cry. He had worked with this man for ages, before pangs of remorse led this man to withdraw from active statecraft and lead a reclusive life in the janapadas.

Meanwhile, the king had called for an urgent meeting to deal with the crisis. That Rudravarman was actually Simhadhwaja had been conveyed to him. Few others were privy to this information as declaring it out in the open would have been counterproductive. While he was convinced that Simhadhwaja was residing in his court under the name of Rudravarman, he wasn't sure if the man was a traitor too. But the very fact that he was an imposter weighed heavily on his mind, leading to Rudra's incarceration. He had now called upon all those who had been involved in exposing Rudravarman to narrate the facts as they had unfolded.

When Aira Kharavela reached the assembly room, Mahamatya Nakiya, Vajramitra, Vikarna, Maitreyi and Bahushalin were already there. They all looked serious and affected, except for Vajramitra, who appeared to be jubilant. They paid respects to the king, who hurriedly took his place and asked Nakiya to commence the proceedings without any formalities.

Nakiya rose, 'Rajan, my head hangs in shame today. I accept the moral responsibility of this debacle. You may punish me with the strictest punishment possible. Alternatively, I will shave my head and become an ascetic and leave for the forest. He was under my direct command. I have been totally fooled into believing that he was who he said he was . . . I don't seek forgiveness, I beg you to punish me severely.'

'Mahamatya, it's not your fault, our spies had verified him fully before we employed him. Amatya Maitreyi, what do you have to say about this?'

'Rajan, he has been constantly under watch, but he was so clever that he never showed any signs of being an imposter. He never had suspicious visitors or dealings, so it was impossible to catch him. Had it not been for Arya Vajramitra, the traitor would have never been caught.'

'How was he caught, Arya Vajramitra?' the king asked, curious.

Vajramitra got up and began strutting like a prince. 'Rajan, when this man came to Tosali, he struck me as a bit queer. He seemed to be too good for his job and position. Then came the Asmaka War, where he was almost single-handedly responsible for our victory. As you know, I had differences of opinion with you about the methods used to win that war. Then I tested him by offering him the position of senapati for helping me overthrow your regime. I remember I had told you that he had successfully passed that test, though he did not reveal the "plot" to anyone.'

'Yes, Vajramitra, I do remember you testing him.'

'Rajan, I was also amazed at his maturity in dealing with problems, which actually made me more suspicious. He consistently exhibited qualities quite rare for a man of his station. I tried to get information about his past, but nothing was known other than his father, Indravarman, being a spy in the service of King Chetaraja, who had died in suspicious circumstances. The family had disappeared later, and nobody had heard anything of them. I then suspected his hand in the attempted poisoning of the royal elephant, but you let him go free.'

'In that case he was innocent. I had personally verified it, Arya Vajramitra.'

'I think he must have staged it to gain your confidence, Rajan.'

'That might be possible, arya. I haven't yet been able to find out who was responsible for it. Could you find out, Maitreyi?'

'Rajan, my apologies, but we have not been able to unravel the conspiracy behind it.'

'I have some inkling of what happened, but I need some more information before I form an opinion,' said the king in a sombre voice. 'Tell me now, Arya Vajramitra, how did you get to Simhadhwaja?'

Vajramitra now produced a document, written on bark paper, which he handed over to the king.

'Rajan, here is incontrovertible evidence of his treachery, in his own hand.'

The king studied the letter then handed it over to Nakiya, who nodded. 'This indeed is his handwriting and seal, Rajan.' Then he read the letter:

Salutations to Dakshinadhipati, Simuka putra Satakarni, I, Simhadhwaja, your loyal and trusted amatya, am still alive. I am writing this to warn you that Aira Kharavela's real mission is to conquer Prathishthanpura, he has sent me with an army through the Mahakantar forests to encircle you before he arrives. I am also supposed to cut off any help from your allies and feudatories. Kharavela will reach the borders of Rathika–Bhojaka in another fourteen days. If you're caught unawares, you will lose your kingdom and your throne . . . Written under the hand of Simhadhwaja.

'Traitor!' wailed Maitreyi.

The king looked at her with curious eyes, then he cast a glance at Nakiya, who responded with a reassuring gaze. It meant that they would have a chat later.

'Tell me, arya, how did *you* get this letter? It means that it never reached the Dakshinapathapati.'

Vajramitra seemed to have been caught off-guard and fumbled a bit. The king continued to observe him keenly. Vajramitra finally spoke. 'Rajan, a disgruntled officer who was punished severely for a small misdemeanour stole this letter from Simhadhwaja's tent. He happened to be from my loyal ancestral troops. It is he who handed over this letter to me.'

Kharavela couldn't help notice the slight tremble in his voice and the arching of his body as he spoke.

'Who is this officer, arya?'

'He is the loyal Devasena, Rajan. It is he who brought this treachery to light by bringing this letter to me. I recommend that you suitably reward him.'

The king nodded in agreement, albeit a bit absent-mindedly. 'Go on.'

Vajramitra looked at Vikarna for support. Clearing his throat, Vikarna said, 'Rajan, when Arya Vajramitra told me about the letter and this treachery, I couldn't believe it. But then everything became crystal clear. Remember his heroism on the first day he entered the royal court? He had apprehended the forest brigand who had escaped. He was trying desperately to make a good impression and gain entry to the royal court at any cost. Alas, he was successful too. So when Arya Vajramitra told me about this imposter being Simhadhwaja, we decided to lay a trap to test him.'

'Who does "we" mean, Nayaka?'

'Rajan, I and Vajramitra discussed it with Amatya Maitreyi, who at first was shocked to hear it, but was later charged with extreme anger and patriotism to hunt this traitor down. We then tracked down his erstwhile bodyguard, Pavaka, from the Andhra days, who had betrayed him, leading to his flight from that country. For some money, Pavaka was happy to write a letter asking his former master to meet him. We guessed that if he *was* Simhadhwaja, he would come. We also planted a person who had known him earlier to identify and confront him.'

'How come nobody felt the need to keep me or the mahamatya informed about this development?' asked the king with sarcasm.

'Rajan, we beg your forgiveness, but we wanted to be sure ourselves before we brought it to your or mahamatya's notice,' said Maitreyi apologetically.

The king nodded. 'Go on,' he said.

Vikarna continued, 'As predicted, he came up to the abandoned Magadhan courthouse, where he met this decoy of ours. Being confronted with his real identity, he attacked and cut his hand. He had actually escaped, but Amatya Maitreyi valiantly fought with him and pinned him down with her sword, and we were able to arrest the traitor.'

'He should be put to death, Rajan.' Maitreyi's eyes were red with anger and indignation. The king looked at her with serious eyes, studying her. Then he suddenly turned to Mahamatya Nakiya and commanded, 'Let him be executed by putting him under the feet of the elephant Mahagiri on the coming full moon. You may all go now.'

He breathed a deep sigh as the others left and gestured to the mahamatya that he wanted to talk to him in confidence.

✦ ✦ ✦

Vikarna returned to the cell, beaming with a cruel euphoria. This time he had brought others with him—skilled torturers and interrogators. With them was the old man who had first met him at the city gates when he had arrived at Tosali.

Oil lamps had been lit in the dark dungeon. Rudra was wide awake. He had lost count of days and nights as there was no source of sunlight in the cell. He tried to calculate the number of days he had spent in captivity from the times he had been served food, but that schedule was too erratic.

Without a word, the men opened his shackles. He felt relieved at first, but then he saw Vikarna smiling viciously. True as his apprehension was, something worse was in the offing. His feet were now bound by several coils of a rough rope, then, in an abrupt manoeuvre, he was lifted and suspended upside down. His legs ached as they pulled his body up. Vikarna now got up and came near Rudra, whose head was now suspended at the height of Vikarna's waist. The nayaka slapped him so hard that he swung from side to side from the suspended rope. He asked him, 'So traitor, have you decided to come clean or not?'

'I have nothing to confess, I have done nothing wrong, nayaka,' said Rudra in a feeble voice. Before he could complete his sentence, the nayaka slapped him again, now on his left cheek. The scab over his wound broke, leading to the gash opening up. As he swung from side to side again, drops and then a thin steady stream of blood trickled to the floor.

'You will not relent, Simhadhwaja. You are a tough prisoner. Why don't you tell the truth and die in peace? The king has already sanctioned your execution.'

'No!' cried Rudra. 'You are all mistaken. I have done nothing, nothing wrong. You all are playing into the hands of that wretched dark prince. You will realize your folly in time.'

'Shut up you snake!' shouted Vikarna, 'I will extract the truth out of your bones now!' Saying this he signalled to his assistants, who brought out a small broad vessel. Some sort of smoke was emerging out of it. He placed the small pot on the floor directly below Rudra's head and blew air into it. Red embers glowed, into which he put a handful of chillies. White smoke rose from the pot burning Rudra's eyes, nostrils and earlobes. He coughed violently, gasped to breathe, shook his head side to side and swung like a pendulum, but to no avail. Vikarna had covered his own face with a thick cloth, and ordered the assistants to hold Rudra steady as he put another batch of fiery chillies into the pot. Rudra cried out in pain, as his eyes burnt and watered as if he had gone blind. He couldn't inhale it anymore, but the men kept holding his head in the smoke till he lost consciousness.

When he came back to his senses, he found that he had been taken off the suspension and shackled again on the floor. Every joint of his body ached as he tried to move, and he moaned in pain.

'Is it hurting badly?' a soft voice asked. Rudra opened his eyes to see the old spy he had met on his first entry to Tosali. He found his presence comforting.

'Yes, old man,' said Rudra, his voice failing, as he breathed with great effort.

'Why don't you end this torture, arya. It's in your hands.'

'How do I do it?'

'They just want the truth, arya, and nothing else. I remember meeting you when you had first come to Tosali, two years ago. My old eyes haven't failed me. I could recognize you even in this darkness. You're a good man.'

'I am a loyal subject of the king, old man. They are mistaking me for a traitor.'

'Get it off your chest, son. Tell me if you can't tell them. I will make all efforts to save you from further torture.'

'I have nothing more to tell. Believe me, even if they kill me, nothing will be achieved. On the contrary, if someone can convey my last message to the king, it will be a great service to this country.'

'What is that, arya?'

'What is the guarantee that my message will reach the king, old man?'

'I cannot guarantee that, son. I am a small man, but I can try my best.'

'Then it is of no use. I will die with it, and the secret will not be revealed to anyone. You want my fate to be like Sage Ani Mandavya, who was impaled even though he was innocent?'

The man didn't say anything, but sat in silence for a long time before he left.

The cycle of torture continued. Now, Rudra had stopped responding to Vikarna's questions. He just cried in pain, which angered the nayaka more and more, leading to increased cruelty. His body was giving way, but his resolve was unbroken. Every day he repeated to himself, 'I have to tell the truth to Rajan and Maitreyi, I will not die like this.'

The torturers were also growing tired of this daily regime. Vikarna kept them interested by trying out a new technique every day. One day it was cold water, the other day it was suspension from the roof, then it was feeding oil, not letting him sleep and a hoard of other methods. He was unhappy that Rudra had still not spoken the 'truth'. The date of execution was nearing, and he felt a sense of failure in not being able to break this man.

There was a lull in the torture as Rudra had been vomiting blood since the previous evening. Vikarna asked for the torture to be suspended for some time till the prisoner showed signs of improvement.

The old spy had come again, but this time he had brought medicine for him. Rudra refused to take anything from his hands. Guessing the reason for his refusal, the man told Rudra, 'Arya, this is medicine, and even if it is poison, you have hardly a day or two to live.'

Rudra's face showed a faint smile. He took the earthen vessel from the old man. 'What poison is it, old man?'

'Son, it's *jatyadi ghrita*, which can heal any wound, internal or external.'

'Does it heal the heart too?'

'Son, I understand what you want to say but I can't do anything.' His eyes were tearful, and he wiped them with his uttariya. 'But there is one thing I can do for you.'

'What is that?' Rudra was hardly audible.

'I can take your message to Mahamatya Nakiya. Don't ask me how. If you can trust me, tell me, if you don't, you may do as you want.'

Rudra thought for a while, then said, 'Okay, tell him this. *Agnih shesham, runah shesham, shatruh shesham, tathaiva cha I punah punah pravardhet, tasman shesham na karyet* (If they remain even in a small trace, fire, loan and enemy, they grow back repeatedly. Hence finish them off altogether, without leaving a trace).

'Also ask him to find out about the whereabouts of the dark prince.'

The old man listened intently, and then fed the medicine to Rudra. He asked him not to have water for some time.

Devabrata had heard about the date of execution—although it was not publicly known, he had access to such facts. He was running a race against time, and his efforts were not bearing fruit. Being Rudra's confidant, he knew that he and other members of the team would be under continuous surveillance. He still risked it all; he couldn't fail his masters a second time in his life. He was successful in asking one particular old gentleman to break his self-imposed exile and come to Tosali.

Rudra saw his death approaching. The day of execution had come. Meanwhile, the old spy had come again, compassionate as ever, to feed him medicine. It had worked wonders on him. He felt that he was healing fast, and this thought made him very sad as he only had a few hours left to live now.

'Old man, I am a good person, remember me as one. I am just an unfortunate wretch who couldn't prove his innocence. Now, I have no hope left. I will die a disgraced death.'

'Shh,' said the old man. 'This will liberate you.' He handed over a small sac containing some powder to him. Rudra looked at him quizzically, but he left immediately without offering any explanation.

With his manacled hands, he opened the small pouch, and an intense aroma arose from it, making him feel instantly dizzy. He felt relieved.

The king had received a message from Rajguru Uddalaka quite late. It was unusual for the royal sage to disturb the king at odd hours. Appreciating that the matter must be of grave importance, the king started towards the sage's quarters. He met Nakiya on the way, and asked him to accompany him.

Maitreyi was vacillating between anger and despair. At one moment she felt intense rage, immediately followed by a sinking feeling at the imminent loss of Rudravarman. Images flashed into her mind—her first encounter with him when he kept staring boldly from the madiralaya window, of the time when she consoled him after the Asmaka War, and when she found him in a semi-dead condition at the jungle camp.

Tears flowed from her eyes as she remembered how he longed for her when he was recovering at her place, and how restrained and honourable his behaviour was. He never had any negativity, even towards his assailants. How boldly he had gotten into her chariot and courted her. She started sobbing when Vikarna suddenly entered her room.

'Maitreyi! What happened? Are you crying?' He came near her and tried to wipe her tears.

'Don't you dare touch me, Vikarna!' She sprang up like a wounded tigress. 'You should have announced your presence before entering my room like this.'

'Why are you so angry, Maitreyi, it isn't the first time I am entering your room.'

'Vikarna, I want to be alone for some time. Will you please . . .'

'What is it, Maitreyi? Why are you being so rude? I too have problems in life, but I don't get affected like you.'

'What problems do you have, nayaka? Let me know a few of them,' she said acerbically.

'Yes, I have huge problems to tackle. This wretched snake Simhadhwaja has not confessed anything till now, even when he is about to be executed! How much I have tortured him every day! He spits blood but does not divulge anything. I am so frustrated. And then you have been behaving in a strange manner nowadays. How much can I take?'

'Will you please go and leave me in peace, nayaka? Yamini, Yamini . . . come here, please escort the nayaka till the door.'

Yamini entered the room and looked at Vikarna with angry eyes. He felt insulted and his eyes were aflame as he left the room.

✦ ✦ ✦

Rudra could feel the weight of time, as he waited for the end to come. He had become impatient. He listened to the dark silence. First, it was like an insect buzzing at a distance, then, it got louder and louder. Now, it seemed like a thousand conch shells being blown simultaneously. He could neither hear his heartbeat nor his breath, such was the deafening silence. He wanted to escape, to run away, even to embrace death. There was no hope left now. He began seeing figures floating in the dark. Agents of the death god Yama were waiting around him. He saw them conspiring at a distance, as they floated effortlessly close to the ceiling. He spat at them but they laughed. Then, he saw a faint shadow of his mother. He wailed. 'Maatey . . . maaatey, I haven't done anything, don't be angry with me. Maatey, your son is innocent, he swears on you . . .'

He cried and wailed till he lost his voice. His chest was heavy, and was breathing in short spurts. He cried with each breath—it was the helpless cry of a victim on the altar who was about to be sacrificed. Suddenly, the door opened, and Vikarna charged in. He went up to Rudra and kicked him in the stomach. Rudra writhed in pain, but didn't utter a cry.

'Traitor, why don't you tell me the truth before you die!'

He kept kicking him and abusing him, and yet Rudra remained silent. Vikarna didn't stop, he removed his shoe and started hitting Rudra with it, the nails in the shoe ripping open his skin each time he hit him. After some time, the nayaka was out of breath. He then addressed Rudra.

'As you are dying now, you insect, I have to ask you if you have any last wish. Then, I can put you under the elephant's feet.'

'Yes, nayaka, I have a last wish. I want to meet Maitreyi and apologize to her for failing her, for everything which I have done or not done, I want to say a last goodbye to her . . .'

'How dare you utter her name!' Vikarna exploded. He pounced upon Rudra's chest and grabbed his throat to strangle him. Rudra struggled hard, but he felt weak and thought this was the end.

He was choking under the nayaka's grip. Immense pain ran down his chest and stomach, he passed urine as his breath abated, his eyes turned blood red and his eyeballs rolled upwards.

Vikarna suddenly realized what he was doing. He retreated with a jerk, then looked with disbelief at the lifeless body lying between his feet. He was struck with panic. What had he done! He had murdered a prisoner on death row! The king was going to skin him alive and cut off his hands too. He reeled under the shock of his own act, streams of cold sweat trickled down his neck, and he felt dizzy and suffocated.

He held Rudra's head with both his hands as he sat near the lifeless body. Seized with frenzy, he began to shake him. He pulled his hair and slapped him in an attempt to revive him, but to no avail . . .

Outside, at the city gates, Kinshuk and Bhadrabahu were returning with a prize catch. They had tracked and hunted down a man who was escaping the city in the guise of a woman. He was Abhisoka, a seasoned poisoner. They entered the city and hurriedly went to Rudra's residence. Devabrata was waiting for them there, with the old recluse Brahman. The grand old man with Devabrata was Maitreyi's father Nagarjun, who used to be chief of spies under Aira Kharavela's father Chetaraja.

Devabrata was caustic, 'It runs in your family revered Nagarjun. You were responsible for Indravarman's death, and your daughter is after Arya Rudravarman's life. I hear that it is she who suggested to the king that Rudra be put to death for his "sins".'

'How much more will you lash me, Devabrata? I have been living with this burden in my heart forever. How I regret the day I suspected poor Indravarman of treachery and despatched men to assassinate him. Later, I came to know that he was as pure as unadulterated milk. When my men returned, they told me that his whole family, including his two children and his wife, had died when they had set fire to their house. I never knew that Rudravarman and his mother had escaped alive. It still brings tears to my eyes, Devabrata. You cannot imagine how much I repented it later.'

'And now your daughter is completing the work that you left unfinished,' said the old fox relentlessly.

'She is a very intelligent woman, Devabrata. When I relinquished the post of chief of spies, she was already an adult. Despite my exhortations to the opposite, the king made her take over my work. She seldom makes mistakes and never forgives anyone but is very just and kind-hearted. I will convince her about Rudravarman's innocence.'

'I don't know how effective that will be virtuous Nagarjun. The time for the execution is approaching.'

'Devabrata, I personally met the rajguru and told him the entire story. He appeared to be convinced by it. He had even promised me that he would convey it to the king personally. We should go and immediately seek his intervention.'

'Yes, worthy Nagarjun. We now have this villain Abhisoka with us. He was the one who had prepared the poison for the royal elephant Mahagiri. He is also the one who murdered the king's mahout and made it look like a snakebite. I suspect that he was also responsible for the poisoned dart which almost took Arya Rudravarman's life in the jungle camp.'

'That is a great achievement, come at a very opportune time, Devabrata. Let's rush to meet the rajguru immediately.'

It was a very secluded place where the prisoner had been kept, the underground cellar was hidden in a thick grove. The guard outside saw Nayaka Vikarna tottering out from the cell, his face covered with a cloth. He saw him hurriedly sit in his chariot and rush towards the city. Something terrible had happened, the guard thought.

Vikarna commanded his charioteer to go to Amatya Maitreyi's residence. The charioteer too sensed that something was seriously wrong, and he sped towards the city. When they reached, he saw an unsteady Vikarna walking in hurriedly.

The attendants tried to stop him, but he beckoned them not to interfere, and they retreated in fear.

Maitreyi was still crying, but she noticed that someone had come into the room. When she saw who it was, she cried out, 'Nayaka Vikarna! Why don't you understand that I want some privacy. Why are you bent upon seeking my wrath? Get out now!'

'I won't, Devi.'

She snapped back in amazement, and when she looked at the man's face, she shrieked, 'Rudra! How . . . how have you come here!'

Rudra gestured to her to lower her voice and then said, 'I will be ready to die after you listen to my side of the story.'

'Why have you come here now!' She was still crying. 'You spoiled everything, you liar, you deceived me!'

'I will surrender to anyone you say after you have heard me, not before that. Your fiancé strangled me and left me for dead.'

'No! It's not possible. Nayaka Vikarna isn't such a cruel person, you are lying again.'

'Amatya Maitreyi, I want one last chance to confess and tell my side of the story. You know that I could've easily escaped the other night when you captured me at the abandoned courthouse. I could have killed the nayaka too, but I did not. So, I am not going to run away. If I have come here, it is with a purpose.'

'What purpose is that, Simhadhwaja?'

'You call me by any name Maitreyi, that does not change the person within me. Let me counter all the allegations made against me. If at the end you still feel that I am guilty, you can call the guards and hand me over to them. If not, I walk out free and chart my own course. Isn't it a fair demand to make? Will you not give me a just opportunity to explain?'

She contemplated, then, regaining her composure, she said, 'If I am not convinced, I won't even call the guards, I will execute you here. You are an escaped prisoner who is on death row, don't forget that.'

Rudra nodded. 'All right, let me explain to you . . .'

She listened intently as Rudra told her everything about himself, including the fact that he felt overwhelming love for her. It was difficult to lie to her; she was a seasoned player, adept at her game.

As he spoke, Yamini hurriedly entered the room and announced that Maitreyi's father Nagarjun had arrived. Maitreyi turned to ask Rudra to wait till she met her father, but he was gone. Her heart sank with worry. She composed herself and got up to receive the old man who had entered the room.

He said, 'Maitreyi, we have to meet the king immediately to stop the execution of Rudravarman! I will tell you the reasons on the way. Do not waste a moment, just accompany me as you are.'

'What happened father? How do you know all this? When did you come to Tosali? And how are you involved in this matter?'

'Maitreyi, come to the chariot before it is too late. As your father I command you to start immediately. I will clear all your doubts later.' Saying this he took her by the hand and made her sit in the chariot, which sped towards the royal palace. She was secretly feeling relieved inside. Maitreyi had access to the king at all times. She was chief of spies but overtly looked after the department of vices. This gave her a very good cover to gather information and carry out operations throughout the kingdom with great ease. Not many people in the mantriparishad knew of her real role. To them she was like any other amatya in the service of the king. Her special access to the king though had set tongues wagging, with people suspecting her of having a secret liaison with him. Many had seen her being received by the king at odd hours of night. In reality, those were intelligence briefings and discussions over vital policy matters.

She was quickly ushered in. The king was getting ready for his evening schedule, but he decided to give her time. Nagarjun was also allowed to enter the king's chamber with her. The king looked at her quizzically, 'There definitely must be a matter of grave national emergency which brings you here like this, Maitreyi. I also see that revered Nagarjun is accompanying you. Please sit and tell me what has happened.'

'Rajan, we are about to commit an unpardonable sin!'

'What is that, Amatya Maitreyi? Speak clearly.'

'Rajan, first please stop the execution of Rudravarman. I will immediately then tell you why you should do it.'

The king thought over it for a moment. Maitreyi could barely breathe. Then, he called for his messenger Trigun. 'Go and immediately inform the nayaka and mahamatya that execution of the traitor will not take place today.'

As Trigun left, the king looked at Nagarjun. The old man took the cue. 'Rajan, this Rudravarman is not a traitor. Putting him to death will be a grave error. He is a patriot who is prepared to die for the country. We have unravelled many secrets which point to a conspiracy against him. He is innocent.'

'How did you get involved with this venerable Nagarjun?'

'Rajan, it's an old debt to be paid, a wrong to be corrected, a sin to be atoned for. Rudravarman's father was called

Indravarman, he was a spy with me. Efficient and brave, he was one of my trusted aides. He was so close to me that he was welcome at my home too. Maitreyi does not know this, but she has played with Rudravarman as a child.'

'But what has this got to do with the present case, Nagarjun?'

'Rajan, I am responsible for the wrongful death of Indravarman and his little daughter and for the displacement of Rudravarman and his mother from Tosali to Prathisthanpura. I have never been able to forgive myself for that!'

'Father!' Maitreyi said, shocked. 'This cannot be true!'

The king was unmoved. 'How did it happen?'

'Under King Chetaraja's reign, there was once a huge conspiracy to overthrow his rule, being hatched at the behest of some Magadhan chiefs. As I was tracking them down, I was informed that Indravarman had been won over and he was playing a double game. So, I put him under surveillance, and the reports indicated that he was having secret meetings with a Magadhan envoy. I personally checked and found that he was indeed meeting a foreigner secretly, which converted my doubt into a certainty. Feeling betrayed and angered, I ordered his execution by assassins. Those people set fire to his house late at night. I was informed that everyone from the family perished in that fire ...'

Tears streamed profusely from Nagarjun's eyes. His throat choked with emotion, he wiped his eyes and continued. 'Later, I was informed that he was actually meeting an official from the Andhras, with a view to get their support if there was any revolt in Tosali. His enemies in the service had fed me with wrong information. I had acted in haste and killed my friend and aide. I also did not spare his innocent little daughter. I have lived with this burden on my heart for all these years. Now, when I learn that his son has survived, we are repeating history by putting him, an innocent man, to death. Till I am alive, I cannot let this sin be committed.'

A grim silence fell on the group. Then, clearing his throat, the king finally spoke, 'What new evidence have you unearthed, Nagarjun, which proves the innocence of Rudravarman?'

'Rajan, we have solved many mysteries. The death of your trusted mahout, the poisoning attempt on Mahagiri, the attack on Rudravarman himself, the attempts to subvert officials and much more. Not only that, we have arrested the poisoner who had participated in this conspiracy.'

'Who is behind all this? Maitreyi, how are you unaware of these machinations?'

'Rajan, I have been trying to find out for a very long time, but there had been no breakthrough. I don't know why my father has acted independently, without even keeping me in the know of things. I apologize profusely for my failure to unearth this.'

'Maitreyi, I will tell you how I got so much information. Some of my old hands have been working with Rudravarman, it is they who have discovered these secrets to save their master. They have also told me that the letter written in his own hand addressed to Satkarni was written when his army was poisoned by the dark prince of Subarnagiri and he was asked to write this letter as a ransom to obtain the antidote. Had he intended to play mischief, why would he have cut off the advance of the Andhra army when he was holding the Rathikas back?'

The king and Maitreyi listened to the old man as he gave proof after proof of Rudravarman's innocence.

Trigun entered the room hurriedly. 'Rajan, I have news for you,' he said. The king called him near. He whispered something in the king's ears; the king looked very alarmed and dismissed Trigun.

'The prisoner has escaped—he tricked the Nayaka Vikarna and has run away. What do you say now, Nagarjun and Maitreyi!'

'Rajan, how did he trick the nayaka? It is impossible!' said Maitreyi, feigning ignorance.

'I don't know, but he escaped wearing Vikarna's clothes and has tied the nayaka in his place in chains. How did this fool allow himself to be overpowered and tricked like this I don't know.'

'Rajan, let us not forget that Rudravarman is Simhadhwaja, a trained warrior, astute statesman and seasoned spy. The nayaka would have been no match for him.'

'Now, how do we find him? Maitreyi, it is your personal responsibility to apprehend him and bring him before me.'

'Rajan, I will put all spies in the city on this one job and will get him here.' Saying this, she left the room, without taking leave of the king.

The king looked at Nagarjun, who was in deep thought. He said, 'It is a very difficult task for your daughter, but I know she will do it properly.'

'Why difficult, Rajan? She is not Nayaka Vikarna.'

'Difficult because she is in love with this Rudravarman. Did you now know this, Nagarjun?'

'No, Rajan. I am absolutely unaware of this! She has never hinted or mentioned this to me. I always thought that the nayaka wanted to marry her, and she too didn't seem unwilling to the proposal.'

'It's a double bind for her, but I know she will choose loyalty over her heart. After all, she is your daughter, Nagarjun.'

'Rajan, I think you are clear about Rudravarman not being a traitor now. Please be considerate with him when he is apprehended.'

'Venerable Nagarjun, you are not the only one who has been speaking to me about Rudravarman. The rajguru has also been advising me. I will make my decision in due course. Meet the mahamatya now and inform him about these developments.'

Nagarjun rose and took his leave.

The disgraced nayaka was meeting the mahamatya, his head hung low in shame. 'I am so ashamed of myself, mahamatya, I am not worthy of this office.'

Nakiya did not react. After a long silence, he said, 'Whenever emotions blind your path, you are bound to go astray. How did it happen, nayaka?'

'Mahamatya, I wanted to find out the whole truth from him. Who were his accomplices, who are the traitors within the court and government and what are they up to? I wanted to find out how they had tried to poison the royal elephant, why had he written that letter to Satkarni and a lot of other questions. Putting him to death would have left them all unanswered . . .'

'What ensued then, nayaka?'

'I lost my temper and beat him up badly. He acted as if he had passed away from the torture, then suddenly he blew some powder at my face. It instantly made me dizzy. Before I could understand anything, I was unconscious.'

'Where did he get that powder from?'

'We are investigating that, mahamatya.'

'So he ran away wearing your clothes, in your own chariot, tying you naked to the chains?'

'He is a trickster, mahamatya. I knew this. I am mortified, but this time I will not spare his life.'

'Nayaka, have patience. Amatya Maitreyi has been given charge of this matter now. Till then you will wait for further orders from me.'

'Mahamatya, this is a matter of my honour and dignity! How can someone else be allowed to deal with it?'

'Let not your personal feelings get the better of you, nayaka. Don't forget, you are working for the king.'

'But mahamatya . . . !'

'You may go now, nayaka. I have other important work to do.'

Hurt, angry, ashamed and full of feelings of revenge, Vikarna left the mahamatya's chamber. As Vikarna left, the mahamatya admitted Devabrata, Nagarjun and Kinshuk. They had come along with a prisoner bound with ropes.

Nagarjun said, 'Mahamatya, this is Abhisoka, the most dreaded poisoner in the whole of Kalinga. He has been working for traitors and saboteurs for a long time. He has a lot to tell you.'

Nakiya looked at the man who seemed to be rather emotionless, but as soon as he looked at him, he assumed an expression of extreme innocence. He pleaded, 'Mahamatya, I am only a small man, doing the dirty job for big people. I just execute orders without knowing for whom they are meant. If you also ask me to prepare a mixture, I will do it for you.'

Before he could complete his sentence, Kinshuk slapped him across the face and the man cringed in pain. Devabrata spoke, 'Mahamatya, look at this shameless man. I don't know how many lives he has taken, but he has the audacity to defend his actions in your presence.'

'What could you get from him venerable Nagarjun? It is good to see you back. I remember, when I was a junior officer in the court, as a young man, we all used to be afraid of you.' Nagarjun smiled at the compliment, then replied, 'Mahamatya, this is more a matter of repaying an old debt than getting back to work. I would not have died a peaceful death, and my soul would have wandered unsatisfied if I hadn't been able to correct an old wrong which I had committed.'

'I am aware of it. I see that you are on the right path.'

Devabrata's face lit up. He looked at Kinshuk who seemed to be relieved by the kind words of the mahamatya.

'Tell me what have you got till now venerable Nagarjun.'

'I think it would be better to listen to the story from the culprit himself, mahamatya,' suggested Nagarjun.

Nakiya nodded in agreement. Devabrata tugged at the rope which had been tied to Abhisoka's wrists. There was a crooked smile on the face of the prisoner. He began, 'Mahamatya, firstly I would like to seek your pardon for my sins.' His face still betraying the opposite, he said, 'Mahamatya, I help anyone who comes to me with a request. You see, recently this old man here had come to me with a job.' He pointed at Devabrata.

Devabrata quipped, 'Tell him what job I had come to you for?'

'He had come for a stupefying powder to be used on the mahamatya.'

'And still you prepared it?' asked Devabrata.

The poisoner was in grave trouble now. He had admitted to participating in treachery right in front of the mahamatya. 'You have no options but to tell the truth now, you scoundrel!' said Devabrata.

'If he does not tell the truth now, feed him to the crocodiles of Daya. I don't have time for his antics.'

'Mahamatya, listen, please, I will tell the whole truth. Please let me live, I have a family to take care of, what will happen to them in my absence? Please give me a chance.'

Nagarjun looked at Abhisoka and warned him, 'If you try to trick us, you go straight to the crocodiles. Tell us your story uninterrupted.'

The wretch was trembling now, he sat down on the floor with folded hands and continued. 'I confess that I have been working for the Prince of Subarnagiri, called the dark prince. He is a great physician and has knowledge of hundreds of poisons and their antidotes. He had come to me around two years back to get a strong paste of kuchila made for an elephant. Believe me, mahamatya, I was not aware that it was to be used on the king's elephant Mahagiri.'

'Continue . . . we know what you were up to,' snapped Devabrata.

'Ah, I forgot to mention, someone who was an enemy of the king's mahout had also taken snake poison from me before the kuchila for the elephant was prepared.'

'Go on, I am listening,' said the mahamatya.

'Then, the dark prince asked me to prepare arrows laced with the poison of the deadly sea snake Alagadda, which is instantly fatal. He used it on one courtier called Rudravarman, who I hear miraculously survived. The dark prince was unhappy that Rudravarman had foiled his attempt to poison Mahagiri.'

'It was you! At that time we had wrongly suspected poor Rudravarman to have done it. He was virtually put to death for it,' lamented Nakiya.

'The poor boy seems to be very unfortunate, mahamatya. Whenever he tries to do good, he is persecuted. My heart bleeds for him,' Nagarjun said.

Devabrata was impatient. He kicked the poisoner. 'What are you listening to? Continue your story!'

The scoundrel cried out in pain. Then, cringing away from Devabrata, he spoke again in a whining tone, 'Many people have been coming to me with jobs. If I talk about each one, it will take days.'

'You know what we are asking for, so don't try to act smart,' said Nagarjun in a cold voice.

'Some days back, this old man Devabrata had come to me, wanting me to make a stupefying powder. He said he would use it on the mahamatya.' He looked at Nakiya, and whined again, 'Mahamatya, please don't believe this man, he had taken the powder for you, you ask him if it is true or not . . .'

'I will ask him that Abhisoka, but tell me where is the dark prince now?'

'How would I know that, mahamatya? He is so mysterious, appears and disappears like a ghost. But I remember something. This time when he came to meet me, I couldn't recognize him. His face has been burnt beyond recognition, his skin oozes pus, and he smells like putrefied meat.'

'What is his aim?'

'Mahamatya, he wanted to be the king of Kalinga, but after he got burnt, he is left with no hope. He wants to seek revenge on Rudravarman, who had caused him to be burnt.'

'Devabrata, take him away to the bandigriha right now. Our specialists will make him speak the whole truth,' Nakiya said. Then, turning to Nagarjun, he admitted 'I see the point in what you are saying about Rudravarman, but I need more proof. Not everything has been explained by the apprehension of this man.'

'Mahamatya, it's a matter of time. The truth will come out like a gem from samudra manthan, the churning of the sea.'

'I hope it does, Nagarjun.'

The old man took leave of the mahamatya after blessing him. The poisoner was taken to the dreaded prison by Devabrata and Kinshuk.

Vijayaka and Bhadrabahu hadn't slept for days. Their only aim was to apprehend the dark prince and his associates. Heartened by Abhisoka's arrest, they now looked for all those who had been a part of the conspiracy against their master. They soon realized that Vajramitra was a sort of innocent fool, who had been conned by the dark prince into a scheme to get even with Rudravarman for the insult he had to face when the latter was given charge of the army contingent marching to Rathika territory. Vajramitra, of course, had a long-standing grouse against Rudra for various reasons.

Both of them were in disguise as Maitreyi's people were all around the city, looking for them in every temple, every eatery, every ganika's residence, every gambling house and every madiralaya. There was also confirmed information that the dark prince was still in Tosali. The question was, where exactly was he?

Devasena had been instrumental in getting the letter which had nailed Rudra. He had been won over by the dark prince when he had treated him for severe bee stings. Devasena couldn't forget his humiliation at the hands of Rudra in the jungle, after which the bees had attacked him. He had gotten his revenge now—the dark prince had instructed Devasena to steal the recovered letter Rudra had written to King Satkarni. The dark prince then brought him to Vajramitra, who had pounced upon the opportunity to expose and destroy Rudra. Vajramitra knew that after the exposé, Rudra's men would look for Devasena and get even with him. Hence, he had made adequate arrangements for Devasena to remain in Tosali undetected, till the storm was over.

Devasena was disguised as a rich merchant from Magadha and wore his hair in the Magadhan topknot fashion. He would go to a gambling house nearby every evening to play dyuta, which was his only solace till things normalized. He had very strict instructions from the dark prince and Vajramitra not to go out as his life would be in danger. This gambling house was a safe place though, as the bets placed were usually very high, so only outstation merchants frequented it and it was avoided by locals. When Devasena reached the gambling house in the evening, some people were playing the game. It was a small boisterous group that appeared to be from Avantikapuri from their language and intonation. Devasena overheard them joking about the liaison of the Prince Agnimitra with a young girl called Malvika, which was the talk of the town there. They laughed and gossiped for some time before most of them left, except two. Devasena, curious about the happenings in Avantikapuri, struck up conversation with one of them. 'What was that about the girl you were talking about friends?'

The merchants looked at each other and then burst out laughing. 'The girl,' they giggled, 'was sent by Queen Dharini's own brother, Viresena, to her. Now, she cannot get her out of the palace!'

Devasena's curiosity was stoked further. He inquired, 'What exactly happened?'

'What else would happen? As expected, Prince Agnimitra has fallen in love with the girl. He wants to marry her and make her the queen!'

The younger of the two added, 'Some people even say that Virasena did this purposefully because he was unhappy with Madhavasena being made king of the acquired territory after war with the Vidarbha king, Yadnasena. He believed that he deserved to be the made the king as he had led the army in the war to release Madhavasena.'

'Whatever it may be, the girl is said to be so beautiful that even gods would not be able to resist her,' the other one chuckled.

As they were about to leave, Devasena requested them for a game of dyuta. They showed reluctance as they already had been playing for a long time. Devasena looked around, but there was no one else for company. He earnestly requested them to stay back and play and they grudgingly assented.

They started with small bets. Devasena seemed to be on a lucky streak and he won repeatedly. The merchants were getting visibly frustrated. They decided to increase the stakes and recover their money. This backfired as Devasena continued to win, and in some time, they had lost most of their money to him. He was beaming; he hadn't hoped for such a good run, but luck was smiling at him.

The merchants were getting agitated. They took a break and consulted amongst themselves, then came back to the game. The younger one made an audacious move—he bet 1000 golden panas in a last-ditch effort. Devasena warned him in a good-natured way, but he seemed adamant. To make things worse for him, it was Devasena's turn to throw the die. He smiled, tossed them in the air . . .

He felt as if he had been stabbed with a knife in his heart. His move had miserably failed, and he had, in a single stroke lost 1000 golden panas! As if his breath had stopped, he couldn't believe his eyes. How could his luck fail him at the most critical moment? Flabbergasted, he broke into a cold sweat.

The merchants at first looked relieved, then, reality sunk in. They had just won a huge amount! They grew jubilant. Devasena was wondering where he would get the money.

He checked his purse and added the amount already won, but it was still way off the mark. It was more than his annual salary. He was in thick trouble now, without the money being made good, he would not be allowed to exit the gambling house. If his conduct was reported to the army, he would lose his job too. What he could do was to go to his benefactor Vajramitra and ask for help. He sheepishly told the two merchants that he didn't have the money to pay up. Livid, one of them got up in a mood to physically assault him. The attendants of the gambling house quickly realized what was happening and intervened in time.

The manager of the facility was a wise old man, and had seen these disputes hundreds of times. He asked Devasena if he could make good his commitment if time was given, to which he replied in the affirmative. He then asked him as to how he would do it. Devasena told him that he was a guest of Vajramitra, who would lend the money to him. The manager asked if the merchants were agreeable to it. They consulted with each other and agreed, albeit with one condition. They would accompany Devasena to Vajramitra's house; he reluctantly agreed.

When they were about to go out, some soldiers came to the gambling house, they were looking for a man with a deep scar on his left cheek. They talked with Devasena and the merchants, and being satisfied about them, they left.

It was a winter night and, as they came out on the street, there were very few people walking. No chariots or riders were seen. Devasena told them that Vajramita's residence was within a krosha and they walked along with him. 'Bhadrabahu,' said the younger one.

'Yes, Vijayaka,' said the other one.

Before Devasena could understand anything, he had been hit on the back of his head with a stone, making him unconscious.

The minor city gate that opened to the north led to the cremation grounds. Dead bodies of persons belonging to particular castes were taken out of the respective gates. This was an inviolable rule, the transgression of which attracted a serious punishment. Chandalas lived beyond the walls of the city, near cremation grounds. They were supposed to be pursuers of dark sciences and rumoured to indulge in occult and magical rituals. People stayed away from chandalas more out of fear than from concerns of ritual purity. They were thought to possess powers of controlling ghosts, demons and minor gods alike. Anyone having the courage to venture near these grounds, especially on new moon and full moon days could see them engaged in savage rituals involving burning of human body parts, animal bones, blood of various organisms and bird feathers. The chanting of magical mantras made the performances appear even more terrifying.

People desirous of obtaining supernatural powers or hidden treasures secretly sneaked into the cremation grounds to ask the Chandalas for help in performing magic rituals. The Chandalas used to keep materials such as snake skins, porcupine quills, owl feathers, human skulls, droppings of crows, tails of foxes and other such things in stock. These would be supplied to those desirous of acquiring dark powers or wanting to conduct a particular ritual to achieve desired ends.

The fearsome Chandala living beyond the north cremation grounds entered the city gates in the morning. People walked away from him looking at his ash covered body and formidable bearing. He wandered about the city, making purchases of objects required for funerary rights. Some city people met him and inquired about certain occult rituals they wanted to conduct for conquering their enemies. He called them to the cremation ground at night.

It was pitch-dark when they reached the cremation grounds, where the Chandala was already busy performing some kind of ceremony. The embers from the burning pyres were the only source of light there. The intense stench of burning flesh coupled with dark smoke created a nauseating atmosphere, as he chanted mantras.

'I invoke Nikumbha, Kumbha, Naraka, Tantukachchha, the great demon, Bali, the son of Vairochana, S'atamáya, S'ambara. I call upon Armálava, Pramíla, Mandolúka, Ghatodbala, and the famous woman, Paulomi.

'Chanting the exalted mantras, I offer to thee the bone of a fresh corpse, productive of my desired ends. May S'alaka demons be victorious. Salutation to them!'

A party of soldiers who were on patrol had stopped by. When their commander approached the Chandala, the men from the city hid in a bush. The commander walked a bold walk until he came near the man, at which point, his confidence gave way to fear. He stood motionless for some time, then turned back and left hurriedly. The Chandala didn't even bother about his presence, but continued with his eerie chanting. Raising his pitch, he frenziedly put oblations in the fire, which bellowed noxious fumes. With hands raised, he cried out to the skies, 'O, Chandali Kumbhi, Tumba Katuka and Sarigha, you possess the bhaga of a woman, oblation to thee too!' Smoke bellowed as he poured oblations into the burning pyre. He picked up a pot of intoxicating liquor and drank it in a single gulp.

The three customers crawled near him and sat in close proximity with each other. The ritual continued for some time, then suddenly, without even looking at them, the Chandala said, 'So you three fools have arrived?'

They shuddered.

The next morning, a funeral procession proceeded slowly on the city streets, as the sons of the deceased wept inconsolably. The north gate guards inquired about the deceased. It was an old potter from the potter lane who had not been keeping well for months. They allowed the procession to go and also offered their prayers as they passed the gates towards the cremation grounds.

When the procession reached the cremation grounds, the dreadful Chandala was informed that the person who had died had a rare and incurable terminal illness, so the body couldn't be burnt, it had to be buried in accordance with the shastras. The Chandala showed them a place at the edge of the forests, where such bodies were buried. He supplied the family members with the implements for digging. The others took a bath at the large well and started returning after reciting mantras and showering flower petals on the body.

Finally, only four of the family members from the funeral procession were left at the site. The Chandala had made all the arrangements required to bury the body, but he was surprised by the absence of a Brahman who would preside over the funeral rituals. As evening fell, the Chandala sat with his three clients from the earlier night for completion of their rituals. One of the men informed him of something very strange: he had seen some movement in the corpse! The Chandala became suspicious, he asked the three men to secretly keep an eye on the grave diggers. They noticed that those people were talking in hushed tones, looking around to see if there were others in the graveyard. The men reported to the Chandala that something very fishy was going on. The Chandala surreptitiously moved close to the corpse and hid himself in the thickets. The three 'fools' also concealed their presence. The men accompanying the corpse let out a sigh of relief as no one was in sight.

The Chandala's clients were getting restless, but there was no other way than to wait it out. The winter sun had set quickly and soon it was dark. To the clients' surprise , the corpse rose and sat. The diggers were not surprised at all. They looked around cautiously, then gave the 'dead' man some water to drink. Then they gave him food to eat. All of them were planning to escape from there.

The Chandala brought out his sword and crawled cautiously towards the grave. There was a faint light from the torch the men had lit. The dead man got up on his feet and stood straight. He only had one arm.

The Chandala pounced upon him from behind and brought him down to the ground. The three men rushed to intervene, but by then, the Chandala's customers also joined in and chased them away. The Chandala said to the one-armed man, 'Dark prince . . . Why the hurry to leave Tosali?'

The one-armed man hissed, 'Arya Rudravarman! You're a real Chandala!'

Chapter 22

Endgame

Maitreyi had learnt about Devasena's abduction. She was worried and terribly angry. Things never had been so out of control in the city. Although maintenance of law and order was not her direct responsibility, being the head of spies entailed preventing crimes and subversion through constant watch, surveillance and advance information. For the first time, she felt that she was losing her grip. Things were happening inexplicably, without forewarning. She also felt a deep sense of failure in not being able to detect Rudra's double identity, although she was sure by now that he wasn't a traitor.

Her heart riled at the knowledge that her own father had been responsible for the death of Rudra's father and the destruction of his family. Her deep affection and admiration for Rudra had put her in a great dilemma. What would she do when she found him or when she received credible information about him? Would she inform the king and the nayaka? No, she wouldn't inform the nayaka. He would put Rudra to death instantly, he had already attempted it once. What about the king? He didn't seem fully convinced about his innocence, would he throw him back in prison again? Her heart was torn with these questions, yet she decided to do her work diligently.

Her assistant had come up with an important development, and spoke in a hurried tone, 'Amatya Maitreyi, the one-armed dark prince escaped from the city through the north gate, pretending to be a corpse carried by the potters. The potters involved were Vajramitra's men. We have arrested five of them, though they claim innocence.'

'Make them speak! Do I need to repeat myself?' she growled. 'And send some good people to escort Arya Vajramita to the palace for questioning. Trick him by saying that the king has called him for a discussion.'

Vajramitra had pre-empted everyone, and was already at the palace making wild allegations. The king was presiding over court with the mahamatya and other ministers. Vajramitra was haughtily gesticulating when Maitreyi arrived. Seeing her got him more incensed. 'All your people have failed you, Aira Kharavela. The Nayaka was tricked and then stripped naked by a prisoner, who tied him to chains and escaped. Three days have passed, but there is no sign of the traitor Rudravarman. None of your spies and policemen have the slightest idea about his whereabouts and activities. None of his accomplices have been picked up or questioned. I demand to know what has been happening! I worked so hard to expose and apprehend the traitor, and these incompetent men of yours can't even keep him in custody. Let them all be fired for their ineptitude, we can do very well without them.'

Maitreyi looked at him with burning eyes. Her father Nagarjun, who was present indicated to her not to react. She held her breath in anger and cast a glance towards Nayaka Vikarna, who hung his head in shame. Mahamatya Nakiya was noncommittal, Rajguru Uddalaka had a beatific calm on his face, while the king looked unfazed. Maitreyi felt that the carved Gandharvas hanging from the pillars were mocking her and the large life-size statues of Yakshas were about to clap in jest. Her chain of thought was broken by someone tugging at her from behind. It was the court messenger Darpak. He said something in her ear, and she left with him hurriedly.

Other members of the mantriparishad were awestruck at these developments. They felt that, for once, Vajramitra had cornered all his enemies and put the king in a tight spot too.

Nakiya finally rose. 'If the King permits, may I seek some answers from Arya Vajramitra?' When the king assented, he continued, 'You called Rudravarman a traitor as he had written a letter to his earlier master. In what circumstances was this letter written, and who brought this letter to you?'

'Ha! Now you have started interrogating the person who exposed the traitor. But I will answer all your questions. This letter was written by Rudravarman when he was leading the army contingent—which I was supposed to lead—to the Rathika territory. He wanted to incite the Andhra king Satkarni into attacking us by providing false information. Fortunately, this letter was found by my loyal Devasena, who brought it to me.'

As he completed the sentence, Maitreyi entered the court room, Rudravarman with her. There was commotion in the room. Nakiya got up and asked everyone to be seated. He asked Maitreyi, 'Amatya, where did you get him?'

'He surrendered to us some time ago, mahamatya.' Then, addressing the king, she said, 'Rajan, since he is here now, he can answer all questions to defend himself. It would be unfair to condemn him without listening to his side.'

'Untie his hands and feet, and let him defend himself like a free man,' said the king in a resounding voice.

Nakiya turned to Vajramitra, 'Arya, you may repeat your allegations.'

Vajramitra was aghast at seeing Rudravarman in the court. He took a moment to stabilize, then renewed his speech with increased vigour. 'Look everyone, look here, this is the traitor I was talking about! How shamelessly he stands here in this court holding his head high.'

'*Ask your questions, arya. I too have questions to ask.*' Rudravarman's voice was like rumbling thunder, his eyes full of pride.

'Oh, the confidence of the criminal! Okay Rudravarman or Simhadhwaja, whoever you are, tell me, did you write the letter to Satkarni, inciting him to fight with us at a very inopportune time?'

'Yes, I did,' Rudra said calmly. A wave of alarm and dismay spread through the court.

'Look, I had told you, this man is a traitor. Rajan why don't you arrest him now and put him under the elephant's feet?'

'Any more questions, Arya Vajramitra?'

'No traitor, now you are free to defend yourself if you can.'

'Devasena, who had given you this letter, did he tell you under what circumstances it was written?'

'I don't know anything about it—what story will you make up to defend yourself now?'

'Why should I defend myself when I have Devasena to tell the truth here, arya?'

Rudra then sought the permission of the king to bring Devasena before him. He was allowed. Devasena was produced, his head hanging in shame and his eyes full of tears. 'Tell us the truth, Devasena. Fear no one. You are under the protection of Aira Kharavela now,' said a concerned Nakiya.

Devasena began with a voice full of remorse. 'I am a junior officer in the royal Kalinga army. In the expedition against the Rathikas, I was under the command of Arya Rudravarman. Just as we were crossing the dreaded Mahakantar region, I misbehaved with a local girl, for which Arya Rudravarman gave me very harsh punishment. As if that was not sufficient, I was badly stung by a swarm of large bees. I was almost dead, but for the efforts of a local mantrik, who miraculously cured me.'

'What does this have to do with the letter, Devasena?' said an agitated Vajramitra.

'Let him speak,' Aira Kharavela commanded. Vajramitra started feeling very uncomfortable.

'The mantrik then gained our confidence. He acted as a guide to help us navigate the dreadful terrain. We did not know that it was a trap. The mantrik, turned out to be the despicable dark prince of Subarnagiri. He later poisoned the whole army. He had the antidote with him, which he promised to distribute on the unconditional surrender of the army. He also asked Arya Rudravarman to write a letter to King Satkarni. The letter was designed to mislead the other king into waging a war with the Kalinga nation. The actual plan must have been to seize the throne of Kalinga at the hands of the Andhras and Shungas acting jointly.'

'So, he didn't write this letter voluntarily?' asked Nakiya.

'No, mahamatya, Arya Rudravarman was forced to write this letter to save the lives of his men, else everyone would have died. He not only saved the lives of each of us but was successful in defeating the dark prince and getting the letter back. So the letter actually never reached the hands of the

Andhra king. Had Arya Rudravarman intended to side with the Andhras or commit any act of treachery, he had ample opportunity when the Andhra army was virtually face to face with us in the Rathika territory.'

'Why did you bring this letter to Vajramitra then?' asked Nakiya.

'Revenge, mahamatya, revenge. It is a very potent feeling that blinds a man and makes him commit every sin he thought was inconceivable for him to commit. I hadn't forgotten my humiliation at the hands of Arya Rudravarman when he physically beat me up in the presence of the army. I decided to get even with him later on. Arya Vajramitra told me that it would be service to the nation if I could help expose the earlier identity of Rudravarman. I fell for the bait.'

'What do you have to say now?' asked the king.

'I have to ask his forgiveness, Rajan. He saved our lives and look at what I have done to him! I have made him a traitor. My conscience has finally woken up. Arya Rudravarman, please forgive me, though I am not worthy of your kindness.'

'You fool!' Vajramitra rushed at him with his sword in hand.

'Arrest him now! Enough is enough!' roared the king.

Soldiers materialized from behind him and pounced upon Vajramitra. They quickly disarmed and overpowered him. The courthouse fell silent in fear and anxiety. Nobody knew what was going to happen next. Rajguru Uddalaka now addressed the king. 'Rajan, I had this apprehension before too and had forewarned you about it. I believe Rudravarman is a victim of conspiracy rather than a perpetrator.'

Nagarjun said, 'Rajan, would you like to see the real face behind these conspiracies?'

'Who is that venerable Nagarjun?'

'He is the dark prince himself, Rajan! We have him with us here in our custody.'

'How did you get hold of him, Nagarjun?'

'It was not me, Rajan. It was Arya Rudravarman who captured this maverick who was escaping Tosali city in the guise of a corpse!'

As they spoke, the dark prince was produced before the king. Everyone cringed in horror at the look of the character. He had only one arm, no ears, virtually no nose and no eyelids. His skin had been badly charred and smelled like putrid flesh. He looked like a ghost straight from the ancient horror tales.

'So we finally meet, Prince of Subarnagiri,' said Aira Kharavela calmly.

'The throne you sit on is rightfully mine,' the dark prince hissed in his deep guttural voice, 'I am the real scion of Kalinga. A descendant of Princess Karubaki of Kalinga and the Chakravartin Devanamapriya Priyadarshi Ashoka. You are a descendant of Ravana, you should die!'

The king laughed at him.

'I knew that I will meet you someday, Aira Kharavela. I have come prepared for that.'

Saying so, he bent down and conjured a porcupine quill laced with poison from his footwear. Nobody could understand what was happening. Nobody other than Rudra, who snatched a sword from the guard near him, swung it and, in a single motion, severed his head from the body. The dreadful headless body still moved, with the quill in hand but Saktimati now sprung into action and cut the arm off. The torso collapsed and twitched for some time, gushing blood before going motionless. Many people from the courtroom ran out in fear. There was a numb silence in the air as the attendants removed the body and cleaned the blood.

The king finally spoke, 'Arya Rudravarman, this is the second time you have saved my life. Ironically, I have almost taken your life on two occasions. When you joined, I put you through many tests, overt and covert. Today, I have no doubts left in my mind about your integrity and ability. You are acceptable to me even as the great Simhadhwaja, whose name is taken with awe and reverence across Bharatavarsha. I have no words to seek your apologies for all that you have gone through, but I promise now, things will be better. I will make good for all the harm that has been done unto you. You are a worthy member of my court and an illustrious son of Kalinga. I hereby restore your position in the court and also announce that you will be the next mahamatya, the day venerable Nakiya decides to retire from the post. Kindly accept my offer and give me a chance to recompense.'

The king got up from the throne and walked towards Rudra. He then undid a necklace of kirata rubies he was wearing and put it around Rudra's neck and embraced him.

The courtroom resounded with cries and hails in praise of Rudra and the king. Rudra touched the king's feet, then sought the blessings of Uddalaka and Nakiya. He then turned to Nagarjun, who just embraced him and burst out in tears. Rudra realized that this man had been his father's friend, whose daughter Mita used to play with him in his childhood days.

The congregation was dismissed. After the king left, everyone flocked around Rudra to talk to him, to congratulate him . . . except Maitreyi. She stood in a corner with tears of joy in her eyes.

After people slowly departed, Rudra looked for Maitreyi as he was going out of the hall, but she was not to be found anywhere. He looked around for her anxiously, but couldn't find her.

His heart sank. After virtually coming back from death and redeeming his life, honour and position, if there was no Maitreyi in it, it was like dust. Life had no meaning without her. Hundreds of questions buzzed in his mind, and a thousand fears and suspicions riled his heart. She had left.

With a heavy heart, he trudged towards his chariot, still looking back with desperate optimism to catch a glimpse of her, but to no avail. When he was about to climb into his vehicle, a voice from the chariot said, 'Whom are you looking for, arya, don't you want to go home?'

'Maitreyi!' he said.

Scan QR code to access the
Penguin Random House India website